The Bard

Aura Weavers, Book 2

LizAnn Carson

The Bard (Aura Weavers, Book 2)
© 2017 Elizabeth Carson
ISBN: 978-0-9949036-7-9

Cover photos used under license from:
Deposit Photos

Thank You

To the wonderful, supportive women of my critique group. You set me right and keep me going!

And always, to Michael, who puts up with my flights of fancy and obsessive streak, and has never been less than encouraging.

Prelude

Bryar, Bryar, pants on fire, fat and lazy, cross-eyed crazy.
Scar face, scar face, eats your baby for breakfast.

Thirteen-year-old Bryar heard them, of course, as he made his way through the village of freezing mud, dirty walls and filthy alleys. He'd been subjected to their taunts his whole life. The girls with their jump-rope chants, the boys lying in wait around every corner, were inevitable products of the hardscrabble mining culture they'd grown up in. But today their words missed their mark, because today the worst had already happened, and life might as well be at an end.

His flute. Irreplaceable, and smashed beyond salvaging.

With winter just around the corner, the sky echoed the uniform gray of the ground. He shivered; he'd bolted from the house without a jacket, too upset to consider practical matters.

Functioning by rote, he let his feet carry him in the direction of his family house, doing everything in his power to man up, not let his parents, especially his da, see his heartbreak. He'd stopped by the icy creek to wash his face, resolved not to cry again.

Cry baby, cry baby...
Bryar blubbers, big fat blubbering blubber baby...

Two boys spotted him. They'd never let him forget he'd given way to tears. Before he had a chance to prepare, they were on him, barreling into him from an alley, pinning his arms.

"Beg, Fatso. Get on your knees and beg for mercy." The punch to his gut dropped him to his knees. But he'd sooner die than beg.

He couldn't take them both, but he could do some damage. He twisted, freed himself, and launched his counter-assault.

Bryar was not so much fat as solid, with the short stature, square face, and blond hair of his father. Not from his father the deep red birthmark that covered most of the left side of his face, though. That was distinctly his own, and an open invitation; as a matter of survival he'd learned to fight early and as viciously as the other boys.

He made a good show of it, inflicting a gouge on one of their faces with a sharp rock, and a punch that left his knuckles throbbing but would net the other a black eye. But both the boys attacking him had already left school to work in the mine, making them leaner, stronger. Meaner. They knocked the breath out of him, kicked him in the kidneys, inflicted a lattice of grazes on his hands and face, and left him sprawled helpless and humiliated in the alley.

After a while he eased himself upright, then to his feet, searching the alley for the pieces of the flute sent flying when the boys launched their assault. The flute was everything to him, the only thing that kept him sane in his bleak northern mining town, lifting his spirits above the blasted land and harsh way of life.

Who would willfully break it? Who would destroy an instrument capable of launching a person into enchantment?

The grim truth was, almost anyone. They all despised him. Most boys his age went down the mine, then with their fathers to the tavern; he'd smelled the cheap liquor on his attackers' breath.

The pieces of his treasured flute in his hand, Bryar hobbled through the alleys to his house.

His ma glanced up from evening meal preparations as he stumbled in the door. "Diou have mercy, not again." Her voice offered him nothing but exasperation.

"It wasn't my fault. They jumped me."

Why did he bother? His ma's attitude changed from irritation to distaste. "The clothier won't replace your tunics anymore. You'll cost your da overtime to buy you a new one."

She sat him at the table and began swabbing his wounds, none too gently.

"I'm sorry." He meant it, though his voice emerged through a haze of indifference.

"Look at you. Grown to your manhood and can't even defend yourself. How do you expect to survive when you go down the mine?"

His ma and da had no use for his music and considered the hours he spent practicing a waste. He escaped when he could, exploring the countryside, swimming in the swift flowing river east of the village, seeking out any remnant of natural beauty in the bleak landscape. His usual reward was a cuff to the side of the head and extra chores.

The thought of the river triggered words he knew he shouldn't say. "I don't want to work the mine, Ma."

Her eyes were like flints above her scowl. "You've no call to look down on your folks as if you're better'n us. As if our honest work isn't good enough for ya." She yanked up his pants leg and began on his skinned knee, which hurt like stink.

He had to tell someone. "Ma, my flute's broken. I don't know who did it. I found it this afternoon." He released his death grip on the pieces, letting them fall to the table.

"High time, too." Fresh from the tavern, his da roared into the room, filling the small space. He studied Bryar's wounds. "How'd the other guy come out?"

"Two of them, and I got in some good licks. They'll show the marks of it tomorrow."

"You given thought to how you plan to pay for that tunic?"

Half a dozen rips, but shouldn't his da be more interested in his injuries than in the fabric? A low, sneering sound escaped before he rallied his wits to stop it. He knew better. That wasn't how life was lived in the village.

"Get out of here," his ma said. "Borrow a needle and sew up those rents. We'll eat within the hour." She tossed the bloody rag into the basin and returned to her cooking without a further glance.

Bryar made his way to the supply depot two streets over and checked out a needle. Even here in the north, where the things were manufactured, needles were too precious for just anyone to own. At home in his room, he changed into his last intact tunic and began the laborious process of patching up the ruined one, struggling to control the needle with his swollen fingers.

Why should he care about his fingers anyhow? It wasn't as if he had a flute to play anymore.

And come to that, why should he care that no one in his family had shown him the kindness of a simple hug? Boys didn't do hugs. Boys grew up to be hard and tough. His da's job was to make a man of him.

Faint consolation that he'd proved his strength and fighting ability this afternoon.

Over supper Bryar found out how the day could get worse.

"I'm done with your nonsense," his da said. "And you're done with school. There's no profit in it. Tomorrow you come with us to the mine. It's past time you earned your keep instead of lollygagging around with music and folderols."

His heart felt like it had frozen in his chest, leaving him lightheaded. "But, Da —"

"Don't argue with me. You've got ideas above your station, and you're costing me coin. It's time you proved your worth."

Bryar started to speak, his spoon hanging forgotten in the air halfway to his mouth, but decided against it. All he'd get for his trouble was boxed ears.

His da wasn't finished. "Ma, see to his hair. He looks like a damn girl."

"Soon's we've eaten," his ma said.

"That toy of yours is history, boy. You don't mention it again, got me?"

The truth hit him hard. His da had smashed the flute, as sure as life.

The rest of the meal passed in silence. Bryar chewed the gristly meat and remembered the Bard who had come through their poor mining town four years ago. His hair falling down his back in a tail, he'd produced magical music, told enchanting stories. And wonder of wonders, before he left he'd given a wide-eyed, marked boy a flute, made from a kind of giant grass that grew far away in the Southlands.

He'd tried to explain to his ma, when he was nine and innocent, holding the precious instrument for the first time.

"It's like there's music in the air. I hear it playing in my head. With this I can capture it, so everyone can hear it."

His ma, who had been softer in those days, had smiled. "Go on, then. Make me some of this music you talk about."

Blowing across the hole as the bard had done, he'd been unable to produce a note, much less use fancy fingering to create a melody.

"Seems to me you can't manage it."

"Not yet, but I will, Ma. Just wait."

It became his obsession. Once he figured out how to blow into the flute, he began with nursery songs, graduating to drinking songs, working out the fingering note by note.

The bard had opened his eyes to another existence, a world filled with richness, that belied the dirt and brutality of his village. But he should have known better than to emulate the bard's ponytail, even if his was just a stub. Juvenile, childish... he lambasted himself as he swallowed the last of his small ale and washed his bowl in the basin.

Today proved one catastrophe too many. His life had descended into a black hell, a future that promised nothing but seven days out of each nine-day spent underground. Work at the mine, drink at the tavern, screw with the girls – not that that would be so bad, if any of them would ever have him – and repeat, all the days of his life.

The next morning, sullen and uncommunicative, Bryar accompanied his parents to the mine office, where they told him what was expected and issued him a sturdy gray coverall, the same as every adult in the village wore each day. The uniform branded him, tying him to the village, to his roots, to everything he didn't want in life. It fit awkwardly, too snug around the middle.

His da sneered. "Proper work'll put some lean on ya."

A trundle cart on a rail took them into the mine, a lantern attached to the front providing the only illumination. The loss of daylight hit him forcibly, clenching his gut, bringing back all his childhood terrors in the night.

And another loss, too. As soon as the cart was properly underground he sensed it. The music in the air was so much a part of him he was hardly aware of it anymore, but its absence frightened him.

"Don't mess this up, Bryar." He heard the threat. There was more at stake than the family's income. His performance in the mine would affect his father's reputation among his cronies, the men who drank every night at the tavern.

A heavy hand thumped his shoulder. "You answer when I speak to you, boy."

"Sorry, Da. I'll do my best."

"See to it you do better'n that."

"Yes, sir."

He fought back against his nerves, the reality of his fate. The weight of the ground overhead, the exhausting labor.

The dark.

He was grown up now, he assured himself. He could handle the dark.

Four hours, he estimated. And five to go. Bryar was filthy, his fingers bruised and scratched, his nails shredded. With the quotas, he never found time enough to rest or stop for a drink. Even discounting his physical discomfort, how could he endure a lifetime underground, where everything was barren and dead? The music that danced through the air failed to penetrate the layers of rock and dirt. Life underground was reduced to its barest essentials.

At least his da, working beside him, seemed pleased with his efforts. Focused toil, extracting the ore, loading the buggies. No one made conversation at the mine face. The other boys glanced at him and away again. They might be judging his work, but taunts and sneers had been left aboveground. Perhaps the gash and the swollen eye he'd delivered the day before had earned him some status.

Above him, he felt the weight of layers of stone and dirt, held at bay by the sagging timbers supporting the shaft. Stark deadness surrounded the murky puddles of light from the lanterns. And the music he'd lived for, swirling through the air, was gone. Gone.

He lasted two days.

On the morning of the third day, shortly before the lunch break, the single lantern provided for the men and women working the face blew out, pitching them into a blackness he had never before experienced, even in his worst nightmares.

His skin went clammy as his hands, his innards, his whole body began to shake. The flood of panic shut down his brain. A howl shattered the dark. Then he was running blindly, tripping, crashing onto the stone floor, huddled into himself and making noises no human ever uttered.

A boot trod on his fingers, then rough hands touched him. The boot nudged his gut. "No son of mine's a coward," his da hissed, broadcasting his shame. "Get to your feet, you, or you've no place in my house more."

He made it half way, then felt his bladder release as another cry ripped from his throat and his legs gave out under him.

They hauled him out of the mine, unceremoniously dumping him in the little cart. The men in the office reclaimed the uncomfortable overall and sent him on his way, humiliated before the entire adult population of the village. He spent most of the day out in the countryside, numb from the catastrophe of the morning. When he returned to his home in the late afternoon, he learned that his da was as good as his word. His few possessions waited by the doorstep, tied in the mended tunic.

He had two options: move into the men's lodge and beg at the mine office for a second chance, or leave. It was no choice at all.

At the food hall, where the single men and women ate, he ignored the stares and whispered comments and got a meal, then helped himself to a generous day's worth of dried meat and bread, the staples prepared for the mine workers. These he folded into the tunic alongside the pair of pants, the broken flute, a striped feather from an unknown bird, a stone that flashed rainbows when placed in bright light.

Hunched in his jacket, he struck out on the track south, aware that the sun would set soon but desperate to make a start, to leave the Northlands behind, to discover where the Bard had come from, so many years ago.

Chapter 1

It had taken Willow all day to descend from the eerie hills, where her last glimpse of Bryar and Joss had been their backs as they set out for home. Tired, hungry, and feeling very alone, she arrived in the town of Orlan at dusk and turned north from the market square toward the black tower.

Could anything but desperation have driven her to return to this cold place? At a minimum, she expected Gauvain, the tower's intimidating Mage, to sneer at her plain tunic. The memory of the fancy dress he'd insisted she wear when she'd been his guest a few nights before brought a fleeting grin to her face. That outfit now lay scrunched at the bottom of her pack, covered in dirt and stains.

She'd be expected, she reassured herself. Given the carrot Gauvain had dangled before her, promising to restore her lost Healing powers, he could hardly think she might refuse his summons.

Drawing on her dwindling courage, she stepped up to the tower's imposing front door, raised the knocker, and let it fall. The sound of metal striking metal wiped out any hint of amusement at Gauvain's sartorial demands. Someone would open the door, and then what? She swallowed and waited.

To her relief, the old, hunched-over servant answered her knock.

"Come in, my dear. The Master instructed me to provide you with a bath and clothing, as before. If you would follow me?"

As Willow stepped into the entry hall she caught a hint of amusement in the man's face. He was laughing at Gauvain, or the situation. Surely that meant she need not worry, or at least not too much. Following a brief tussle over who should carry her pack, a tussle she won, the old man closed the door behind them and turned to the stairs.

"I am Willow," she said as they climbed. "Will you tell me your name?"

"Leo, Miss. The Master informs me that eventually you will join the apprentice class, but he wishes you to reside here rather than in the apprentices' hall. A good choice, I believe, for all that he has his own ways."

The stairs wound up the curve of the tower. Willow had been too exhausted and traumatized by Bryar's injury to pay attention before. Now she did. Small, high windows provided daylight that fought to gain purchase against the black stone. The reddish wood of the banister and stairs gleamed, but the narrow staircase encroached on Willow's love of open spaces, leaving her slightly claustrophobic. There were no decorations, no hangings or implements on the walls. Not a welcoming ascent.

She was to stay in the same room she had occupied before. "I have laid out bathing things," Leo told her, "and provided a mirror, although the Master believes they contribute to female students' vanity. The wardrobe is well stocked. For classes, there is a black student's gown. At any other time, he will wish you to be 'suitably attired'. Please inform me if you need anything else. And I will handle your laundry."

"Yes, clean her up, for all our sakes."

Willow turned. Gauvain stood in the doorway, filling it. She abruptly felt penned in, which made her want to fly to freedom. Instead, she swallowed again and resolved not to be intimidated. This man intended to restore her Entrée, reconnect her to the life-enhancing power of the planetary Aura, as an educational experiment of sorts, and so far had done her no harm other than with his harsh words.

"Good day. As you see, I am here."

"As I expected." Gauvain strode into the room, stopped in front of her, and surveyed her top to toes. "I don't suppose you could teach her to style her hair?" he asked Leo. "No, I mustn't hope for miracles." He returned his attention to her. "Bathe, I beseech you, and do not be late for dinner. There is much to discuss. And I am eager to begin your first treatment. I find myself curious to get inside that head of yours. Your case is unique."

Willow had just parted from her friends and walked an entire day through the summer heat. Tired and in no mood to deal with his rude demands, she stood straighter. "You will not explore my head tonight. I am weary, I feel the start of a headache, and I want nothing more than to be clean and fed. Tomorrow, when I am rested, we can discuss the treatment."

Gauvain's cold gaze locked onto hers, his eyes dark blue flints set in the tense muscles of his face. "This once I am willing to accede to your wishes. Do not make defiance a habit, however. Leo, see that she presents herself on time. And please, burn that thing." He gestured at her tunic, then wheeled and left the room.

She looked at Leo. "He sucks the energy out of a place, doesn't he?"

"You are brave, Miss. Not many dare stand up to him."

Maybe, but at the moment that surge of defiance was deserting her. She sank onto a cushioned chair that formed part of a comfortable seating area tucked in the corner. "Please don't destroy my tunic. I will need it when I return home."

"The Master doesn't believe you will ever return. The tunic will be safe on the top shelf of the wardrobe."

"Thank you. You've done a lot to make me feel welcome."

"Tonight I shall ring a gong for dinner. I apologize for not doing so before. I understand he was... cranky? Tomorrow I will be pleased to show you the kitchen. Should you need my services, you can usually find me there, and I suspect it might be more compatible with your tastes." Leo bustled to the window, opened the glass, peeked into the bathing chamber and nodded at whatever arrangements he had made, then bowed to her as best he could, given his hunched-over frame. "Listen for the gong, Miss."

When the door closed on the elderly servant, Willow allowed herself to sag against the back of the chair. So this was it. Alone in a foreign land, in a black tower that felt...

alien. And then there was Gauvain. She straightened her spine, got to her feet, and stripped out of her tunic and trousers. She had dealt with him before, and she could do it again. Full of renewed determination, she crossed the room to the bathing chamber, more than ready to sink into the unimaginable luxury of hot water.

"Passable," Gauvain pronounced.

Willow paused in the doorway, subjecting him to equal scrutiny. He wore black, as always. His shirt tucked into the waistband of his trousers and fit close to his body, a style unknown in the Midland. A short cape draped over his shoulders emitted a metallic shimmer in the light from the Aura-powered globes scattered around the room.

"Less comfortable than a tunic, but the fabric is lovely." It hadn't taken her long to discover the wonders of the mirror, something altogether new to her. Leo's choice of dress was a low-cut blue gown encrusted with silver embroidery. With its wide skirt, the thing held enough fabric for two or three tunics. It itched where it clung to her skin, and the dip in the bodice made her uneasy, but despite the drawbacks Willow had been astonished, then bemused by her appearance. Her clean, pale blonde hair lay over her shoulders in a sheet of cornsilk. The shoes matching the dress were too small, so instead of reassuming her hiking boots she had opted to go barefoot to this meal. A pair of simple sandals should be adequate footwear even for such elaborate outfits; she resolved to ask Leo for a pair. No doubt she risked offending Gauvain's fashion sense, but she respected her own limits of discomfort in what she wore.

She shifted her gaze from the man to his setting. Objects positively encrusted the dining room. Tables and shelves bore as many articles as they could hold, almost none of which conveyed any meaning to her, but she suspected they were not merely decorative. Gauvain had uses for them. Heavy wine-red drapes shrouded parts of the walls in a fabric that alternately caught and rejected the light. The walls matched the draperies, creating an obscurity that could be intimidating, should she allow herself to be intimidated. The better for the Master of the room to remain in command, she reflected, then took her place at the table across from him as Leo appeared carrying two plates.

Gauvain poured a ruby wine into the patterned silver goblet before her. "I ask that you at least attempt to develop a taste for this. Besides enhancing the meal, it will help relax your mind, which will make our work go more smoothly."

He toasted her and drank. In return, she lifted her goblet and sipped. "As I told you before, I prefer beer," she said.

His mouth tightened in annoyance. "Be careful, you risk boring me. You speak like a peasant."

"By your standards, I come from a peasant culture. I like it. It is a place of kindness and sharing."

Gauvain looked up from his chicken, which swam in a pale sauce. "Oh, please, Willow-who-is-not-Willow. Don't give me that romantic nonsense about the wonderful civilization on your side of the hills. Let me guess. No one ever is cruel, there is no crime, sickness and depression and loneliness have been banished. The sun shines always, no one goes hungry. Have I got it right so far?"

The chicken was excellent. Willow ignored his outburst in favor of food. She knew from her previous stay that when Gauvain finished his meal, the plates would be whisked away. Tonight she intended to eat her fill before that happened.

"Well?"

She swallowed. "Of course not. But being a Weaver in my land is rewarding. By contrast, I found the people in your town unfriendly, and nothing is green here." And she faced two seasons, minimum, in this bleak place.

"I will have a plant placed in your room," he replied coldly.

The meal progressed in silence. Willow risked a few more sips of the wine. If its consumption aided his work to restore her Aura connection, she'd try it.

Gauvain rested his fork on his plate. "Your attention, please, while I outline my expectations." He cleared his throat. "You will attend my apprentice classes as soon as we sense even a trickle of Entrée. Practice assiduously and remember that you are not a Weaver here, but merely an older woman whose powers are late developing."

Older woman? "What ages are the apprentices?" she asked. "And how many are there? Boys or girls?"

The tightening around his eyes told her she had annoyed him again. Clearly, no one questioned Gauvain, or interrupted him. "Four, and they are thirteen years old or thereabouts. One girl. For the most part, females that age are too flighty to attend to their lessons."

"Puberty is powerful," she murmured, more to herself than to him.

He ignored her. "Until you are ready to join the class, practice your manners. I entertain occasionally. You will serve as hostess in my home, and display the grace and confidence that implies. I have retained a woman to instruct you. Now, regarding your clothing – Leo has provided you with a suitable wardrobe?"

"A wardrobe, certainly. I cannot speak to its suitability."

"Never wear the same outfit to both breakfast and dinner. I trust you to learn the difference between morning and evening attire. You will present yourself promptly and fall in with my plans – without demur."

"That might be a problem."

Their eyes met and clashed across the table.

"And why?"

Willow took another bite of the chicken, chewed and swallowed, while Gauvain radiated annoyance. "Because I may be ill, for instance, or suffer from my monthly courses. I might —"

His hand hit the dark, polished wood beside his plate. "You *never* mention such things. Deal with it as you must, but keep your female problems to yourself."

Her eyebrows went up. "Is it a secret that women bleed? What is so mysterious?"

"Here, it is not mentioned. Do not forget."

"Very well." With his pontificating, she had finished her dinner. She took a last bite of vegetables, then said, "Please go on."

His face gradually resumed its disapproving mien. "On occasion, we will venture out to a social event. Again, I expect the utmost in manners and discretion. I daresay a rumor will take root that you are my new paramour; do nothing to disabuse them of that idea."

"Impossible," Willow said. "I am not and will not be your lover."

His nostrils flared. "Undoubtedly. That I would choose to consort with a peasant-grown chit like you is absurd. But in society, that may be the assumption. Do not cause me embarrassment by denying it."

She stared at him. Leo came in and whisked away their plates while they hung in impasse.

"Now, what else?" Gauvain leaned back and steepled his hands before his face. "When we begin your treatments, you will be subject to my command and submit entirely to my wishes. Your recovery depends on this, so do not disappoint me. Undoubtedly it will be unpleasant."

"How unpleasant?"

"I cannot say. As I told you, your case is unique. You will endure, and report progress. When you begin attending classes, be quiet and absorb the lessons. It must be assumed you have knowledge the other students do not, but you will keep such learning to yourself. I will not have you fomenting agitation among my apprentices."

"You needn't worry. I know it is risky to learn things too early in training."

"Excellent. Your first proper response tonight. To continue, I require you to be rested. Yawning is insufferable, and the ignorant believe that a yawn allows malevolent spirits to enter. Nonsense, obviously, but one cannot rely on society's intelligence. These myths are pernicious. Have you questions?"

"Yes. How long has this town been here?"

"What else?" He passed over her question. Willow suspected he didn't know the answer. She was beginning to build a picture of the man, his assumptions about himself.

"Will I have free time to explore it?"

"Why would you wish to? A dirty place filled with people who can't be bothered to speak properly."

"I am not convinced I will like it, but I don't want to feel myself a prisoner here."

Again that meeting of eyes. His never softened. "Given the primitive nature of your culture, I'm quite certain you have no money, so I will arrange with Leo for you to receive an allowance. When I do not require your presence, you may do as you please, as long as you do not embarrass me. But I recommend you devote yourself to your studies. Because if you fail, I will turn you out."

"I'm no more than human, but I will do my best."

"Can you read, by any chance?"

"It forms part of our studies, although we have little use for it." She didn't mention that because of her early training as an archivist, she was handier with letters and reading than most.

"In time I may allow you access to my library. You must earn that privilege, however. You may use the lounge and the dining room, and eventually the apprentices' workroom. Do not enter my study without permission."

"I expect to visit the kitchen as well."

Gauvain made a dismissive gesture with his hand, then reached for his goblet. "It is plain and unadorned. Leo prefers it that way. I suppose it is functional for him."

"Functional suits me well." She saw no way that the objects filling the tables and walls could enhance her life.

Gauvain drained the goblet and dropped his napkin onto the table. "This meal is over. Your lessons in comportment begin tomorrow after breakfast. I will instruct Judith to teach you first to hold your tongue."

After he stalked from the room, she rose and located the candleholder she had used the last time she dined here. There was no fire starter, and the comfortable glow from the Aura-fueled globes was fading. Her fire stone was upstairs in her pack. Trusting the lingering evening to provide enough light for her to mount the dark staircase safely, she took the candle holder, and a second candle besides, and made her way up the stairs.

Chapter 2

"Sit still. Assuming you understand the concept?" The hands enclosing her skull fell away. Gauvain wielded sarcasm like a bludgeon.

"I'm doing my best." Willow had believed she was immobile, but even when she was young the people of her hamlet delighted in pointing out how little able she was to be still. A restless, twitchy girl, they'd said, and not with admiration.

Gauvain required her to dress in a white robe that covered her to her ankles and cinched at the waist with a cord. Her hair fell loose over her shoulders, which had tensed almost to her ears under the robe. She forced herself to relax the muscles.

He had placed her on a straight-backed chair without arms or padding and required her to sit upright, not leaning back, and to focus on the one candle left burning in the small, unadorned room he'd chosen for her treatments. So she had remained for at least an hour as his fingers prodded her scalp.

With her head free of his hands' pressure, she risked twisting around to look at him. Same black clothing and disapproving expression as always. "Is anything happening?"

"Perhaps you are bored and prefer to quit now?"

Willow sighed and settled once again into position.

"Better." From behind, those hands returned to her head, gripping firmly.

For a long, tedious time she experienced nothing, the same as before. Then a jolt shot through her brain from the left, followed by vertigo so acute she gripped the sides of the chair. The candle flickered and swayed in her vision.

"Hold *still*." Gauvain's voice showed his impatience, and more, an urgency she hadn't noticed before.

"I'm about to be sick," she choked out.

"Sustainer help us." A hand reached around to pass her a basin.

Willow didn't take it. "I can't..." She keeled over, off the chair and onto her knees on the thin floor covering, as her dinner retched from her stomach. By some miracle, the basin made it to the floor at the same time. Gauvain stepped away. After a minute, during which she hovered helplessly over the basin, enduring wave after wave of nausea, Leo entered the room and handed her a cloth, placing a supportive hand on her neck, catching back her hair.

When her stomach settled, she attempted to straighten, but couldn't. Instead, she remained hunched over the malodorous contents of the basin, too weak to move. Pain shot through her head like a hammer pounding a wedge into her left temple.

"Is this to be a regular feature of our sessions?" Gauvain's voice reflected his disgust. "If so, the sooner we complete the treatment, the better. I abhor such displays."

"Not as much as I do." Speech was a struggle. The nausea retreated, but the agony in her head shot stars through her wavering vision. She couldn't focus on Gauvain, much less care about his disapproval. Unable to remain even minimally upright, she collapsed onto the floor covering and curled into a ball, wanting above all to be free of the unbelievable pain.

Above her, Gauvain said, "Take her away and make her a tisane with a dose of heal-all tincture. Notify me when she improves."

Heavy footsteps crossed the room; a door closed. Leo's voice said, "Let me help you, Miss. You will be more comfortable in your own quarters."

She struggled to her feet and leaned heavily on the stooped old man as she stumbled, half blinded, up the stairs. When Leo brought her a lukewarm tisane, a few minutes after she'd settled in her bed, the liquid refused to stay down. As she emptied her stomach again and again, Leo provided a steady supply of cool, wet clothes and water to wash her mouth.

A solitary candle in the bathing room provided the only light. Willow lay curled on her bed, grateful for the darkness as she battled heat and cold, dizziness and nausea, her head locked in an agony unrivaled even by childbirth.

Two days later Willow faced Gauvain across the breakfast table, wrapped in a robe. The garment felt loose on her frame; the illness had cost her weight she couldn't afford to lose. Leo had stayed as close as his duties allowed, encouraging her to drink the healing tisane, sponging her feverish head, calming her when she thought she'd die from the misery in her body.

She had debated the wisdom of joining Gauvain for breakfast without dressing to his specifications, but decided if ever there was a time to ignore his dictates, this was it. Physical agony had at last given way to hunger and a desire to learn what had caused such a strong negative reaction.

Thanks to an earlier consultation with Leo about breakfast, her plate contained a pared-down meal, two pieces of dry, toasted bread and a pat of butter. She needed simple food to settle her stomach, and avoided looking at Gauvain's serving of eggs, bacon, and a kidney.

His cold eyes scanned her body. "I believe I stipulated that you appear before me only clean and well attired," he said. "You look like hell."

Willow was in no mood to put up with his attitude. Traces of the headache remained, and she didn't trust her eyes not to throw her into another spell of vertigo, or her stomach into nausea. "I will take my plate to my room, if I offend you so much."

"Oh, stop being such a martyr. I warned you it would be unpleasant."

"There are degrees," she muttered, and nibbled the toast.

"When you speak, speak so I can hear you. How do you feel?" It was a command, not a question. He shoveled a bite of egg and kidney into his mouth; she looked away.

"Dizzy, headache, slightly nauseous, but overall much better. With food and rest, I should be well soon."

"Are you in the least curious to learn what happened to you?"

"Very curious, in fact. That is why I am here. But be brief, please. My strength is fading already."

He swallowed and sipped from a mug of caff. Her system responded favorably to the aroma. "Will you pass me a mug, please? I am too weak to risk pouring for myself."

Gauvain glanced around, as if hoping for Leo to appear, then reached for the heavy pot. "You are not allowed milk until you are fully restored. A little honey, if you wish."

What she would recommend herself, although more curtly expressed. "I do."

He grimaced but added a generous helping of honey to her drink. While she stirred, he said, "An energy field surrounds your mind, barring signals from the Aura. I made minimal progress toward breaking through it. You felt it, the moment you cried out—"

"I cried out?"

"Yes, and then informed me you intended to vomit. I doubt you will notice a difference, but it's a start. The next time will be as distressful for you, I don't doubt, but I know of no way to avoid it."

Her shudder equaled his own obvious distaste. It was enough to make her question whether she wanted her powers back that badly.

She reminded herself of her stated claim she'd endure any agony for the sake of restoring her Entrée. Quite apart from her longing to Heal again, the memory of life lived in the glow of the Aura haunted her waking dreams.

Willow took another bite of toast, then added more honey to the caff – Gauvain noticed and frowned even more deeply – and took a sip. Bliss. The sweet liquid surged into her body, giving her energy and alertness long before it logically should, perhaps triggered by the simple pleasure of drinking it again.

"It may be possible to ameliorate the effect," she said.

"Oh? And what do you propose?"

"Lighter meals. A plain potato, an egg or meat without garnish. Sauces and condiments don't sit easily in the stomach."

Gauvain shrugged. "I consider it a mark of civilized living to acquire a taste for the finer things—"

"Which depends on the definition of finer things, I suppose. Simpler fare suits me better."

His nostrils flared. "I have spoken to you about contradicting me."

"And I responded that I speak my mind. I am not being rude, and I do not want to lose another meal."

She caught a glimmer in his eyes. It might have been respect. At least he didn't snap at her. "Very well, that can be arranged. Leo seems to be fond of you. I am sure he will be delighted to cook specially for you when a treatment is scheduled. Kindly enlighten me as to when that is likely to be."

Willow had eaten the toast, and the caff was almost gone. She longed to ask for more, but knew it would be both an indulgence and a mistake. Maybe later, when she assessed how well her breakfast digested, she could enjoy a mug in the kitchen, away from Gauvain's glare.

"At dinnertime, when I know how my system responds to this meal, I will give you an estimate."

"I await your words of wisdom." Again she caught that flash of... admiration? Surely not. But at least he'd kept his customary annoyance in check, and that was miracle enough for one day.

Gauvain left the table without further conversation. She lingered over the last of her caff before returning to her chamber, anticipating the pleasure of a hot bath and clean hair.

Chapter 3

Walking through the hills toward the Midland and home, Bryar endured surely the worst autumn equinox of his adult life.

As the Midland celebrated the first harvest, he should be performing on some plaza or other, feasting on the fruits of summer labors, making love in a patch of dappled sunlight. He'd compose a new tale, a selection of music and song. Always, in his memory, the sun shone.

Bryar trudged along the path, a corner of his mind appreciating the soft warmth of the air and the relatively level track. The rest of his mind registered every lingering ache and exhausted muscle from the force that had felled him almost two nine-days ago, when he'd crested the last rise for his first and only glimpse of the land on the other side of the hills.

Joss walked several paces ahead of him, as he had since they'd left Willow and struck out for home. It had taken all Bryar's willpower to let her go. He hated, at a visceral level, her descending alone into that new land, placing herself in the power of the man she'd brought to the campsite to restore him to consciousness. His brief encounter with Gauvain chilled him. But she made her own choices, and no one changed Willow's mind once she'd set it.

At least the core of himself, his energy connection, was intact. Given what the Aura had done to him – and to Willow before him – he supposed he should be grateful for that.

He and Joss steamed in the heat after last night's rain. His beard itched. His clothing felt both uncomfortably damp and annoyingly ripe; neither of them had been able to wash properly in days. No place for fastidiousness on this trek.

They had barely exchanged a dozen words in the four days they'd traveled together so far. Even faced with another six or seven days on the trail, Bryar was grateful for the mutually agreed silence. His current mood was scarcely conducive to conversation.

Each day, Joss set the pace until Bryar's uncertain strength gave out. He hunted, hauled water, and prepared their skimpy dinners. He set strips of meat over the fire to dry overnight, to sustain them through the next day's walk. And he never complained.

And Bryar's own contribution? Nothing. An anger he hadn't felt in years tightened his shoulders. He should pull his weight. He should be recovered from the overflow of Aura energy that had knocked him senseless. He should –

"You're being too hard on yourself," Joss said. His first words in days not related to survival.

"What are you talking about?"

Joss stopped walking. His mouth straightened into tight-lipped determination. "You're agonizing when you don't need to. After what you went through, I'm grateful you can walk at all. No one's mollycoddling you."

"Willow said you'd been in my head." Bryar couldn't help the hostility. Willow had told him about Joss reading his emotions while he was out cold, unable to defend himself. The man's budding animal whisperer skills weren't his fault, but what went on in his head was nobody's business. What gave this giant foreigner the right to invade his thoughts —

"You've got that wrong," Joss said, inadvertently causing another spike in Bryar's anger. He was doing it again, invading his mind. "The way this whisperer thing works is, I don't have a clue what you're thinking. But feelings, that I sense, when they're strong. At least I'd rather deal with you getting mad than those poor-me vibes. Made me damn uncomfortable."

Furious now, Bryar shrugged out of his pack, ready to attack the man for his taunt. He stopped short, remembering where he was, who he had become.

Joss sighed and settled onto a boulder jutting into the path. "Not what I meant. Sorry."

"Yeah."

"You're awfully prickly. I'd turn this stuff off if I knew how."

Bryar dropped the pack and sat next to the other man. He stared out across yet another valley, filled with its own collection of ferns and giant big-leafed trees. Each had its own personality. The lowlands might be swampy or hold swift rivers bordered by lush riparian growth. A few were nearly barren, the vegetation scant and underdeveloped, but verdant, untouched forest blanketed most of them. A mist rose from the foliage, filtering the light until the trail ahead was rendered unworldly.

Unworldly. Unreal. That summed it up. Nothing fit into his understanding anymore. He'd never dreamed the Aura could deal him such a blow. Its inherent danger had been easy to ignore, expressed only as a risk to Quinn, should she probe too far into a template's depths. But somehow no one translated that into a more generalized menace. Just as no one ever crossed the hills, almost as if the thought had been blocked from Weavers' minds.

Everything in him ached to create songs, poems praising the landscape, the path, the murmuring breeze caressing the silence. Commemorating the pilgrimage they had set out on, so innocently. So damn stupidly.

But it wasn't in him, not yet. His body still hurt. His mind felt bruised and tired. Music was far away. He sensed its distant presence, and he had begun to be impatient for the day it filled him again. For now, though, life condensed into putting one foot ahead of the other on the rough path, keeping up with Joss.

But Joss showed no hurry to move from their impromptu resting place. Bryar seized the opportunity to remove a boot and pick at a blister on the side of his toe, wishing Willow was there to tend to it.

"Grew up in a barracks," Joss said. "Everybody figured I was slow, because I didn't say much, and my size. Big dumb guy, you know? I had to beat up a few to make them leave me alone, but then they got sneaky – or plain mean. Things I couldn't catch them at. Want an apple? Found a few on a tree yesterday. May not be edible, but worth a try."

"Sure." Bryar rested his foot on top of his boot and accepted the proffered fruit. It was green and hard. He took a tentative bite. Not as sour as it might be, just coming into its ripeness.

Joss bit into his, winced, chewed, and continued. "You have one of those childhoods, too?"

The easy casualness of the question made it possible for him to answer, if obliquely. "Mining towns are tough. No welcome for men in my occupation. Music? Not unless it's leading a song in the tavern."

"You look like a scrapper."

Bryar didn't respond. He'd sooner forget those days.

"There's always a jerk out there, I reckon," Joss continued as if not noticing Bryar's lack of response. "Needing somebody to pick on. That ended when I got promoted out of the workers' barracks, but then they ignored me. Everyone assumes I'm stupid or deaf."

"Even here? I never heard that."

Joss took another bite of the sour fruit. "No. You're right. Not so much here. Or on the ship. There they respected my skills. It gave me credibility. And companionship."

Those companions were lost now, Bryar knew. Four of Joss's crewmates had died before he and the commander of the thing crash landed not an hour's walk from Willow's waysite, throwing their whole world into chaos.

Willow. How was she managing in Borgonne, on the other side of the hills? His mind held only foggy impressions of the Mage. The man had straightened out his brain after the energy waves of the Aura felled him, but through the treatment he'd been aware of arrogance in the man's personal aura. His restoration had been accomplished for self-serving, not altruistic reasons. Now Willow had put herself in his hands, hoping to regain her own powers. By all that sustained them, he hoped she was right.

"I'm worried about her, too," Joss said.

Bryar stood, pitched the apple core into the valley, and confronted the larger man, making no effort to mask the anger in his voice. "Stop it. Maybe you can't help it, but I hate you throwing my thoughts back at me that way."

Joss nodded. "I don't mean to be rude. But I told you, it's not thoughts. Feelings, yes, and I share that one. I miss her."

"I bet you do." It was a snarl, and uncalled for. He'd seen no overt sign of a shift in Willow's relationship with Joss during their long trek east into the hills. Nevertheless, he sensed a new connection between the two of them, disrupting his own easy rapport with her.

Like him, Joss had been staring out across the valley. He spoke without turning his head, addressing the vast space between them and the next hill. "I get it. I mean, I get how you react to me, but I don't know what to do about it. In my culture, men and women never even meet each other. The social structures are different here, so you tell me what to do." Joss spread his enormous hands wide, shifting to focus on Bryar.

"She's a free agent," he muttered. "She makes her own decisions."

"We should go."

Bryar laced on his boot. Both men stood, resumed their packs, and carried on along the track.

A full day passed before Joss spoke again, other than commonplace words concerning campsite, dinner, sleep.

"So you got picked on, growing up."

"Yeah."

"You don't like to talk about it."

"No, I don't. That was a different life."

They were climbing out of one of the innumerable places the trail dipped into a valley, this one shrouded in a cold mist so thick it soaked into his clothing, chilling him and making the climb back out that much harder. Bryar lacked breath for conversation and focused on keeping up.

"Once they found a snake and put it in my bed," Joss said conversationally. "They didn't know it was poisonous. Damn near killed me. Or maybe they did know. I don't understand how anyone can be that mean, though. Especially kids no more than twelve years or so."

"I mostly got taunts, but plenty of fights, too. My ma grew sick of patching up my clothes."

"Bet they had a field day with that mark on your face."

"Yeah. I got to be a good scrapper." Joss didn't skirt around the subject of his birthmark, which was rare. It embarrassed people. Bryar found it a relief that Joss dealt with it matter-of-factly.

"For me it was my size. Still is, even here. The kids on the plaza in Stanstead got a game going where they cast me as a boogie-man. Lots of running and screeching. A kid tripped and fell right at my feet, but I terrified him when I stooped to see if he was okay. Like I'd hurt a kid." Bryar heard insult in Joss's voice.

"What did you do?"

"Got out of the way. A couple of women came over to help. I think kids might be kind of neat. I can't imagine what a baby must be like."

Odd statement. Bryar let it go.

An hour on, the path leveled out, the trees thinned, and a pale sun filtered through the treetops. Bryar stopped and stared, then smiled. The beauty of the scene made it easier to get out of the sullen mood which, he recognized now, had dogged him since they struck out on the trail. In truth, his strength was returning. Slowly, given the limits to their food supply, but steadily. Tonight he'd start the fire – it had been painful, watching Joss struggle every night with a fire stone when he required only a flick of his hand, provided he could find the energy reserves – and set up the camp while Joss went out hunting. Perhaps he'd play the little flute tucked in his pack. Best he could offer at the moment, but as the sunlight rippled over the path through the shifting leaves, he experienced a trickle of faith in the future.

Chapter 4

"We're home." Bryar leaned against a tree and surveyed the track that crossed the end of theirs, running north and south into the green forest. "Four hours to the Motherhouse."

"Can you make it on your own from here?" Joss asked.

"Yes." They could be home in time for the evening meal. The last couple of days had seen an upsurge in his wellbeing, fueled by their breaking out of the hills and traversing land that was a part of the Midland. Vegetation he was familiar with. A sense of normality, something he couldn't put his finger on but had been missing in the hills.

"Do you have a different plan?" Bryar asked.

"I might try to find Ezra."

"Why?" Bryar shifted his pack to the side of the track and sat on the ground beside it. His hand brushed the low vegetation, rocks and mulch, under the canopy. Home.

"Got some questions."

I bet you do. He and Joss had grown more comfortable with each other since their talk on the trail, sharing reminiscences and experiences late in the night, when the campfire burned low. Talking about everything except Willow.

Both of them shied from any mention of her, for all that she occupied Bryar's thoughts. Missing her, wondering how she fared in Borgonne, if the Mage Gauvain really could restore an Auric connection as he'd promised. He knew more about her experience of losing of the Aura than he had ever revealed, because he remembered, far too vividly, his experience in the mine so many years ago, where he'd first experienced its absence. And then the time on the hillside, locked in terror, unable to move or communicate until Gauvain broke the shell his body had built around his mind...

"Will you write about it?" Joss asked.

"Hmm?" Bryar's thoughts had drifted as he soaked up the dappled sunlight, birdsong from somewhere deep in the forest.

"Will you write a saga about this? About what happened to you?"

"I'm not sure. Perhaps when it isn't so raw. Are you ready to go?"

"If you are. And safe journey to you."

Bryar stood and shouldered his pack. He hadn't planned it, but he had a few questions of his own for the Old Man. "I'm coming with you."

Joss nodded. "That's good."

The men headed north, away from the known comforts of the Motherhouse.

Two days later, Bryar questioned the wisdom of his decision. Not only had they found no sign of Ezra's residence, a relentless autumn rain pummeled them every step of the way through the rolling landscape.

It only took two days to get to Ezra's. they should be there by now.

You knew this, Bryar reminded himself. In addition to the rain, everyone said Ezra's compound was well shielded, and no one found it unless he wanted them to.

Joss had turned sullen, so next to no conversation passed between them.

Mid-afternoon they drew to a halt above a low scarp bordering a vast bowl covered with loose rubble and boulders. Bryar studied the concavity; it would require half an hour or more to cross it. He hoped for better hunting on the other side; the squirrel Joss had snared the day before was long since consumed.

"Want to turn back?" Joss asked. "I'm cold and hungry and we're wasting time here."

Joss looked ill, in fact. Bryar suspected his own appearance was a match. But they'd come so far already...

"The Old Man couldn't travel much farther than this to get to the Motherhouse, could he?"

"Maybe we missed a turnoff somewhere."

They stood looking out over the scree-filled bowl, taking minimal shelter from the pounding rain under a coniferous tree clinging to the edge, undecided.

"Any chance of connecting with Ezra through the Aura?" Joss asked.

"I've tried. He isn't making things easy, assuming he's paying any attention at all."

"I bet he knows we're here. It's like he's psychic."

"He was a Scribe, once."

"You reckon this is a test?"

"Hell, I don't know." Bryar straightened. Sensing the despondency in the big man, he decided for them both. "One more day. We'll camp once we're across, and we'll both hunt. There's bound to be game here. We can find it."

"Fair enough. Watch your ankles."

Is this your best course? The thought appeared from nowhere. He frowned and shook it aside.

They scrambled down the scarp and had advanced perhaps twenty paces when a low, rumbling noise filled the air. They both froze.

"I know that sound," Joss said.

"So do I." Earthquake. With the weight of the steep bowl above them. "This isn't a good place to be right now."

They turned back. Before he had taken five steps, the ground lurched underfoot. Joss went down, scrambled up again. Bryar fought against his own legs, gone weak from the quake.

The rumbling deepened, coming from far above them. He looked up in the instant the entire top of the bowl face released.

"Run!"

He hadn't known how quickly a landslide moved. They pelted for safety, stumbling over the boulders. Bryar crested the scarp as the first debris hit behind him. Deafened by the roar as the full force of the slide reached the lower slope, he scrabbled away on hands and knees, then collapsed unbelieving as the vast bowl disappeared under tons of rock spiked with uprooted trees from the torn edge, including the tree that had sheltered them.

In the wake of the landslide and earthquake, an eerie silence hovered over the landscape.

Still unsure of his legs, Bryar made his cautious way downslope. He located Joss south of the trail. Like him, Joss had made it to safety, and like him he bore the marks of flying debris. Joss, however, lay unmoving on the slope, face down.

At least he breathed.

"Joss?"

He groaned.

"Can you move?"

No reply.

Bryar sat and did his best to remember the experience of linking with Willow to assist a Healing. No Healer himself, he still might support the other man. After settling his mind as much as possible, given the events of the last few minutes, he attempted to tap into Joss's body.

Pain. It arrived in his consciousness with such force that he recoiled and lost his connection. How did Willow bear it? Day after day, allowing herself to explore others' illnesses and wounds, subjecting herself to whatever the person experienced…

Years of training. The answer trickled into his mind as if some other mind had put it there.

He claimed the Aura again and reached out to Joss, this time more cautiously, using his instincts to build a filter between the two of them.

There. Headache. Bryar rarely suffered from headaches; the intensity of this one appalled him. He emerged from his trance and ran his hands over Joss's head, but detected nothing broken.

"Sweet Christopher." Joss's voice grated, as if his throat pinched on the words. He moved his arms as if to raise himself, then gave it up and collapsed.

"Talk to me," Bryar commanded. "Are you okay?"

"Give me a minute."

Bryar watched as Joss tested one limb after another, then his torso, turning himself over.

"Thought I'd bit it when this boulder came sailing through the air and knocked me flat. Must have smacked my head. My eyes aren't working right."

"Concussion. You made it up the slope, though."

"It's over?"

"Yeah."

Nothing was dry or warm in the pouring rain, and the sound of the landslide still echoed in Bryar's ears. He got them into the forest for minimal cover, helping Joss to half stumble, half crawl over the uneven ground. The tarp slung between two branches gave some protection. Then he poured a cup of water, added a few drops of willow bark tincture from their small collection of remedies, and encouraged Joss to drink.

The rubble filling the bowl periodically shifted, setting up minor slides that were big enough to break a bone, or bash in a man's head. The constant movement set his nerve endings on edge. Joss seemed to pay no attention.

After a while, the rain stopped, but the heavy cloud lingered. Bryar's fingers were frozen, his stomach queasy. In the aftermath of the slide, an uncontrollable tremor gripped his body, not only from the cold but exacerbated by it.

He had just reflected that there was now no possible way they could continue when, to his open-mouthed amazement, a figure appeared on the far side of the bowl and started across, hopping from stone to stone as if it were no more than a jaunt before dinner.

A teenager, Bryar concluded as the person got closer. Young and skinny and very well coordinated. What was an unknown kid doing out here in the middle of the wilderness, nonchalantly crossing a landslide?

The boy worked his way over the rubble. Bryar waited, watching his progress until he dropped to the ground beside them. He released a breath he hadn't been aware of holding.

No more than middle height, the kid had an unruly mop of brownish hair shot with gold and eyes that matched. He – or she? – wore sturdy sandals, trousers, and a tunic cinched at the waist. He spoke to Joss. "I'm Tai. Here, take this. Gran says it'll help." The kid, whose voice was low pitched and slightly gravelly, rummaged in a pouch attached to the rope belt and urged a small pill between Joss's lips. He grimaced. Tai looked at Bryar. "Water? Those things are bitter."

With Tai supporting his head, Joss sipped, muttered, "Thanks," and subsided into a near trance, staring up at the scudding clouds.

Tai's clothes were dry. He frowned, puzzled.

"Granddad wants you to come with me, the sooner the better. Gran's making a stew, that'll warm you up." Tai seized one of Bryar's hands in both of his own. "Crikey. You're freezing. And only a few days past equinox, too. That was nasty." He nodded toward the slide. "We didn't expect that. Are you all right?"

"Bumps and bruises," Bryar said. "Who are you?"

"I told you. I'm Tai. You're Bryar. Ezra's my granddad. He's waiting for you both. He says it's vital I get you to him. Life changing." Tai stood, shaking out gangly arms and legs. "In this case, lifesaving, or at least we hope so."

A thin shaft of sunlight pierced the cloud, the first since they had passed the intersection leading to the Motherhouse. Joss pushed himself up and sat, one hand shielding his eyes. "Then let's go. No point in delay."

"I'm not going across that," Bryar said. "It's suicide."

"Is there an option?" Joss asked. "I'm still feeling kind of woozy."

"That's the long way around," Tai said. "We go back along the path and take the cut-off. It's a lot easier."

"But you came from over there." Bryar gestured at the bowl.

Tai shrugged. "I spend lots of hours roaming. Days, sometimes."

"There is no cut-off."

"Everyone misses it first time. Can you stand?" Tai asked Joss. "I'll help you. I'm stronger than I look."

Joss staggered to his feet. It took their combined effort to steady him, but once upright he looked better, not so pale. "I can't move fast. I hurt all over, and my head's not right."

"That's why I'm here." Tai's bubbly optimism both encouraged and annoyed Bryar. The idea of help close at hand – not to mention the promised stew – lifted his spirits, but did Tai have to be so insufferably upbeat? The kid could prove to be obnoxious.

And who knew Ezra had a grandson?

Granddaughter? Tai didn't shave, he'd bet on it. But the gamine figure under the shapeless tunic resembled an immature boy's more than any girl's form he'd known.

Walking proved to be problematic, but united in intent, they struggled from the site of their near calamity. Based on the signals radiating from most of his body, Bryar anticipated a mass of bruises tomorrow. Joss sported the beginnings of a black eye and had lost a boot so he walked half shod. After half an hour of staggering forward, the turn from the main trail appeared on their right, just as Tai promised. Impossible to miss – yet neither of them had seen it. Tai stayed alongside Joss, often tucked under the big man's arm when his energy flagged. He distributed dried fruit from his pouch; the sweet treat revived Bryar and Joss both as they stumbled along the track. Half an hour later they reached Ezra's compound.

When the trail opened into a clearing surrounding a rambling structure, and Bryar saw Ezra sitting in a comfortable chair more suited for indoors, on a porch in front of an open door, he could have wept with relief.

As they drew closer, though, he realized that Ezra sat wrapped in blankets, and his elderly wife stood behind him, a protective hand on his shoulder.

As Bryar observed the scene, his connection to Auric energy flickered, then disappeared. Before him the Old Man slumped in his chair.

No longer upbeat, Tai spoke. "He's weaker every day. Gran's worrying herself sick." He paused. "So am I, actually."

Chapter 5

Gauvain was in a foul mood. Willow knew why, but there was little she could do about it. He prowled the tower, snapping at the apprentices in the adjoining workroom, making unreasonable demands of Leo, snarling at her attire, her way of speaking, her very existence. As if the vanishing of the Aura were her fault.

Over breakfast, she faced him down. "I assume nothing has changed." Before the current disruption, they had managed two treatments, and occasionally, after the second one, she had thought she detected a trickle of energy. Now, the Aura's disappearance left Gauvain as helpless as she was.

"Go over it again. You *must* have more insight into this power cell. Though I concede you may not be aware of your own knowledge." He glowered at her over the lip of his caff mug.

"There is nothing more I can tell you. Be content and don't push me."

"Who controls it now? Where is it?"

A spoonful of Leo's excellent porridge bought her a few moments to ignore his insistence. Leo had proved more than pleased to prepare a cooked cereal, plain toast, or an ungarnished egg for her. After she swallowed, she said, "No Weaver has it, I'm sure. No Weaver would allow this extended fracturing to happen."

"This is beyond fractured, as you well know."

"No, I don't."

She no longer feared matching his hostile tone with defiance of her own. In fact, she had begun to suspect that he enjoyed their sparring.

"Who, then? One of your beloved peasants stumbled upon it, perhaps?"

"Highly unlikely. We've covered this, Gauvain."

"The strangers are most familiar with the cell, and arguably have an interest in it."

"Kiril is more likely than Joss, since Joss shows rudimentary Auric awareness. He wouldn't put the Weavers at risk. But this is speculation. I have been away from home a long time."

"Humph." He swallowed the last of his caff. "The one redeeming aspect to this is that I've begun analyzing the disruption. Revealing the underlying principles."

Good. Gauvain had switched into teaching mode. He pontificated, but that was better than his silences or veiled hostility.

"I'm curious to hear what you have learned."

He poured himself a fresh cup of caff and even topped up her mug before speaking again. "I modified one of my instruments to capture and map whatever energies are present. The Aura is not gone, exactly. The energies conflict, overriding each other. I theorize that a brain such as yours – or mine, I suppose, underneath the defenses around it – cannot sort out the competing vibrations. With what we call the Aura in the way, determining the effect of the new radiation becomes impossible. I am attempting to isolate its energy." Something that almost passed for excitement softened his haughty face. "Think of it. The person who understands how to use the new energy controls the world. Once we learn to tap into its capabilities, just as we've used the Aura... who can say? It might prove to be more powerful still. But its potential is hidden while the two cancel each other out. When I discover a protocol to mask the original energy—"

"You can't do that," she blurted, horrified by what she understood him to be saying.

"Given the right tools..." Her words sank in. Even more than being contradicted, Gauvain hated having his limitations pointed out to him. He looked at her coldly. "I am confident I *can* do this, if I choose."

"The Aura does originate from a... a thing, then. You've never been explicit."

"You have no need for that information."

"In that case, I'm forced to suspect you don't have the information."

"You are mistaken."

Probably true, but the direction his research had taken him shocked and dismayed her. She pushed her point. "It would be a terrible wrong. The Aura governs our entire civilization."

"In the interests of science, one must make sacrifices. Just as you sacrifice a few days of good health in the interest of restoring your powers... which, I confess, I find a fascinating process. Watching your mind break open, bit by bit—"

"Stop. I dislike that analogy."

"Nonetheless, that is what I am doing. And should I gain access to this new energy, make no doubt that I will exercise all my abilities, and any feasible tools, to learn its qualities."

Willow's caff mug hit the table with unnecessary force. "And I will do all in my power to block you, if you attempt to affect the Aura."

He looked down his nose. "Given your pitiful powers, woman, you cannot prevent me. And I recommend you not try."

"Not so pitiful, once fully restored. Without boasting, I can say I was considered an expert at working with the Healing templates."

"You will never be another Ezra, and you may end up being nothing. Please remember that your fate is in my hands."

By now she was used to his oblique references to people from the Midland, so his mention of Ezra failed to shock her. She shook her head. "I am not an inert recipient in this process. Of necessity, I participate. Perhaps I learned enough from our two sessions to return to the Motherhouse and let them continue the treatments. Or I might decide to live as I am. I am not your puppet, nor will I ever be."

He smiled, though without warmth. "You are feisty, Willow-who-is-not-Willow. I look forward to our debates. So few dare be combative around me, it is refreshing. As soon as the Aura returns, I will execute another treatment. At that point, I believe you will be ready to join the apprentices. Your unfolding fascinates me."

She had no words to answer his implied compliment. Instead she sipped at her caff and watched him. But however fascinating she might be, he clearly had finished with her. He rose and stalked from the room, as usual giving her no further acknowledgment.

Chapter 6

The Aura flickered back into life three days after its abrupt disappearance. Nonetheless, the nine-day following the landslide, a nine-day filled with sunshine, Rebecca's nourishing cooking and healing salves, Tai's chatter, and concern for the largely silent Ezra, left Bryar on edge. Several times he and Tai had gone out into the countryside; he'd sung and played the little flute for her but suffered from a lack of vitality behind the performance. Was this his future if the Aura never returned? With the terror of the slide receding, its absence weighed on him more and more.

He'd sought Joss that morning. Joss's vision had cleared, and his bruises and wounds had healed, although he still endured the occasional headache. He spent most of his days around the small barn, tending to the livestock, even milking the cow and goats. Never loquacious, now Joss was positively taciturn. At most he had tolerated Bryar's presence, but it was comforting to spend time with someone familiar.

Tai popped up at his elbow after lunch as he wandered the edges of the compound seeking the mental focus to compose. "Granddad's looking for you. He's in a serious mood today," Tai added in a mock whisper, then took one of his hands and tugged. "He's really relieved you're here, you know. Let's go see what he wants."

This wasn't the first time he'd held Tai's rough, callused hand in his. He liked the fit of their fingers and palms. When they met, Tai's enthusiasm had grated on his nerves, but as the days progressed, he found himself looking forward to their hours together. In fact, Tai intrigued him more and more. So different from him, and yet there was a spark there, unlike any he'd felt before. He couldn't define it, so contented himself with looking forward to their expeditions into the wilderness surrounding the compound.

They started across the grassy lawn toward the front porch where Ezra waited in the old, padded chair, tucked under a woolen blanket despite the renewed summer heat in the wake of the unprecedented thunderstorm the day of the slide.

"You plan to listen in?" Bryar hoped not. Ezra had summoned him once before for an intensely personal discussion, delving into Bryar's life and loves, his use of templates, his dreams for the land and for himself. Tai had been off somewhere else, not there to overhear his secrets.

"Granddad says he can't afford to exclude me, that it's the only way I'll ever learn enough to gain wisdom. I have a hard time staying still."

Bryar believed it. Tai was a will-o'-the-wisp, never in one place for more than a blink.

"You're air and fire, aren't you?"

Tai grinned. "About equal, and a little of the others. Gran calls me a hodgepodge." That odd, rough voice blended with the background sounds from the compound; even without the Aura, Bryar had sensed the underlying rhythms.

He smiled. "That's powerful, logic and passion combined."

The Old Man had faded over the last nine-day. Instead of the vigorous man Bryar had known since his teen years, these days he exemplified the reality behind the nickname. He had indeed become old. Bryar settled on the porch floor, his legs stretched out over the steps; Tai folded down next to Ezra, leaning on the arm of his chair.

"It was a joke at first," Ezra said, unnerving Bryar by his uncanny ability to read his thoughts. "I showed gray in my hair while I was still a student at the Motherhouse. I've been called Old Man since I was sixteen. Which, as I recall, was also the age you finally confronted your demons." Ezra's hand rested on Tai's arm for a moment, squeezed and let go.

Bryar blushed, to his annoyance. The council had held him back a full two seasons, half a year, in his training because of his residual anger over the birthmark and the cruel treatment by his home town. A time he strove to keep private, his own personal shame.

Ezra was relentless. "Tell us how that felt. And how it is now."

Bryar hesitated. Since Ezra already knew all his secrets, it took a moment to figure out why. Simple, really; he didn't want to share those days with Tai.

Why not? The words appearing once again in his head.

"I beg your pardon," Ezra continued. "I understand your reluctance. But you need to consider these questions. They are more important than you realize. Please answer me."

When did the Old Man ever give him a choice? The memories arose far too readily. He steadied his voice to neutrality, using techniques he'd learned over years of performance, before he spoke. "Rough days. Willow and Quinn were moving on with their training, even though they both faced – challenges, I guess – from their own childhoods. Nobody held them back..." As the words formed, he became involved in his own story, wrapping the long suppressed emotions around him, letting them color his words. "I hated it. I hated being malformed. I hated the mind exercises, as if you expected me to pretend it didn't exist, when it did." The red mark burned on his skin. "Constantly confronting this... *thing* on my face. Wanting to ignore it. Wanting it to go away."

"Until the day you released it, or seemed to. Because no one cared about the birthmark except you."

"Yeah." That much was true.

"And now?"

He turned from Ezra, twisting his fingers into a knot. "I don't notice it, usually."

"Because it's easier, or because it genuinely doesn't matter?"

Questions he hadn't been forced to confront in years. "I'm not sure."

"While you're here, I want you to spend half an hour each day dealing with that question, and the role the birthmark plays in your life. Your work as a Bard isn't affected. Give me the deeper truth, the part that still hurts.

Because for what you'll be facing, you can't afford to carry any wounds or weaknesses."

Bryar looked up at Ezra, who sat in his chair with his eyes closed, hands folded in his lap. The valley housing Ezra's compound grew silent. Bryar's trained ears constantly registered the sounds of chickens scratching, birds scolding from the trees, the goats foraging in the pasture, a clatter of pots from the kitchen. But for a moment everything was still.

Tai's gaze changed from worshipful to worried. "Can I bring you anything, Granddad?"

"No, child, I'm well enough. I need to organize my thoughts."

The imp in Tai resurfaced. "Not like you to be disorganized."

"Hush." Quietly, even lovingly spoken, but Tai immediately subsided.

After a time, during which Bryar emptied his mind to regain equanimity, daily sounds penetrated his consciousness again.

"Good," Ezra said. "Now, to begin. When you walk the Midland, what do you observe? Is there a difference since the day the power cell fell from the sky?"

Relieved to return to the ordinary, Bryar frowned as he reflected. "I haven't traveled since then, other than around Stanstead. I don't remember noticing anything in particular, though. What's changed?"

Ezra ignored the question. "And yourself. What is the state of your own wellbeing? I don't mean in the wake of the Aura's disappearance. In general. What is different?"

He reflected. "Fatigue, perhaps. I sometimes wonder if my thoughts are as sharp as they used to be. I've attributed that to either the down times or getting felled by that energy blast. When the Aura comes back, it sets everyone reeling for a while – doesn't it?"

"Yes, it does. And you yourself have experienced the power of the Aura to affect your mind, even do harm. So let me tell you what is true. The corn grew straight and tall as always, but the cobs failed to fill out properly. Further west a blight struck the wheat crop. Tomatoes are not as plump and the chickens lay erratically – just ask Rebecca, it's driving her crazy," he added with a note of humor. "And the weather. That downpour was unprecedented, but so is the dearth of rain since then, a disruption in the storm patterns. Shall I go on?"

"I get the idea. This is happening because of the Aura?"

"Not the Aura, but its sporadic absence. As you spend that half hour in introspection each day, inquire into your own health. By now you should be fully recovered from the strike you received in the hills, but you aren't. Your bruises are mostly healed from the landslide, but not completely. You're still a young man, Bryar, and vital, but less healthy than you should be."

Ezra paused, looking at the two of them, then at a goat trotting across the farmyard, before going on. "I'm a bellwether, in a sense. Because my Entrée is unusually strong, I experience these changes sooner and with more force. But it's more than that, much more. To be blunt, the Aura sustains us, and its loss may well destroy us."

"What should we do about it, Granddad?" Tai's eyes focused on Ezra.

"Possibly nothing. But that decision is up to Bryar. Because" —He looked Bryar square in the face— "you're the only one who can change it."

"What do you mean?" He was on his feet before he registered his intention. "I can't affect what's happening. I'm a Bard. My template skills are just average. I don't have the kind of power—"

"The quest will not involve a template. It will be physical, plain and simple. Listen." Ezra let his hand drop from Tai's head and leaned back, his eyes closed again. "Years ago, when you and Willow and Quinn first formed your friendship – or perhaps we should call it a bonding – you presented us with an unusual, even unprecedented situation. You are children of destiny, although none of us could explain how. As I told Willow at the Motherhouse, before the calamity that felled her, the three of you are entangled in the threat to our land, but I couldn't provide any specifics. I assume her injury and her stay east of the hills have a purpose. But it is evident to me that saving our home from the ravages of the power cell is your calling, and yours only."

He had backed down the two porch steps as Ezra spoke, and rested his hand on the newel post at the foot of the steps to steady himself. "Impossible. That's not me. I sing. I don't—"

"Fight? But you can, and well. Listen closely – and you too, Tai, because you also have a role to play. The calamities of the last few nine-days, the unconsciousness in the hills, the downpour, the landslide... those weren't natural. None of it. They were directed at you." Ezra fixed his blue eyes on Bryar. "Only you. Joss's injuries were unfortunate, but he wasn't the target. The Aura demands you, if the Midland is to be saved."

"That's ridiculous. You make it sound as if the Aura's alive, capable of making decisions." The desperation came out in his voice; he couldn't hide it. Again he wished Tai were not there for this discussion.

"I'm not being fanciful, although it's reasonable for you to suspect so," Ezra said. "It falls to you to find the power cell and return it to the Motherhouse for disposal. Only you can do it. I have seen it in various templates, and I have watched you. I believe this as fervently as I have ever believed anything. The choice remains yours, but I do not intend to make it easy for you to refuse. If nothing else, you will watch me die, because that is the first logical outcome, before the famine, the disruption in personal relationships, the potential warfare when the Borgonnian civilization decides it wants control of the Midland. Which they will, or at least a few of them will.

"I'm not going to sugar-coat this. The risk to you will be great. But you are the only hope. We must reclaim the cell, whatever the cost."

Ezra's flat words passed through him with the same force as the earthquake, the landslide. He sank onto the bottom step, his hand still on the post. "I can't."

Ezra ignored his statement. "I will help you prepare."

"How does he prepare, Granddad?" Tai asked, her voice hushed.

"Besides what we spoke of earlier? Strength training. Joss may assist us there. And more formal fighting techniques.

You're a scrapper. We can enhance those skills. Also..." Ezra's voice tapered off.

"Tell..." Bryar cleared the hoarseness from his throat and tried again. "Tell me." He didn't want the answer, but better to get everything on the table.

"We need to find a way to shut down your Entrée. For the challenges ahead, access to the Aura can only hurt you. I'd like to give you the tools to switch it on and off at will, but that may not be possible. You and I must experiment. It's dangerous. It might cost you the Aura permanently. But I see no alternative."

"Thanks," Bryar muttered under his breath.

The Old Man showed a flash of impatience. "Work with me. We're facing a crisis."

Bryar looked up. "I can't do this."

"You can. I believe you will. Go now, and think. Weigh it in the balance."

"You want me to sacrifice myself. Give up who I am."

Ezra shook his head. "Who you are is what happens without the Aura. The energies merely enhance, they don't alter. You mustn't downplay your essential nature. Return tomorrow, and we'll talk again."

"Where is the power cell?"

"In the hills. I expect it back in the Midland soon."

"Who has it?"

"That I don't know, although I have my suspicions. Tai, take Bryar and see if Rebecca can provide something sweet in the kitchen, and maybe a cup of caff."

Tai unfolded and bent to kiss the old man. "Later you'll tell me my role in this?"

"That, you must figure out for yourself. Go, both of you. I'm tired." Ezra closed his eyes once again, effectively ending their discussion.

Bryar felt a touch on his shoulder. Numb, he stood and followed Tai to the kitchen.

Chapter 7

Once inside the rambling house, Tai led him straight through the kitchen, pausing only long enough to kiss Rebecca's cheek and claim a couple of abricoe pastries in a linen napkin, and out the back door. With nothing else to do, and his thoughts in too much turmoil to make decisions, Bryar followed.

The path Tai chose led to the river. Bryar had been along and in the river several times, drawn like a magnet to its clear water. He suspected this was the same river that rushed in a dangerous torrent past the Motherhouse. Here, upstream, it was swift but without rapids or whirlpools. Still not safe for poor swimmers, but for him it provided a form of surcease.

"There's a nice spot a little way downriver," he said. "We could go sit —"

Tai didn't give him time to finish, but set the pastries on the bank, kicked off her sandals, and —

No!

—and disappeared under the water.

"Tai!" Panic flooded him. The androgynous boy-girl couldn't possibly be a good enough swimmer to handle the current. His own sandals joined Tai's as he scanned the water, watching for movement. When nothing happened, he dove in himself, trusting the flow to carry them in the same direction.

Bryar surfaced close to the far bank of the river. As he shook his eyes clear, he heard Tai call, "Over here!" A waving arm caught his attention, then a lithe form stroking toward a low-hanging tree.

Bryar followed, and found himself in a backwater, a pool that had warmed in the summer's heat. The tree's branches sheltered them and afforded a dappled, otherworldly light. Tai sat chest deep in the shallows, hair made dark by the water sticking up as it freed itself from the slicked-back effect of swimming, gesturing him over and grinning.

"I figured you'd find me."

He thrust himself through the water and settled on the sandy bottom. "You scared me out of half a lifetime. You shouldn't be in this river."

"Bryar," Tai said patiently, "I've been in and out of the river since I started walking. I know its moods. After the storm last nine-day, I wouldn't go near it. At low flow like this, it's easy. And I was right, wasn't I? You need this more than you need sugar and caff. You looked positively dehydrated, talking to Granddad."

"I hadn't thought of it that way," he murmured.

"I recognize things, patterns. Just so you know, I never notice the birthmark. It's there, sure, but somehow it doesn't register. I'm sorry it gives you so much grief."

Bryar gazed across the river, up into the tree; anywhere but at Tai. "I don't talk about it."

A callused hand touched his bicep. "But you should. And who better to talk to than me?"

He could think of at least two people. Why should Tai assume a right to that role in his life?

"Because I'm here." Ezra's grandchild, reading his mind the way the Old Man did. "And we have something. I'd be surprised if you weren't aware of it, too."

In his irritation, he decided he might as well ease his curiosity. "Hell, Tai. I can't even figure out if you're boy or girl. Not what I'd call a deep connection."

"Neither." Tai drew away, affronted. "I am neither boy nor girl. I am twenty-eight years old, full grown. I've paid my dues at the Motherhouse, same as you. Don't you dare think I'm a child."

Bryar sighed and leaned back in the water, studying the gently swaying leaves, still green but a few tinged with gold. "That's not what I meant."

"Well, why does it matter?"

"Damn it, Tai..."

But why did it matter? His attraction was undeniable and growing, and he had taken men as well as women as lovers over the years. When the two of them...

He shook the idea away. Whatever was going on with Tai, it wasn't casual like most of his liaisons. Only with Willow and Quinn had he established any lasting connection, and he doubted he was ready for a new one. He might never be ready, because to be brutally honest with himself, that wasn't how he lived his life.

"Okay. Perhaps it doesn't matter. But why won't you tell me?"

Tai shrugged and sank down until only that pixie face remained above water. "I live independent, a little wild. Alone, although Granddad and Gran keep an eye on me. Usually I'm out there, seeing what I can find." Tai's hand described a broad sweep that he took to encompass most of the northeast Midland.

"Scribes' Guild?"

She smiled. "I choose not to allow myself to be defined. With all my potential clans, I defy categorization. How do you suppose I'll figure in this story of yours, anyway? We'll be lovers one day, that's a given. But what else?"

He blinked at the abrupt change of topic. "You sound mighty confident of that."

"And you're not?" Tai laughed. "Scribe, remember? And Ezra's kin."

He leaned his head back, letting water dance through his hair, and closed his eyes. "I don't know what Ezra expects me to do. I'm nothing special. A minstrel can't save the world."

Tai's hand worked its way under his tunic, which had ballooned in the water. Fingers touched his chest, stroked. Normally such a touch aroused him, but this time he felt comforted. Tai's magic, he supposed.

"Look at you. You're sturdy and strong, the furthest thing from typical water clan. You fought as a kid, didn't you? On top of that, the Aura says so. You can save the world, once you put your mind to it."

"Your faith is misplaced."

"Nope."

He was silent.

"Do you like my hideaway?" Tai withdrew the hand and leaned back next to him. "It's one of my secret places. Nobody else knows about it. I used to spend hours down here or up in the tree. Hiding, when I was supposed to be doing housework or milking the goats."

Another old wound opened, but this time, talking to Tai there in the river, he was less hesitant to vocalize it. "I never had a place of my own. A room barely bigger than a bed, and one day my da went in and smashed my flute. My only instrument, back then. Something died in me along with the flute."

"Oh, sweet hosanna, that's it." Tai sat, grasped his tunic in a fist, and stared at him. "You've got to find that piece that died. To make yourself whole again, because I intend you to survive whatever Granddad sends you to do, and he's right. You'll never get through this quest if you're fragmented. We both believed it was the mark on your face, but it's not. It's what you just said."

Bryar pulled himself more upright. The waterline rippled across his chest and back. He shivered; the water in this little pool was warmer than the air. "Don't, Tai. Let it go, please. I can't handle it right now."

"Later, then. That piece is still out there. I'll teach you techniques. Between us we can fix this." Tai left it a beat, then nodded and pointed across the channel. "See downriver, that gap in the trees? To get home, we aim for that. It's an easy walk back to where we left our pastries."

Without waiting for him, Tai launched into the river. He followed, swimming strongly, so they reached the opposite bank at the same time. Walking to the compound, munching the abricoe pastry and listening to Tai narrate tales of the natural world around them, contributed to a temporary calm but did little to lessen his dread at whatever Ezra foresaw for him.

More, as their wet tunics clung to them, he finally saw underneath, to the shape of her body. Breasts, small but perfect, and a waist that flared to hips definitely womanly.

Tai had been right about one thing; he'd needed the water. None of it felt good, and he anticipated an uneasy night, but for the moment he felt more himself, with a better chance of sorting out the information he'd received from the Old Man and his grandchild.

Chapter 8

Above all else, Willow did not want to open her eyes and admit to her miserable self that she was awake. While she slept, she avoided facing how completely wretched the treatments left her. The third one, the night before, had been the worst so far, and she'd paid the price in blindness, headache and nausea, and an almost complete loss of control of her limbs. Based on past experience, she faced two days of illness, then another several as her body recovered its alignment.

Light penetrated her eyelids. Oddly, she could swear she heard a bird outside. Birdsong was rare in Orlan, so that made no sense.

Willing herself to sleep again, she lay unmoving. But it was hopeless; she was fully awake. Abruptly, she realized the nausea had vanished, and the headache.

She felt whole.

Impossible.

The bird launched another note into the sky. In a bid to avoid the sun pouring in the window, she rolled over, and gradually opened her eyes.

Dust motes danced in the sunlight reflecting off the highly polished wardrobe. She had slept in the white robe she donned for the treatment sessions, but a simple shift in a teal green, with matching, darker trousers, both made of a fabric that shimmered in the brightness, waited on the chair. Leo's doing, no doubt. Someone in this cold place cared about her wellbeing.

Willow hauled herself upright. The entire room shone with light, for the first time since she'd arrived. The obscurity that seemed to surround her in the tower had vanished, drowned by the sun pouring in the window. Even the stones of the outer wall, though still black, sparkled with glints of white and silver.

She sat motionless, in case the wonder dissipated.

Then full realization hit. *Gauvain had done it. He'd cracked her open.*

The Aura.

Through all the long, gray days since this glory had been wrested from her, she had begun to forget.

Let us never forget. Let me never become complaisant. Let me always be awake to the wonders and richness of life.

She shoved back the covers and dropped barefoot to the floor. There it was, the texture of the boards rich against her bare feet. A step took her into the sunbeam, which instantly warmed her, made her hair shine.

It was all... right.

Her chin trembled; she fought the emotion back. She wouldn't pollute the moment with clogged sinuses brought on by tears.

Experimentally, she waved her hand at the candle on the mantle. Nothing happened.

She readied her palm and called up light. Nothing.

Chastened, Willow perched on the edge of the bed, swallowing back disappointment. Surely she hadn't forgotten how to manipulate these simple templates, so it must be that her Entrée was as yet insufficient. Gauvain must know what he had done. She needed to find out.

The sunbeam drew her to it, irresistibly. Its warmth ignited something in her, sending her into a delighted twirl around the room. No illness, no pain, and the Aura within her grasp once again, even if its strength was no more than she'd known as a ten-year-old.

Willow hastened to wash and dress, delighted by the touch of warm water, the brush of the fabric against her skin. She forced herself to do a full morning ritual rather than bolting down the stairs to breakfast.

"Good morning."

Gauvain looked up from his plate. "I did not expect you, much less sounding so insufferably cheerful."

Leo appeared on her heels. "Breakfast, Miss? And allow me to say, I'm pleased to see you looking well."

"Thank you, I'm starving. I'd love two eggs soft boiled, please, with toast."

"Shall I slice a tomato?"

"That sounds so good."

Leo disappeared, and Willow crossed the intimidating room, pausing to reach for the carafe and pour herself a mug of caff before sitting.

"I take it you have at long last found cause for celebration in your treatments?" Gauvain glowered at her, as if to imply that she had no right to high spirits, since he was the one doing the work.

Willow reined in her excitement in favor of customary irritation at his attitude. "You know very well what you accomplished. The only reason for you to be surprised is that I feel so good this morning. It's against the pattern."

"Naturally, I am pleased." Sounding more bored than overjoyed, he returned his attention to his breakfast.

Neither of them spoke until her eggs arrived. She took a bite, sighing with pleasure. Leo gave her a smile as he backed out of the room.

She swallowed. "You may be dour all you want, but I intend to enjoy this day."

"I will expect you in the apprentices' hall at the start of class."

After another taste of her perfect egg, she said, "No, I do not wish to. Not today."

Gauvain shoved aside his plate and poured caff, reaching across the table to refill her mug, an unusual gesture of courtesy. "I daresay I can understand your elation. However, I must remind you of our agreement." He gulped the hot liquid, then set down his mug and stood.

"Yes, and part of that agreement concerned you keeping me apprised of what is happening to me. I would like an account of last night's activity. I know my own experience, but that isn't the same as understanding what you did, and how, and how long you believe it will be before my capabilities are fully restored."

He folded his arms over his chest and glowered down at her. She met his gaze calmly, waiting.

"I did nothing different, merely whittled away at the barrier around your mind. Last night I found a weakness in the grid and exploited it."

"Where was it?"

"In the left hemisphere, slightly above your ear. Is that relevant?"

"Probably not." It was, though. The left side of her head had faced the propelling force, that day in the meadow. She stored the information away for the future consideration. "Can you explain my absence of headache or nausea?"

"I suspect it is because enough Auric energy filters through to your brain to stabilize you and ameliorate any negative effect. I gather you have ascertained the extent of your current powers?"

She nodded and picked up her knife to spread butter on a piece of toast. "Almost nil, other than perception. The world feels more alive today."

His mouth twitched, whether in irritation or satisfaction she couldn't tell. "If you insist, I will excuse you from classes. Expect another session tonight, and assuming you continue to improve, you *will* attend class tomorrow."

As usual, Gauvain afforded her no opportunity to reply, but left the room without further acknowledgement.

She finished her meal and went in search of Leo, determined to use the day for her first exploration of Orlan.

Willow dressed for dinner more cheerfully than had been her habit, still excited by the events of her day. With sun and freedom, enhanced by the Aura, her hours in Orlan had pleased her beyond expectation.

A smile. People respond to your energy. That's all it takes.

Leo had provided her with the promised allowance of money – not an unfamiliar concept, but uncommon in the Midland – and coached her on the denominations and how to shop, and had even walked with her to the market, lending her his credence as a member of Gauvain's household. After he placed an order for a joint of late-season lamb for dinner, he left her to wander among the stalls.

She'd occasionally asked questions or passed the time of day, but mostly contented herself with looking around. After a while she purchased an apple, then later a pair of hair barrettes in a bluish shade the stall owner said came from a kind of shell. She had no idea what a reasonable price should be, but regardless of whether they were a bargain – she doubted it – she didn't care. They were her own, a souvenir.

And all day, the black tower loomed over the town, absorbing the sun.

Leo had approved the barrettes and chose a dress to pair with them, the blue silk that shifted and changed in the light. Willow had never concerned herself with external appearances before, but tonight, descending the stairs, she felt like a princess from one of Bryar's fantasy stories.

That ended abruptly enough. Gauvain was not alone in the dining room.

He stood when she entered. "Come in. Duncan, meet the object of my experiment. Willow, be seated. Duncan is a colleague, a fellow Mage."

"Although to hear Gauvain, in a different league. You mustn't believe all he tells you, however. Hello, my dear. Allow me to say, a stunning ensemble on a lovely woman." Duncan stood, reaching toward her in what she'd learned from her coaching in deportment was a mark of gallantry. When she placed her hand in his, and he raised it to his mouth, she caught a flash of contempt on Gauvain's face. The touch of the man's lips on her skin sent a shiver through her, which she hastily suppressed.

As they settled into their seats, Gauvain elaborated. "Duncan learned of my experiments with you and decided to see for himself. I invited him to observe our session tonight."

Showing off, Willow thought. Two Mages strutting for supremacy like cockerels.

Over the meal – as expected, Leo had worked wonders with the lamb – she assessed the newcomer and his relationship with Gauvain. Duncan showed himself as avuncular, kind, and interested, all the things he should be. He dressed more elaborately than Gauvain, although by now she knew that the unrelieved black was in fact the most expensive dye available. Duncan's jewel-tone green waistcoat stretched across an ample middle which must test the band of his trousers to the limit. His sleeves gathered at the shoulder, allowing quantities of fabric to drape down over his arms. He managed to consume quantities of the meal with enjoyment and overstated manners, asked the right questions of both her and Gauvain, and gleaned an abbreviated version of her story between bites of mint-infused lamb and patate.

She didn't trust him.

Willow kept her own counsel, allowing Gauvain to carry the conversation. For reasons she couldn't immediately discern, she did not want Duncan to know any more of her than manners dictated. Gauvain, however, had other ideas.

"You see, the hexagonal matrix formed by interlocking currents provided a near impenetrable barrier, a form of defense, I speculate, but that will require further research. Expectedly, my techniques succeeded in parting the array. The work is not complete, not yet, but that is for the best. With her mind attuned to life in the Midland, a full exposure to the energies in Borgonne would probably kill her. A little at a time."

Conveniently leaving out the part about the flaw in the matrix, which made your progress possible.

But by now she understood Gauvain and his attitudes. He would never acknowledge any such weakness to Duncan, who she concluded was a serious rival. Even with her attenuated Entrée, she was aware of him brushing her mind. She tried to erect the barrier she relied on when doing healing work, screening herself from the thoughts and pains of others, but without success.

A long way to go.

Wine flowed freely, at least to Duncan. Willow, as usual, limited herself to a few sips. Gauvain accepted one refill of his goblet, but drank little of it. Duncan drained a second goblet and helped himself to a third. She watched, maintaining silence whenever she could, as the meal unfolded.

"Naturally, Willow is impatient," Gauvain said after an interlude of polite chewing, swallowing, and trivial talk. "That pleases me. She will be a welcome addition to my current class of apprentices, most of whom are irresponsible, silly teenagers. Do you find the same with your students?"

"Dreadful. I refuse to believe we were ever that unfocused."

The talk rambled on, leaving her to finish her lamb and vegetables in peace.

Following dessert, roasted apples with thin slices of cheese, Duncan excused himself to, as he put it, "... relax and freshen up before the session this evening. I'll need to be on my toes to keep up with Gauvain." He winked at her on his way out of the dining room.

Gauvain stood over her, at his most commanding self. She suspected the onslaught of Duncan's good humor had drained what little of his own he possessed. "Go and rest for a while. I expect you to be at your best, and two treatments in as many days is certain to tax you."

"Is it wise to push forward so? I would prefer to wait."

"No, we don't wait. You are strong today. The energy suits you. Duncan is correct about one thing, although he gets most things wrong. You are a lovely woman, Willow, despite a hint of sunburn."

"I..." What was she supposed to answer?

"An example of the positive effect of the Aura on an otherwise ordinary visage, I suppose. You have an hour."

"I... yes." The unexpected compliment, followed by the equally unexpected derogation, left her stammering.

The light was failing as she made her way back to her room. She had hoped to delay this session, not because of her state of health, but because she truly did not want Duncan anywhere near them when Gauvain manipulated her mind.

Chapter 9

Willow had paid only token attention to the lesson in the apprentices' hall the next morning, her mind still battling the aftereffect of Duncan's presence at her session with Gauvain the night before. She hadn't been able to detect him, any more than she ever did Gauvain, but he put paid to any doubt of his invasion when, after the work concluded, he took her hands in his plump, slightly damp ones. "My dear," he'd said, "what an enchanting essence surrounds your thoughts. So pure. I would be honored to learn what combination of background and training created such perfection."

Gauvain had turned away, busying himself with his own post-session ritual, while she attempted to free her hands from Duncan's grasp. With no success; his grip tightened.

"I am very tired."

"Ah, but a glass of wine will relax you before you sleep. And we have much to share with each other." He had lifted one of her hands toward his lips, stopping only when Gauvain spoke from his stance at a cabinet against the far wall.

"Willow, report to me. Have you a headache? Nausea?"

"Only a slight headache. But I would like to go to my room." She tried again, unsuccessfully, to free her hands.

"I've often found that women don't truly know their minds, or what's good for them. I insist you join me."

Gauvain had finally become aware of the exchange and intervened. She could have kissed him. "Release her, Duncan. Willow dislikes wine, and she needs rest."

He had let go of her hands then, to her great relief. "Thank you," she said to Gauvain, not specifying what she was thanking him for. With an effort, she refrained from wiping her hands on her white robe, contenting herself with moving swiftly to the door. "Good night."

She had fled up the stairs praying not to be followed. Much later, she had been disturbed by a jiggling at her door, as if someone was trying to turn the handle; thankfully, for the first time since arriving at the tower, she had obeyed her instincts and locked herself in.

The memory wasn't pleasant, and she'd barely been able to eat her breakfast that morning with Duncan present.

Shrugging off her annoyance, she remembered she was in the classroom and forced her attention back to the aftermath of Gauvain's lecture on the transformation of water to either ice or steam. The material itself was familiar to her.

Which didn't mean she could do the exercises.

Gauvain had stepped from the room on some errand of his own, so she waited as the four youngsters hurled self-created snowballs at each other, stifled shrieks and giggles, and generally proved themselves to be teenagers. She couldn't blame them. Dark and cramped, the classroom held only two wooden tables, each cluttered with esoteric equipment, surrounded by high stools. At one end, a dais provided Gauvain with an elevated view of the students' work, as well as reminding them constantly of his rank and authority. The classroom sat adjacent to the tower and attached to it, so that a black-stoned, concave wall abutted the limited space. Several windows allowed in light, none of them low enough to look through. Outside was the perfection of autumn, sunny with a crispness in the air. The few trees around Orlan had begun to show their colors. She ached to be in the open air instead of cooped up in this pokey room, and she was sure the apprentices felt the same.

Autumn at the Motherhouse... her mind again wandered from Gauvain's teaching, this time to roam back over her youth. They had been equally hard to discipline, except that even at fourteen, she and her classmates never disrespected their teachers. They had saved their high-spirited shenanigans for after class, when pitched snowball battles out behind the outbuildings were the norm. Willow suspected that neither Gauvain nor Borgonnian society in general gave these young people many outlets for their energies, so they made opportunities wherever they could.

"*Stop this instant!*"

Gauvain reappeared at the front of the room, catching more than one guilty expression and melting snowball.

After leaving the students to cower for a space of time, he thundered, "You are disgraces. If you wish to become Mages, you will behave as such. Beginning now, or so help me, I will throw you out on the street. John, forward."

The boy named John sheepishly approached the dais. Gauvain appeared larger than usual, more intimidating, as his apprentice stood before him. Willow suspected him of using illusion to cower the students, for Gauvain was more wiry than large.

"Demonstrate the process for transmuting ice to steam, without an intermediate step."

The entire class held its collective breath. Even Willow froze, waiting to see what would happen next. This hadn't been included in Gauvain's lecture.

The boy turned pink. "I... I don't know how, sir. You never said —"

"Of course I never said, fool. If you showed the least attention to your studies, you'd have worked it out for yourself." He left the shamefaced John standing in front of the small class. "Anyone else? Not you," he added to Willow, "although being a sensible adult, I had reason to expect you to contain these... *children.*" The contempt dripped from his voice on the last word.

Willow had no intention of riding herd on the other apprentices; her position among them was already tenuous. They clearly viewed her as somewhere between an interloper and a spy, at best a person they couldn't explain and so didn't fully trust. But she'd never say these things to Gauvain, especially with the class present. She sat a little straighter and tossed her hair back.

The only girl, Amalie, raised a tentative hand. "I believe I know, sir."

"Unlikely. Come forward." Gauvain had made it clear that his faith in any woman's ability to work with the energies was nonexistent. That she had been admitted to the class at all bordered on a miracle.

She stepped to the front of the room, caught a glimpse of Gauvain, arms folded, glowering down at her, and froze.

You can do it. Show him. Once upon a time, Willow had been able to send simple thought messages when in proximity to others. Now she doubted her thought went anywhere, or that she had the power to screen it from Gauvain if it did. But for whatever reason, Amalie lifted her gaze from the melting snowball on the floor at her feet and said, "It's a matter of finding a way to bridge the gap where the water phase should be. If we twist the working like this..." She picked up the remains of the snowball and made a gesture over it. "I believe that should seal the ice so that the water phase becomes impossible. Then the incantation to create steam can..." She ran out of words as the limitations in her method became evident.

Gauvain kept his customary contempt in check, however. "You are very close. Instead of sealing it, surround it in a matrix. Then apply the formula, keeping all thought of water firmly away."

Amalie stood next to John, uncertain.

"Well, go ahead, girl. Do as I say."

"Yes, sir." Willow noted that Amalie's voice was neither timid nor abashed. Good for you, she thought. But when Amalie tried the formulaic exercise, she screeched and dropped the snowball.

John picked it up. "You heated the matrix, not the snow," he said. Willow and the other two apprentices kept their attention fixed on the tableau in front. "I think you need to use focused, directional application of the energies, and target the gaps in the matrix. May I try, sir?"

Gauvain waved a bored hand at the boy.

John carefully held the snowball, constructed the matrix, and performed the incantation. A cloud of steam formed around the ball before he, too, yelped and dropped the now sodden chunk of snow.

Willow bit back a sigh. This working and the technique were familiar to her, as was a smoother, more professional way to perform the same operation – but she had been unable to perceive the matrix or sense the power of the incantation. She felt a flicker of energy caroming around in the classroom from time to time, but no more. Perhaps she'd speak to Gauvain later about speeding up the restoring of her mind; it would be worth risking any number of nauseous, headachy episodes to feel the fullness of the Aura in her hands again.

"Not bad," Gauvain said. "Return to your stools. We have several more things to cover this morning."

Willow heard the collective groan. If Gauvain did, he ignored it and continued lecturing on the nature of matter.

Chapter 10

The afternoon sun baked down as Bryar took a blow – another blow – and collapsed on what was left of the lawn, covered in sweat and dirt and anticipating a healthy bruise. A tough way to learn, but he wouldn't be making that mistake again. He and Joss were both pulling their punches, but it didn't follow that either of them was immune to hard strikes. Tai watched the mock battle from the porch steps, next to the pile where they'd dropped their tunics. The little herd of goats regarded them solemnly from the edge of the grass. In four days, the two men had managed to largely destroy the lawn in front of the house, but when they'd apologized, shamefaced, Rebecca waved them off. "Bosh. The grass will grow back. I leave the window open so he can hear you. He enjoys it."

Because Ezra's chair sat empty. He had taken to his bed. Tai had been allowed one visit, yesterday, but neither he nor Joss had seen the Old Man since the fateful conversation on the porch.

Joss offered him a hand up. Once, Bryar would have disdained the helping hand; now he accepted it willingly. Sparring with Joss served as a useful reminder that he wasn't as young, or as fit, as he once had been.

"You okay?" Tai called.

"Mostly."

"Debatable," Joss rumbled. Bryar smirked under the dirt coating his face; he'd landed a telling blow or two himself. Good. He'd already picked up several valuable techniques from Joss, and he intended to use them. He backed away and readied himself.

"Adjust your feet," Joss said. "Like so. You'll get better leverage."

Bryar made the change, felt the improvement in his balance, and braced himself for Joss's next attack.

This time they both ended up in the dirt. Instead of grappling, they collapsed there, content to abandon their practice bout. Tai came over and stood above them, hands on hips. "Fine defenders you two will be, if this is the best you can do."

Bryar reached up a hand and grabbed hers, tugging her down, his mind flashing to her gently rounded breasts... He let the memory go, though he'd certainly return to it. She intrigued him more each day, it seemed. The three of them lolled on the remains of the grass.

"Me, I'm good with you defending yourself for a while," Joss said. "I'd forgotten what hard work this is."

"I suspect you don't need any defending," Bryar added.

"Gran made fresh ointment for your bruises," Tai said. "You've both taken a pummeling this time. I'll go get it."

"Not yet," Bryar said. "Give us a chance to clean up first."

"Did you know you can make a whistle from grass? Listen." With a blade of grass anchored along her joined thumbs, she blew. At the shriek she produced, Rebecca rushed out onto the porch, only to shake her head and return inside.

"That's horrible. Whistles should be musical, not sound like a dying animal."

"Makes me glad there wasn't much available grass on Terra."

Tai sat back and grinned.

Bryar resisted turning his mind to the reason he was subjecting himself to a daily battering at Joss's hands, but he had to admit their bouts felt good. Muscles unused for years ached pleasurably at the end of the day, and the river soothed the cuts and bruises.

Tai's almost constant presence didn't hurt, either.

Rebecca reappeared. "Tai, I need you."

"Sure, Gran." She scrambled up and headed for the house.

"That it for today?" Joss asked.

"I hope so. Some of what hurts needs time to heal."

"Same here. You're a fighter. Didn't expect that."

Bryar experimentally plucked a thick blade of grass and mimicked Tai's position with his thumbs. He blew. Nothing much happened. "Must be the angle of the breath, like when you play a flute. I'll practice."

"Not when I'm around. I can still take you, you know." Joss got to his feet. "I'm cleaning up, then going in search of food. You're swimming?"

"I need the water." Joss, being both earth clan and a novice swimmer, kept himself well away from the river, but for Bryar it was as essential as life blood.

He emerged an hour later, refreshed, clean, and ready for Tai's ointment. Several new bruises decorated his arms and torso, and he suspected he'd have to forego practice tomorrow to give his muscles a chance to catch up. He used his walk back to the compound to start his mandated half hour exercise, trying to find what Ezra sought, what Tai had forced into his focus, the old, broken-off pieces of himself from his years enduring taunts, the cataclysmic loss of his first flute. But it was hopeless. He understood with words the importance of moving past those long-ago hurts, but he lacked the techniques to restore the parts of himself that she swore had gone into hiding for safekeeping. Instead, he paid attention to the vegetation, the patterns on the forest floor where animals had foraged or run. Every time he and Tai ventured anywhere, he got an earful, how the world worked, the interdependencies among the plants, the soil, the water.

Thunder rumbled overhead as he reached the edge of the lawn surrounding the house. Ezra once again sat in his chair, relaxed and peaceful, as if waiting for the rain.

Bryar trotted across the grass with a friendly goat at his heels. He bolted up the steps and sank down on the porch floor beside the Old Man. "You're..."

"Better, yes." Ezra's clawed hand clutched his arm, squeezed, and let go. "And you owe me a conversation. And a decision."

Tussling with Joss was a game. The words that came out of his mouth next would seal his fate. With every fiber of his being, he didn't want to say those words, and couldn't keep the tinge of bitterness from his voice. "Did you ever doubt?"

"I'm afraid I did." Ezra leaned back and closed his eyes. "I appreciate your reluctance, Bryar. You wouldn't be the man I believe you to be if you came into this without doubts. It's one thing to ride helter-skelter into battle without preparation – and I don't mean physical exercises – and quite another to do the work. If it comforts you at all, trust me when I say that the way of life you long for is dying. You might have been given a year or two to roam the Midland and perform, but the end is inevitable. Until that power cell is disposed of, all we love is under threat."

"Joss is a good fighter —"

"And Joss is fulfilling his role. The rest is yours to do. The decisions, the primary action. Have you been working with memories of your lost flute?"

"Tai told you?"

"Yes. I was convinced the birthmark caused the rupture, but I see now it's much more. A loss like that, right at puberty, too..."

"I don't know how to do what you want. I get the concept, but there must be some technique, something I'm not seeing. Tai talked about finding missing parts of myself."

"Exactly. I will arrange for Tai to help you. There is a form of trance work, unrelated to the Aura. It may break this blockage for you."

"Okay." Ezra probably heard his reluctance. Even back in his training days at the Motherhouse, he hadn't been sure which was the more painful, the physical beatings he'd endured as part of his childhood or being forced to confront and come to terms with them.

"Be still. Let's watch the storm roll in."

The sky had darkened, the first sign of rain since the storm that accompanied their arrival in Ezra's neighborhood. Joss emerged from the house, his arms shiny with ointment. Wordlessly he settled against the house wall.

"Give us a show," the Old Man muttered, and the heavens opened. Lightning danced from cloud to cloud, thunder added a bass counterpoint to the rush of falling rain. Bryar closed his eyes, sheltered by the roof but also by the power of the man in the chair next to him, and heard music dancing through the air. He listened, hypnotized, as the harmonies seeped into him. Not since they left to cross the hills had music entered him this way.

Feeling as if he'd been given his life back, he swallowed hard, unable to speak.

"Record it," Ezra murmured. "Make it yours. You won't get many more opportunities."

"I will." His voice came out a whisper.

Later, when the thunder died out and the rain settled into a steady pounding, Ezra said, "We will develop a plan to use our remaining time wisely. From now on, your days will be fully occupied. Physical and mental training, and I will require your assistance to devise a template that will block your Auric connection. We have never explored such techniques, but this is crucial for your safety, possibly your survival." He paused, then added, "Joss, I know we must talk, but for the moment your help here is vital. I hope you will stay."

"Sure, if you need me. There's nothing urgent in my life."

"You want to go to the Motherhouse. I understand that. But your whisperer skills can wait for now." Ezra relaxed in his chair and closed his eyes, ending the discussion.

Bryar and Joss looked at each other across the porch. Committed, Bryar thought. You and me. Willow, far away in Borgonne. Tai and Ezra and Rebecca, the Motherhouse, the Midland. Mari, his daughter. The weight of it might rest on his shoulders, but for this afternoon it didn't matter. Because today the music had returned. Today, he'd found peace.

Chapter 11

Another few days, another batch of bruises, Joss reflected ruefully as he headed toward the compound. He liked them all, Ezra and Rebecca, the odd Tai, Bryar. In the sparring match that morning, Bryar had taken him down. The man now fought with a terrifying focus and intensity – and then sat on the porch with his flute and played the sweetest music Joss had ever heard.

Weary of the others' constant presence, he'd headed to the landslide site, to see it with fresh eyes. So many mysteries shielded Ezra's compound that he no longer trusted his memory. Illusion protected the Old Man's privacy, he supposed, but for the life of him he didn't understand what the fuss was about.

At least he was confident he'd find his way to the slide. Once Ezra accepted you, the illusions became no more than vapors. But he agreed with Bryar; there had been no turnoff from the main trail when they'd first traversed the path.

The landslide was no illusion. Debris filled what had already been a bleak bowl in the hillside, a sure invitation to a twisted ankle – or worse, to being caught in the middle when the earth released again, raining boulders the size of a small house down on you. He had overheard Ezra instructing Tai to stay away from it, part of a gentle chiding for that first crossing she'd made, right after the slide. She pushed ahead through life accepting no boundaries, in Joss's opinion, but at times a person needed rules and regulations to guide him – or her.

The whole earthquake business puzzled him. Earthquakes on Terra brought devastation. He'd experienced several in his season here, yet the glass in the windows at the

Motherhouse seemed impervious. How did they do that? More of their magical hocus-pocus?

Our magical hocus-pocus, he corrected himself. He'd become one of them, if a minor player. No point denying it any longer.

After the thunderstorm four days ago, the world had dried out and crisped up. The air held a tang he now associated with apples. On Terra, fruit of any kind was a once-every-few-months treat; non-essential, and so not grown. Here, he couldn't get enough. Overhead, reds and golds such as he'd never seen tinged the leaves; the few trees in his part of Northam Corporation turned a turgid, dirty gold, nothing approaching this radiance. The sun warming his skin, filtering through the branches, carried a gentler warmth with a hint of cold weather to come. Joss sensed the change in the seasons and wondered what winter would bring. Rebecca might be his best source of information, as Ezra showed little practical sense about things such as food and clothing, assuming – rightly – that all he needed would be there for him.

Ezra gestured to him when he emerged at the edge of the clearing that surrounded the compound of house, barn, and outbuildings. Joss ambled over to the porch, but before he could sit, Ezra struggled to his feet and held out a hand. "Help me please. I want to see the orchard, but my legs are unsteady."

"Happy to." Joss allowed the Old Man to grasp his arm and assisted him down the stairs and across the lawn, where a trail headed south through the woods.

"You respond to the change," Ezra observed as they walked slowly toward the orchard. "More than mere observation, it's in your bones."

"Seems so."

"How are the livestock?"

"Goat one, the big nanny, is bored. You can expect mischief there. The chickens are quite a bunch, chatting all day long." Joss grinned. "Everyone's healthy."

"Good. Let's hope it stays that way."

On the edge of the orchard they found a small table and two chairs awaiting them. The table held a caff pot with matching miniature mugs and a plate of pastries. He shook his head in mild amazement. "Rebecca?"

"Tai, more likely." Ezra dismissed the mysterious appearance of caff with a gesture. "We maintain our own resources, but when the apples and abricoes are ripe, we welcome assistance. The fruit is stored, dried, pressed into cider, processed into jelly, and baked into these excellent pastries. You could lend a hand if you're willing."

"Sure." He eased the older man into a chair and took the other. Ezra poured from the caff pot. By now Joss knew about Ezra's fondness for caff. The stuff waited ready on one table or another throughout the day.

"This is pleasant. Everyone responds to the passing of seasons, even those like me who are not earth clan. Expect snow before Solstice."

Joss did the mental calculation; sixty days or so. Two months, back on Terra.

"Are you getting used to making decisions for yourself?"

The Old Man's questions always poked at a sensitive spot, not that questions about his own nature and the way of life on his new planet didn't teem in his mind. "It's hard sometimes. Like working weak muscles. After a lifetime of people telling me what to do..." He shrugged, offered the pastries to Ezra, then took one himself.

"So you work that muscle, learn to use your brain to discern your best course. Now, you want to improve your whisperer skills. And spend more time in the Hallan valley. You hope Willow will return – to you, unless I miss my guess." Ezra bit into his pastry and gazed out across the apple trees, laden with red, yellow, and green fruits, the overripe ones littering the ground and filling the air with a fruity, yeasty aroma.

Willow. The rituals surrounding men and women on this planet remained a mystery to him, and he never quite mustered the courage to ask about them. But he'd learned that Ezra not only seemed to know everything, but was willing to hear anything Joss wanted to talk about. And he'd longed to explore the topic of Willow ever since that day in the meadow.

He plunged in, aware of the heat on his face and grateful for Ezra's fixed gaze on the fruit trees.

"Willow and I, we..." The words wouldn't come; he hoped Ezra would figure out what he meant. "It changed things, for me, anyway. Did it affect her the same way? Or was it just... I know about her and Bryar. And probably others. I feel a bit lost, to be honest."

Ezra picked up his little caff mug, but cradled it rather than drinking. "You're on your own when it comes to learning Willow's feelings. I will say that here, some people form exclusive sexual relationships, while some take many partners. There's nothing preventing either type of relationship, and no predominance of one over the other. It is unusual, however, for a Weaver to mate with a single person. The nature of our lives precludes it, and probably some oddity about our minds. For a while, after Romarin's birth, I expected Willow and Bryar to commit, but it wasn't to be. They traveled together for three years with Mari before they separated, so there will always be a special understanding between them. You need to accept that."

"But for Willow and me?"

"Be honest, and it will sort out. But recognize, too, that Willow, Bryar, and Quinn are involved in this mess with the power cell. Willow may have already fulfilled her part. Bryar is starting his. And Quinn..." Ezra stopped and smiled. "After training, a journey Weaver works with a mentor for a year. You've met Dal, he was Willow's mentor. I was Quinn's. I care about that girl, and I worry. Because of her ability to walk templates, she may find herself in danger – not to mention that she's far too willing to put herself at risk."

Joss's mouth twitched at Ezra's use of the word 'girl' for Quinn.

The two men ate pastries, sipped caff, and said nothing. A breeze rippled the yellowing leaves on the apple trees, sending a few of them skittering along the ground.

"What do you expect of me?" Joss asked.

Ezra cleaned his fingers on a linen napkin before answering. "For you to recognize your own worth. I do believe you must return to the Motherhouse. We haven't plumbed the full scope of your gift, nor have you mastered it, but it may prove to be a valuable resource. There are people in the world who mean no good to us. If you could read them—"

"Are you talking about Kiril? He's having a hard time adapting, but he's a good man. His life was a lot more tied to the hierarchy on Terra than mine."

"No, not Kiril. Two at least, the other side of the hills."

"Do you know the man Willow found? The one who healed Bryar?" Gauvain had spooked him; he sensed the man's power, and his pride.

"Yes, from years ago. He exhibited the brashness of youth and confidence in his own abilities, a presaging, I believe, of how he must be today. That's a big part of the reason for the shielding around the compound. I am confident I could triumph, should it come to a battle, but the older I get, the less I choose to test that belief. I don't want Gauvain, or Duncan, to find me."

"Duncan... the other one?"

"Yes, and in his own way possibly more dangerous. They both seek supremacy. Life in Borgonne has always been predicated on hierarchy, one of several reasons we discourage – shall we call them adventures? – in the hills. Your party was an exception, and against my better judgment. Kiril tried to move the cell through the hills, but a confusion weave prevented him from going more than a day's journey before he found himself back where he started. He's determined and enterprising, so it required two more forays before he gave it up. And while he fought the confusion, we suffered the loss of the Aura, because he didn't keep it shielded. Even packing it in dirt would have helped. But Kiril probably wasn't aware of that, nor did he realize how detrimental it can be. He too wants power, but as a means to save himself, not for its own sake. As you said, he's confused about his place here. He'll find it, so he doesn't concern me so much. I am concerned, however, about securing the cell, wherever it is."

"You don't know?" Joss had assumed Ezra knew everything.

"In general terms. We need to claim it, and soon, before Gauvain and Duncan find it."

"So my abilities, if trained, could tell us what they're feeling – I can't read thoughts."

"No, but that may be enough. Suppose, for instance, someone enters the hills. He might elect to bring pack animals with him, or goats for meat. But the spells in the hills would spook any domestic animal. And you could pick up on that, as well as on Gauvain's own feelings. Despite his bravado, I doubt he's happy in the hills."

Joss stretched back in his chair, allowing the sun to dance on his face, and rubbed his chin; shaving was not a simple task on this world, but he disliked not being clean shaven. "I'd love to hear how you met those guys."

"It was a long time ago." Ezra made a small, dismissive gesture with his hand. Whatever the backstory, Joss wouldn't learn it today.

"So, I'll stay here and work with Bryar, and help with the harvest, then go to the Motherhouse around Solstice?"

"The weather may turn before then, but that's likely the best compromise. I'll notify Arwen to expect you, since she'll need time to develop a training plan. You're an anomaly, arriving full grown with powers that only occur once in generations. I've never met an animal whisperer before."

"I still don't understand it." But he couldn't regret it, either. Reading the thoughts, if you could call them that, of the animals was a joy. The cow tended to be stand-offish, but both the goats and the chickens in Ezra's compound had become his friends. Despite that, sometimes he needed a break. On his own he'd begun devising ways to shut out the incessant chatter from the henhouse, with limited success.

Ezra read his thoughts. "It's a standard technique, Joss. All Weavers shield their minds. We'd go mad otherwise. You'll learn how at the Motherhouse. I regret I don't have time to teach you."

"Then why can't Bryar just shield himself? Why the need for new protocols?"

Ezra made a quick, dismissive gesture. "Shielding from others is one thing. Shielding from the Aura itself is quite another. Bryar could never handle his quest with his Auric connection unshielded, quite apart from the fact that both his main rivals are stronger in power than he is."

"Okay, I get it. But after seeing what happened to Willow..."

"Nobody wants that. I'll do my best to prevent it."

Everything centers on the thirst to control the power cell, Joss concluded as he returned to the compound with Ezra on his arm, his free hand carrying the linen cloth with the dishes wrapped inside it. The damned thing was his and Kiril's responsibility, so he'd make himself available to Ezra and Bryar, he'd train and become adept at being a whisperer, he'd do what he could.

Chapter 12

Once, it was so easy.

"Are you coming tonight?" Amalie bounced on the balls of her feet, radiating excitement although her voice had dropped to a whisper. Gauvain's energy dominated the apprentices' workroom, even when he himself was absent.

Willow shook her head. Two nine-days after she once again began to sense the Aura, she was no closer to working a weave. For sure the colors of the world glowed more brightly, the breezes carried intimations of seasons to come, food tasted better... all in all, her senses responded with delight to the return of the world's magic. But as far as actually using that magic – nothing. She strove to perform the simple workings, practicing into the night to build the energy and release it for a focused task. But while the Aura tantalized her, template work remained a distant memory.

And no Bryar to talk to, no Quinn. No Joss.

Gauvain's impatience taunted her. Given that each treatment resulted in greater access to the Aura, he failed to understand her inability, time and time again, to produce a functioning template. His cold silences made it clear he considered it her fault. She was doing something wrong.

But I'm not.

She followed Gauvain's protocols, and when she manifested no result she reviewed her early training at the Motherhouse, recalling the techniques she had been taught then. With no success at all.

Her presence in the class puzzled the apprentices. An older woman who showed no Entrée? She didn't blame them. Amalie and Reed at least made an effort to include her in their activities, some approved, many surreptitious. Gauvain had no idea what went on under his nose.

The other two apprentices, John and Conor, remained aloof and appeared indifferent to her presence.

For tonight Amalie proposed an authorized venture to the town square, where musicians promised an evening of dance and revelry. Willow remembered last summer at the Motherhouse, Bryar's strong body not quite touching hers as they undulated to the music, his eyes smoldering into hers... the last time she'd danced.

Since then there had been Joss.

"Thank you, but I think I will stay here. I'm a little tired."

"You never go out."

"Not too often, no."

"Why not? Does he lock you up?"

That said a lot about the apprentices' idea of their master.

Willow laughed. "No, nothing like that. Things aren't working for me right now, as you know. Once..." She let the memory hang.

"All you do is work. You need fun in your life, if you ask me."

I didn't ask you. You're a child.

But Willow forced herself to accept the possible truth in Amalie's words. Gauvain's and her own efforts had intensified as they strove to unlock her Entrée. The girl might be right that she needed a counterbalance.

"About tonight, I'll let you know later. I hadn't considered it, but I wonder..."

"You're no fun. Even my mum goes out to the dances."

Willow was old enough to be this young woman's mother. In fact, Amalie was only a year older than Romarin.

Romarin. She missed her daughter, another weight on her heart. The hills imposed a separation greater than walking the byways of the Midland.

Gauvain arrived, and the classroom settled into its usual somber studiousness.

Later, in her room, Willow consciously relaxed, accessed the Aura, performed the movements that should create a glow between her hands, and… nothing. Despondent, she turned to her window and stared out at her unprepossessing view, mainly rooftops. Off in the distance she could see the near fields, now mowed as Borgonne battened down for the winter. She'd picked up the rumor from Leo that the harvest would barely meet winter's needs; the grain heads had failed to fill properly despite the good weather.

The Aura again? Or the power cell?

More likely the lack of rain.

Disgusted and bored with herself, Willow turned from the window to study the clothes in her wardrobe. Neither her scholar's gown nor the elaborate outfits Gauvain provided for her would do for a village square. But…

She reached up and fingered her old tunic, washed and even pressed, thanks to Leo. Paired with one of Gauvain's plainer skirts…

Why not? It wasn't as if staying in the tower was doing her any good.

She rushed down the stairs and made her way to the kitchen, where promising aromas rose from the cookfire. Leo turned and smiled when he saw her. "My dear. How lovely to see you."

"You, too." She hugged the hunched man. Leo had proven to be a kind light in an otherwise bleak experience. "I need your help."

"With pleasure."

She left the kitchen with coins in her pocket, protocols regarding Orlan dances in her head, Leo's promise to alert Gauvain to her absence at dinnertime, and a determination to leave the tower behind for a few hours and maybe, just maybe, enjoy herself.

Orlan's style of dancing involved everyone pairing up in two lines to perform an assortment of moves, most of them familiar to Willow. Residents of the Midland danced heys, do-si-dos, right-and-left and swing, the same as here. For new steps, your Borgonnian partner more or less threw you in the direction they expected you to go until you caught on.

Everybody participated; a single dance lasted for a quarter of an hour or more.

Willow pulled to a stop after a final flourish from the musicians. "My side hurts."

From laughing. How long had it been?

"Yeah, I know what you mean." Her current partner, a woman a few years older than Willow and considerably heavier, gave her a shoulder hug. "I've not seen you around."

"I have lived here for almost half a season, but I don't go out much."

"Where ya from?" The two women worked their way through the milling crowd toward the food stalls.

Should she tell? Why not? "A place called the Midland."

"Never heard of it. Like here?" Few of the people she encountered outside Gauvain's dining room spoke in complete sentences.

Willow looked around, remembering her grim reception, noting the dingy, reddish buildings, the absence of trees. "No, not much. It's more agrarian. Structures are white or timbered, not red."

"Ever try one of these?" The woman held up a pastry, then flipped a small coin to the boy behind the counter of the stall. "Mutton."

Willow dug a matching coin from her pouch and accepted the treat, wrinkling her nose as grease coated her fingers. Mutton pastries weren't greasy in the Midland. But the first bite tasted like... home. Friends, work, familiar food, ways of life she understood.

Diou, but she was homesick.

"Catch ya later." The woman disappeared in the crowd. Willow used one hand to push her hair out of her face, then found a quiet corner and munched the pastry. In the twilight, she absentmindedly flicked her wrist, without considering her actions.

A small light globe appeared in her palm.

She hastily closed her hand around it and muttered the words to smother the light. Not knowing the prevailing attitudes toward those with such skills, but well aware of the distrust held by much of the populace for Gauvain and, presumably, other Mages, she watched and waited to see if anyone had noticed. And if so, what they would do about it.

Nothing happened. She finished her pastry, wondering why she didn't feel more elated.

Amalie spotted her and pushed through the crowd, dragging Reed along with her. "Saw you in the line earlier. Enjoy the festival? Come with us, we know where there's ale they'll sell to those not yet sixteen."

"I'm tired." True enough, after dancing for over two hours, nearly nonstop. "It's time for me to go home, but thank you." She pulled Amalie closer and whispered, "About having fun... you were right."

Amalie spun on her toes, her giddiness suggesting that either she thoroughly entered into the spirit of the evening or she'd already found the rumored beer stall. "Told you."

The two teens left her in favor of their own search for what made for a fun evening.

Willow crossed the square, dodging the lines forming for the next dance, and struck out along the avenue that led to the tower, which was deserted and eerie in the semi-dark. She had been to the square a few times now and knew the route well, so she decided not to risk casting another light globe to show her the way.

Halfway to the tower, a man came out of the shadows of an alley and grabbed her by the arm, his fingers digging into her flesh through the thin linen of her tunic. He was unremarkable, in his mid-twenties, of average height, with sallow skin and greasy dark hair. He stank of beer. "Yer not welcome here," he snarled, then jerked her up against a wall.

Too astounded to panic, she frantically scanned the deserted street for help.

His hand pinched her cheeks, holding her still. His body shoved up against hers, his face not a handspan distant, his breath foul. Unable to move, she twisted her head away. "I've no argument with you," she gasped. "Let me go."

"We got no truck with witches around here. Don't you deny." He shook her roughly; the brick wall grazed her shoulder. "I saw that light ya made back there. Just watch where ya show yerself from now on, or we'll teach ya where ya belong."

"Teach 'er now, Rafe." Another man appeared, this one slighter, with tousled, greasy blond hair. "Let 'er know we mean business."

Diou, he means it. Fighting panic, Willow struggled against Rafe's hands. He laughed at her.

"Not a bad idea at that. Lookit, I c'd do with some of this." He twisted his hand into her hair and yanked her head back. "We're fixin' to have fun here."

He pulled her away from the wall and shoved her toward the alley.

A flare lit the night, momentarily blinding her. Rafe screamed, released his grip on her arm, and fell to his knees. The other man looked around, his eyes wide, then fled.

"You will be both impotent and incontinent throughout the winter season. Perhaps that will teach you to respect women – and to be careful whom you call a witch." The voice, never so welcome as now, came from the man wrapped in a black cape who stepped out of the obscurity.

Rafe writhed where he lay.

"Come," Gauvain commanded, and reached out to her. Numb, Willow allowed him to tuck her hand under his arm. He set off toward the tower, pulling her stumbling beside him.

"Kindly explain what you thought you were doing, walking the streets alone at night. I don't expect such behavior from you."

Uncertain of her voice, she stammered, "I didn't know… in the Midland, it's safe, even in the bigger towns. Nothing like this… he meant to hurt me," she added incredulously.

"The man's drunk. He would have raped you and left you dumped in an alley. Whatever possessed you to dress like that?"

She stopped walking and blinked at him. He'd just saved her from pain at the hands of another man, and now he questioned her dress? "The outfits you chose for me are not suitable for a dance on the square."

He started her moving again. "Had you spoken to me, I could have escorted you to a gathering in a different part of town, where your gowns would have suited extremely well. Not to mention it is safer, and you would have been under my protection. This was foolish, Willow."

Feeling steadier on her feet as they walked, she said, "I wanted this type of festival. Loose and... fun. I miss dancing. Being free from worry."

"I assure you, the other dance was delightful."

"And required conformity to rules and manners I don't understand. But I never expected —" The enormity of what had just happened rushed over her; her knees failed as she burst into tears.

"Oh, by the Sustainer." But Gauvain turned and gathered her up against his chest. "Do try to control yourself until we get home. I'll arrange for Leo to draw you a bath, if he isn't out making a fool of himself at the festivities."

"He said he planned to go, but only for a short time." Her voice came out roughly as she struggled to stop the sobs.

Gauvain uttered an exasperated sigh and hustled her forward. "I sometimes believe that however I attempt to improve the lives of those in my household, you all still prefer these low occupations. I suppose the apprentices are there as well."

She wiped her face on her sleeve and gulped. "I believe you gave them permission."

"Much joy may it give them. They will be fit for nothing tomorrow."

She wanted to keep it to herself, but Amalie was sure to speak up. "Look. Some good has come of this evening." She used her free arm to reach out, move her fingers in the weave, and cast a light globe before them.

Gauvain stared at the light, then at her. "Excellent, although it took unconscionably long. Now we can accelerate your treatments."

She'd hoped for something positive, like *I'm so happy for you.* But this was Gauvain. She extinguished the globe.

Neither spoke again until he deposited her in Leo's care.

Chapter 13

They'd gone to a rough meadow at some distance from Ezra's compound, he and Tai, stopping in the orchard for pears on their way. Much of the fruit had been gathered, and giant flagons of brewing cider filled the outbuildings. Bryar inhaled deeply; the air was heady with the scents of fermenting apples.

"You're limping," Tai said.

"Joss landed a blow across my ankle. It's just bruised."

"I saw that. Why didn't you block him?"

"I tried. Truth is, I need a break. I'm getting worse, not better, I'm so tired."

Tai said nothing, merely led them along the path.

The meadow formed a loose pattern of golds and browns, with only a hint of green remaining, and one red wildflower in bloom. Bryar stopped and seized Tai's hand. "Wait. Stand still. Feel this day."

Everything he was willing to fight for flooded his senses. The colors of the Aura, which so few could see, danced overhead, russet reds fading into the palest blue of the sky. Music teased at the edges of his mind; if he weren't so weary, he'd reach out and claim those notes, weave them into perfect harmonies...

Wordlessly, Tai led him to a sheltered hollow where they'd sat together before, sharing their lives, their responses, their enjoyment of each other's company. As they settled onto a ground blanket, she knelt behind him and placed hands on his shoulders. "I've brought a potion."

He leaned back, their bodies touching. "Why?"

"To relax and empty your mind. We must try again, Bryar. Something's missing. You need to be... I *want* you to be whole again."

"Rebecca's potions taste nasty." He'd taken a few, to keep his body going under its daily drubbing at Joss's hands.

His fighting skills had improved, though. Joss bore an equal share of grazes and bruises. Furthermore, their jousts reinforced a camaraderie between them. Relaxing with Joss at the end of the day, drinking Rebecca's cider, proved to be a connection he sorely needed.

Tai released his shoulders and twisted to the side. He dropped back, onto the fragrant ground.

"My potions are no better. But this is nothing to do with Gran."

Lying there, Bryar couldn't care less about missing pieces of himself and all Tai's meditative mumbo-jumbo. With the mild autumn breeze on his face and the radiance of the sunshine brushing the meadow around him – not to mention Tai's presence, which made it that much more perfect – he wanted for nothing.

"I'm serious." She shook Bryar's shoulder, then stood and rummaged in their pack. "My potion will help."

Later, after gagging down the drink, he found it even easier to lie still, letting the day soothe him, listening to the music in the susurrating grasses, the occasional bird call from the surrounding trees. He claimed Tai's hand again and felt himself dozing off...

"Oh, no, you don't. Shall I tell you what we're going to do?"

"Sure." Because it was Tai doing the telling.

"It's like template work, but different, and it's important to keep them separate. Just let go of everything – but don't connect to the Aura. Okay?"

Doubtful, Bryar thought. "None of us release the Aura completely, ever. You know that."

"Do your best. I'm going to link with your mind, but not like Weavers usually do, so it might feel strange. If you let me in, we'll journey together to find this missing piece. Or pieces." At his sigh, Tai added, "You don't make it easy."

"I don't make it hard, either. I want this as much as you do." Mainly so they would leave him alone about it. Get it over and done.

He sat up to look around, soak in the richness of the autumn palette. She gave him a minute or two. "Try not to go to sleep, okay? Let the drum carry you. I'll be along for the ride."

Obediently, he stretched out and closed his eyes. Tai began drumming, a repetitive, non-musical beat played with impeccable rhythm. There was little to fault in Tai.

She was...

He found himself lost in an unexpected trance, aware dimly of Tai's energy nearby. The Aura intruded, alive with color and hints of melody; he remembered her injunction and pushed it away. Without it, he saw only swirling gray patterns.

And words, sounding clearly through the mist. *Bryar, Bryar, pants on fire...*

No! He slammed the door on that memory, only to find that Tai kicked it open again. She wouldn't allow him to suppress it.

More pieces of his childhood came to him. Enduring one of so many beatings, humiliations, pain not from the fists. His broken flute, which he'd vowed never to think of again. His appalling failure in the mine. He groaned; his body thrashed against the ground. Tai's leg crossed his, giving him an anchor, while the drumming captured his nerve endings, claiming him.

"Follow me." Tai's voice. He felt himself pulled through an opening...

They were in a cave, dark and dank. A thin shaft of light provided minimum illumination. A blond child, a boy, perhaps eight years old but small for his age, huddled in a corner, his feet bare and his clothing no more than rags. Bryar sensed pain... physical, but more than that...

Tai spoke to the child. "Hello, little one."

He turned from them. Fear pervaded the bleak atmosphere, clenching Bryar's gut... but more, a wounding deeper than words could heal as the child sank back against the hard stone corner.

Bryar watched as Tai cajoled the boy, assuring him of comfort and welcome.

A sob pulsed through the cave. Something in Bryar tore open.

"We've come to take you home. Your true home," Tai said, and reached a hand toward the miserable child in the corner. "It's safe, and you'll be okay. I promise."

The boy moved his hand, then sank back, distrusting.

Tai looked toward the entrance. "Join us, my beauty," she called. An instant later Bryar became aware of the batting of wings, a hooting such as sometimes echoed through the night sky, a suggestion of breeze in the air. A chouette, the largest he'd ever seen, landed next to Tai. "This is my friend," she told the boy. "You can pet him if you want to. He won't hurt you."

As if hypnotized by the bird, which was almost as large as he was, the boy slowly lifted his hand. The chouette hopped closer and butted its head against the hand. He jerked back, then reached out again, gingerly. As he stroked the bird, his eyes opened wider. Then, as if a deal had been struck, the child pitched forward and flung his arms around the chouette's neck, burying his head in the down on its chest.

"I have a gift for you." The boy peeked at her. Tai held out a small flute, similar to the one Bryar's father had smashed so many years ago. "For you. Try it. People all over the Midland love to hear you play."

The child was paying little heed to Tai now. His attention swiveled between the chouette, one arm around the bird, and the instrument. With a sudden lunge, he snatched the flute and retreated to his corner. His hands stroked it, then he raised it to his lips.

Tentative notes formed the lead-in to a basic tune, swirling through the cave, singing like an echo in Bryar's mind.

"You can keep it," Tai said. "But I wish you would come with us. There's so much more music out there."

The child gripped the flute. With his free hand, he wiped the tears from his face, then stood and spoke for the first time. "You promise?"

"Yeah, I do." She smiled.

After a great, shuddering breath, the boy said, "Okay." He reached for Tai.

She shook her head. "Not me. Him."

Bryar couldn't work out what happened next. He doubled over with unbelievable pain, his heart thudding. Not physical... he curled into himself, clutching his middle, as something invaded him, broke through his carefully constructed walls.

The rhythm changed, faster, urgent. Tai's voice overrode the pulsating beat, calling him home.

Home. The rough ground under the blanket, the air tinged with apples.

When Bryar emerged from the trance, Tai had shifted away, stowing the drum in its case. He stretched, rose to his knees, and looked around. The sun was sinking behind the low hills, casting long shadows and filling the sky with peach and purple. An autumn chill touched his skin; there would be frost that night.

Next to him lay the primitive flute Tai had given the child.

He stared, then snatched up the instrument and stood, his feet wide placed for stability, abruptly understanding what had happened.

"The notes are pure, as you heard." She nodded at the flute. "I'm going back to the house, but you take all the time you need. It'll be many nine-days before you finish integrating this, but I'll be close." Then, unbelievably, she stepped up and kissed him. Very gently. "Come home for dinner, or Rebecca will worry."

She turned away and crossed the meadow to the path leading to the compound.

Bryar dropped back to the ground, clutching the flute, too overwhelmed to answer.

He couldn't deny the lost boy any longer.

In the solitude of the meadow, he cried.

Chapter 14

In the late afternoon light, Joss stood on the edge of the compound everyone called the Motherhouse, wondering for the umpteenth time in the last two days why he'd been summarily dismissed from Ezra's home and sent here. Everything had changed five days ago. Bryar had retreated from them all, moving into a small room in the main house instead of the one adjacent to the barn they'd shared since their arrival. Ezra said little but seemed subtly relieved. There had been no practice bouts, no collapsing with Bryar on the ruins of the lawn, exhausted but content. Tai was nowhere to be found, but Rebecca continued as usual, feeding and mothering them.

He'd have liked to say goodbye to Bryar, at least. Instead, Ezra told him to go, Rebecca stocked his pack with enough food to carry him to the Motherhouse twice over, and now here he was.

Emotion – not his own – bombarded him. The Motherhouse didn't exactly project scholarly camaraderie. Maybe it never had, and this was merely another manifestation of his maturing powers. Only the strongest, or the most focused, human emotions registered in his mind, so for him to experience the intense force of anxiety assaulting him meant something was wrong.

Great. Just what he needed. If he didn't find a way to shield himself from others' feelings, and soon, he'd be so drained he'd be useless.

Arwen emerged from the main admin building, which they all called the Centra, and headed in his direction, Quinn on her heels, both with looks of serious intent on their faces.

Free will be damned, right now he wouldn't mind having orders to follow. Facing these two formidable women without a roadmap gave him a cramp in his gut.

"Where is everybody?" he asked when they drew alongside him. "The place seems pretty quiet."

Arwen looked at him as if questioning his intellect. "Traveling, naturally. It's what we do."

"There didn't seem to be a point in holding everyone here any longer," Quinn added. "We exist to work out in the world. Those who aren't too far distant can be recalled, should we need their help."

"Let's go," Arwen commanded. "The bell's about to ring for evening meal, but afterwards we'll meet. I want to hear from you directly what you can and can't do."

"I'd rather not tonight." The gray-haired woman intimidated him, but hell, he'd just spent two days on the trail. "Food sounds great, but the rest? No."

He and Arwen locked eyes. "Yes, tonight. It won't take long, but I need a place to start with you. The sooner you have some control, the better. You'll be more useful."

"Useful how?"

"That's what we need to find out. For your sake and ours." Joss picked up a note of weariness in her voice, though his whisperer senses detected no emotions from either of the powerful women studying him like a specimen, despite the prevailing tension. Shielding themselves, he'd bet. He remembered the incessant chatter of Ezra's chickens and fervently hoped shielding would be high on their list of priorities for his training.

Arwen wheeled and strode away.

Quinn came closer. "She's under a lot of stress," she said quietly. "We all are. Between Willow being gone, and the possibility of actually crossing the hills, and the cell and its effect on the Aura..." They both set out in the direction of the guest lodge, Joss thinking more about kicking off his boots and having a bath and a shave, followed by a good meal, than about Quinn's words. "Arwen sees you as a tool. A feather in our quiver. How's Bryar?"

"I don't know."

She spun in front of him to block his passage. Her dark skin picked up warm, almost rosy undertones in the failing light, but her sharp voice belied her gentle appearance. "What exactly do you mean?"

Joss shrugged and stepped forward, forcing her to move aside and walk with him. "He was in seclusion for three days before I left, and no one's talking. He's at Ezra's, nothing's changed there. But he hasn't been training, hasn't been to meals, so I can't answer your question."

Quinn went silent and seemed to disappear into her mind; it was like walking with a ghost across the green. When they reached the lodge, she emerged from her reverie and said, "Yes, I believe that. I can't reach him. He's shut me out."

"Can he do that? I thought you Scribes had all these powers —"

"Don't be ridiculous," she snapped. But then she caught her breath, as if questioning the wisdom of her last words. "You're right. There's an energetic cost, but usually I'm able to connect with others, especially Willow and Bryar."

Joss leaned against the wall next to the door of the guest lodge. "Have you heard anything from Ezra?"

"Nothing but silence. I wonder what he's up to." Her fingers interlaced, forming a loose fist. "I want to know, Joss."

He hesitated, then shrugged. "Well, there was talk about how Bryar needs to be whole for this quest Ezra's sending him on. I wasn't privy to those discussions, so I don't really get what that means."

"Whole." Quinn sighed. "There's a lot in his past... but I thought that had all been dealt with during his training. If Tai's involved, I wonder... She knows techniques that aren't part of the Aura."

"Bryar's... he likes Tai. They're always together."

Quinn's mouth quirked, the first sign of humor he'd seen since arriving at the Motherhouse. Few people were about, but those they passed as they crossed the compound had appeared preoccupied. The tension in the air was palpable.

"Get yourself settled. I suspect we all need a decent meal. It's been a long afternoon, with too many unsolvable riddles."

"It is pretty intense around here." He rubbed his chin, grimacing at the stubble.

"And you pick up on that."

"I'd rather not."

Quinn snorted. "Welcome to the Motherhouse." She turned and left him at the door.

Joss checked in and headed straight to the bathing room, thinking over his meeting – confrontation? – with the two Scribes. Arwen had issued a command, and he'd made a stab at rejecting it. She'd won this one, but maybe he was growing comfortable with making his own decisions after all.

Chapter 15

In Borgonne, the crisp autumn days ended in frigid air trapped by low, gray cloud. Chill permeated the stone walls of the tower; Willow spent her afternoons wrapped in a cozy, pale yellow shawl Leo procured after seeing her shiver one day as she downed a hot tisane at his big kitchen table.

Gauvain didn't approve of the shawl, as being both inelegant and unsuited to a plain black student gown. Mornings, she left it in her satchel whenever possible, but at times she needed its warmth to fend off the bleakness of the classroom, while keeping it well away from their student experiments.

On this particular morning, Gauvain was lecturing on the nature of matter and the relative permeability of physical objects, including living beings. Willow followed closely, although, as a Healer, she already understood his subject in depth, at least as it applied to people. She suspected her knowledge of the subject was greater than his – not that she would ever say so.

When he placed a cage full of mice on their worktable, however, and outlined their experiment for the day, she decided to speak up. The technique he proposed was adequate, but there was a more elegant way to obtain the same results, with less potential harm to the mice.

"May I make an observation?"

"If you must." His eyes showed curiosity mixed with disdain; she almost never spoke in class.

"As an alternative, a method I've used frequently... if you start with a deep weave, isolating the injury... then work outward, expanding the weave... the gaps in the matrix won't matter so much, in most cases, because the steps you've outlined tie it off..." She heard the hesitation in her explanation and hated herself for it. She knew this technique inside out, but in the classroom Gauvain still intimidated her.

"And you take twice as long and risk your patient bleeding out in the meantime. We will follow my protocol, which is proven. Any questions?"

The apprentices, who had listened to the exchange wide-eyed, shook their heads in unison. No one spoke up when Gauvain took that tone.

Willow sent a mental apology to the mice, and the class resumed. Suspecting the poor things were likely to be traumatized by the unskilled practice, she planned to visit them after lunch for a Healing.

That afternoon, as Willow made her way along the corridor toward the kitchen, hoping for a warming drink from Leo, Gauvain's voice stopped her.

"You. In my study. Now."

She followed him into his private domain, steeling herself to indifference, on the surface at least. His tone left no question about his displeasure. Intense displeasure.

She chose to stand in front of his desk, pulling the offending shawl more closely around her shoulders.

He took his seat, his posture rigid. When he finally spoke, it was through clenched teeth. "You will never contradict me, especially in front of the apprentices."

"I didn't contradict you." Oddly, his barely contained anger served to calm her. She had done nothing wrong, and many nine-days of Gauvain had taught her enough about his usual way of operating that he might intimidate her, but he never overwhelmed her.

He showed no emotion, outside of barely contained rage. "You undermined my authority. That is not acceptable and not permitted. If you persist, I shall—"

"Shall what? Throw me out of the class?"

His control was slipping. A tremor shook his clenched hands on the desk. "And out of my home, if need be. You aren't fully restored yet, woman. Don't force me to discontinue your treatments. I can toss you onto the street, penniless."

"As I arrived? Somehow that doesn't frighten me."

"It should."

Yes, it should. The part of her brain that wasn't insulted by his tone reminded her to stay centered. Hoping to appear less confrontational, she perched on her accustomed chair and folded her hands in her lap.

"I am a Healer." She kept her voice neutral. "Naturally I have evolved other ways to approach the human body. I did not challenge your authority, nor did I criticize your technique. I merely contributed to it."

"These youngsters are not destined to be Healers. My working provides a more certain and secure binding. Yours..." He waved a dismissive hand in the air. "Undoable with no effort at all."

"By someone who set out to undo it, yes, I suppose so. But why would anyone want to? To Heal—"

"Are you really so obtuse?" He paused. "Now that I consider it, you probably are. I repeat, these young people will not be Healers, but Mages."

"And the primary focus of a Mage is power." She had gleaned that much from her time in the tower.

"Knowing how to build strong templates, to wield the weaves safely and competently. Understanding the underlying basis of the spells. Building on that knowledge – why do I even try? That Motherhouse of yours blinds you to the true scope of the Aura. I thought you might be adaptable once you saw the truth for yourself. Now, I despair."

"As do I, if that is your hope for me."

"Leave my study. At once. And *do not* speak that way in my class again. Am I clear?"

"You are. You are wrong, but your wishes are perfectly clear."

Willow rose with dignity, turned on her heel, and left without a backward glance, trusting to receive a warmer welcome and friendlier conversation in the kitchen.

Gauvain and his Mage work could just... just... in her suppressed fury she couldn't think of a curse bad enough for Mage magic.

Chapter 16

It had been almost four long nine-days since the cataclysmic afternoon with Tai's trancework, days during which the leaves fell and the first early snowfall blanketed Ezra's compound. Bryar had emerged from a self-imposed seclusion after most of a nine-day to find Joss gone, Rebecca and Tai involved in cheese making, and Ezra sitting on the porch staring out over the lawn toward the orchard.

He missed the sparring sessions with Joss, the chats in the evening before they retired.

Not that training had ended with Joss's departure. Ezra devised fiendish ways to build muscle tone and nimble reflexes, so that most nights he fell into bed exhausted. And that didn't even take into account the mental exercises. He hadn't composed a new melody in days; inspiration fled under the onslaught of fatigue.

Ezra was unsympathetic. "When you leave, this is how it will be. You may as well get used to it," he'd say. He'd then assign another exercise, most likely one leaving Bryar dripping with sweat despite the near freezing temperatures. And doing his best not to think ahead or wonder why he had agreed to this quest in the first place.

Ezra's unwelcome message demanding his presence came as Bryar enjoyed a rare break, exploring the snow-draped woods with Tai and soaking up her mystical and, to his mind, romantic view of the changed landscape.

They tensed at the same time.

"Did you get that?" Tai asked.

"Yeah. I wonder what he wants." The command had appeared in his head, just as occasional messages from the Motherhouse or private communications from Quinn did. At the moment, he wished Ezra wasn't quite so adept at template communications.

"I'm in no hurry to go back." A rare flash of defiance from Tai.

"Neither am I." Bryar looked at their mittenless hands, joined as usual. "But..."

She sighed. "I have work to do in the barn, anyway. And Gran wants me to start supper. This weather gets to her rheumatism."

"Too bad there's no Healer here."

"I do what I can, and so does Granddad. It's not always enough." Tai directed their steps back toward the compound, taking a roundabout way through the snow-shrouded trees. "Look."

He stopped, his gaze following where she pointed. "A violette?" he asked.

"The snow insulates, but the poor thing will freeze before it comes into bloom." Tai bent to touch the little plant with a finger, then straightened and led them toward the house.

Ezra wasn't in his usual spot. He'd been a fixture by the front door, even as the weather turned cold, wrapped up under a mountain of quilts and furs. Bryar frowned.

"He's in his workroom." Tai knew things she shouldn't, but because she was almost always right, he didn't argue. They left their wet boots by the fire in the lounge. Tai disappeared into the kitchen, and he headed down the hall to the far end of the building where Ezra maintained his private sanctum.

Bryar had been invited into the remarkable workroom only once before and was eager to see it again. Glassed windows graced two adjoining walls, so light always reflected off the highly polished wood floor. Shelves on either side of the door held books – a miracle in itself, for he had hardly ever seen a book other than the ones maintained in the villages to record births and deaths – and odd implements that might be practical or decorative, because he couldn't discern their function and Ezra wasn't saying. Elaborate hangings, a few of them faded and tattered, covered the wooden walls. Newer tapestries exhibited jewel tones unfamiliar to him in Midland textiles. A workbench filled the center of the room; Ezra perched on a stool on the far side, scowling.

"Took you long enough."

"We went to the woods."

"And would rather linger than return. Despite Tai's charms, you have more important things to deal with now."

"Sorry." Chastised and resenting it, Bryar claimed the stool opposite Ezra.

The Old Man got right to the point. "I can go no further with my experimentation without your participation. I wish to try out a weave to shield you from the Aura – I hope temporarily, but I make no guarantees."

The import of the words hit his gut. This was it. The day he stood to lose all he loved, all he was, if something went wrong.

"You're certain this is necessary?"

"You doubt my understanding?" Ezra retorted. "They're out there. They want the cell. We have to get there first"

Bryar recoiled. He had never seen the Old Man so on edge. "Maybe I'd be better off tracking it with my Entrée intact. I might—"

"No." Ezra was curt. "First, direct handling of the cell without shielding could destroy you. Men who cannot touch the Aura are unaffected by it, seemingly. Second, the enemies you will face are much stronger in Auric energy than you are. Your best hope is to activate the cell and cripple them. We've been over this before," he added with a huff of breath that told Bryar a lot about his worry and his frustration.

"Am I ready for this?"

"No. This is merely an experiment—"

"Which might well cost me the Aura."

"This quest may well cost you your life, so I recommend you do as I say. And one other thing – starting tomorrow, I plan for you to train with Tai."

His life? But he'd known that from the start. Hearing it in such unadorned words, though...

Wait. *Tai?*

"Train how?"

"As you did with Joss." Ezra's impatience pulled the words into the air as if thrown from a slingshot.

"But I don't want to risk... I mean, Tai could get hurt."

"That's the point. Someone you believed a friend may prove to be an enemy. You need the moral certainty to destroy that person, if necessary. From today forth, you are to treat Tai as a potential foe. Jousts every morning, no matter the weather."

"Have you told Tai?"

"Not yet. Now, please stop stalling. I don't know for sure the effect of this weave, so I prefer that you lie on the table. That way you won't fall."

Their eyes met. Ezra's had become hard blue crystals, piercing and dominating.

Bryar hadn't been so tempted to lash out since he left Newcastle, his childhood home in the Northlands. And at Ezra, of all people. The man he had learned to trust, almost like a father, or what he believed a father could be.

"Hold fast to your rage, Bryar. Until this is settled, you must keep your anger foremost. It will fuel you."

"Or drive me do something I shouldn't," he muttered.

"You won't. I've trained you better than that."

His uncertainty stood no chance against Ezra's absolute conviction. He heaved himself onto the workbench and stretched out. "What should I expect?"

"No pain, I hope. Possibly disorientation. Time will tell. Close your eyes."

He did, although he remained alert to every shifting movement or touch of energy. Ezra didn't seem to care. He sensed the older man, hands passing around him, then energy moving in ways he'd never experienced. The template gripped him and held him fast before releasing him and disappearing. Everything dissolved.

"Sit up."

Bryar opened his eyes. "How long has it been?" The space looked different, the shadows darker. Was the sun setting? Light returned, then faded, as if filtered by cloud.

"About half an hour. Sit up, boy. Look around."

Responding to Ezra's impatience, he dragged himself upright, part of his brain wondering why he bothered.

Then it hit him. Only half an hour? But the richness had bled from the room, leaving murky colors, flat light...

Fighting panic, he moved to climb down from the workbench, but stopped when he realized there was no place to go. Everywhere would be the same, rendered with the same lack of life.

This is what Willow lives with. Sweet Diou, no.

"Report. Tell me your perceptions. Can you touch the Aura?"

Numb, he shook his head, fighting the fear that filled him. "Damn it, Ezra..."

The Old Man rubbed his hands together. "Not perfect. There are gaps, and the working won't hold beyond an hour or so. But a good first try. Now we will attempt to undo it. This is trickier, so I need you to—"

"You have to." Bryar spoke quickly, barely quelling the terror seizing his nerve endings. "How can anyone live like this? It's the same as being underground..."

Ezra's face tightened. "I do my best, always. Lie down. And this time, relax. It doesn't help when you fight me."

As if he had any choice. His entire body stiffened at the realization that the Aura was gone. Purposely gone.

Given no option, he stretched out on the table again, sending out a heartfelt wish for Ezra's reversal technique to succeed.

Later that night, exhausted but too anxious to sleep, Bryar sensed rather than saw a presence hovering over him. He knew without opening his eyes that it was Ezra.

A thread of energy entered him, just enough to untangle his rampant emotions.

He felt it. Praise be, he felt Ezra's healing. He'd never, *ever*, take his Auric connection for granted again.

A hand brushed the hair from his forehead, and he heard, more with his mind than with his ears, a soft whisper. "I'm sorry, my son. Truly, I am sorry."

The presence vanished. He took a breath, his muscles relaxed, and he settled into sleep.

Chapter 17

Bryar had been trying to kill Tai for a nine-day and a half. To his alternating delight and dismay, she'd proved herself a worthy opponent. Now, on the afternoon of Winter Solstice, Ezra had granted them a well-deserved break.

He'd hurt her, more than once. They both bore abrasions and bruises. Tai's agility and unexpected moves counterpointed the measured, rehearsed attacks he'd learned from Joss. She kept him on his toes every instant, because he couldn't be sure what she would try next. She never held back, whereas he had to force himself to knock her down, hold a wooden sword to her throat.

Thinking of Tai as an enemy for a morning's bout, then reverting to best friends in the afternoon, warred in his mind.

Mercifully, Ezra hadn't repeated his experiment with Bryar's Auric contact, leaving him free to meld familiar templates into melodies that told of battles, of winter... and increasingly of the slight, nearly androgynous woman beside him, although he kept those compositions private.

They spent the early afternoon tramping through the snow-filled woods under a vast blue sky. The session that morning had been strenuous, and they both suffered from it in sore muscles and bruises.

"I don't like this," he said.

"Neither do I, but it's necessary." As usual, Tai read his meaning – the bouts, not their walk.

He smiled. "You'll never be an enemy."

"Ezra's right, though. You can't know who will betray you, once you're out there." She shivered.

"Cold?"

"No. More like a premonition. I'm uneasy about where this is going. It's safe here. I wish..."

"No point to wishing." He was committed. And the training had changed him. His mind felt clearer, harder. And his body... looking back, he realized how soft he'd become over the years.

No softness now.

At the house, they propped their snow-sodden boots by the fire in the lounge and settled in front of it themselves. Tai stretched out on a chaise and sighed, and almost immediately fell asleep. Given the work she did, helping in the barns and the kitchen, training with him, always available, always willing, he knew she must be exhausted, but it was rare to see her unmoving.

He sat on the floor in front of the chaise, leaning his head back against the seat. No one else was around. Rebecca's rheumatism flared in the cold weather, and Ezra wore his fatigue for them all to see, each day seeming more stooped, the lines on his face deeper. The Old Man's worry hadn't lessened, although the Aura had been stable since mid-autumn, which almost caused Bryar to doubt the utility of his training.

Rebecca had filled the room with pine boughs, cones, and garlands. Strings of hard berries and aromas of cooking brought up in him a nostalgic longing for the innocent days at the Motherhouse, when the kitchen spared no effort to give the children under their care the finest holiday possible. Homesickness had never been a problem for him, or for Quinn or Willow, but they'd been more than pleased to benefit from the kitchen's efforts.

Tonight they would feast. And now Tai slept.

He got up and crossed the room to the corner where Ezra kept a chitarre. After giving it a tuning, he settled down again, plucking idle notes and chords. The still mystery of Solstice touched the space, the silence broken only by the occasional crack from the fire. Words flooded him. He quietly sang them into the silent room.

"...veins of ore, like veins of cold, when every kid wants home...

"...no one to say goodbye to...

"...the road lies ahead, long and winding ...

"...the music lives in me. It lives in everything...

"...it lives in you."

The chords flew from his hands in a cascade of sound, played in a minor key that spoke of the Solstice, but also of loss and yearning and uncertainty.

Tai's hand touched his head, her fingers running through his hair. He barely moved, the feeling so right, but let the instrument speak for him as the music changed into a major key, promising hope and...

Love.

He twisted around; Tai's hand dropped to his cheek – the disfigured one, the red blemish he'd longed to be free of. Their eyes met.

No words. No words needed. She smiled.

Solstice.

Sustainer of all, preserve this. Let me live in this moment.

Nothing lasts forever. Rebecca bustled into the room. "Tai, where are you?"

"Here, Gran," she replied from the hidden comfort of the chaise.

"Let's go, girl. We've a farce to prepare, and pastries and custard."

"On my way."

The whole tableau unwove as Tai rose, leaving behind a lingering touch of cool fingers brushing his face, a look that told him all he needed to know.

Chapter 18

Willow had never participated in a Winter Solstice celebration like this year's. Dressed in heavy red velvet, she had accompanied Gauvain to a gathering of what she now recognized as high society in Orlan. Rich food, candles, greenery, dancing... she doubted the people she met were truly attuned to the earth and its seasons, but the celebration had assuaged the hollow feeling she'd endured as the holiday approached and no seasonal decorations appeared in the tower.

She had even seen Gauvain smile. More than once.

If she had a complaint, it was that the velvet quickly became too warm. Sometimes she longed for the comfort of the linen and woolen tunics of her old life.

Her old life – did that mean she accepted this as her new life?

Gauvain had been absent since Solstice. She had no idea where he had gone. The meals she shared with Leo in the kitchen were just as succulent, less rich, and much more relaxing.

Natural light wouldn't hurt, she grumbled to herself as she entered the formal dining room. There were no windows on the ground floor of the tower, although heavy curtains covered niches where windows should be. Gauvain created scenes in them when he entertained, as if his friends looked out on seascapes, or the hills, or whatever he chose. Willow's attempt to create such a scene on a wall, depicting the view downslope to Hallan Hot Springs, met with limited success. It turned out more like a shadow.

This morning marked her first encounter with Gauvain since the party.

"I trust you enjoyed the celebration?" he asked as she seated herself for breakfast, his tone implying that any admission of pleasure would be dismissed as frivolous.

"Yes. To my surprise."

"And you have used the time since then productively?"

"Once I recovered from the excesses of the party, yes."

He gestured with the caff pot. She held her mug out for him to fill it.

"Tell me. A full recounting, if you please."

"The clouds yesterday —"

"I thought those were yours," he said impatiently. "Go on."

"Small things, but practical. Boiling water for a tisane, triggering new growth on the plant in my room."

Juggling light globes. But Gauvain didn't need to know about such childish activities.

"Healing? Leo spoke to me of your treatment."

On the day following Solstice, she had ventured into the market in search of particular herbs, and these she infused to make a salve to ameliorate Leo's ongoing backaches. The joy of creating a medicine again, pouring Auric energy into it to heighten its powers, thrilled her beyond anything Gauvain taught her. She'd devoted most of that day to the elderly servant, assisting in the kitchen and chatting about revels long past.

Now she frowned at the underlying tone of disapproval in his voice. "He is my friend, and his back pains him."

"A local healer provides him with herbs."

"The local healer cannot bolster those herbs with Auric energy. You know that as well as I do."

Gauvain apparently had no riposte. He made a grumbling sound in his throat and turned his attention to his breakfast. "I wish to explore an advanced working with you, which will be to your benefit," he said without looking up from his egg. "We will discuss it after breakfast, in my study."

"Very well." Willow recognized an unexpected undercurrent of excitement as he spoke of this teaching. For herself, the oatmeal and caff before her provided quite enough pleasure. With the happiness of Solstice fading, tendrils of homesickness once again intruded on her consciousness. The gentle melancholy suited her today, grounding her in memories of home.

When she presented herself in Gauvain's study later, she found him standing in front of his shelves, running a finger across the spines of the books there. She sensed his unease immediately – and that he tried to hide it as he turned to face her.

"Tell me about the new technique."

"One that I personally use only rarely." He swallowed. "Willow, would you like to be able to glimpse your Motherhouse? See what is happening there?"

Her eyes widened. "I've never been able to communicate across distances easily, much less do distant viewing."

"I believe that with the right – ambience – you can do these things, if only for an instant. Your potential... this may further unlock it. Although I must inform you yet again, your stubborn unwillingness to divulge your true name inhibits your powers."

That argument again. Her past was her own, and none of his business. "My name is Willow."

"But was not always."

She couldn't deny it, so she deflected it. "About the technique..."

Gauvain cleared his throat and returned to fiddling with the books. His back to her, he said, "There is a time, between a man and a woman, when boundaries dissolve. With the proper preparation, greater magic than usual may be enacted. I believe you are ready for this step."

Sex magic. The apprentices giggled about it. Borgonnian culture being considerably more prudish concerning such matters than in the Midland, she doubted any of them had experienced the joys of sex yet.

But...

"Are you suggesting that you and I...?"

"Yes. Yes, I am."

She wished he would face her; his books could not possibly be *that* interesting. Especially when he had just proposed that he and she should...

Sex with Gauvain?

Willow sat, her voluminous skirts – green the shade of new grass this morning – tucked around her. She studied his black hair, neatly confined in a tail by a black binding ribbon, and thought, or attempted to. He had always been compelling, drawing her to him in ways she didn't fully understand and didn't completely trust. But...

There was a physical allure. No point denying it. Willow tucked her hands into her skirt to hide their shaking. His suggestion left her stunned and scrambling for words.

But...

But the chance to catch a glimpse of Mari, maybe Bryar or Quinn, if they were resident at the Motherhouse?

And Joss. Where would Joss be now?

Gauvain offered her a transaction, not a seduction. Thinking practically, to give in to the release of sex, the slackening of the low-grade tension that haunted her days and especially her nights...

"There is an expression," she said. "It regards dangling a carrot."

He finally turned. "I have no need to bribe you into my bed." His voice was haughty; she had insulted him. "This suggestion is for your benefit, not mine."

That restored her to level ground. "You make it less alluring by the moment."

"Listen, foolish woman." Gauvain's temper, as usual, was held in check by a thread. He leaned on the desk, glowering at her. "I am trying to further your education in the magical uses of the Aura. Considerable effort went into assuring that the method will produce the desired results. I am prepared to teach this to you. And you raise this *ridiculous* resistance —"

She stood, hands on her hips. "And you choose to treat me like an object. No woman wishes to be viewed in the same way a man views his shaving razor, or his favorite pair of walking boots, whatever the reason. Are you so divorced from—" Her voice hitched; to her amazement and annoyance, she found herself hovering on the edge of tears.

Gauvain sat and gestured that she should do the same. "I apologize," he said stiffly. "I failed to take into consideration your sentimental nature. Which, I might add, also inhibits you as you progress in Auric workings."

"I am not convinced of the benefit of further training. My Healing abilities have been restored."

"And stronger than before, for which you may thank me. But you have much to learn still."

"Not much that I need to learn, however."

"You made a commitment. Two seasons as apprentice."

And one completed. Bleak winter stretched ahead before spring would bring freedom...

"Do you wish this?" she asked.

Gauvain customarily kept his eyes shielded; when they locked on hers across his elaborate desk, their black depths came as a jolt. His expression was unreadable. Silence surrounded them.

"Yes," he said. "I wish it."

"Then I will consider it." Willow rose as steadily as she could, given that her legs felt like custard, and walked with her head held high out his door.

Willow waited four days before she spoke to Gauvain about his proposal. Too much was unclear. His motives, for instance. Did he desire her, or was this simply another experiment? The enticement of a glimpse of life at the Motherhouse drew her like one of those magnetic rocks that attach to knives or needles. But did she want to combine this vision with a physical experience that ought to be all-consuming?

And Gauvain. Willow admitted the allure, at least to herself. But did she trust him enough to share herself with him? He'd been true to his promises, yet a part of her resisted.

Magic. She'd heard some of the common workings referred to as magic, but had never related to the Aura that way. For her, templates promoted Healing, allowed her to do her work. For Gauvain, was sex anything more than another esoteric practice?

And that circled her right back to the beginning, and the certainty that the unspoken tension between them needed resolution.

Over breakfast she said, without preamble, "How does this work? The image of the Motherhouse – how long will it last? How much control will I have? Can I see what I choose, or only what you, or the Aura, show me?"

He had looked up from his eggs and ham when she began her questions. He sat unmoving, his eyes fixed on her, until she stopped.

"Appreciate, please, that I cannot guarantee the content of the vision, only that it will occur. From my experiments, I can say that the Motherhouse is blanketed in snow, the children shriek altogether too much, and Arwen appears tense. That giant of a man is there, too."

"How long?" she demanded.

"Ten seconds at the most."

She eyed him. "If your experiments allowed you to see my home, you could teach me to attain the vision on my own, without requiring your participation."

At her veiled mention of solitary sexual practices, color tinged his face. He returned his gaze to his plate and waited a moment before he spoke. "Certainly not. You are not strong enough. You could never perform this working unassisted."

"Oh."

"The idea is... unpalatable to you?"

"No. But—"

"For the love of—" He cut off the curse and rose. "Do you expect a courtship full of pretty words and out-of-season flowers? I thought you had more sense."

She folded her hands in her lap. "I'm a woman, Gauvain."

"I am teaching you to think like a Mage."

"And succeeding. But I practice within my own body and using my own capabilities."

"Very well." He strode around the table, seized her elbow, and raised her to her feet. Willow sensed anger or frustration or ... passion? As for herself, the single bite of porridge lay uneasily in her stomach as he pulled her close.

"I will tell you this, although I fail to understand the necessity. You are a very attractive woman, and I find myself drawn to you, even anticipating a liaison. I believe you feel the same, however you cloak your reactions in sentiment."

He drew her closer still, and then his mouth was on hers, gently but with command.

Without further debate, she gave in to him as he explored her with his lips and, gradually, his hands. Pressed against him, even through the luxurious skirts of her morning outfit, she was aware of his desire.

After a dizzying time, he stepped back. "Do you continue to doubt me?"

Not exactly the romantic words she might have enjoyed, but typical of Gauvain. "No, I don't doubt."

"Excellent. It seems the Motherhouse is on some sort of holiday for the Solstice. Your chances of seeing those you care about will be heightened. Now, I wish to finish my breakfast, and I suggest you do the same."

Willow sat, wondering what had just happened.

Around mid-afternoon, Leo tapped on her door. "The Master wishes to see you in the workroom."

"Thank you."

"Miss..."

"Is something wrong, Leo?"

The elderly servant hesitated, fingering the fabric of his black coat, a frown adding to his wrinkles. "Be careful, Miss. The Master... I'm not sure what he's planning. He means you no harm, I'm sure of that, but his ways aren't yours."

She took his hand and squeezed. "I know. It's part of my training. Please don't worry."

Leo left, the frown still creasing his face.

The workroom? Hardly conducive to a romantic interlude. But she supposed he had his reasons. She abandoned any notion of seduction and changed into the white robe she'd worn for her evening treatments, then descended the stairs.

Gauvain stood in the center of the room. Willow caught a fleeting whiff of an unfamiliar incense as she closed the door. He came forward and raised her hand to his lips, for all the world like a courtier in one of Bryar's tales. He led her formally to another door, which she had always assumed was a closet. Instead it opened onto a small room holding a thick pallet on a frame, covered with a plump duvet. The room was undecorated, the duvet the basic beige of undyed linen. "I occasionally wish to rest," he explained. "This is convenient. Why did you change?"

"An experiment, yes? This is what I wear when you use me for your experiments."

He released her hand. "Your treatments are at an end."

"This is a new phase of experimentation, then."

"You insult me."

"That was not my intention."

"Very well. An experiment. If that is what you wish." He reached out and touched her.

She had believed Gauvain to be almost entirely air clan, but now she learned a new aspect to him. Fire. She responded viscerally to the passion weaving through the room. He moved slowly, building the desire between them.

His body, naked in the light of the Aura globes, was a thing of beauty, dark and sinewy, desiring her... She allowed him to lead, passion spiraling toward its peak.

Until...

Abruptly, a deep voice imposed itself on her mind. A strong, pale body. A man afraid of what they created together, but willing to learn. Quietly there when she needed him.

She jerked away, freeing herself from Gauvain's clasp.

"Did I hurt you?"

"That's not it."

He stiffened. "Tell me. Surely your Midland conscience isn't interfering with our pleasure."

Disdain filled his voice, but that didn't surprise her. Breaking off a liaison at this juncture was insulting. She knew it, and couldn't help it. She picked up her robe and donned it under his disapproving eyes.

"I just... can't. I'm so sorry."

"Leave me," he commanded. "This instant."

"Let me explain —"

"I do not want your explanations, pitiful as I'm sure they are. Go."

Later, over supper, she addressed his unresponsive face. "Sex is magical, yes, but there is more. This afternoon another man intruded into my thoughts. His presence in my mind curtailed my response to you. I love him, Gauvain. I only realized this when..." She waved her hand a little desperately to indicate their aborted liaison.

"Naturally, I am delighted to assist you in understanding yourself," he said. Then he began eating his dinner and didn't speak again, not even to offer to fill her wine goblet.

Willow ate a few bites and left the table. She would beg a sandwich from Leo later. But she couldn't stay in Gauvain's presence any longer.

Chapter 19

The Solstice celebration had been lighthearted fun. The village and the Motherhouse combined for an afternoon of revelry, food, and small gifts for the children, many of which Joss had carved in his free time. These days the shapes came naturally to his knife – the one Quinn had slipped him, which he'd never returned – as if they were hidden in the wood, waiting to be revealed.

Joss liked the kids. The apprentices accepted his presence, the local urchins treated him like a giant play toy, and that was fine with him. It eased the loneliness of his life these days.

Such thoughts occupied him as he trudged toward the village, whose inhabitants provided support services for the Motherhouse. The forests and fields were snow-covered and silent, but the path bore enough traffic to thaw into a muddy slush. His destination was one of the long barns, his intention to check on the cows. Since he'd been stuck with these whisperer skills, he'd learn how to use them.

He kept his thoughts well away from Willow. Or from Bryar, or Ezra and his family. Simplest to focus on the present.

The present, for Joss, meant mornings with Quinn as she put him through his paces. No, he'd never be able to create a light globe. The best he got was a feeble glow that sat in his hand like a pet. But with her not so gentle tutoring, he was beginning to understand template work, the basic manipulation of the weaves. To sense the different energies, earth always the strongest. He struggled to detect fire, but the others, air and water, came more clearly. Phlegmatic, not passionate, Quinn had said with her usual detachment.

Passion. Sometimes he did think about Willow, far away with that intimidating man, in the land across the hills. Memory struck at night, or when the sun shone just so, reminding him of the meadow.

The afternoon was crisp and clear. With another day free of lessons, the younger apprentices would be out in the snow, the older ones gathered in their rooms – or paired off for some personal time. The sexual mores of the Midland still confounded him.

At the barn, he scraped the muck from his boots and ranged along the ranks of the cows. One forlorn lady lay on her side and had barely touched her hay. He registered discomfort. Fear.

"Hey, girl." Joss stepped into the stall, ran his hand over her great, bony head, and emptied his mind, or did his best to. Her pain came through, as did another image...

Aha. He stood and crossed to a nearby store of apples. Choosing a healthy-looking one, he returned to the stall and held it out. The cow raised her head; Joss felt her craving. He grinned, replaced the fruit in the pile, then went to find Robby, the chief agriculturist.

"This girl's been in apples," he said. "That's why she's bloated."

"Figures. Must have happened when we turned them out in the field a few days ago, before the last snow. There's always windfalls. I'm gonna punch into her before the bloat gets worse."

"Punch?" Had he heard right? But the man crossed to the workbench and returned with a small bottle, a knife, and a narrow tube that looked like bamboo.

"Yeah, punch. She won't be impressed. Better stand back."

Joss would swear the cow was begging him to ease her distress. Surely not, though. He was getting fanciful.

Robby swabbed the cow's side and the tools with the liquid from the bottle – alcohol, Joss concluded – and rammed the knife into her side. He removed the knife and stuck the tube into the incision.

Joss stood frozen, unbelieving. But the cow seemed more irritated than pained.

"Now we wait," Robby said, and clambered to his feet. While he cleaned and stowed his tools, Joss watched the cow. After a moment a greenish, slimy mess of gas bubbles emerged from the tube. The smell almost drove him from the stall.

"We'll leave it in for five or six days, I reckon. It heals on its own once the tube comes out, so long as it doesn't get infected. There's a plant in the hedges the cows eat, dunno what it's called but we keep some of it around, dried. Makes 'em burp. I'll add it to her hay; she ought to start eating soon. She'll be worrying about the young'un she's carrying, like as not."

"I'm not picking up any worry," Joss said. "Mostly, just relief." The bubbles continued to pour from the tube.

The cow looked hopefully toward the apples. Joss laughed. "Not going to happen, girl. Stick to your hay."

"Let's check the sheep while you're here. Problem with their feet, some of 'em."

"I'll look, but I never learn much from sheep."

They left the cow lazing in her stall and visited the other animal enclosures. Robby was as vital to Joss's education as Quinn. By the time he finished his stint at the Motherhouse, he'd know enough to be truly useful as an agriculturist somewhere in the Midland. Hallan, by preference.

Once again, as happened so often these days, his thoughts wandered to Willow's cabin. He yanked them away. She would return, or she wouldn't. She would be healed, or not. She would move to Hallan, or she would travel. All imponderables now, and he had to learn to earn a living.

Before leaving the village, he stopped by the cow's stall. A nasty-looking pile of froth had accumulated on the straw, and she had managed to take a mouthful of hay. She looked content, as if nothing had ever bothered her.

He'd help birth her calf in a month or two, he supposed.

❖

At the Motherhouse, Joss headed first to the dining hall for a cup of caff, dodging through an old-fashioned game of tag. He took his mug and a pastry with him and escaped the chaos. He'd been upgraded to a small suite in the guest lodge, giving him a bedroom and a sitting room, and it was to the table in the sitting room he went now. Quinn had diagrammed a couple of weaves for him. They didn't make sense, yet. But they would. He settled his large frame into the chair, used the fire stone – not the Aura, he lacked the power – to light a lantern, and bent over his studies. The weaves weren't so different from engineering, mastering the connections, the cause and effect.

Except to master these, he had to shut down his logical brain, turning himself over to the Aura to grasp the complexities in the diagram. He was battling his way through ephemeral realities now. So maybe not like engineering after all.

After an hour of study, he found himself staring out his narrow window, seeing nothing. He'd talked to Arwen about these moments of blankness. They hollowed him out, but she'd been unconcerned. It was only logical, she'd pointed out, that the magnitude of change to his life, however beneficial, occasionally threatened to overwhelm him.

Chapter 20

Trying to pay attention to Ezra across the workroom table, but without much success, Bryar remembered the lingering touch of Tai's lips on his. Last night, touching Tai, kissing Tai for the first time... he'd had hundreds of first times, but last night was the kind of experience he wrote ballads about.

He'd made a restrained exploration of her curves and angles, holding himself forcibly in check. A woman... a future, together... they could make babies...

"Bryar." Ezra's usually patient voice held an edge.

"Sorry."

"You didn't hear a word I said."

He grinned. "No, probably not."

"Where is your mind this morning?" He hesitated. "It's Tai, isn't it?"

Bryar nodded.

"I was afraid of this. Tai wouldn't want it."

The grin faded. "She does." *Her small body nestling into his, her bold hands...*

Ezra turned away to pull out a stool and sit. The Old Man had enjoyed a period of strength and vigor for the last couple of nine-days, but Bryar's statement seemed to deplete his energy. "That isn't good. She at least appreciates the seriousness of our work here."

"And you think I don't?" Bryar bristled at the criticism, but the memories overwhelmed his touchiness, softening his reply. "I feel ready for anything. She's..." He struggled for the right words. "Living like we do, moving around constantly... even with Willow, I never knew."

"Weavers. We live in our insular world. Love is everywhere, but we avoid it. Your timing is inconvenient."

Bryar sobered. "I just need a day or two—"

"We don't have a day or two," Ezra snapped. "There's far too much to do still."

His own ire burst forth. "There are six or seven nine-days before spring. The cell isn't moving. No one knows where Kiril is, assuming he's got the thing. I'm fit and your protocol works, it just needs refinement—"

"Which I'd hoped to pursue today. But I need your focused attention."

"I want a couple of days off."

"You're not a sixteen-year-old."

"You should remember that," Bryar said, his voice cold. "I'm a man grown. I make my own decisions."

Ezra pounded the workbench, then sighed. "Lovesick puppy. You're no good to me this way. But Bryar..."

He met Ezra's gaze. What he saw there chilled him.

"If this continues to interfere with our work, I'll send Tai away. You have a job to do. I expect you to do it. Tai's future is as much at stake as yours or anyone's. Don't forget that."

"I'm not likely to." Just a day or two, that's all he asked, time to hang out with Tai, complete the song growing in his head, kiss her some more... He didn't let his thoughts go to what came after the kissing. That would happen in its own good time.

"Since you're useless today, I suggest you exercise this morning." Ezra reeled off a list of drills. "That should keep your libido in check, and I'm concerned that your left ankle needs strengthening."

Bryar lifted his leg and rotated the foot. "I broke it, years ago. It'll always be weaker."

"Do it anyway. Go."

Glad to escape the disapproval, Bryar made for the training arena in the barn. Tai might come watch, or even spar with him. Although how he was supposed to fight her, hold a wooden sword to her throat, after last night... He stripped out of his tunic and got to work.

Tai didn't appear for lunch. He wondered, but she took off on her own regularly. Scribe, he told himself. Scribes devoted their lives to learning. Tai followed her curiosity and instincts, wherever they led.

He had good tracking skills. He'd find her.

Rebecca was quiet over the meal and kept shooting him these motherly, concerned looks. Possibly she sensed the tension between him and Ezra, who was tight-lipped. Rebecca, he gathered from Tai, had been a drop-out, one of the handful of apprentices every year whose connection, when put to the test, proved insufficient to allow her to become a Weaver. But during her time at the Motherhouse she met Ezra.

And had been his mainstay ever since, Bryar thought, watching the restrained interactions between the two elderly people. Ezra built his power on the foundation of her quiet strength.

After lunch Bryar donned coat and boots and set out to find Tai. The weather had turned mild over the last few days, resulting in muddy trails and dripping trees; even from the compound he heard the river as it raged over shattered ice. Ezra predicted a hard freeze that night, locking everything up again.

He followed her prints to the clearing by the river. The maelstrom of the current had drowned her quiet refuge on the other side. But Tai had more sense than to go anywhere near the river today; even he wouldn't dare —

Tai's boots lay propped against a nearby tree trunk.

He found no other signs. No indication she had slipped and fallen in. No other articles of clothing. Nothing. Just her boots.

When he shouted her name, the surrounding hills seemed to vibrate to the timbre of his voice, but here was no answer.

His heart thudding in his throat, he took the trail downriver, scanning the torrent, every rapid and eddy, stopping regularly to search. To cry out. After an hour he reversed the journey, always watching, listening for any sign of Tai.

When Bryar returned to the clearing, Ezra stood on the bank staring at the boots. When the other man looked up, he said, "She's not – I'm going in. See where the current might have —"

"No." Ezra's hand gripped his arm, hard, then the Old Man collapsed, clinging to Bryar's arm. "Even you can't go into that. It would be suicide."

"But Tai..." Bryar helped Ezra toward a tree for support, the two of them alone on the wet bank.

Alone.

He released Ezra and approached the river, as close as he dared. "*Tai!*" he screamed. The single, lonely word came back to him from the surrounding hills, hollow and inhuman.

"Take me home," Ezra whispered.

Beyond comprehension, he surveyed the river one last time. Then he stooped and lifted the Old Man into his arms, and staggered toward the compound.

That night Rebecca gave him a spicy tisane with honey for his raw throat. Nobody spoke much, although Rebecca did say, more than once, "Tai isn't gone. I would know it." Bryar put it down to a grandmother's wishful thinking.

That night he plunged into an ague, his body gripped in shivering fits, dragging him between burning fever and icy cold. Rebecca dosed him with her vile-tasting remedies. It didn't help. Nothing helped. Nothing would ever help. Tai was gone. What was the point of it all, with Tai gone?

When the ague lessened its grip, Ezra sat beside his bed as he finished a bowl of chicken soup, his first nourishment for days. "I'm sorry," Ezra said. "I pushed you too hard. Your body rebelled."

"Tai," he said. His voice barely worked, more croak than baritone.

"If Rebecca says she's alive, then she is. But where or why? I don't know."

Bryar allowed Ezra to take the bowl from his shaking hands. "She'd need her boots. But there was no trace. She didn't walk away from that bank."

"Never underestimate her. Even I don't fully understand all she's capable of."

He collapsed back on his pillows. Despite Ezra's words, Rebecca's confidence, he forced himself to face the truth. The one person in the Midland who completed him – a line from the partially composed song – was gone.

It was five days before Bryar could to do more than sit by the fire with Ezra and Rebecca, and almost two nine-days before he resumed his training. That afternoon he walked again to the river, scouring the bank, looking for any trace of Tai. As he half expected, half dreaded, he found nothing.

The extent of his anger and bitterness astounded him. Even in his darkest moments he had never experienced this level of pure hatred for the Aura, for life itself.

Although it took him days to build up his strength again, he threw himself into the training with a fury, ready to destroy. He was distant with Rebecca, surly with Ezra, locked in his own aggressive need to pummel something, anything, for taking Tai away from him.

Chapter 21

Willow sat in Leo's kitchen, idly tracing a scar on the worn table and watching the elderly man assemble the ingredients for supper. Leo had a brace of some kind of bird, which he planned to stuff with breadcrumbs and castanya nuts, one of Willow's favorite winter treats, although at home they usually were pureed and sweetened as a filling for pastries.

Leo's sure touch would sweeten the food, if not the atmosphere created by those partaking of it.

She rarely saw Gauvain apart from meals and lessons. Not surprising, given that she suspected he was avoiding her as much as she avoided him. Unresolved tension underlay life in the tower. Willow stuck to her room and the kitchen, and longed to venture out into the town, but Leo informed her that the market had shrunk to only a handful of stalls, the merchants bunkered against the cold in unwelcoming hovels of stores.

"I do wish I could find the formula to cheer you, Miss," Leo commented, his eyes never leaving his chopping. "It grieves me to see you so desolate."

"Sometimes you make the right decision, but to the wrong effect."

"True. But when the decision is correct, in the long term all will be well."

"I wish he weren't so angry, though. He's... I don't want his mood to overflow onto you."

Leo chuckled. "I've known Gauvain since he was a lad, and we on his staff are used to his moods. The unusual thing was his cheerful demeanor until now. This is much more typical."

"Nevertheless..."

Leo set his knife on the table and leaned toward her. "Take your tisane and a pastry and go up to your room, Miss. You haven't been sleeping well. Give yourself an afternoon off. If your schedule is free, accompany me to the butcher's tomorrow. There are one or two shops nearby you might enjoy."

"Thank you." Willow stood. "As for free, though, Gauvain acts as if the break at Solstice destroyed all the work from the autumn. He drives the apprentices as if he wielded a whip."

"A hard taskmaster. Go now. Things may look better in the morning."

Maybe, she thought as she climbed the curved stairs. But not likely to be. Gauvain had been frigid since their aborted liaison, refusing to hear or acknowledge her explanation. Proof enough that she hadn't handled it well. In the past, she had given her body, just as she gave her affections, where she chose, and it never occurred to her that this time would be any different. Joss had changed her unexpectedly, and deeply.

But now, faced with this new awareness, she'd done the only thing possible. The fulfillment of love far outweighed the magic of sex, and she was no longer willing to exchange the one for the other.

She grimaced as she passed through her door and settled into her chair, wondering what Joss himself would say about all this.

The tisane finished, she stood to stare out the window. The bare limbs of a solitary tree, only just visible behind a bank of buildings, tossed in the chill wind driving gray, scudding clouds. Stalks of weeds thrashed against the base of the tower. A cover of snow softened the distant view, but she knew it to be a thin layer, insufficient to provide moisture come spring.

The high hills must be waist deep in snow by now; like it or not, she was trapped in this place until after the melt.

Another season before she could go home.

Willow nodded to herself and began preparations for a leisurely bath. Hot water on demand still thrilled her.

Given no other options, she'd accept Gauvain's teachings, assessing each weave's potential for Healing work. Other lessons, the esoteric stuff dealing more with probing the mysteries of esoteric templates, twisting them to a person's bidding, she might carry home for Quinn and the other Scribes.

Borgonne offered nothing Bryar would value. Borgonnian music differed little from music in the Midland, and Willow had heard no stories or legends at all. A pragmatic culture, Borgonnnians showed no interest in history or fantasy.

Before Solstice, as her powers strengthened, she had approached Gauvain about setting up a clinic in Orlan, renewing her Healing skills by helping the populace. He had flatly denied her, and even Leo had explained that such a move would undermine the resident healers and create resentment toward the inhabitants of the tower.

No Healing, then. But the ability lay dormant, waiting. Relaxing in the warm water, she practiced a few weaves, just enough to experience the joy of working with templates again.

Warm and dry, again at her window, she reached out with her mind to the land. She received only a trickle of sensation in response, nothing like the rich connection of the Midland. The Aura might be stronger in Borgonne, but it seemed to require a harsher, more demanding touch to awaken it. Gauvain's, perhaps. She wondered if, had she opened a clinic, her Healing templates would even have worked here. The energy felt different, as if the earth itself bowed to the will of the people living here, a colder, less welcoming society.

In the hours before Leo rang the supper bell, as she watched the bleak landscape and revisited all she was learning – or, more often, reviewing – in the apprentice class, she was led to one inexorable conclusion. She did not belong here. As soon as the snow receded, she would replace Gauvain's fine silks and satins with her old tunic and boots, and strike out for home.

Chapter 22

The ferocity of his feelings, not to mention his actions, horrified and consumed Bryar in equal measure. No trace of the mild-mannered Bard remained; he tore through his daily routines as if his goal were to destroy anything in his path, to inflict injury on whoever got in his way.

Rebecca watched, cooked, and changed his sweat-soaked sheets. Ezra ignored his moods and continued his research.

After tense meals with the elderly couple, afternoons found him at the riverside. Although he no longer sought Tai, alone by the river he screamed his pain, bellowing her name, letting the tumultuous water carry it downstream.

After days spent combing the riverbank, he had visited the landslide, the land around the orchard and the meadow, and far beyond, everywhere she might have gone, clinging to the hope she lived.

Every evening Rebecca gave him a tisane with soporific herbs to aid his sleep, and honey and a touch of citrus to soothe his throat. He was perpetually hoarse, and couldn't have sung if his life depended on it.

While the tisanes helped, most nights he slept only if he had exhausted himself enough with physical training. Failed sleep meant long, dark periods with no escape from the layers of pain and anger. Four nine-days since Tai vanished, with no sign, nothing to restore him to sanity.

Until the day came when the overload of emotion burned out, leaving him emptied. Devoid of purpose, he neglected his regimen, sitting on his bed in the main house – for Rebecca had not permitted him to return to the room he'd shared with Joss beside the barn – staring into space.

At mid-morning he received the summons to the workroom. He went, reluctantly.

"Lie down," Ezra commanded. "I will apply the shield. Rebecca is preparing rations for you. You're leaving for the Motherhouse this afternoon."

Like hell. Leave Tai's home, the place she might reappear? "I'm not ready."

"You are. She's not coming back, Bryar. The trail is open, and Arwen's expecting you."

"Not today." He heard the petulance in his voice.

"You will never be more prepared." Ezra advanced on him and jabbed a bony finger into his chest. "You need no more time or training. I've located the power cell, and I have no wish to go to the effort of locating it again, should it be moved."

A vague curiosity tickled his mind, a novelty since Tai's loss. "How did you do it?"

"A combination of the slow seepage into the earth and spies. Don't look surprised. I maintain a well orchestrated network of people who tell me what I need to know."

"Scribes?"

"A few. And others."

Ezra's voice was matter-of-fact, brooking no argument. But today he couldn't face... "Ezra, listen. This just isn't a good day —"

"A perfect day, and you will lie down. Now. I'll not have you keeling over under the force of the working."

He didn't bother to lock eyes with the Old Man; since he knew he'd lose any such war of wills, he hoisted himself onto the workbench and stretched out.

Ezra's capable hands grasped Bryar's head, weaving a template that felt like a knitted cap. Bryar released himself into a trance, his mind no longer in the workroom but probably somewhere in the Aura with its energy patterns swirling around him.

Until it vanished, leaving only emptiness. He opened his eyes.

Ezra backed the pressure off slightly, then made the moves to tie the weave off and said, "I have no way of knowing how long your shield will hold, or the extent it will withstand trauma. But I can do no better. See Rebecca for food, pack, and go. Arwen expects you tomorrow."

Bryar sat and swung his legs off the workbench. Ezra had never allowed him to venture from the room with the weave in place, and facing the world without the Aura brought up in him a new vulnerability. He remembered Willow's misery and wondered if it would be as difficult for him.

With his senses dulled, his memory of Tai developed hazy edges. Ezra might have unwittingly offered him respite.

"Hold on to that pent-up anger," Ezra said, correctly reading him yet again. "Never forget Tai. And all she stands for."

Released from the workroom with a handclasp, he packed Rebecca's food and his few belongings, allowed the old woman to kiss his cheek, and left.

The compound bade him no goodbye. Neither Ezra nor Rebecca watched him go. The stable hid the cow and goats, the chickens ignored his footsteps. It was the same as when he turned his back on his childhood home in the Northlands.

A surge of acrimony welled up as he turned onto the path that lead to the Motherhouse. He had touched true happiness, and lost it. His future held much risk, and no certainty. But he was damned if he'd let this bleakness become the norm, as might happen if the power cell fell into the wrong hands.

It was the first charitable thought he'd entertained since Tai left him.

And the last. To attain the Motherhouse by the end of the next day, he walked until it was fully dark. By then, an icy drizzle destroyed any hope of a comfortable camp. The next morning, after a miserable night huddled under his tarp, the drizzle had become a rain that threatened to change to sleet. Impossible even for his freezing hands to rummage in his pack, protected by his lanolin-infused cape, to dig out something to eat. The trail became a morass of semi-frozen mud; ice-cold water soaked through his boots within an hour.

There hadn't been a cloud in the sky when he left Ezra's compound. Had the Old Man orchestrated this particular piece of torture, one final test?

A full day to the Motherhouse. The dense cloud washed out color. Uneasy in the flattened light, Bryar doggedly put one foot ahead of the other, frozen, exhausted, starving, more like a mongrel than a Weaver – *former* Weaver – as he walked through the long, miserable hours.

The Motherhouse, when it came into view, looked as bleak and lonely as the trail. Nobody crossed the green and few lights shone from windows. From the slight rise as the path entered the circle of buildings, he couldn't see into the dining hall, but guessed everyone would be there, food and warmth and friendship...

Skirting the green, Bryar turned right toward the Bards' lodge and deposited his cape, boots, hat and mitts in the anteroom. From there he headed directly for the bathing room, not stopping to drop his pack in his quarters. The urge to relieve his physical misery surpassed even his grief over Tai.

It took an hour, much of it spent slowly easing his frozen feet into ever warmer water, before the chill left his body. Eschewing the damp spare tunic he'd brought from Ezra's, he wrapped himself in a towel and hurried to his second floor room. A welcome fire burned in the grate, further relaxing his exhausted muscles. He rapidly changed into dry clothing and boots, and returned to the anteroom, where he claimed a cape and ventured out to the dining hall.

As expected, chaos reigned.

In the twilight gloom and devoid of his Aura-enhanced senses, Bryar had lost track of time, but it must be after supper. He managed a half smile at the healthy, optimistic teens barreling around the big room, involved in some complicated game that included dodging under and vaulting over the tables. He remembered these cold, rainy days and the joyous romps they'd shared as apprentices, but it wasn't what he sought now. He found a table in a corner of the area reserved for Weavers and sat, waiting for a group to clear the buffet line.

Joss appeared unexpectedly, bearing a tray with steaming bowls, thick slices of bread, butter, and a dish of honey. He set the tray down and settled opposite Bryar. "Lentil stew. There's meat in it." His big hands distributed bowls and cutlery. Then, without further speech, Joss dug into the meal.

"Thanks."

"Welcome. Good to see you."

"You, too."

Bryar was almost too hungry to face the rich aromas of the stew. He tore off a hunk of bread and gave it a heavy coating of butter and honey. After a couple of bites, his stomach began to settle.

Shrieks penetrated his corner from across the room. Whatever the rules, someone had just pulled off a dramatic move. He involuntarily sought the flows that would tell him the kids were practicing their new weaves as part of the game – but that didn't work anymore, did it? He felt like a eunuch, unable to touch what everyone else here took for granted.

Joss downed his stew in short order. "I'm going for more. Want me to bring you another?"

Bryar shook his head. The lingering uncertainty in his stomach, brought on by a day of next to no food, warned him not to overdo now.

Joss returned with his fresh bowl and said, "We heard about Tai. That's tough."

The bread in his mouth turned to chalk. He forced it down. "Yeah."

"Sorry."

"Me, too."

"You sure you're okay? They've been worried. Quinn's been fussing like a damn mother hen."

Given all he and Joss had endured together, Bryar felt obliged to be honest. "Not so good."

"They plan on putting you through your paces, but I don't know what they have in mind. Did Ezra get the shield to work? I can't sense your energy."

"I'll be glad when this is over with." He finally picked up the spoon and took a tentative bite of stew. Ambrosia. He moaned quietly as the savory concoction hit his taste buds. He'd missed the cooking at the Motherhouse. Almost two seasons since last autumn when he, Joss, and Willow set off on their trek into the hills.

He hadn't come back – come home – before going to Ezra's. Why not? Why had the pull to locate Ezra been so strong?

Dumb question. Ezra had wanted him at the compound. Expected his presence.

"How are you doing?" he asked. "Are you learning anything?"

Joss dropped his spoon in his nearly empty bowl. "I'm developing a new appreciation for Weavers, that's for sure. By evening my mind's on overload. Arwen, Quinn, and Dal – they figure to work with animals I need Healing skills, so they've added some of the basic Healers' training to the curriculum. With any luck, they'll spring me after six months. How you endured it for years is beyond me."

Months. Months were about women, their rhythms, their bodies. Tai would think in months... Bryar shook the thought from his mind.

"We were young." Another cheer from kids. They'd eat well and sleep soundly tonight. "I don't feel young anymore."

"No. Me either."

The lentils in his bowl had disappeared almost without his noticing. Bryar debated joining the line for more stew and decided against it. Considered a warming mug of caff and rejected that, too. He desperately needed to sleep tonight. "Tisane?"

"Sure. There's cake, too. Abricoe, I think."

Bryar took the tray and returned with mugs of tisane and generous slabs of cake. The abatement of his hunger made him more amenable to chatting. "You've settled in here well."

"Tolerably well. They gave me a suite over in the guest lodge, and I divide my time between the Motherhouse and the village. I'm learning, that's the important thing. I can't earn a living here without a marketable skill."

Bryar got where Joss was coming from. He needed to be useful. Made sense. If his Auric connection never returned, he would need to do the same. He remembered Willow, her struggle to find her place in a redefined world. What had happened to her? Was she a Healer again? Touching the Aura again, weaving her Healing around all she came in contact with? Or had that man...

"Any word from Willow?"

"Quinn believes she's okay. They're constantly scanning for her, but the hills block them."

"I hope Quinn's right. I don't think I could bear another loss."

The significant news exchanged, they ate their cake in silence. Bryar had just swallowed a bite and raised his mug to his lips when a new shout pierced the air.

"*Dad!*"

He sprang to his feet. Romarin barreled into him, clutching him in a fierce hug.

His daughter. His beautiful daughter, grown so much in the last half year.

"Mari." It came out choked. Standing there, his child in his arms, his face buried in her hair so like his own and soaking up his tears while his heart did its best to block his windpipe, Bryar knew his first true peace since the Aura had turned on him, far away in the hills, so long ago.

Chapter 23

Early spring appeared in the fields just visible from Willow's window, in the form of a tentative green tinge. She shared in the awakening of the land, as if the winter had been a long dream.

By her reckoning, thirty days remained until equinox, thirty days before the agreement with Gauvain expired and she would be free to leave. She wondered if the trail through the hills was clear of snow this early.

Cross-legged on her bed, her voluminous lavender skirts bunched around her in a way Gauvain would be certain to disapprove of, she created half a dozen small light globes and began a game, seeing how many she could toss against the wall and catch on the rebound before they dropped to the floor. Bryar was a master at this, as at any kind of juggling. That she tried at all testified to her boredom.

Lately Gauvain's lessons failed to engage her. What she didn't already know she dismissed as either a game or a weave with no practical value. Still, she remained in the class, enjoying the energy of the teenagers, who in some ways reminded her of Romarin.

She gathered up the globes and dispersed them into the Aura, then turned to the piece of metal lying on the small, inlaid table by the window. The task, to change iron into gold. Even Gauvain's magic failed to accomplish this; the assignment was merely to show the apprentices the types of challenges awaiting at the end of their training.

Not that Gauvain wouldn't be willing to take advantage of any discovery they might make.

Items made of iron, and its more useful alloy, steel, were rare in the Midland, to the extent that communities held almost all metal objects in common. As a Weaver, she carried her own knife and needle, but most didn't. The Motherhouse had received a gift of metal spoons many years ago, but in towns, even those as big as Stanstead, wooden spoons were the norm.

Willow saw no practical use for gold or for the proposed weave. Here in Borgonne its use was limited to ornaments such as those worn by Gauvain's friends.

She allowed her mind to explore the inner organization of the strip of iron. Gauvain kept the gold used for teaching locked in his study when the apprentices weren't experimenting with it, but she had memorized its structure.

The connection, the small similarity that would form the core template for changing one to the other, eluded her. And even should she uncover the secret, the energy required would leave an average Weaver depleted for days.

Quinn might like to try, though.

Quinn. Spring at the Motherhouse, the first fresh greens served in the dining hall...

Abandoning the iron, she returned her attention to the window. With approaching evening, the colors faded into gray with no hint of a sunset to warm them. Something smelled tantalizing from the kitchen; Leo had gone into Orlan that morning and came back with two packs full of foodstuffs.

Just to be sure – and despite having done the same thing numerous times during her months in the tower – she checked the wardrobe. Tunic and trousers, waterproof cape, sheepskin vest, pack and boots, all waited on the shelves. The fabric of the tunic felt well worn and soft under her fingers.

A gentle knock sounded from the door. She opened it to find Leo with oceans of fabric draped across his arm.

"I've cleaned and pressed your blue silk, Miss. Shall I lay it out for you to wear this evening?"

Willow groaned. On nights when Gauvain entertained, she was on stage as much as ever Bryar was, acting as his hostess and expected to produce a flawless performance.

"Thank you, yes. Whatever you're cooking downstairs, it smells delicious."

"The Master's guests are important in the town." Leo provided quick summary of the six men and women attending the dinner. "You'll be fine, Miss."

"They won't like me. I'm too..." she frowned. "Basic, I guess. The social chatter fails to interest me, and I don't understand Borgonnian politics."

"But you listen, so the gossip will be that the Master's hostess performs her duties impeccably. Would you like me to prepare a bath?"

"Thank you, but I'll do it. You have enough to attend to downstairs."

"So I do, Miss. I will see you later." The old man backed out of the room, possibly bowing as he went. Willow couldn't be certain, because Leo's hunched frame had worsened during the winter.

Proving there is some good in Gauvain. Anyone else in this indifferent place would have tossed Leo out onto the street.

With a sigh, she turned her attention from the window, the iron, and the gorgeous blue outfit, a textured skirt with a multi-hued silk overtunic, and stepped into the bathing room to relax in hot water and herbs.

The evening progressed according to Leo's prediction. Willow listened, said little, and nodded at appropriate times. The mildly scornful looks were no worse than usual, and the food considerably better. Nonetheless, she was exhausted when the last couple departed.

As he closed the door, Gauvain turned his sardonic gaze on her. "You did well."

Courage defeated fatigue in the face of the unexpected compliment. "Truth to tell, I wonder why you bother. They are boring."

"Local politics is necessary."

A détente of sorts had emerged from the wreckage of her rejection of him soon after Solstice. Gauvain remained as formal as ever, but a tentative truce existed between them now. Enough so, at any rate, that he placed a hand on her elbow and led her into the reception room, a space marginally brighter and more cheerful than his study, workroom, or dining room. "Think of it as a competition. Practicality demands I participate, although it takes me away from less trivial pursuits."

"Competition for... power?"

"Of course." He removed his hand from her elbow. "Will you join me in a brandy?"

"No, thank you, I am too tired. Do you require anything else of me tonight?"

"I require nothing of you, and pray do not speak as if you were my servant."

She smiled, rendering her words mild rather than aggressive. "Am I not? A servant or an experiment. There isn't much difference."

"There is every difference, and our experiment is at an end."

"Truly?" Certain he knew more about the workings of her mind than he admitted, she plunged on. "What do you gain by my presence? Am I such an intriguing specimen?"

Annoyance flashed over his features, but he didn't deny her allegation. "If you insist. Your connection to the Aura is only slightly above average, but you perform well above an average level, as if you amplify a template, forcing it to respond more strongly than it should. I have yet to penetrate your method."

"I believe it to be nothing more than focus on my task."

"You don't seem surprised."

"Others have said similar things."

"A focus to the detriment of all else. Come, Willow, don't be stubborn. Have a brandy."

She did like the stuff. "A small one, please." She sat on a nearby chair, allowing her finger to trace the brocade on the arm.

He nodded. "You are much too slender. Perhaps you are right to be cautious." He crossed the room to the table of bottles and glasses. As he poured he said, "A glass of wine, even of the quality I serve, might send you to bed with a headache."

Remembering celebrations past, the quantities of beer she and her companions consumed, she managed a half smile. "I enjoy alcoholic beverages occasionally, but a clear mind is a necessity in my work. I have saved lives by not indulging."

Gauvain handed her the small glass and claimed the chair next to hers. Glass, one of so many marvels common here, in the Midland was exotic.

"You found the company tedious," he informed her. "I assure you, I also prefer to engage in other pursuits."

"Magic," she murmured.

"Your blasted Motherhouse again. Magic isn't an evil."

"But I am a Healer, not a Mage."

"The two are not mutually exclusive. With your penchant for matters relating to earth, combining your talents and mine, I believe we may find the solution to the transformation of metals."

So that was his plan, or a part of it. Her skills were useful to him. She sipped the brandy, letting its warmth work down until her toes tingled. "And you are almost entirely air, with a suppressed hint of fire. I'm sure you envision a weave to trap the iron in a gold state. But without my earth, you can't stabilize it. It will not hold."

"True," he said.

For a brief time as they sat silently, Willow amused herself by watching the fire sputter in the grate; it would burn itself out soon. Her tiny sips of the brandy contributed to a sense of wellbeing she almost never experienced in the tower, or anywhere in Borgonne.

Borgonne. Inevitably perhaps, her spirits turned melancholic.

"Something is bothering you. Do you lack for anything?"

His question startled her. Was she so transparent?

"No, I thank you. Please don't trouble yourself." She hesitated. "Gauvain..."

"I'm listening."

And judging, no doubt.

She grasped the opportunity to explain her rejection. "I am grateful. You restored me to life. It means everything to me."

He made a dismissive move with his hand and a sound resembling a growl, low and quiet in his throat.

"That I was unable to share myself... I didn't expect that. But I must be true to my own truth. I... I did want to."

He stood, rigid. Insulted or embarrassed? She wondered. But at least she had given him her explanation, and her apology. He took the glass from her hand and returned it to the table beside the brandy bottle, then gave her a stiff bow and left the room. Almost immediately the light began to fade, so she cast a light globe, retrieved her half finished glass of brandy, and made her way up the stairs.

Willow awoke to an overcast dawn, resolved. After her morning ritual, she went straight to the kitchen.

Leo looked up from his breakfast preparations. "Miss? Can I do anything for you?"

She smiled. Leo never, ever used her name. "Maybe. Do you know if it's possible to cross the hills yet?"

He shook his head. "Nobody goes there. Unless the Master...?"

"I'll ask him, but I don't know how indignant he will be."

Leo snorted. "His levels of indignation have decreased markedly since you arrived, Miss. You needn't fear him."

"As you told me, my first day here. Now, I want to go home."

"I expected that, but I am sorry. The tower is a different place with your presence."

Her answering smile was wistful. "Could you make porridge, please? Last night's meal was magnificent, but so rich."

"With pleasure, Miss." Leo picked up a tray holding caff and mugs, and led the way to the dining room.

Gauvain stood when she entered, nodded, and reseated himself. His breakfast had yet to be served. Leo set the tray on the table and scurried away. Willow sat and waited until Gauvain had poured caff for them both before she said, "I long to return to the Midland."

"In thirty-two days you may do so, although I recommend against it." His voice conveyed no emotion.

His precise accounting of the days unnerved her, but she shook her head. "I am of no further use to you here. I am learning nothing that interests me, and my mind refuses to focus. Despite our agreement, I need to leave."

"I choose not to release you."

"I do not believe you can prevent me. But I would rather depart on good terms."

His two hands smacked the table, a reflection of the cold anger in his voice. "You are a fool. Your training is incomplete. Given your earth connection and your supreme mental control, you have the potential to rank among the most powerful Mages of your generation. With so much still to learn, I refuse to allow you to reject the opportunities here."

She drank down the mug of caff. "If the hills can be traversed, I must go."

"Obdurate woman."

"Tell me about the trail, Gauvain. Will I be able to pass?"

Leo entered again, carrying a large tray that undoubtedly pained his hunched back. He hustled around the table, serving Gauvain with bacon, pan cakes, and a dish of spiced, sautéed apples, placing the plain bowl of porridge in front of her, and a second pot of caff between them. After he scuttered away, Gauvain said, "Did you really believe the route to be impassable? Any half decent Mage could open it. The road leading to it presents a barrier, but not the hills themselves." He scooped apples over his pan cakes, ignoring her.

As a treat, Willow added some of his apples to her porridge and followed suit. Not until she had emptied her bowl did she say, "I won't beg permission. But I prefer that my departure be congenial, not hostile."

"Understand this, Willow-who-is-not-Willow." He had not used his old appellation for her in months. Today he spoke it with scorn. "Once you set foot on the path to the hills, you are no longer under my protection. You will receive nothing from me, no further training or favor. When you return to my door begging, you will not be welcome. You have experienced my power and my hospitality. I recommend you abuse neither."

"I am not." She rose from the table. "I regret this. But I am suffocating here."

"Then go. It is no concern of mine."

Did that count as Gauvain's blessing? She supposed so.

Chapter 24

Arwen's idea of training differed radically from Ezra's.

Bryar sat across from her in the plain, stone-walled workroom, battling his way through the exercises. Today that meant counting backwards from one hundred, in threes.

Who cared?

Yesterday, it had been reading. As a student, he had learned to read and write, but the skill was seldom called for among Weavers. He was rusty. This particular folio, with fading, blotched ink made from berries on yellowish paper imported from the Southlands, had been one of their texts back then, when he was about fifteen. At least the story held his interest.

In between the school lessons and tests, Arwen badgered him, forcing him to talk about the trip through the hills, his birthmark, the techniques he used to create his poetry and songs. Her choice of topics at first had felt random, but after a day or two, he sorted out that she was assessing his psychological fitness for the task they'd given him. Poking at his mind.

He'd rather be sparring with Joss, as happened every afternoon in the practice field out beyond the amphitheater.

Arwen interrupted his counting at thirty-one. "Excellent. That's far enough."

"I'm not likely to count backwards when I'm looking for the cell." He didn't hide the impatience in his voice.

"No, but you will need to concentrate. Focus on the mission. Now," she said in an abrupt turnaround, "tell me about Tai."

His heart lurched. "No."

She raised her slate gray brows, filling him with the same trepidation he'd experienced when hauled before her desk for some infraction or other, twenty-five years ago.

"Explain."

"No again. I won't go there."

"Because you're afraid. You believe she's dead."

Arwen's flat words landed in his heart like a jagged stone. He sprang to his feet. "She's gone. And that's the end of it."

Arwen also stood, glaring.

"Sit down, Bryar."

"I think we're done for today." Bryar turned and strode toward the door of her workroom.

Arwen's voice stopped him as she hurled a challenge. "Can you keep Tai out of your head? Can you prevent her memory from interfering with your work?" Her sandaled feet padded across the flagstone floor, then she seized his arm and raised it straight out to the side. "Keep your arm strong," she commanded. "Don't let me move it."

He just had time to tighten his muscles before she pushed down. To his horror, he couldn't resist the pressure; his arm collapsed.

She removed her hands. "Sit down," she said again, quietly but with an undercurrent of iron.

As he grudgingly returned to his chair, she added, "Memories that bring upset or sadness weaken you, as you well know. If I could block your memories, I would. But I can insist that you learn to compartmentalize them. Weakness is a luxury you can't afford. Not given what may lie ahead."

"Yeah." He sat and hunched forward, elbows on his knees, his antagonism forgotten. "But damn it, Arwen. How much do I have to pay? I'm like half a man as it is, with Ezra's mask. To strip away the things I care about—"

"Nobody can measure the cost to you. But according to Ezra, you are the one chosen for this."

The anger he'd lived with in the nine-days after Tai's disappearance resurfaced. "It's time I go and get it over with."

Arwen shook her head. "Soon, but not yet. Controlling your impatience is another part of it. You must be master of many types of strength, in addition to the physical tasks Ezra set for you."

"I'm fine to leave now."

"You are not. Talk about Tai. Describe her, explain how her mind works, what she likes to eat and how she sleeps. Paint me a picture with your words. Everything you know."

"Why?" Given Arwen's lecture on not letting Tai into his mind, what was the point?

"Memory work."

"I'm a Weaver and a Bard. My memory's excellent."

"Prove it."

Arwen was indomitable. Tempted beyond resistance by the opportunity to relive all he'd found in Tai, Bryar reluctantly began speaking. "She's so slight, but she doesn't get cold like the rest of us. She's healthy, never even a sniffle. She loves Ezra and Rebecca, and wildflowers, anything orange, and pastries – the same as Willow. Her mind, it's... luminous, I guess. More than curious. Rich and shiny. Does that make sense?"

"Knowing Tai, yes. Go on."

Bryar settled into his memories, weaving the words much as if he were composing an ode. Only later, when he ran out of things to say – because he wasn't about to tell Arwen about Tai's softness under his hands, the taste of her – did he realize that the exercise did far more than prove his memory. Arwen had provided him with the opportunity to relieve some of the emptiness left behind in the wake of Tai's loss. To rebuild a sense of wholeness for himself, knowing that Tai, whether or not she still lived, was woven inextricably into the fabric of his being. He'd bet Arwen would tuck his words into a template somewhere since he couldn't do it himself. Waiting for him when he came home again.

He tackled Joss with renewed creativity that afternoon. It felt good.

Chapter 25

Leo had spared no effort for Willow's last dinner in the tower, which did nothing to relieve the currents of tension between Gauvain and herself. He persistently rebuffed her occasional attempts at conversation and waved off her repeated thanks for restoring her and sheltering her through the winter.

He looked older, and tired; the lines etched between his eyebrows and around his mouth seemed deeper. He would hate her seeing him as careworn, but that was the image he conveyed as she ate the scrumptious dish of poultry with cranberries.

Much she wanted to tell him was left unsaid, but it was nonetheless a relief when he stood with his usual abruptness, gave her a curt nod, and left the room. He had eaten little, which surprised her; one of the few traits they shared was a hearty appetite.

She returned to her room, to find on her bed a cloak. She approached it slowly; even in the dim illumination from her solitary light globe, she could see this was special. Her hands trembled as she lifted it. Crafted in a soft green, tightly woven wool, the hooded, fleece-lined, and waterproofed garment promised far more defense against the elements than the woolen vest and standard waterproof cloak she had worn to cross the hills last autumn. She stroked the soft fabric, then swung it around her shoulders, luxuriating in its warmth and softness.

More than at any time since she arrived in Borgonne, she felt sheltered, even loved.

But who? Gauvain or Leo?

The materials were finer than she believed Leo could afford. And she sensed something that spoke of more than ordinary protection, as if a defensive template had been worked into the fabric itself.

She draped it over an arm and headed for the kitchen.

Leo had almost finished clean-up from dinner. He smiled as she entered, then turned and shelved a platter before giving her his full attention.

"You like it. I'm glad."

"Is this from you, my friend? It feels costly."

He shrugged. "A few people in town owed me favors. For your journey through the hills, I wanted the best. The trail is unpredictable, or so they say." He pulled a canister from a shelf, lifted the kettle from the cookfire, and began preparing mugs of tisane.

"I don't know how to thank you."

"Your presence has lightened the dark of winter. To be confident of your safety eases my heart."

"I wish there were a way to let you know."

"Gauvain will tell me."

That stopped her. "He can do that? Track my progress?"

"He is most unhappy about your departure. And your venturing alone into the hills concerns him."

Willow sat at the time-worn table as Leo placed a mug before her. "Gauvain told me that the path is open, but I admit I'm nervous. I will miss you, too. Little else, to be honest."

Leo put away the last of the crockery and eased himself into a chair opposite her. "You cannot appreciate the changes you've brought here. Gauvain is more peaceful, less likely to explode into tantrums. He will suffer your absence as much as I will. I could almost swear the light shines more brightly through the windows, but perhaps that's only an old man's fancy."

Willow smiled and sipped the tisane. Chamomile, and other flavors she couldn't identify, herbs unique to Borgonne.

"To answer your question, he wove a spell into the cloak. To keep you safe... and to allow him to track your progress, but you are not to know that. Be sure to wear it."

As she suspected. And Gauvain had forgiven her after all. "I'd like to thank him."

Leo shook his head. "Not recommended. However, he commanded that I arrange a horse and cart to take you to the trailhead, to spare you most of a day's walking. But you mustn't let on that I told you of his hand in these arrangements."

"Why does he insist on being so distant?"

"Old history, Miss."

Certain that Leo would not betray Gauvain's deepest secrets, Willow relaxed over the tisane, occasionally reaching out to stroke the cloak, now draped across another chair. "It is perfect."

"Simpler styles suit you, and will be of more use when you get home."

Home. She was going home. Home to the Motherhouse. To laugh with Mari, to travel again, to catch up with Bryar and Quinn. To visit her cabin at Hallan, giving herself solitude to recharge.

To see Joss. To be with Joss.

"Traveling in the hills is rough. The cloak will become soiled."

"It can be cleaned."

"I'll try to stay in touch with you."

Leo covered her hand with his gnarled one. "The prohibition against communication between your culture and mine is long standing, for whatever reason. I am simply grateful to have shared your life for this short time. Your presence has been an unexpected gift, Miss Willow."

"And you made my stay here possible, even comfortable. Without your care, I might well have sunk into abject misery."

"The Master did his best, providing you with everything he believed you might like. But you never craved luxuries, did you?"

She shook her head. "No. The clothing, for instance, conveys no meaning beyond opulence. People I work with and treat with my Healing create our linen garments, from flax in the fields to weaving and sewing."

Leo chuckled. "An unfathomable attitude here. Not even Gauvain grasps it." He rose and took their mugs to the sink. "The horse is expected before breakfast, but stop here before you go. I am preparing food, most of it dried. It should carry you through many days in the hills."

She stood and wrapped the old man in her arms, swallowing hard. She couldn't regret leaving Borgonne, or the tower, and she was uncertain how she felt about leaving Gauvain, his irascibility and hauteur. But she would miss Leo.

The morning dawned cold and clear. Willow tiptoed through the tower to the kitchen, where a compact bundle awaited her on the table. Inside, Leo had wrapped each day's rations separately, including bread enfolding a meat paste for her to begin her journey. She stowed the sandwich in a pocket of the cloak and shoved the rest into her pack. Then, because neither Leo nor Gauvain appeared, she slipped out for the last time.

The cart waited at the door. The driver, a weathered man of middle years in a coarse brown cloak, nodded but didn't speak. She tossed the pack aboard and climbed onto the seat next to him. He clucked to the horse, and she was on her way.

Home, she reminded herself. But leaving the tower caused more of a wrench in her heart than she had predicted. She watched it recede in the distance until they were halfway to the hills. Then she turned her attention to the sandwich. She needed its energy to handle the first climb.

Late that same afternoon, on the other side of the hills, Quinn raised her head from the weave taking shape between her hands and sat very still, much as if she were listening to a silent voice, a ripple in the Aura. Nothing moved in the Scribes' lodge, and the world around her grew silent as her attention focused on events far away.

The template before her had no practical use, but was for her own amusement. She'd been attempting to create an eddy and tie the air into an overhand knot. The eddy was simple, the knot less so. That she hovered on the verge of success mattered not at all.

The weave collapsed. She stood, shoved her feet in sandals, and crossed from the Scribes' lodge to the Centra, heedless of the drizzle. She barged in on Arwen without knocking.

"Willow's coming."

"Already?" The older woman looked up, studied Quinn for a moment, then moved her quill and paper to the side. "I sensed a disruption, but I didn't have time to explore it."

"She's in the hills, since this morning. I thought so earlier, and now I'm sure."

"Are you going?"

The turmoil of the last three seasons had etched permanent lines on Arwen's face. She seldom smiled anymore, and never joked. Quinn felt a stab of guilt at adding to her burdens. But this time it couldn't be helped. She longed to be with Willow, if only to assure her safe arrival at the Motherhouse.

"Yes."

Arwen let the bald answer hang in the air for a moment. "I thought so. Plan with care, Quinn," she added unnecessarily. "We don't know if she has adequate food, and it will be cold. You'll both need survival gear."

"I made my preparations a nine-day ago. I can be ready in an hour."

"Notify the kitchen. And do *not* leave today, however eager you are. Start fresh in the morning. Oh – and don't tell Bryar."

Quinn frowned. "Are you sure about that?" Keeping secrets from Bryar threatened one of the pillars of her life, her deep bond with him and Willow.

"I am. He'll hear soon enough. I have no time to waste convincing him not to go with you. It would be doubly dangerous, with his shield."

"Good point. But you should give him more credit."

"Oh, I do. He's still on edge since Tai chose to disappear. The best all around, but —"

"I could kick that girl."

"So could I." Arwen's mouth twisted into a wry smile. "But she was right. Her presence had become a distraction, and her absence tests him in unpredicted ways. Bryar's not your typical hero. He's forced himself into a mold of gentleness. Unleashing the fighter inside isn't easy."

Quinn grinned. "I find him very tempting these days."

Arwen snorted, but said, "Leave him alone. He's not recovered from Tai yet."

The grin faded; Bryar's troubles touched her more deeply than she let on. "I'll set off first thing tomorrow."

"It isn't necessary for you to go alone. I'd be happier if you took someone else with you. Another Healer?"

"No. I need the time with Willow, just the two of us." Quinn leaned forward and propped her hands on the back of a chair, considering what her explorations in the Aura over the winter had taught her. "The hills... I don't believe safety, or even survival, depend on how many go. If the spells on the hills choose to protect you, you'll be protected."

"That's my intuition, too. Not that I could stop you. Be safe, Quinn."

The women's eyes met briefly. She and Arwen understood each other well. Apart from the note of humor around Tai, their meeting had been businesslike and unemotional. With a nod, Quinn left to begin her final preparations. Scribes tended to keep to themselves more than other Weavers, and Quinn was among the most solitary. She would quietly slip out, taking the path north as if she were heading to Ezra's before turning east to skirt the massif that towered over the Motherhouse complex, and few would notice she was gone.

Chapter 26

Half way there, Willow speculated, based on days spent in the hills.

But she had no accurate idea of how far she'd progressed. The landscape looked very different from the one she, Joss, and Bryar crossed last autumn, a function of both the changed season and her restored powers. On their trip to Borgonne, she had walked with a dogged determination and a focus on finding something, anything, to heal her mind – and possibly assist in destroying the cell. This time she appreciated the surreal beauty of the mists in the dales. The peaks towered overhead, majestic as they caught the changing light.

Barely a hint of spring touched the crisp air, and she kept the cloak wrapped securely around her to ward off the lingering chill. Hunting supplemented her food supply, but Leo had packed enough to carry her most of the way to the Motherhouse. That didn't help the blister on the side of her big toe, but she supposed minor injuries were to be expected. With half a year or more since she'd last traveled, her feet, back, and leg muscles protested every step.

But the weather held, and nothing occurred to make her feel unsafe or threatened, despite the prevailing eeriness.

Snow mounded on either side of the clear, but occasionally muddy, trail. The sound of rushing water dominated the valleys. One ford frightened her, flowing knee deep and fast, but she crossed successfully – barefoot, pants rolled high, and the precious cloak bundled in her arms. She'd been forced to stop afterwards, setting up camp and lighting a fire to thaw her frozen legs before shoving her feet back into her boots.

A magical place. She wondered again why the hills formed a barrier between her world and Borgonne. And what sort of spells made them inviolate.

The trail rounded a corner and opened onto a wide valley. From her vantage point half way up the slope, she could see how the path snaked its way up the far side and through a gap in the hills. She stopped to enjoy the view and munch a handful of dried fruits and seeds.

A figure emerged from the gap.

Alarmed, Willow's gut tightened. Then she made the connection. After twenty-five years of friendship, she would recognize that gait, that body shape, anywhere.

"*Quinn!*"

Her voice echoed across the valley. She couldn't hear an answering cry, but Quinn raised both hands, waving them in greeting, before disappearing around a bend.

Willow forgot all about the view. At her fastest pace, it would be hours before they met. Still munching the dried fruit, she strode downhill and through the valley until she came to the river.

It was more a torrent than a stream. There was no sign of a ford.

She looked both ways, hoped for the best, and set off upstream. After most of an hour fighting her way through rampant vegetation, she found a downed tree spanning the channel from the opposite side.

It would have to do.

It wouldn't be easy, though. Her thoughts visited a trick or two Bryar had taught her, back when he first studied gymnastics for his performances, but she couldn't see any immediate application. Levitation might be more of a help.

She considered crawling across, trusting the density of the branches to support her. A quarter hour's experimentation proved the unfeasibility of that idea. She decided to use the lower branches as hand grips to keep herself from shooting down the river. Gingerly, she stripped. She stuffed her clothing in the pack, securing boots and cloak to it with twine. The tightly packed branches jutted toward her; if she crossed upstream she risked impalement as the vicious current slammed into the tree. She waded in just downstream, clutching one branch, then the next.

She'd made it three-quarters of the way across when she lost her left-hand grip and her tenuous footing simultaneously. The river seized her, pulling her horizontal. Only her right hand grasping one spiky branch kept her from being swept away.

She screamed.

Quinn crashed through the undergrowth on the far side of the river, shouting right back. *"Don't let go!"* She toed off her boots and plunged in, clinging to the tree, until she was close enough to grip Willow's flailing hand and haul it to a branch.

"I can't do it," Willow gasped. The shaking, a combination of the frigid water and fright, consumed the last of her strength.

"Yes, you can," Quinn shouted above the river's roar. "I'll steady you. You just hold on. Hard. You're almost there."

Almost there. Fighting panic, Willow recited the mantra over and over as the two women edged to safety in the lee of the tree's roots. Then her legs, and the remains of her energy, gave out. Quinn caught her before she could sink into the water.

Safely on land, Quinn pulled Willow's pack free and shook out the cloak, which miraculously was damp but not sodden. She draped it over Willow's huddled figure. "Warmth," she decreed. "I'm freezing myself, and I have clothes on. Makes it worse, actually. I'll get a fire going."

Later, dry and warm, after tending the assortment of gashes and grazes they had both sustained from the tree, Willow cradled a mug of hot caff – trust Quinn to pack along a supply of the ground root – and said, "You don't know how glad I am to see you. But what are you doing out here?"

"I've missed you." Quinn shrugged, as if missing Willow were just another everyday occurrence. "And I was worried."

"Worried? Why? I suppose you predicted I'd almost drown?"

Beside her Quinn chuckled and stretched, moving her feet closer to the warmth. "I'm pretty sure you'd have been okay. The hills take care of their own. But not even Bryar could top this river story. No, it's more that no one knew what was happening to you."

"I'll never believe you didn't find a way to spy on me."

"Believe it. Signals from Borgonne get tangled up in the spells and lose their meaning. Until you entered the hills, we weren't sure you were alive. But—" Quinn shut up and pushed back the hood of the cloak, then placed her hands on Willow's still-damp hair. "The connection – I feel it. You're whole again." She grabbed Willow in a tight hug. "You did it."

"I did. There's so much to tell you." She sagged into Quinn's embrace. Five days. Five days with her best friend, and then they'd be home.

"Nice cloak," Quinn said as she pulled free and reclaimed her caff mug. "Who put the spell on it?"

"His name's Gauvain. He's a Mage."

"The guy who healed Bryar."

"That's him."

"Tell me everything."

"Later, there's so much. And I want to know... Bryar and Mari?" She didn't ask after Joss, although she would sooner or later, unless Quinn volunteered. The whole Joss thing had precipitated her return to the Midland, but she didn't understand it and wasn't ready to discuss him. Not yet.

"Both fine. Bryar's at the Motherhouse, and Mari's thrilled. Your daughter's got a great future, Wils."

Her world made right, the days flew by as she and Quinn walked and exchanged their news. Willow dealt with Quinn's blisters and aches – worse than her own, testimony to the Scribes' more sedentary lifestyle – and lived with bubbling joy and anticipation. Whatever she had gained by being in the tower, this was where she belonged.

Chapter 27

The hubbub on the green told Bryar they were back. Bruised, filthy, and sweaty – and chilled as a result, because the temperature had dipped to close-to-freezing levels – he watched the excitement swirling around Quinn and Willow from the top of the slope forming the amphitheater.

He spotted Mari in the scrum, clinging to her mother. Quinn did her best to ease herself free; the first chance she got, she'd bolt for the Scribes' lodge.

Arwen hovered a distance from the small crowd. The woman missed nothing, and Quinn was growing more and more like her.

"That's a relief." Joss stood behind him, pulling his shirt over his head. "You want a part of that? I'm heading for a bath."

"No, I'll catch up later." Today's workout had been strenuous and unusually intentional, for both of them. Bryar suspected the underlying tension of Willow's and Quinn's imminent arrival, and maybe of his own departure, was on both their minds. He smiled and clapped the other man's shoulder; Joss had got the worse of it this time. He turned away, heading toward the Bards' lodge.

When he got there, he found a summons. Arwen's workroom. As soon as he could get there. Please. The polite word clearly an afterthought.

Well, he expected nothing else from Arwen. But he wasn't going anywhere until he'd eased his aching muscles in a heated bath.

Midafternoon, when he presented himself at Arwen's door, she gestured him into a seat and wasted no time on niceties.

"You're ready?" Her brusque tone reflected her usual efficiency, but with an overlay of fatigue. Arwen, he realized with a jolt, was aging. She was no longer the dynamo who kept them in line when they were teenagers.

"Yes." He matched her terseness with his own.

"And you accept that this is not a suicide mission?"

Bryar's eyes widened. Had they thought he'd...?

"There's Mari to consider, and others," he snapped. "Suicide never crossed my mind."

Arwen stared at him, as if she could delve right into his deepest, most private self.

"By the Aura." He was offended and let her see it. "No. Not even those first days."

His outrage failed to penetrate her calm. "Good. You leave tomorrow. We've been monitoring the energy the cell leaks into the ground. Almost every member of earth clan helped to refine Ezra's positioning, and we believe we have a reasonably accurate location." She slid a scrap of paper across the table to him. "The waymarks are here. You'll need four or five days past Stanstead, toward the northwest but primarily on well-used tracks. Can you travel as a Bard? If not, you'll still be recognized, so we'll develop a cover story."

He shook his head. "Without the Aura, I'd find it hard to produce a decent performance, and I haven't practiced in a nine-day or more."

"Say you're returning to your home village. Perhaps an illness or death? What works best for you?"

He mulled it over. "A father's death would work. In the Northlands, men's lives carry more value than women's."

"So it is, then. When you return, go to Ezra's. There's a route that doesn't pass through the Motherhouse."

Bryar studied the paper. "Through the landslide."

"He says it's stable now."

"It was stable then."

Arwen shrugged. "This route's the best option. I don't want that thing anywhere near here. And obviously, shield it. Fill your pack with dirt, whatever it takes. Otherwise we'll endure the loss of the Aura until you get it to Ezra. Those tracks are rougher, so probably six or seven days. There are

Healers out there, Bryar. More than the other guilds, they need the Aura."

Her urgency puzzled him. "You think I don't know that?"

Arwen's mouth twitched, a minor sign of contrition. "Sorry. A couple of Weavers are in the healing rooms now, some new virus. The treatments aren't going that well."

"Heard about that." He was on the verge of telling Arwen to keep the kids away, but bit his tongue in time. She'd be insulted. For all that the children residing at the Motherhouse imagined they lived a life of comparative freedom, they were closely guarded, even cosseted.

"Memorize the waypoints. The cell's been stable for a while, so we're confident Kiril won't shift it in the next nine-day. Reasonably confident."

"If I can't find it?"

"Ask around. Locate Kiril. Make him tell you."

"I'd almost like that." His fingers rolled into fists. Fair or not, he, along with everyone else, blamed Kiril for the Auric disruptions.

Arwen's smile was grim. "Good luck."

Willow waited in the lobby when he emerged. She looked exhausted, a little gaunt, in need of a bath... and the most beautiful thing, other than Mari, he'd seen all winter. Wordlessly they locked arms around each other, her face nestling in his neck, her body molded to his. Even blocked from the Aura, even with Tai's disappearance and probable death, and the overkill training – because locating and returning the power cell sounded straightforward – he knew where he belonged and what mattered.

She stepped back, her touch so familiar as her fingers rested on his biceps. "Quinn says you're going tomorrow. There's so much to share, but when?"

"This evening, the three of us?"

"Over supper? I expect to be in bed soon after."

He fingered the soiled green cape she wore. "It's lovely."

"It was a gift. Borgonnians adore fine things for their own sakes, not for utility, although this is practical as well. I must go. I promised Mari, and then Arwen... you know Arwen."

"And there went your afternoon, when you'd be better off napping."

"Yes. I suppose you can't tell that my connection is restored. I'm whole again, Bryar." Her hands cupped his face; her gaze conveyed wonder, and worry.

"Don't concern yourself about me." He kissed the tip of her nose. "It's temporary."

"Or so we hope. Quinn told me."

"May I join you this afternoon? Together, you, Mari, and me."

"Mari would be happy. I need a bath first."

Bryar watched Willow walk toward the Healers' lodge, the green cape swishing around her ankles, then turned to the dining hall. He could use the time to study the waypoints on Arwen's scrap of paper.

Willow tidied her room and enacted her morning invocation there, rather than in the herb garden. She'd managed the first few days at the Motherhouse. What she hadn't been able to do was get enough rest, or sufficient time to herself to sort out the conflicting memories and emotions doing battle inside her.

Gauvain and Joss. The long walk with Quinn. Bryar leaving to who knew where, facing unknown risk. Orlan, the men who had attacked her, magic, Healing... Idly she formed a weave from one of Gauvain's teachings. Its utility was limited, extracting water from the air but in a restricted way that wouldn't affect the weather... Perhaps she could modify it to hasten the drying of clothing caught in the rain? An idle musing, but the idea tickled her.

She delayed her breakfast until most people had left the dining hall, then gathered a bowl of porridge with dried abricoes and settled into a corner.

Home.

Traveling, when she set out once again, would ground her. She just needed more time. Anyone who had experienced all she had must feel the same, her mind a jumble, incapable of focus or rest.

Bryar should be near the power cell by now. Was he all right? She had never worried before. Two or three seasons might pass without their seeing each other. But this was different. This wasn't traveling.

Gauvain. Did he miss her? Leo implied as much. While her winter in the tower had been challenging, maybe he had done his best to make it pleasant. The fine clothing, the plant in her room, his determination to improve her Auric skills... his offer of himself.

The pain and nausea, the fatigue. The disdain that followed her every attempt at template work.

Leo. The apprentices, refusing to let Gauvain suck the youth from them.

So much to remember. She closed her eyes.

When she opened them again, Joss was pulling out the chair across from her, his plate of scrambled eggs already on the table along with two mugs of caff.

Wordlessly, they studied each other for a moment. Then he sat. "I wanted to wait until some of the flurry had died down. You had enough to contend with."

"How are you, Joss?" She heard the slight quaver in her voice.

He nodded. "Doing good. But I think Arwen's trying to squeeze years of training into six months. My mind's more tired than my body. It's worse than cramming for exams back on Terra."

She smiled; her mood, which had become heavy with memories, lightened. "Must it be six months? Could you stay longer?"

"I suppose. I work in the village most days. We're building a new barn, and the animals always need something. Lambing's just started, and a couple of cows are ready to drop. And the chickens – the less said the better. Bunch of gossips."

She laughed. "You're kidding."

"Nope. Biddies, the lot of them." He grinned when she did, then attacked the eggs. After a while he put the spoon on his plate and said, more seriously, "It keeps me fit, and it's valuable training. When I'm done, I'll be useful in a team of agriculturists." His face took on a boyish mien. "And look." He squinted in concentration, and a glow appeared on his open palm. "Is that magic or what? Arwen says I'll never produce a proper globe like you do, but heck, even this little bit is a wonder." He dismissed the luminance and returned to his breakfast.

Willow pushed her empty bowl aside and picked up her mug. "Where will you go? Do you plan on walking the Midland to find where you belong?"

He shook his head, swallowed, and said, "If you're agreeable, I'm heading back to Hallan. It's small, but it feels right. The men's lodge is comfortable, and they need an extra hand, especially when the tourists come."

As if she minded. Having Joss close – how close?

"Stay in my cabin. You are welcome, whether or not I'm there."

"Willow..." He turned red and twisted his big body so his back was to the room. "Thing is, that's still a long way in the future. Since you're home... I'd like to see you before then."

He didn't mean going for walks with her, sharing meals. Or not only.

Denying Gauvain had been worth it.

She covered his hand with her own, then lifted it to his cheek. Newly shaved.

"You never liked having a beard."

"Still don't."

"Join me for supper. There are rooms in the guest lodge—"

"I have a suite."

Of course he did. Arwen might be a slave driver, but council took care of its own.

Oh, she wanted this man. With time and distance, she had almost allowed the memory to fade. Not the connection, but the flare of desire.

But Arwen and Quinn awaited her, expecting her to allow them to uncover every crumb of information and technique from her brain. "This evening. It's good to be with you again."

"For me, too." He consumed the last of his eggs, then drank the small mug of caff in one swallow. "Since Arwen's tied up with you this morning, I have work to do in the barns."

"See you later," she said, glad for a commitment to the future. In this case, the near future.

He gathered his cutlery, plate, and mug, and hurried away, leaving her to contemplate yet another exhausting session with Quinn and Arwen.

Chapter 28

Whatever Kiril had done with the cell, finding it wouldn't be simple.

After four days on the road, Bryar felt wonderful. Even without the Aura, even though his muscles, however toned by his bouts with Joss, were unaccustomed to long-distance treks, he recognized the imperative of his need to travel.

He'd taken the track to Stanstead, then crossed the ford and struck out on the northern trail, the one where Willow first encountered the two strangers, Joss and Kiril. The land west of Stanstead gradually flattened from rolling hills to plain. Fields lay fallow or planted in winter legumes, although vast swaths bore no trace of human habitation. Rivers recently wakened from their seasonal freeze carried their burden of spring melt, spreading to fill their valleys. Branches of deciduous trees, bearing tiny chartreuse pinpricks of leaves, rustled in the chilly wind. Forest replaced fields before he reached his goal. The weather held fine, and he enjoyed the solitary walk, following the waypoints to the end, somewhere in the woods.

Logically, Kiril wouldn't have hidden the cell close to habitation, but there had to be a predominant landmark, natural or manmade. But which? And what?

Bryar made an unobtrusive camp well off the trail, grabbed a quick lunch, and set off into the forest to look around and get his bearings. The journey from the Motherhouse provided a fine lesson in how much he relied on the Aura to guide his steps, but he was an adequate tracker, a skill learned in boyhood. He sought the incongruity that would remind Kiril of the location of his treasure.

Joss had told him about their wilderness survival training. He didn't dare assume he was dealing with an amateur.

He found his first clue as the sun neared the horizon. Moving slowly and cautiously through the forest, he had been following an animal track which broke out into a natural meadow. The land was soggy, studded with boulders, the grass already greening. A few trees, still barren, punctuated the bog. As he looked across the clearing in the low-level light, he could see evidence of compacted snow, not yet fully melted, spaced to a man's stride.

Kiril had been here sometime in the late winter. Or *someone* had. He couldn't discount the possibility that a local hunter left the trail, but he thought it unlikely. The last village he passed was most of a day's walk away; he wouldn't find another for two or three days more. Plenty of game closer to home, surely.

He squelched across the meadow and paused at the far side.

Now where?

Within a day or so, the warm weather would remove these traces of footprints. He scanned his surroundings. A long-dead tree, its top branches victim to years of harsh winters, formed the only anomaly in the landscape. Twice his height and his arm's breadth around, it stood about ten paces in from the edge of the forest and fifty to his left.

Bryar cautiously explored the snag. No footprints to guide him now; the snow, where it remained, edged toward wet mud.

He'd find the cell near ground level; Arwen and her team had traced it by its seepage into the earth. It had to be shielded now, because there had been no further disruptions to the Aura.

On the far side, a deep cleft split the trunk. Generations of ice-cold, composting leaves and dirt filled the hollow.

Only one way to find out. He plunged his hands blindly into the waste. When he touched a hard, unnaturally smooth surface, he could have wept.

He'd done it.

Piece of luck.

Luck, the combined work of Weavers, and his willingness to close himself off from the Aura. He detected no discernable effect from the box's proximity.

Ezra had been unable to devise a sure weave to shield the cell. Dirt provided the best protection they knew of. Bryar had never seen it before and studied it in wonder. So this was the source of all their trouble, this box about the size of his large hand, a little over a thumb's width thick, gleaming gold in the daylight. After a moment's contemplation, he dropped his pack to the ground and pulled out a large bag of tightly woven linen. Within minutes he had transferred the cell, mulch and all, into the bag.

He reminded himself to be cautious as he followed his own trail back through the woods. He had no reason to believe Kiril was anywhere near, but the man clearly meant to hold onto the cell with minimal regard for its effect on life in the Midland. However, the meadow and surrounding forest remained quiet, with only the occasional skittering of some small animal in the undergrowth, as he made his way to his campsite.

Chapter 29

Willow crossed from the Centra toward the Healers' lodge, Quinn hard on her heels, in full harangue mode.

"You can't leave. There's so much we haven't learned yet about your recovery. And everything you can teach us about his techniques, his so-called magic."

"Arwen was furious when I left without saying anything before, remember? So I'm telling you now. I cannot bear another minute of having my head poked and prodded. I want to go home. Don't you understand that?" Willow shot back over her shoulder. Quinn had followed her from Arwen's workroom and, unusual for Quinn, hadn't been quiet for an instant.

She touched Willow's arm to slow her down so the two of them could walk side by side. "I do. But a flaw in whatever closed off your Entrée... it defies logic."

Willow shrugged. "When I started to regain my powers, I was so happy I didn't consider the 'how' of it. But the more you force me to think about it, the more I don't accept the idea of a blockage. I wonder if our Auric connection's more like an extra layer, and it got ripped away. Think of it like a scar, or maybe like a navel, a tiny remnant of whatever gives us access, not big enough to use, but enough for Gauvain to build on, not tear down. Given his pride, he'd never admit to any assistance or shortcut if he could avoid it. If he says he found a flaw, he found a flaw. About here." She tapped the left side of her head.

"Even if you leave, it won't be until tomorrow, and it'll take you all of ten minutes to get ready. Let's grab a caff."

Suppressing a sigh, Willow allowed herself to be turned from her destination and shunted into the dining hall. Quinn more or less shoved her into a seat, then went to the cafeteria line for mugs and a caff pot.

This was Quinn at her most bossy and infuriating. But she was right. Willow had the day free; the packing could wait until after supper.

"Hallan's a solid two-day walk. Haven't you had enough walking for a while?" Quinn asked as she sat at their table.

"Since I got home I haven't had a moment's peace, and now I need it." Except for the night with Joss, but she wasn't ready to share that, even with her best friend. "Too much has happened. I've been where no one has ventured in a lifetime or more. I miss friends I left behind in Orlan. I've barely seen Bryar, and now he's gone, too. Mari's safe and happy, and I crave time to myself."

Quinn brooded over her caff mug. "Are you going to be all right, Wils?"

"Yes."

"Spoken with your usual stubborn determination. That tells me you aren't all right now."

"Which is what I've been trying to tell you." The caff was an enjoyable mid-morning treat. If this was to be a day of relaxation, she might as well make it complete. Willow rose and fetched seed pastries. Leo's cooking was superb, but he hadn't mastered these flaky delicacies.

Instead of protesting, Quinn bit into hers with gusto. "When you're around, you give me permission to indulge."

"You won't stay as skinny as you are if you indulge too much."

"Pot calling kettle."

"But I'm a Healer. I burn through a lot of food in the course of a day."

"I'll miss you."

"Come see me. But not too soon. I need time to myself, not to mention cleaning and restocking. I want to visit Hallan, hold a clinic, ease myself into Healing again. Don't argue with me, Quinn."

"It wouldn't be the same if I didn't, would it?"

Willow fought back her grin until she had swallowed her mouthful of pastry. "No, but it might be a pleasant change."

Quinn's sandaled foot connected with Willow's leg under the table. Willow giggled.

"On another topic," Quinn said, "did you feel the disruption yesterday?"

She nodded, her mouth once again occupied with the succulent treat.

"Bryar's found the cell. We expected a short spell like that while he repacked it. He'll be heading to Ezra's, Sustainer willing."

"Good. I want this over. More than I can say."

"You think it will be?"

"Do you know something?"

Quinn shook her head. "Not for sure. Just a sort of intimation. This is almost too easy."

So much for leaving with a light heart and worry-free mind.

Quinn's hand reached for her shoulder and gave a gentle shake; her reaction must have shown on her face. "Once it's here, we can start figuring out how to neutralize it. Maybe, if Ezra's weave shields Bryar from it, then a similar weave will shield it from everything. Sort of overlay it on the one we tried before."

Willow stretched out her legs and leaned back, balancing her caff mug in her hands. "Sadly, I hardly care. I thought I'd be able to realign myself on the walk home, but it didn't work that way. I'm so tired, Quinn."

"It's been pretty intense for you." A rare concession from her friend. "I have commitments here for a while. Once the cell's at Ezra's, I'll be expected there. We're approaching equinox. By my estimate, it'll be Solstice before I can get to Hallan."

"I could well be traveling this summer."

"Might be the best thing for you."

Willow tracked Joss down as he crossed the green to the guest lodge an hour before the supper bell. He looked stunned, his eyes slightly unfocused and his reactions slower.

"Arwen?" she asked.

"Everyone swears it's good for me," he said by explanation, making her laugh.

"You're ungrounded."

"Tell me about it. That woman's intense. Are you still leaving?"

"Tomorrow."

An unspoken message passed between them. Joss took her hand, played with her fingers. "You're sure?"

"More than."

"I'll... well, I wish you weren't. But I understand." His voice was subdued. With lovemaking so new to him, he treated it, and her, as rare and fragile. As perhaps it was.

"I'm going by the dining hall later," she said. "Once the crowd dies down."

He grinned. "Weavers' rations?"

"And supper. Until then I've arranged to spend time with Mari."

Suddenly the path outside the Centra swarmed with pre-teens released from their studies. "Later?" Willow said.

The grin grew wider. Joss never used to smile. "I hope so."

He at least didn't question her leaving. He fought his own demons and, without a physical home, he retreated into himself when he needed to. Her time in Borgonne had given her an appreciation for what he faced with everything familiar gone, making his way in a new land.

She wondered if he knew how much he gave her when she lay wrapped in his arms. Twice, only twice. But their times together had changed her world.

Chapter 30

Because he wasn't familiar with the track Arwen had laid out for him to take to Ezra's compound, Bryar would have been more comfortable taking the busier routes through Stanstead and the Motherhouse. The total absence of habitation along the heavily timbered route felt unnatural. He had walked most of the Midland in his days as a Weaver, and he couldn't remember ever experiencing such complete isolation.

Still, the barely budding trees allowed sunlight through, warming both his body and his spirits. There were songs embedded in this land. As soon as Ezra removed the shield, he'd return and find them. His mind tingled at the prospect. By his reckoning he'd reach Ezra's tomorrow, deliver the cell, and be free to resume his life.

He set up his camp later than usual, in a small, natural clearing a few paces off the trail. The ground was stony and uneven, but the best option in the dense woodland. Nights still arrived early, although equinox had to be soon. He ate his simple meal of dried meat, waybread, and a handful of abricoes, by the light of a laboriously created fire – if ever he missed access to templates, it was in fire building – and rolled himself into his blankets almost immediately afterwards, the pack with its dangerous cargo beside him. For three days, the cell had never been more than an arm's length away.

He woke abruptly, sometime in the night. Had there been a noise, or a change in the quality of the darkness?

Through slitted eyes he watched as a man hunched over the pack, silhouetted by the embers of his fire.

His months of training stood him in good stead. Bryar moved smoothly out of his bedroll and approached, relying on the noise created by the man's unguarded rummaging to cover any sound.

He'd pin the guy down, then find out where he came from and how he knew there was anything in the pack worth stealing. His Weaver's sash kept him safe from the ordinary criminals who populated the more isolated parts of the Midland, but this was different. Intentional.

Bryar lunged. His arm locked around the man's neck as he pounded his lower ribs with his free hand. The man bucked, but Bryar knocked him off balance, throwing him to the ground.

From out of nowhere, a weight slammed into his back, sending him flying onto the dying embers of the fire.

He screamed.

"Hold 'im, Jeffy." The first man staggered to his feet even as iron hands hauled him up, locking his arms.

This wasn't sparring with Joss. This was real.

The burn set his chest on fire. He ignored it. He kicked back and high; years of acrobatic performances had given him the flexibility he needed. The man holding him howled and relaxed his grip. Bryar pulled free, wheeled, and launched a vicious fist toward the man's face.

Only to be grabbed from behind again and thrown, his cheekbone smashing into a jagged rock as the man seized the pack and spilled its contents onto the ground.

Jeffy took advantage of the opportunity and landed blows to Bryar's face, his gut. The pain and loss of air paralyzed him just long enough for the first man to call out, "Got it." He held up the cell. Its golden surface glinted in the remnants of firelight.

"What else's in there?"

"Dirt." He upended the bag, dumping the protective mulch. Bryar watched through eyes half closed against the pain, struggling to catch his breath. "Who the hell carries a bag full of dirt?"

"Reckon we should leave it packed that way. That's what he said to do."

"And he'll never know, will he? I ain't carryin' that weight. We can replace it when we're close."

"Suits me. Anything else worth havin' in there?"

"Nah. Bunch of primitives this side." The man tossed the power cell into the air, caught it. "This here's treasure, man. Pure and simple."

With Jeffy's attention diverted, Bryar gathered every bit of strength he had left and dove low. He caught the first man's ankle and yanked. Man and cell went flying.

Jeffy landed on him, nailing him to the ground. A series of brutal kicks pummeled his midsection. The world grew darker, then blinked out entirely.

When Bryar came to in the dim pre-dawn light, the men were gone, leaving his plundered pack and the pile of mulch behind.

One day to Ezra's, assuming he could walk. More cuts and bruises than he could count, unable to breathe through his nose, his chest blistered from the fire, an eye swollen shut, and his insides pounded into mush.

And his mission a failure, the unshielded cell almost certainly creating havoc among Weavers all over the Midland.

Diou, but he needed a Healer.

Panic-stricken, Willow jolted from sleep in the depths of night, to find herself lost in a far too familiar feeling.

The Aura. Gone.

A relentless pounding filled the suite, not stemming from a dream. Struggling to get her heart rate under control, she pulled on a robe and opened the door to an anxious messenger kid. "Sorry to disturb you, Sister. It's Quinn, from Scribes. She says it's urgent."

"Send her up, please."

"No, she wants that you meet in the conference room, over in the Centra. Fast as you can get there, she said."

Her prevailing nightmare was that Gauvain's repair work would fail, casting her once again into the flatness of a world without the Aura. But it wasn't just her. This was worse.

Quinn's call to concrete action dispelled the lingering miasma of dread. "I'll be there," she assured the girl, then closed the door and swiftly donned a tunic and sandals. With a shawl thrown around her shoulders, she rushed across the green.

In the meeting room, she found the entire board assembled. Even Fergus, usually the most light-hearted of them, looked rumpled and troubled. Arwen alone appeared alert, her clothing and hair impeccable. "Speak," she demanded of the council, wasting no time.

Willow circled the table and chose a seat next to Quinn, who gave her hand a quick squeeze.

"We need to find Bryar. Someone's taken the cell, sure as anything." Daren spoke with assurance, although his demeanor suggested as much annoyance as concern. Willow suspected he hadn't been alone when the call to meet went out.

"How?" Arwen's question fell like a... like a pod from space, Willow decided, crashing among them and leaving more problems than answers. They had no way of tracking Bryar, other than hoping to find him on the trail to either Ezra's or the Motherhouse.

Until that moment, she hadn't been sufficiently awake to think past those possibilities. He could be lying wounded or...

Sustainer, help him. Help us.

Shaken, she missed the next part of the conversation, snapping back when Daren, as her guild leader, spoke directly to her.

"Willow, you're the logical person to go. I'm sorry about your planned return to Hallan, but this takes precedence."

"I beg your pardon, I—"

"He'll be all right, lass," Fergus said. "There never was a harder head than Bryar's. He's too stubborn to let this kill him."

"He may need a Healer, though," Daren said.

"But the Aura...," Willow began.

"It is what it is. You have healing skills, and your presence will be an assurance." Arwen's voice told them she brooked no argument. "You're already packed. We will assume he was on his way to Ezra's. You and Quinn be prepared to leave at daybreak. Check with me before you go."

Quinn gave a brusque nod. So far, she hadn't contributed to the discussion.

"Any thought about what might have happened?" Cynth asked.

Daren shook his head. "Not for sure. But that distant from settlements, and unshielding the thing... my gut says it isn't one of the local robbers."

"Surely it couldn't be... not Gauvain." Willow stammered over the question, stunned by the prospect, however unlikely, of his world invading hers.

"Why not?" Arwen's eyebrows rose as her gaze bored into Willow, challenging her statement.

"Because... he wouldn't... would he? Is he this side of the hills? Could he send anyone else? How?" The questions chased each other, forming a whirlwind in her head.

Quinn's cool hand rested on her arm. She took a breath.

"Possibly," Daren said. "Not long after you returned, we noticed activity in the hills. You tell us, Willow. Is he powerful enough to get a henchman through the spells? Or desperate enough to come himself?"

Quinn's touch worked its magic; Willow allowed her mind to calm. "Desperate, no. Powerful... maybe. They don't have a comprehensive training program like we do. He may well know people with Entrée but minimal or no training, who'd be willing to risk the hills."

"Cutthroats," Fergus muttered.

"It is possible it's someone from our side," Cynth pointed out.

"Yes," Arwen agreed. "It's possible. But I don't believe it."

"We could talk around this all night," Daren said. "I suggest we let Willow and Quinn get some sleep. If it helps," he added to Quinn, "I'll arrange your trail rations with the kitchen. Then the two of you can grab them in the morning, talk to Arwen, and go."

"Thanks."

Willow watched as Quinn and Daren exchanged a smile, one that answered her idle curiosity about who Daren had been with tonight. She'd suspected for a while that they were occasional lovers; now she was sure.

"That's it, then." Arwen dismissed them, and the council showed little desire to linger to discuss the Aura's disappearance as they drifted back to their lodges.

At the sight of Ezra's homestead, Bryar went weak in the knees with relief. Two days of agony to complete an easy one-day journey. The pain in his side was the worst; he suspected a broken or bruised rib. Swelling prevented the use of his left eye. He hadn't dared remove his clothing to check on the welts and bruises. If he did, he'd likely never find the energy to dress again and push forward.

He stumbled up the steps to the front porch. Even Rebecca's vile potions sounded better than the pain and exhaustion assaulting him. Although much lighter without the cell and its protective contents, his pack still felt like a dead weight. He let it drop.

Failure. And worse, because the bastards didn't have the sense to shield their prize.

Before he could do more than step over the threshold, they were with him, his two oldest friends, Quinn supporting him, Willow soothing his hair back from his face.

Later, after they'd stripped and bathed him, doctored his wounds and eased him into bed, he finally allowed himself to relax. The ordeal over, he gave them an abbreviated version of what had happened.

No detail needed. His battered body told the story.

For the next two days, they were in and out, pouring healing tisanes down his throat, changing the poultices on his wounds. On the third morning, he sat up on his own, allowed Willow to administer to the nasty bruise under his eye, and ate every bite of the porridge Rebecca brought him. "Caff?" he asked, almost the first words he'd risked.

"Tisanes only, until you're better." Willow was brisk.

"The Aura?"

She smiled sadly. "It's good to see you're curious. Let me call the others. It's time for a confab."

Ezra and Rebecca, Quinn and Willow gathered around his bed and gave him the grim news. "We don't believe these were ordinary brigands. We believe the cell's on its way across the hills." That was Quinn, not sugar-coating her words.

"Gauvain?" he asked. The man had saved his life, but he radiated a sinister energy. Bryar had hated watching Willow descend into Borgonne to be with him.

"Perhaps," Ezra said.

"If they cross the hills, they'll need twelve or thirteen days," Quinn said. "Hopefully, the cell will end up with Gauvain, because he'll shield it immediately. This affects him as much as us."

"How is your head?" Ezra asked Bryar. "Do you sense the weave?"

"What's caused by the weave and what by the cell... I can't tell."

"I would remove it if I could, to lessen the pressure on your head. Unfortunately, without the Aura, I can't guarantee it's even there." Ezra's hand twitched as it moved toward Bryar, as if to work with the currently inaccessible energy, then fell back.

"In the meantime," Quinn said to Ezra, "teach me what you've done. More than one person should understand the template, and I found nothing in the Aura."

"We'll work together today. The screening weave needs to be added to our fund of knowledge – but for this, we rely on written records. The Mages of Borgonne may be able to access our records in the Aura – we've certainly tried to retrieve theirs. The potential value of this is too great to risk losing control."

"Agreed." Quinn's voice was grim, as it had been most of the time since they'd reunited.

Bryar swallowed hard. "I'm sorry. I'll do whatever —"

"Hush, dear." Rebecca's hand soothed his arm, as if she really were his mother.

"You are not at fault, Bryar," Ezra said. "We never expected an assault like this. It means only that our work is not done."

"We must get it back somehow," Willow said softly from her perch on his bed. "But if it means going to Borgonne... I'm not sure I can agree to that."

Bryar sagged against his pillows. "I can't even contemplate it yet. But I promise." He stopped and swallowed again, both because his throat pained him and for courage. "I'll retrieve the cell. Here, Borgonne, wherever. I'll do it."

Willow planted a gentle kiss on his less scarred cheek – by chance, the right one, without the birthmark. Ezra ushered Rebecca from the room, Willow in their wake. Quinn lingered.

"What?" He was exhausted. Couldn't she just go and let him sleep?

"Something else is bothering you."

"You're imagining things."

"I'm not. I know you too well."

She perched on the edge of his bed and waited. Bryar sighed. Knowing Quinn, she'd still be there if he dozed off. "Tai," he said.

"Being here brings it all back?"

"Yeah. Quinn..." He hesitated, knowing that even speaking the words risked rending his heart open. "...do you think there's any chance...."

"That she's alive? Yes, I do." Quinn rested her hand on his bare arm, her fingers smoothing the blond hairs. "No one in Scribes thinks Tai's dead." She studied him for a moment. "I don't have an answer. Tai's always been like this, following her own path. Years ago I vowed never to seek leadership of the Scribes' guild, for that very reason. I don't want to try to control her."

"Neither do I. But damn it —"

"Let it go, Bry. She goes her own way. I don't know where she is, and I suspect she disappeared so she wouldn't be a distraction, but I have no proof of that. There's nothing to do but wait."

"I've been to hell and back."

"Maybe that's what she planned. You're a warrior now. Her going tempered you."

"I'm so tired, Quinn," he whispered.

"You'll get your strength back. We rely on you, love."

He smiled. Quinn never used endearments. The brush of her fingers on his arm was soothing. He let weariness overtake him.

Quinn leaned over and dropped a kiss on his forehead, an echo of Willow's.

Not Tai, but they cared.

He drifted into sleep.

Chapter 31

After a two-day trek from Ezra's, Bryar had barely rounded the furthest building of the Motherhouse complex when Romarin spotted him, broke away from her class, and ran across the green. He didn't mind the stab in his ribs; her strong arms wrapped around him provided the best succor imaginable.

Her cheeks were wet.

"Hey. I'm okay." He brushed her cheek with a finger. "Don't, Mari. I'm fine."

It was the truth. He wouldn't dare be less than healthy after Willow and Rebecca's fussing.

"But the Aura." She pulled away, re-establishing her fourteen-year-old dignity. "It's awful, Dad. I've never felt so empty."

"Because your powers are maturing. It's bound to affect you more."

The tears evaporated with her grin. "Your little girl's growing up, huh?" The cocky smile gave way to a frown. "You're a mess."

"You might say that." Two days' journey, his face every color of the rainbow, his nose still puffy and swollen. With an arm across her shoulders he piloted them in the direction of the Bards' lodge.

"Arwen's going to interrogate you."

"I just hope she doesn't flay me. Your mom and Quinn should be here soon. They're communing with a wildflower."

"For all the good it'll do. Damn dead times."

His daughter was picking up adult vocabulary, as well as adult attitudes. "Nothing we can do. Remember, this is what it's always like for most people. Only they never experience what we do, so they don't mind."

Mari's thumped his chest lightly with a fist. He mentally thanked Rebecca for the salve that had mostly healed the burn. "You'd better get cleaned up. Arwen's a bear these days."

"Love you." At the gate to the lodge, Bryar kissed her cheek, taking care not to disturb the bruising around his nose and eye. "If you see Arwen, tell her I'll meet with her after lunch, okay?"

The first person Kiril saw as he entered the Motherhouse complex the next morning was Joss. That surprised him; he'd assumed his sergeant would have moved on by now, found some farmer's field where he could commune with cows.

Unfair.

True. But Joss's unwillingness to cooperate, much less accede to his plans, still grated.

Over the course of his winter ramblings, Kiril had developed a reasonable mental map of the Midland, reflecting with every step that he'd kill for paper and a decent pen. Holding everything you knew in your head was a challenge after a life of computerized records.

From all he'd gathered, the further west you went, the lighter the population. Which would be perfect for his – for Terra's – needs. He'd also made an abortive attempt to cross the hills to the east, but even without ever finding a fork in the trail and navigating by the sun, he kept ending up where he'd started. He remembered the bolt of pain shooting up his leg, after he and Joss were brought to the Motherhouse for the first time. Willow had assured him it had been nothing more than a pinched nerve, but it forced him to wonder if these people's skills extended to turning the hills into a maze.

The cell troubled him. When he'd checked, just a few days ago, it was gone, and whoever took it made no effort to hide the theft. He'd encountered a Healer on the road to

Stanstead and learned that once again it was wreaking havoc with Auric energy.

Kiril expected the Motherhouse to be in a stew. He hadn't expected to find Joss in the middle of it.

The morning was crisp and clear, with the scent of grass and something floral in the air. A few people, mainly workers from the village, stood talking or carried bundles to and from the stone buildings. Joss strode across the green to meet him. "I'm holding off from punching you out," he said with deceptive mildness. "But the temptation's there."

Kiril leaned against the wall of the Centra and surveyed Joss up and down. Despite the harsh words, he appeared relaxed, as if he were in his home barracks.

Deceptive. Joss ran deeper than he'd ever given him credit for, back on the space pod.

"Nice to see you, too. Whatever's going on, don't blame me. I secured the damn thing."

"Not enough. Could be nothing's secure enough. Let's get a caff." Joss turned and walked away.

In the dining hall, which was nearly deserted at midmorning, Joss challenged him. "So who's got it?" He poured the hot brown liquid into two tiny mugs and shoved one over to Kiril's side of the table. The other he raised to his mouth, draining the liquid in one gulp.

"Damned if I know. I told you, I took precautions. Besides its value to us, I didn't want to screw up your precious Aura."

"Ezra and Arwen pegged it to within about a football field. The thing leaks energy into the ground, different from whatever radiation's messing up the Aura. The earth clan Weavers noticed it, back when they tried that crazy circle. Willow's okay, by the way."

"Glad to hear it." He meant it. She had saved his life; he figured there was a debt owing.

"They got back yesterday, so you'll probably run into her while you're here. Anyway, it seems Bryar found it first. But whoever has it now doesn't give a damn about the Aura or keeping it shielded."

"What are you doing at the Motherhouse?"

Joss poured a second helping of caff. The miniscule mug looked ridiculous in his big hands, but he handled the caff equipment as if he'd been born to it. "It's the animal thing. Everyone agreed I'd be better off with training, and they're right. Another few months and I'll be really useful. Easier on me, too, learning how to turn it off. Then the Aura disappeared. You aren't going to be popular around here, sir."

Joss had used his honorific. Good.

"They can believe what they want. I don't have the cell."

The door crashed open.

"I get that," Joss said, deadpan. "But you're about to meet the hounds of hell."

The statuesque, dark-skinned woman from the inquisition loomed over their table. Kiril looked up at her and smiled.

She wound up and slapped him.

"What the —?"

Joss had the nerve to chuckle. "Welcome back, Quinn. He isn't responsible for the latest disaster."

"And you believe him." Controlled rage colored her voice. But for Joss's presence, Kiril suspected she'd willingly eviscerate him.

"Yes. Events aren't consistent with his usual modus operandi."

Typical of Joss to reduce everything to patterns. Kiril's hand had crept toward his stinging cheek; he lowered it back to the table. There'd be a bruise, maybe a black eye; Quinn packed a punch. But he had perfected an air of casual nonchalance over the winter. That, plus a charming smile, had kept him fed and sheltered as he wandered the eastern Midland. Survival skills. Not hunting and foraging, but survival nonetheless. "Caff?" he asked her, allowing the corners of his mouth to quirk up as if she hadn't just tried to knock his head halfway across the dining hall.

Quinn was gorgeous. He'd never met a woman to rival her, especially when worked up the way she was now.

Joss's big hand touched her arm. "Sit down. I'll get you a mug."

"Making him a part of the solution?" she sneered.

"Better than having him work against us." Joss left the table. By the time he returned, bearing another mug, a fresh caff pot, and containers of milk and honey, Quinn had pulled a third chair over and sat, her tense body radiating hostility.

Interesting that Joss knew Quinn well enough to cater to her caff preferences. An undefinable twinge crossed his chest at the obvious closeness between them; he ignored it.

"We work together," Joss said, anticipating his thoughts. "Quinn's helped me a lot with constructing templates in my head, sorting out what I can use and what I can't."

The three of them silently sipped the bitter drink.

Finally, she set her mug on the table with a thump and locked her glare on Kiril. "Do you expect to be of any value around here?"

The desire to goad her, flatten some of her pompous posturing, was irresistible. "Haven't a clue." He leaned back, casting a casual arm over the back of the chair. "I don't know who's got the thing or where it is," he added. "Get over it."

"What are you doing here, anyway? This isn't exactly a travel hub."

She apparently wasn't prepared to give up her fury. Kiril shrugged. "I was in Stanstead. Nothing more sinister than that."

"Are you staying long?" Joss asked.

"Until we're willing to let him go," Quinn answered, overriding him. "You've been a thorn in our sides since you got here. We don't need you out there trying to find the cell and hiding it again."

"Suit yourself."

Her mouth twitched, settling into a scowl. "I'll alert Arwen that you've turned up. Get yourself a place in the guest lodge. Too bad the Motherhouse doesn't have a lockup."

"Your faith in me is overwhelming."

"Lowlife." She shoved the chair back and stormed away.

Joss waited until the door slammed before he laughed. "Gotta love that gal," he said.

"Yeah, I bet she's a fabulous teacher." Kiril had enjoyed their confrontation and chose to turn his goading on Joss. "You bedding her?"

Joss didn't blink. "Nope. Just learning from her. Let's get you settled. You'll want time to clean up before Arwen gets her claws into you."

A bath and the prospect of a comfortable bed sounded wonderful after nights on the trail. He waited while Joss delivered the caff supplies to the hatch at the back of the dining hall, then accompanied his ex-sergeant to the guest lodge.

Chapter 32

Bryar spent the afternoon huddled in the conference room with Arwen, the council, and, surprisingly, Joss.

"I kept my Bard's sash prominent, so I was safe from ordinary robbers," he said, filling them in. "Ezra figures they were mercenaries, possibly from the other side of the hills. The power cell was a secret, but they knew to look for it."

"The blame lies elsewhere, not with you," Arwen said. "I'm sorry for your injuries."

Bryar managed a half smile. "Thanks. Sometimes I wonder if I shouldn't have hidden it at night —"

"And possibly been killed instead of beaten up," Joss said. "Ezra should have sent two. You needed a lookout."

"With hindsight, yes," Arwen said. "But given the situation then, maintaining a plausible cover story required that Bryar travel alone."

He considered mentioning the effect of the broken nose on his singing voice, but thought better of it. Enough consternation filled the room without adding to it. He trusted his vocal prowess would heal along with his face. "We relied on secrecy. Whoever they were, they weren't from the Midland. They spoke with strange accents. And that they knew about the cell at all..."

"It's by far the worst disruption we've experienced," Fergus said.

"They dumped out the mulch I'd used to screen it. Didn't want to lug the extra weight. Whoever's controlling them, they said he'd never know and they'd add fresh dirt before they delivered the cell. When the Aura comes back it'll be close to where they're taking it."

"Gauvain, do you figure?"

"Willow's Mage? Wouldn't surprise me. Ezra thinks so."

"Next steps?" Arwen asked.

"When it gets to where it's going, we'll track it like we did before," Joss said.

Quinn spoke up. "Which we were able to do because of seepage into the earth. Gauvain, or whoever, probably did the same. He may be smart enough to keep it elevated."

"Good point," Arwen said. "Which leaves us with supposition."

"Maybe not," Bryar said. "Given the strange accent, and the level of secrecy, it's on its way to Borgonne. There's no other explanation. And that means Gauvain."

"Not necessarily." Arwen was silent a moment. "This should be kept confidential." Her gaze surveyed them, hesitating on Joss.

"This is my home," he said. "I intend to do all I can to preserve it."

"Good." Arwen measured her words carefully. "Borgonne developed a system of Mages, similar to our Weavers here but with no central training. A Mage may or may not take in apprentices, and they become part of his lineage. *His* lineage – they are almost always men. Female Mages are rare and tend to be scorned, or so I gather. These days, two wield the most power, Gauvain and another man named Duncan. They are both in their fifties and at the peak of their abilities. They can be charming, but trustworthy? No."

Bryar tamped down a surge of anger, forcing his speech to factual rather than heated. "And yet you let three of us cross the hills with no preparation. You let Willow—"

"Do you honestly believe I could have stopped Willow? There are good people, honorable Mages, and I'd hoped... well, never mind. Gauvain and Duncan have fought for supremacy their whole lives. I feel certain that one or the other of them orchestrated this assault."

"Then it's simple," Bryar said. "From the general location, we narrow it down to which Mage and go after it."

"Given their powers? They're much stronger than anyone here."

"That's why Ezra insisted I reclaim it without my Auric connection. I'd be outclassed."

"So we get it the old-fashioned way," Joss added. "Break and enter."

Quinn had been silent. Now she said, "Where is this Duncan's headquarters?"

"I'm not sure," Arwen replied. "He used to be based a day or so east of Orlan. Personally, I'm betting on Gauvain. He's the nimbler mind of the two, and he's had recent contact with our people. Duncan may not know of the cell's existence. It's the kind of information Gauvain would keep to himself."

Bryar wondered how Arwen came by her knowledge of these Mages, but didn't ask. His time with Ezra had taught him that the older generation of Weavers held their secrets.

"So Bryar and I should prepare to cross the hills again," Joss said.

"No." Arwen's gaze swept over them again, then she nodded as if confirming a conclusion she'd already drawn. "Joss, I want you to leave for Hallan a few days after Willow. The disruption's hard on everyone, but for her it will be even more so. She needs the contact. No..." She drummed her fingers on the table. "I think we've just found a use for your friend. Tell Kiril to report here in an hour. I expect him and Bryar to be on the road as soon as we locate the cell."

Stunned silence met her command. "We can't trust him," Bryar finally sputtered. Beside him he could feel Quinn virtually quivering with indignation.

"Think of it as supporting him while he finds his place here. He strikes me as an excellent choice for a – what did Joss call it? – a break and enter."

"Cat burglar," Joss chuckled, clearly amused by the idea. "I've told you before, he's a good man. It's just taking him a while to settle into life here."

"And we can't send the two of them," Daren put in. "Neither of them has Auric access. They can't cross the hills."

"I think they can," Arwen said. "Bryar has access. It's just shielded from him at the moment. But we'll formulate a backup plan, in case I'm wrong." She stood. "Joss, make your preparations. The rest of you, one hour."

As Arwen left, Fergus touched Bryar's arm. "Check with the Healers, son. They'll see to it your voice comes back good as new."

Bryar grimaced. "You knew, huh?"

"That nasal twang when you speak, hard to miss. Get yourself to the healing rooms."

Fergus followed the others trailing out in Arwen's wake as Joss clapped a heavy hand on Bryar's shoulder. "Good to see you."

"You, too. I'd be more comfortable with you having my back."

"Care for a tisane?"

"Caff. I've been subjected to Rebecca's tisanes for the last five days."

Joss chortled. "Lucky you."

Strolling to the dining hall, Bryar took a deep breath and slowly released it. Coming home always felt right. Seeing Mari again yesterday had given his spirits a boost. And Joss; the bond between him and the big man had strengthened with the training.

But sentimentality held no place in his life nowadays. He hadn't tasted a mug of caff since the attack, and nothing sounded better.

That evening, Bryar faced Kiril across mushroom cutlets and mounds of soft patates. "Why'd you agreed to this, anyway?" he asked. The hours they had spent with Arwen had failed to assuage his distrust. Kiril had complied with Arwen's demands, but Bryar could think of no one less eligible to accompany him.

From his scowl, Kiril was no more thrilled than Bryar. "It's something to do. And getting the cell back is important to you people."

"In case it's not clear, I'm reluctant to take this on with someone I don't trust."

Kiril set his fork on his plate with more force than necessary. "Laying it on the line?"

"Better we understand each other."

"Arwen's already subjected me to an inquisition. Drop it, will you?"

Bryar kept his voice carefully unemotional. "You tried to take the cell from us. More than once."

"I said drop it." Kiril hissed. "As it happens, I don't want your damn cell anymore."

"Well, that's a change."

Kiril masked his feelings well; he betrayed little outward sign beyond a tightness around his mouth. "I'm no happier about this than you are. But I'll babysit you until we get the damn thing back. Who knows, I might like Orlan. It sounds more sophisticated than this backwoods."

"It sounds nasty. But maybe you'd fit in better."

Both men glared, the meal forgotten. Then they both looked up as Quinn appeared beside their table. Bryar knew her too well to miss the set of her shoulders, way her eyes narrowed. Quinn was more than capable of carrying a ton of attitude, and hurling it like a weapon at whoever got in her way. "Gee, you guys will have such a nice walk together," she said sweetly.

Bryar watched as tension flared between Quinn and Kiril, so strong as to be almost visible, sparks from a fire stone kindling a conflagration.

Kiril's scowl turned into a cocky smile. "Tell me, Miss Know-It-All. How come the hills are so sacrosanct? What's kept people from going back and forth whenever they please?"

"Like you tried to?" she asked, her voice almost dripping honey.

He didn't rise to the bait, although the smile faded. "I have damn good tracking skills. I should have been able to get through."

"Maybe you should reassess your skills," Quinn said. "As for why... why should we tell you?"

"Any chance of finishing my meal in peace without you two sniping at each other?" Bryar asked.

Quinn touched his shoulder, exchanged one last smoldering look with Kiril, then turned on her heel and joined the buffet line.

With a nod in Bryar's direction, Kiril carried his bowl to the hatch. On his way out, he passed Quinn and pointed a finger at her, a smug grin plastered on his face.

Bryar could sense Quinn fuming from across the room.

Chapter 33

A full nine-day ago, one of the monitors, a Scribe from earth clan, had finally picked up the briefest flash of energy through the ground, enough for them to place the cell not far from the hills. Gauvain had masterminded the heist, then, from his tower in Orlan.

The Aura had returned shortly after, and the next day Bryar and Kiril struck out for Borgonne.

Crossing the hills was no fun, Bryar thought as he plodded onward, despite the spectacular vistas and relatively easy trail. Eerie mists pervaded the valleys; giant birds unknown in the Midland sailed over the peaks, their bone-jarring cries echoing from the hillsides. Nothing overtly threatening, but unnatural just the same. With his Entrée cut off by Ezra's renewed weave, the feeling was attenuated but still noticeable, a constant reminder that however benign the scenery, undefined threat surrounded them.

Despite traveling together with only themselves for company, Bryar had developed no fellow-feeling for Kiril. Filthy and unshaven, they walked for hours, mostly in silence. Hunted, cooked, slept, walked some more.

On the eighth day, they pitched a camp alongside the trail on a gentle slope about halfway up a hill. The trees were sparser here as the rolling terrain opened into meadowland. After an unsuccessful hunt, Kiril studied their store of waybread and dried meat from the Motherhouse kitchen, grimaced, and said, "Not if I can help it. There's got to be game around here somewhere."

"It's not so bad. The meat cooks into a reasonable soup."

"Yeah, then you soak the bread so you won't break a tooth. Get a fire going. I intend to find us a decent supper."

Kiril took off uphill from the trail. Bryar watched him go until one of the numerous rock outcrops hid him from view, then started shaving curls of wood from a branch to kindle the fire.

Nothing glorious about this quest.

No one promised glory. In fact, quite the opposite. Bryar scoffed at himself; he had told too many mythical stories about heroic adventures. The reality was very different.

The pile of shavings had just caught when he heard the shout, abruptly cut off. After a moment, a cry rent the air.

He abandoned the recalcitrant blaze, snatched up his knife, and ran.

Another cry.

He followed the sound until he rounded a giant boulder and skidded to a halt.

Growling, a huge, drooling, lizard-like creature with a long neck and gray-brown scales pinned Kiril down. He had thrown up an arm to protect his head. With its enormous jaws, the beast savaged it, pointed teeth sunk into Kiril's flesh.

Bryar bellowed and threw himself at the animal's back, ramming the knife into a flank. A greenish, slimy substance squirted from the wound and drenched his tunic. The lizard released Kiril and turned on him, lashing out with a viciously clawed foot. Bryar felt a slash rip his tunic at the hip as he rolled and sprang away.

Strings of saliva dripped from the lizard's mouth. Its golden eyes held no intelligence. A mindless killer, it took a step toward him. Freed, Kiril staggered to his feet and reached for his knife.

Bryar slashed, catching the animal on the shoulder, then stumbled back. Kiril drove at the beast's face, cutting the tip of its nose.

The lizard shrieked, a high, unearthly cry, and wheeled on Kiril. Bryar attacked again, this time sinking the blade into its belly from the side. With another furious call, it spun and lurched toward Bryar, two paces, three, before its short legs gave out and it pitched forward. Stumbling in from behind, Kiril sank his knife up to the hilt into the beast's eye.

In the sudden stillness, Kiril dropped to the ground where he stood, his head in his hands. Bryar turned away and retched bile at the stink from the viscous liquid oozing from the animal's wounds. He kept one hand on the boulder as he straightened, until he could muster some strength in his shaking knees again. Then he supported Kiril back to their campsite.

Both men dropped by the now-dead fire, chests heaving. They reeked of sour sweat and blood, and stench from the dead animal.

"Your arm?"

"Not bad." Kiril tried, and failed, to flex the arm, now covered in the beast's thick saliva, and fingered the shredded sleeve.

"Don't lie to me. Puncture wounds can be dangerous." Bryar took hold of the arm, grimacing at the slime, and studied the wounds. The beast had torn Kiril's flesh half way to the bone.

For once Kiril didn't protest. He looked pale, but he hadn't lost his insouciant humor. "Excellent hunting, in terms of weight anyway. You want to cook any of that?" he gestured with his head in the direction of the carcass.

"I don't think so. You?"

"No way."

With a sigh Bryar started a new fire, regretting his missing Aura-based skills. Fire stones worked but weren't efficient, especially with trembling hands. "We'll need to boil our clothes," he said. The smell still caught in his throat, making him gag.

"Or throw them out. You ever see anything like that before?" Kiril asked, his voice unsteady.

The fire caught. Bryar added water from his flask to their cookpot and cautiously positioned it, taking care not to extinguish the struggling flame. Then he pulled his tunic over his head, cringing at the foul ooze coating the front. He ripped it in two and tossed the polluted half downslope. With the remainder, he began cleaning his knife, noting that the slash on his hip had not bled heavily. A superficial wound, with any luck. "Never. What happened?"

"Damned if I know." A spasm crossed Kiril's face. He shifted his arm carefully to ease it. "It came up behind me, and the next thing I knew I was on the ground with the air knocked out of me."

Dal had provided a supply of medicinal herbs, with instructions. As the water reached a simmer, Bryar found the packets he wanted and added a measure of herbs to the cookpot. He pulled the pot off the heat and covered it. "This steeps until it's lukewarm. In the meantime, we'll use alcohol."

Kiril shuddered. "What if it was rabid?"

For the first time Bryar detected fear in the other man's voice. "What's that?"

"You get it from infected animals. It kills you without the right medicine."

"You're probably safe. I'd be more worried about infection. But... by the Sustainer. That thing—"

He let the thought go as Kiril's tunic followed his own into the brush. He used clean rags to doctor Kiril's puncture wounds, saturating them with their limited supply of alcohol. Kiril grunted, then was silent, braced against the sting. When the herbal concoction was ready, Bryar used it to swab their cuts and scratches. Then he made a poultice from the herbs in the pot and tied them to Kiril's arm. "This will help. It's not ideal, but we're short of options. Nobody ever predicted this."

Night fell quickly in the hills, accompanied by a wind that whistled through the peaks. They hastily donned spare tunics and huddled in their bedrolls for warmth, although Bryar doubted either of them would stop shaking any time soon.

"Personally, I'd rather push on," Kiril said. "This campsite..."

"I agree. But moving wouldn't be smart. It's already too dark, and we're both shaken up." He placed the blade of his knife in the fire to sterilize it, then held out his hand. "Want me to do yours?"

"Thanks." Kiril handed over his gory knife.

After a silence that lasted too long, given the dark, the dead beast in the meadow, and the susurrating wind whistling above them, Kiril said, "Suppose it has a mate."

Sustainer, please not. Lighten up, he told himself. Don't give in to the fear.

"Remind me to invite you to tell ghost stories some night. The kids love them."

Kiril managed a brief chuckle. "Except when they're real."

"Yeah."

Neither ate. They both slept with their knives in hand, but met with no further disturbance.

Chapter 34

Bryar crouched in the filth of the alleyway, watching the back entrance to the tower.

The place matched Willow's description. Forbidding, its height and the black of its stone walls set it apart from the rest of Orlan. How Willow had borne it for a winter, he couldn't fathom.

He was at least as dirty as the narrow back passages that hid him. Kiril had insisted on that in the interests of tight surveillance. He hated it. For two days, he'd crawled Orlan's alleys, eating remnants from his pack, sleeping rough in corners where he wouldn't be found.

Once a day they met, near nightfall, to share what they'd learned. Since the confrontation with the lizard, they had achieved a grudging mutual respect that stopped well short of friendship but made their current assignment easier. Kiril was brittle, undoubtedly still hurting after the attack, although he had refused to allow that to slow them.

Borgonne, and the sprawling, dirty city of Orlan, repeled him. The day before, he'd glimpsed a flogging; his stomach roiled at the memory of the blood, the howls of agony from the two men tied to poles in the main square, the crowd urging the floggers on. With a sick certainty, he believed the men to be Jeffy and his companion. The Midland caught and punished its criminals, but never like that brutal public spectacle.

The door opened, and the ancient man who must be Leo, Gauvain's servant, secured the entrance, turned left, and vanished down the alley. This happened almost every mid-morning; he would return in an hour's time or less with a bag of food. The aromas that wafted from the tower in the evening drove Bryar's stomach into a cramp.

Willow had liked and trusted Leo. He'd use that, if he could.

❖

That night, his plan made, his resolve high, and as clean as he could make himself with the help of a scum-coated rain barrel in a hidden corner behind a row of shops, Bryar presented himself at the back door of the tower.

In answer to his knock, a voice spoke through a small hole next to the door. "If you seek the Master, go to the front."

He took a breath. "I'm a friend of Willow's."

In the uncomfortable pause that followed, Bryar heard a rustle and spun around, but saw nothing in the gloom. Rats, probably. The cold wind drove clouds that promised freezing temperatures by morning. He shuddered.

"Your name?" the voice demanded.

"Bryar."

The pause stretched longer this time. Bryar shuffled from foot to foot in the near-frozen mud of the alley. Then the old man unlatched the door and jumped back as it opened, a knife at the ready. "I am skilled in the use of this," he said. "More than Miss Willow knew."

Bryar's heartbeat ratcheted up, but he detected no overt menace. "You are Leo? I must talk to you."

The man nodded, his eyes distrustful, and gestured with the knife for him to step inside, keeping his distance.

Bryar quietly closed the door behind him. "Willow sends her best. Her trip through the hills was uneventful. She tells me you gave her a cloak."

"I did, to defend her against the weather. The Master spelled it for protection. Sit, but beware, I soldiered before I came to work for Gauvain. A false move, and you will rue it." The hunched man swung a kettle over the cookfire. "A tisane, I think. To warm you. It was Miss Willow's favorite."

"I need your help."

"Wait."

Leo shuffled from pantry to counter to cookfire, although his attention remained on Bryar and he never released the wicked-looking knife. Bryar studied the large, plain room. Cooking facilities took up the left half, and pantries lined the right-hand wall. There were no windows. Facing him, another door presumably led to the tower's living quarters. Through a door to the right of the cookfire, he could see the corner of a cot. A battered wooden table and chairs filled the center of the space.

Of indeterminate but advanced age, Leo himself had gray hair and sharp brown eyes set in nests of wrinkles. He was severely hunched, but Bryar detected the musculature of a man accustomed to defending himself. An aging warrior, and not one to be crossed. Meeting him, nobody would believe him to be a servant.

The elderly man placed two mugs on the table and eased himself into a second chair, all the while keeping his hand on the weapon. "Now. You are the one whom Gauvain restored to life last autumn in the hills. Am I correct?"

"You are." Bryar accepted Leo's questions and met them with as much equanimity as he could muster, given the urgency of his task.

"The more powerful Auric energy in Borgonne felled you, as I understand. And yet here you are."

"A template protects me from its effects. Unfortunately, we don't know how strong it is, or how long it will last. It's imperative I complete my assignment as quickly as possible."

"And this assignment... I suggest you tell me, succinctly, what you want here."

Bryar slumped forward over the mug, inhaling the fragrance of thyme and something else he couldn't identify as he sorted out his thoughts. "The disruptions... in my land, the Aura assists us in any number of ways, the most important being Healing."

"Like Miss Willow."

"Exactly. Are you aware of Gauvain's activities?"

"My job is to know everything. More than even the Master realizes."

"When the Aura vanishes...?"

"I notice, but my connection is rudimentary. Not enough to use, but it does assist me in my duties." Leo sat up a little straighter, with effort. People like him lived scattered throughout the Midland, Bryar knew, men and women who sensed the Aura, but with insufficient strength to work with templates. Many of them became hedge healers, or dowsers, or weather-tellers for their communities.

"A box about this size causes the disruptions." Bryar gestured with his hands. "It's shiny gold and heavier than you expect it to be. It must be kept shielded, or the Aura disappears."

"As happened recently."

"Yes, following an assault on me." His hand brushed his face. Few traces of the bruising remained, but his nose was still tender. "Two men. Not Midlanders, I'm sure of that. When they took the cell from me, they didn't bother shielding it. I believe Gauvain has it now."

"He would not have liked that," Leo mused. "Assuming the device came to him, he would have insisted on the shielding. That might account for —"

"The flogging on the square?"

"Probably. His temper has been uneven of late. Ever since Willow left here, in fact."

Both men sipped their tisanes. The kitchen was silent other than occasional gurgles and hisses from the kettle suspended over the cookfire.

"The box – the power cell – emits several forms of energy. Did Willow tell you how it arrived among us? The aliens?"

Leo nodded. "Rather like a tale from school, isn't it? And this is the same device that cost Miss Willow her connection?"

"Through a failed effort to shield it, yes. But it wasn't the box directly. That came from the Aura itself, as far as we've been able to gather."

"And that led her to put herself in Gauvain's power." At Bryar's horrified look, Leo shook his head. "Not like that. He would never harm her, but she could not have discerned at the beginning whether he be healer or destroyer." Leo's voice dropped as he muttered, "I wasn't sure myself, at first."

"She's happy and healthy, and speaks of you with affection." Bryar took a swig of the tisane, now tepid in the mug. "You can see the risk, should the cell fall into the wrong hands."

The old man's lips tightened into a grim line as he considered this. "The struggle for ascendancy. To sum, you believe Gauvain's hands are the wrong ones. And you want my assistance to steal the device back. You ask me to trust you not to use it as you imply Gauvain might – for his own reasons without concern for others."

Bryar sat quietly for a minute, meeting Leo's eyes. "We've developed a plan to secure it so it can't be found or leak its poison into the earth. It does that. It's a different energy from the one that masks the Aura, insidious and just as dangerous. But our first priority is to retrieve it."

Leo finally removed his hand from the knife. Bryar relaxed, releasing a tension he'd only vaguely been aware of. "The mark on your face convinced me you are who you say you are. Such birthmarks are rare. Willow is very fond of you."

He smiled. "And I of her. We have a daughter together. She'll always be a part of me."

"Romarin. Miss Willow often spoke of her. Of her ability with herbs and her joy at making music. And you, a Weaver from the Midland, risk exposure to this cell to return it to your Motherhouse."

"And secure the future of those I care about. Will you help me get it back?"

Leo now fell quiet, considering before he spoke. "Lately the Master has been so fractious he's no pleasure to himself or anyone else. This concerns me. I distrust erratic behavior."

Bryar leaned forward, his voice low and urgent. "Then give me your support."

Leo sipped the tisane before replying. "I believe you are correct that the device is here in the tower. Gauvain has social engagements tomorrow. As I always do, I will take the opportunity to dust, which is an excellent way to learn things others might wish me not to. You say it is best shielded by earth?"

"As far as we know."

Leo's expression held neither disbelief nor censure. "Come tomorrow night at this time. I'll attempt to give you an answer."

"Thank you."

The elderly servant rose and cleared away the mugs, clattering them into the wash basin. "Have you a place to sleep?" he asked over his shoulder.

"I've found a spot under a chimney."

"I cannot risk you staying here, but if you turn right..." Leo gave him directions to a stable not far from the tower. Bryar noted the information but didn't plan on using it. This meeting had gone smoothly, but he sensed a wiliness in the old man. Until he was sure whose side he was on, he'd make his own arrangements.

"I'm in," Bryar told Kiril the next evening when they met behind a pile of rubbish to share a pitiful meal of rock-hard waybread with questionable vegetables Kiril had stolen from the compost pile at the back of a magnificent home on the outskirts of town. The cold wind hadn't let up. It whisked clouds across the sky, but so far there was no sign of rain.

"Good. Our time's running out. I almost got nabbed this afternoon. If nothing else, the authorities know someone's snooping around." Kiril scratched at his arm. He'd complained a couple of times about the itching as the puncture wounds healed.

"Not to mention we'll starve." Hunger made Bryar irritable. "Is this the best you could do?"

Kiril smirked. "You got anything better to offer?"

He didn't, so he kept quiet and poked at the mess in his travel bowl, picking out the worst of the moldy vegetables.

"You talked to the servant, did you?" Kiril continued. "He probably went straight to Gauvain."

"I doubt it. He's worried about Gauvain's stability. And he misses Willow, that much is clear."

"Next steps?" Kiril tossed a particularly unsavory scrap into the sewer running down the center of the alley.

The smell was enough to put Bryar off his food, almost. After a day with little sustenance, he forced himself to ignore the stench and, like Kiril, poke through the half rotten vegetables for morsels worth consuming.

"Stay close when I go back tonight. If Leo's going to betray us, it's likely to be now. He promised to scout around for the cell."

"You pick up on the chatter in the square today?"

"No, what?"

Kiril held up something green, frowned at it, then shrugged and popped it into his mouth. His nose wrinkled, but he chewed and swallowed. "Seems your precious Aura hiccupped this afternoon. A few seconds, hardly anything. I overheard some men talking about it."

Bryar nodded. "Good. Leo found the cell."

"And probably got beaten for his trouble. Gauvain felt the disruption, too, don't forget."

"I hadn't thought of that."

"You're no strategist. That's why you should have left this to me." Kiril's disapproval ricocheted between them.

"We need Leo. On our own, we could search forever."

Kiril touched his arm, cautioning him, as four men dressed identically in tunics with wide green leather belts rounded the rubbish pile and stopped. Bryar had narrowly avoided them more than once in his short stay in Orlan. They drew wooden truncheons as one stepped forward. "You there. Explain yourselves."

Bryar left the interaction in Kiril's hands.

"Sorry, sir. We'll be moving on." Kiril's voice dripped with a subservience that Bryar knew to be wholly false.

"See to it you do. Next time we'll drag you to the stocks. Shift it." The man made a threatening gesture with the truncheon.

Bryar rose when Kiril did and stood hunched, keeping himself small.

"Yes, sir," Kiril said. "Our apologies, sir."

Volunteer nothing beyond what you must. Be submissive, a mouse. If it comes to a confrontation, you can't win. Lessons

Kiril had pounded into him during their last few days in the hills. Survival training.

As they emerged from the alley, the four policemen hard on their heels, one of the green-belted men called out, "Find a better place to hide out from the womenfolk."

Kiril looked back at the man, a completely unnatural sheepishness masking his face. "Good advice, thanks."

When the troop left, Kiril hastened them to another rendezvous point they'd chosen, this one farther out from Orlan's town square. Neither spoke until they were crouched hidden in a warren of alleys. No windows opened above them, but even so they kept their voices low.

"We're known now," Kiril said. "We need to wrap this up and get out of here."

Bryar nodded. "Tonight, then. Assuming Leo's found the cell, I'll stay in the kitchen until the household retires for the night, grab it, and go."

"Don't forget the dirt. You won't be able to tell if it's masked or not, but Gauvain will."

"I'm well aware of that," Bryar said, annoyed. He wasn't the idiot Kiril took him for.

No, a niggling voice in his mind pointed out, but less experienced. They'd only survive this by pulling together.

"Can you get me in with you?"

"I'd rather not. I have an excuse if Gauvain should turn up. Willow's friend, come to pay my respects to Leo. I'll be sure the door's unlatched, but I don't want you in there unless things go wrong."

"Meet me in the alley beforehand. Damn, I could have used more food tonight." Kiril straightened and tossed the remains of his meal into the alley.

Typical. They were living on the edge of danger, and he complained about his stomach.

Bryar watched Kiril fade into the darkness.

Chapter 35

Leo met Bryar at the kitchen door before he had a chance to knock. "Very quiet, if you please," the elderly man said in a near whisper. "The gentlemen have not yet retired."

"Gentlemen?"

Leo closed the door gently behind him. "Yes, and for the Master, the worst that could happen, or so I believe. Another Mage. They've been rivals for years. Possibly their whole lives."

Uneasiness crept up Bryar's spine. "Duncan? I've heard of him."

Leo nodded once. "They have just requested brandy. I must hurry."

Bryar took a seat at the table, thinking it the best place to stay out of Leo's way as he scuttled about preparing a decanter and glasses. He left carrying the tray, returning empty-handed a short time later. "I dislike this. Brandy makes the Master loquacious. He fails to see the danger of revealing too much. The two of them will boast and brag half the night away."

Leo busied himself with the kettle, making another tisane, or so Bryar surmised. "You don't want Duncan to learn of the cell."

"It's too late for that. I overheard some of their grandiosity earlier. Gauvain leaves no doubt in Duncan's mind that he possesses it. Whether he has revealed its location, I can't say. Duncan is corpulent, and this makes him appear harmless. But he is dangerous, more so than Gauvain. Miss Willow distrusted him."

"That tells me all I need to know. You found the cell, Leo?"

"I did." Leo set the tisane on the table, along with a plate of flatbreads and a soft cheese. "I suspect you have eaten little today."

"You're right." He consumed a cracker, then another. "Thanks."

"I was a soldier once. I'm acquainted with the perils of long marches and poor rations."

Bryar washed the crackers down with a swallow of tisane. "I want to take the cell tonight. There are men in green belts —"

"The police. We require them to control crime."

"We've been noticed. I can't risk waiting any longer."

Leo's hand froze over his mug. The cautious friendliness fled his voice. "We?"

"I'm here with one other, not a friend of Willow's."

"She dislikes him?"

"No. She finds him frustrating. But she saw the merit of his accompanying me."

"I don't like this. You didn't mention another, yesterday."

"He's back-up. If all goes well, you'll never see him."

The men's eyes met across the table. Uncertainty tightened the skin around Leo's. Bryar schooled his face to openness.

Leo twisted in his chair, then rose, seeming to accept Bryar's statement. He began scraping the Mages' plates. "I agreed to your scheme because of recent events, which I am helpless to counteract. The change in the Master since Miss Willow left... I believe he became more attached to her than he ever let on. She spoke her mind, which would have been a new experience for him. With her absence, he's become unlike himself. Unpredictable. A few days ago, he lost his customary control and hurled an instrument at the wall. The apprentices have noticed, too. The girl, Amalie, visits with me. She finds it hard, as generally women are not considered candidates for elevation to Mage. Harder still, with Gauvain in this mood. It's not healthy, and it may color his decisions."

"The person who controls the cell controls the world."

"Aye. And Gauvain intends to be that man. I'm sure of that now."

"How long a wait before they go to bed?"

"Probably two or three hours yet."

Bryar didn't dare nap. "Have you any caff? I have to stay alert."

"I do, and the finest. The Master buys only the best."

Leo brewed the caff, and they waited, Leo periodically leaving to serve the men in the dining room.

Leo proved his worth, staying up past midnight, swapping tales. The man's stories of army life amused Bryar, the more so because he suspected them to be true. "You never told Willow any of this," he said as the tower settled into a quiet that suggested its inhabitants had retired.

"No. Some stories aren't for the lasses. Soldier's creed."

Bryar hadn't heard of a soldier's creed, or for that matter that soldiers actually existed outside of the fanciful tales he spun for entertainment. Something else he didn't much like about life on this side of the hills.

When the last caff had been drunk, the last story told, and the exact location of the power cell explained, they sat in silence for a while, listening. Bryar longed once again for his enhanced senses, even knowing the energy in Borgonne would destroy them. No, this was a job for an ordinary man, even if it meant, as a last resort, exposing the cell, neutralizing both Gauvain and Duncan's Auric connections.

Finally, Leo rose to make a final pass through the tower. "As I do every night, nothing suspicious about it," he assured Bryar. On his return, he said, "All is quiet. It's time, lad."

"Thank you for your help."

"All for the greater good, including the Master's. Safety go with ye." The old man turned from him and disappeared into his private quarters. Bryar was on his own.

He unlatched the outer door and set it ajar, then took the one remaining candle in its wrought iron holder and carried it, following Leo's directions, into Gauvain's study.

The room left him slack-jawed. Even in the uncertain candlelight the richness of the cloths and tapestries, the fine, elaborate working of the many ornaments – or whatever they were – filled his senses, making him wish to abandon the task, just for a night, and explore the wonders before him.

Like a boy under an enchantment in one of your stories.

He set the candleholder on the high mantel. Behind Gauvain's desk, on a separate table, he found what he was looking for. A nondescript boulder, oblong, the size of a serving tray in cross section, was at odds with the rest of the furnishings by its very plainness. With his fingers, he explored the stone and detected the line of the cut around its circumference.

Lift the lid. Remove the cell, and go.

Simple steps, which should take no more than seconds to accomplish.

The two halves fit perfectly together; Bryar couldn't get so much as a fingernail between them. Considering that, and the probable weight, he shifted the top half to the side, rather than try to lift it. The edges made a grating noise as they moved against each other.

A soft shuffling disturbed the dark quiet of the tower. He froze. When the sound didn't recur, he told himself to relax, but he broke out into a cold sweat.

The moment he uncovered the cell, Gauvain would know. Could he make it out of the tower without detection?

He had to. There was no other option.

A final shove revealed the interior of the hollow boulder. The light from the candle shattered into a thousand flashes. Purple crystals surrounded the power cell, unlike anything he had ever seen. The sight hypnotized him.

From the vicinity of the door came a gasp, as if from pain. He wheeled.

"Not the only one, I see." A man entered the room and approached the desk. Considerably taller and heavier than Bryar, he wore a reddish gown that caught the light almost as much as the crystals did.

Duncan.

"Kind of you to locate it for me," the man growled.

"It's not yours." The words fought to emerge from Bryar's suddenly dry throat. He smelled his own fear, which threatened to drain away his strength. He couldn't let that happen.

Duncan strode around the desk and reached toward the boulder. Bryar shoved the top of the stone back in place, slamming it into the man's fingers.

Duncan howled – pain and fury blatant on his face.

Bryar shifted the stone again to give himself leverage, pried up the top, and heaved it away. It landed with a heavy thud and rocked once before settling. The lower half shuddered on its stand, sending the forest of crystals into wild dances of color in the candlelight.

Judging by the way the other man gasped, he had just unmasked the power cell. And leveled the playing field.

Physical, plain and simple, Ezra had said.

Moving with a swiftness that belied his size, Duncan lifted the cell from its crystal bed and started for the door, circling the desk.

Bryar sprang, chopping the larger man's wrist. The cell shot from Duncan's grasp; Bryar kicked it farther away before landing a punch under the older man's eye.

Duncan might be overweight, but he wasn't weak or unskilled in fighting techniques. He crashed into Bryar, sending them both tumbling onto Gauvain's desk. Something hard jabbed into Bryar's back before their struggle pitched them both to the floor. Duncan caught him in a leg lock, pinning him. He bucked and gained enough leverage to shove the man off and roll to a crouch.

He lunged for the cell. Duncan seized him from behind, his arms locked around his chest and squeezing. *Diou*, but the man was strong. Unable to break the grip, Bryar used a move learned from Joss, sending Duncan flying over his head to sprawl on the floor.

The Mage rolled to his feet, the cell in his hand. Bryar dove for his knees and pulled him to the floor. A small table holding fancy glass implements collapsed on top of them, shattering to shards on the floor.

The two men grappled, sending the cell shooting across the room. Neither was able to get an advantage. Bryar twisted free and staggered to his feet.

The knife in Duncan's hand appeared from nowhere, glinting in the light. He approached Bryar, feinting with it; Bryar danced aside. Then he grabbed Duncan's raised arm, and they were locked together, struggling for control of the weapon. The other man's eyes had become tiny pinpricks reflecting the candlelight.

Bryar felt sweat pouring off him, slickening his hands. With Duncan's face close to his own, he could see spittle gathered at the corners of his mouth, smell breath soured by rich food and wine.

Duncan was larger and had the advantage of leverage. The blade crept closer.

He had one chance. Desperate, Bryar mustered all his strength and training. But his left hand slipped from the knife an instant before he spun, pulled Duncan off balance, and jerked the weapon down.

Duncan's face registered shock, then puzzlement. He slumped to the floor. The hilt of the knife protruded from his abdomen.

No. He couldn't be dead.

Pain, the worst of Bryar's life, shot from his left hand and into his arm. He screamed as his legs gave way. Then the world went black.

Kiril burst through the door as the hunched old man rushed into the kitchen. Kiril shoved past him, darted into the main part of the tower, and followed the faint light to the study.

Two men down. As he approached Bryar, he trod on something. When he bent down to see what it was, what he found made him sick. But he had no time for that now. He quickly checked Bryar and was about to bellow for help when Leo appeared in the doorway.

"Thin bindings," Kiril barked. "For tourniquets."

The man didn't hesitate.

As soon as Leo left, Kiril nudged the larger man with his foot and nodded grimly. One less problem.

Bryar had landed on his side. Kiril flipped him onto his back, hooked hands under his shoulders, and dragged him toward the kitchen.

Another man stepped through the door and crossed the room, barely hesitating at the chaotic scene before him. Kiril slowly straightened and watched as the newcomer, dressed completely in black, bent and picked up the power cell.

Gauvain. It had to be.

"You're not keeping that." Kiril pitched his voice to be threatening.

Gauvain turned a contemptuous glance toward him. "You are mistaken. Once its shield is restored —"

Rather than argue, Kiril released Bryar and launched forward, ramming a shoulder into Gauvain's solar plexus. They crashed against the shelving. Gauvain's head ricocheted against a heavy metal instrument. The cell fell from his slack fingers. Kiril snatched it up and stowed it in a pocket.

Then his good sense fled. He yanked out his own knife from its sheath at his ankle and turned back to Gauvain, who stood leaning against the shelves, as if stunned. "A souvenir," Kiril growled. He slashed the blade along the side of Gauvain's face, deep enough to scar him from eyebrow to chin. "That's for Bryar, asshole," he muttered.

Gauvain screamed once, then sank to the floor and crouched among the jumble of objects that had fallen from the shelves.

By the time Kiril had dragged Bryar to the kitchen, several lengths of torn rags waited in a pot simmering over the cookfire. "Pressure," he commanded. "Fast." With difficulty, he hoisted Bryar's limp body onto the table.

"You apply the pressure, I will handle the binding."

The old man tended to the remains of Bryar's fingers efficiently, twisting wooden skewers inserted in the bandages to tighten the tourniquets, while Kiril held the arm upright, trusting gravity to assist in slowing the flow of blood. Their patient lay motionless on the scrubbed table.

"Name's Kiril."

"Leo. Be sure to release the bindings as soon as possible, or the remaining limbs will die."

"I know," Kiril replied. "I'm surprised you do."

Leo shrugged. "Soldier, once."

"Same here."

With the bleeding under control, Kiril stretched, hands on his lower back, and studied the other man as he sank into a chair, his eyes closed. "Now what? Can he stay here?"

"No. The Master will be furious." Leo didn't look up.

"It's a bloodbath in there. Your boss needs you. He's cut up some."

Leo's look morphed from exhausted to hostile. "By whose hand?"

Kiril chose not to answer. "He'll live. But he's going to hurt like hell, and there's a lot of blood. Where can I take Bryar?"

Their gazes met and held. "There's a place," Leo said at last. "Turn right, then right again, then a few doors further you'll come to a stable. If anyone's there, tell them I sent you." He opened a cabinet and extracted two flasks. He filled the first with water from the simmering pot, the second with a golden liquid that, from its scent, contained alcohol. "You will need these. I'll bring you some clean rags when I can. Go now. I must see to the Master."

Go. As if it were that easy. Bryar was average height but heavily built, and a dead weight. He needed... he looked around the kitchen and spotted a board covered in cloth propped against a wall.

"What's that?"

"I use it to press the Master's clothing."

A primitive ironing board. It would do.

"Help me."

"I really must—"

"Now, damn it," Kiril hissed.

Between them they moved the board to the table, rolled Bryar onto it, and lifted it down.

Grimly, Kiril remembered his own first journey in this benighted world, the lashed litter on the rough trails. This wouldn't be any better, and the risk of being seen by the police once they emerged from the alley frankly terrified him, but there was nothing else to do.

Leo stopped at the door. "The cell?"

He patted his pocket.

"Thank the Sustainer for that." The old man shuffled from the room.

The puncture wound on Kiril's arm throbbed; he ignored it. He stuffed the flagons into Bryar's pack and threw it over one shoulder, his own over the other. Then he lifted the head of the board and eased it and its load over the threshold. "Sorry, buddy," he muttered. "This is going to be bad." Very slowly, stooping to reduce the angle, unsure how much blood Bryar had lost or even if he stood a chance of surviving, he dragged his cargo through the muck of the alley.

Chapter 36

Quinn jerked upright from a restless sleep, scanning her room in the Scribes' lodge.

What had just happened? She sat still, sensing, listening.

A jolt through the energetic imprint of the Aura, but at a time when the Aura itself had vanished. Now it hummed quietly in the back of her mind. But more than that...

She frowned, stretched her senses, seeking the difference.

And found it. Indistinct – so very weak.

She estimated it was nearer dawn than midnight. Never one to bother with anything as unnecessary as a sleep shirt, she threw on a tunic for warmth and bolted for the stairs, taking the flight from her suite on the second floor to Arwen's on the third.

Arwen was up and waiting for her at the door. "Your energy's scrambled. Calm down, you'll wake the whole lodge."

Quinn stepped into the older woman's living quarters and pulled a chair out from the plain wooden table. She sagged into it. "The Aura?"

"Stable now, but that was frankly scary. Any thoughts?"

"This isn't right. I'm worried."

Arwen sat across from her. "Ground yourself, Quinn."

Palpable silence filled the room. She felt Arwen's scrutiny, but after twenty-five years or so she was used to it.

When she was sure she wasn't dreaming, she leaned forward. "Something's going on in Borgonne. You felt that massive energy release?" Arwen nodded. "I'd swear it came from Borgonne. There's more, though. We shouldn't get anything, should we? Not with the barrier of the hills."

"No, we shouldn't. But there are many imponderables. While Willow was there, things were stable for the most part, and any disruptions came from the Midland. I don't know what the energy surge meant. When I was in training, one of the Scribes died. I remember because he had been Ezra's mentor. The same kind of energy surge happened then, if my child's memory can be trusted."

Quinn's stomach sank. "Bryar?"

"No, or at least I doubt it. He isn't powerful enough. It's rare. Someone of Ezra's caliber might trigger it, for example."

Quinn frowned. "I didn't think so. We've always had this crazy connection, Willow and Bryar and me," she mused. "A vague awareness that the others are in our world."

"Are you reading Bryar?" She couldn't miss the urgency in Arwen's voice.

"I don't know. It's similar to signals I got when Ezra was experimenting with his weave. But I shouldn't, should I? I never picked up Willow."

"No. But that blast of energy... *Sustainer*, Quinn. I don't know what it means. Gauvain? Has something happened to him?" Arwen's lips compressed. "I don't like this. I'm contacting Ezra."

"Do you need me to link?"

"Yes, please. My energy is low."

Quinn reached across the table. Arwen took her hand, then extinguished the single light globe, allowing the room's quiet to merge with the darkness. They sat for a quarter of an hour, unmoving.

When Arwen released her with a gentle squeeze, she rubbed her forehead. "Ow."

"That was hard."

"But worthwhile?" As the secondary, not controlling the link but merely supplementing the energy, Quinn had not been privy to Arwen's communication.

Arwen nodded. "Ezra believes we may be picking up signals from Bryar, fueled by the energy release. The weave is predicated on life force. It can't survive death. Based on the unevenness of Bryar's connection... and that there *is* a connection... Ezra thinks he's injured."

"A serious injury would have to damage the weave," Quinn mused. "An erratic signal could stem from the weave, or from Bryar himself." She shivered.

Arwen stood. "Possibly. At this point, speculation does no good. He's alive, and we rely on his staying that way. I'll make you a tisane to calm you, because you need to sleep, even sleep late. But as soon as you're up, you have a lot to do."

"I have to find him."

"Nobody could stop you, but in this instance, you and I agree. I want an experienced Healer with you, so take Dal. Tell him to emphasize remedies for injury, shock, and fever. I'll notify the kitchen, they must be starting the morning bread by now. They'll arrange for your provisions. Plan to leave right after midday meal."

Quinn watched the other woman bustling around the compact cookfire in her suite, choosing from a select assortment of herbs, and let her mind drift to the near future. Even contemplating another venture into the hills chilled her, especially with Borgonne as the destination – assuming she could master Ezra's weave for herself and Dal, to prevent them suffering the same fate as Bryar's the previous autumn. It didn't help that she dreaded what she might find when she arrived.

Bryar. They couldn't lose him.

"Drink this, then go."

She sighed. Fatigue seeped into her pores; what sleep she'd managed hadn't been restful.

"I'll prepare a message for Gauvain. Use your discretion. The man can be a bastard, but he's not without redeeming qualities."

Quinn sipped the tisane. As she expected, the taste wasn't one to linger over. "I'd love to know how you met a Mage from the other side of the hills."

"Another story, another time."

She quirked an eyebrow, wondering about history hidden to her, but shared by Arwen, Ezra, and the sinister, man from Borgonne.

"Relax," Arwen said. "I'm not going to die with the tale untold. But not yet."

211

She gulped the rest of the tisane, that being easier than sipping the vile stuff. Already she felt it at work in her muscles.

As she left, Arwen hugged her, uncharacteristically. "We're not helpless. Although the probability of success..." She shrugged.

Two days to get to the hills, then ten to cross them. If Bryar was injured, would she and Dal make it in time? Willow said they didn't have Healers in Borgonne. And what role did Kiril play in all this?

The thought of Kiril irritated her, like an itch on her back she couldn't quite reach to scratch.

In her own room, she dropped the tunic on the floor, dropped herself onto her bed, and was asleep within minutes.

Chapter 37

Surely goodness and mercy shall follow me all the days of my life...

The blasted chant was back in his head. He'd been free of it for months, and now he couldn't shake it.

Leaning against the wall of the stable, Kiril stretched his legs out. Bryar lay on a bed of clean hay, the wounded hand propped upright. While he slept, Kiril had released the tension on the tourniquets, then reapplied them more gently. Blood oozed from the wounds. They needed a medic, desperately, to cauterize the ends of the mangled fingers. The sight was enough to make even a grown man, a hardened leader, squeamish.

Bryar hadn't wakened, although he had cried out a couple of times during the appalling trip to the stables with Kiril grasping the ironing board and dragging it over the ruts, Bryar's feet trailing in the muck of the road.

They could both do with a bath. He'd check with Leo.

At least the stable was warm. He slung his pack, now weighted with dirt to screen the cell, against the wall, then scooted down until it formed a pillow. Hard and uncomfortable, but better than nothing. Marginally.

How was he supposed to get any sleep, with an injured man in his care?

Forgotten your leadership skills already?

He set his mouth in a grim line, remembering all he had pledged years ago, that day he assumed command of the pod. A leader does whatever is necessary. That meant getting Bryar and the cell back to the Midland, and by damn, he'd do it. They hadn't exactly bonded, but he understood Bryar's single-minded determination, and increasingly appreciated the necessity of his mission.

He reached over. Bryar jerked when he touched his forehead, as if it pained him.

Too hot.

The stable door opened, then closed. "Kiril?" The whisper threaded through the air.

"Over here." His eyes now accustomed to the dark, he watched as Leo made his way past the animals to the pile of hay.

"I've brought clean rags." Weariness tinged his voice. "Also a tisane we used when on campaign for injuries, to numb the pain and help with shock. Can he drink?"

"I doubt it. He hasn't wakened."

"For the best, I suppose. I would like to know what happened to the Master's face." Leo stared at him, tight-lipped, across Bryar's inert body, a look that made Kiril wonder about the old man's military rank. He was no follower, that much was evident.

"I guess I went a little mad. I wanted to make it clear he'd better not try to take the cell again."

"Gauvain is more stunned by the turn of events than by the actual injury. I dare say the scar will draw admiration. There's a story to be spun of an intruder, a confrontation. Ladies seem to like such trivial things."

All hope of rest gone, Kiril sat upright again. "The other man?"

Leo shook his head. "Steps are being taken to hide, or at least disguise, the events of tonight. Nevertheless, the sooner we can get you out of Orlan, the better. Challenging, because a horse and cart heading for the hills is always suspicious. But they expect odd behavior from Gauvain, and so from his servant."

"We can't move him. Not until he's healing."

"For the moment, you're safe. Keep the wounds clean. Tomorrow we will reassess."

"He needs a medic," Kiril insisted.

"Inquiries will be made, very discreetly." Leo stood still, looking down at Bryar. "Now I must go. Many things require my attention this night."

"I'm grateful, but find that medic."

Leo nodded, then crossed the stable and slipped out the door. Kiril watched him leave, wondering what other skills the wily old servant had at his disposal.

Leo apparently maintained a network of allies in Orlan, people he trusted to keep secrets. Bryar had awakened from a stupor shot through with torment in the early hours of the morning, to find himself being hauled up onto the hay-strewn bed of a cart and jostled to some other part of town. Being awake was worse. He couldn't pretend the physical anguish, his helplessness, or his fragmented memory were simply a transient nightmare.

Kiril was nowhere in sight; Leo and another man did the hauling, and Leo's voice spoke quietly to the animal – a donkey? Not worth wondering about. Bryar faded in and out of consciousness during the jolting drive.

The cart stopped, and the stranger appeared above him. "Okay, let's move him in. Quiet, now."

They carried him into a place that smelled like the Healers' workroom at the Motherhouse, calming scents he associated with restored health.

When he next surfaced, he lay on a hard bed in a whitewashed room that radiated cleanliness and light. He felt as if he'd fallen from a high cliff onto rocks. Every muscle in his body protested whenever he shifted.

Had he killed Duncan? Bryar's memory of the struggle in Gauvain's study was vague, at best.

The agony in his hand chased off all other ruminations. He didn't know the severity of his injury. He remembered only the knife descending, the hilt shivering from Duncan's abdomen. The stink of blood and sweat, vomit and urine. And then the searing pain.

The stranger's strong arm supported his head. "Excellent. Try to stay awake for a few minutes, would ya? We need to get some of this into ya."

'This' proved to be an exceptionally nasty tisane. Given all the wondrous plants in the world, why couldn't anyone mask the horrid tastes?

He choked down the first sip. "You're a healer?"

"Herbalist. Come on, take more."

The repulsive drink filled his mouth. He swallowed and choked. The man backed off, but held the mug to his lips again as soon as he caught his breath. "The more you can keep down the better."

He managed another mouthful of the drink, then said, "Kiril?"

"That a person? Don't know him. Leo said he'd drop by later. Maybe he's got your friend." The man patted his shoulder to show he was satisfied with his work and eased him onto the pillows. "In a while I'll medic your hand. Stitched you up, but it'll want alcohol, regular, to fight off the infection."

"Stitched? What...?" He found he lacked the courage to finish the query.

"Never you mind. No point fretting. Get some rest." The herbalist patted his good shoulder in a way that was probably meant to be reassuring, then left him alone.

As if he had a choice, Bryar thought grimly. He was incapable of escaping the tension-laced miasma that passed for sleep. A wave of heat enveloped him, and now-familiar pain throbbed through his left hand and down his arm. He drifted in a fog, unclear where nightmare ended and waking awareness began.

Later, during a lucid interval, he dragged his attention to a larger and potentially more urgent problem dancing on the edges of his consciousness. The Aura. He sensed it, here in Orlan. Attenuated, as if it flowed through gauze, but there. Ezra had worried about his weave's stability. Were it to dissolve completely, the Aura would fell him, as it had the first time he crossed the hills. If it was degrading, he had to get out of Borgonne before it destroyed his mind.

Wouldn't it be better for the cell to be unshielded, to neutralize Gauvain's powers?

But that would destroy the Weavers' ability to work with templates.

Where was the cell, anyway?

The fight. Had he really...?

He drifted off, into the haze of suffering and memory.

Kiril paced the small room. At dusk he'd arrived with Leo, who studied Bryar, grunted, and disappeared without comment. As night fell, the herbalist's wife, a round, older woman with her hair in a kerchief, had lit candles and drawn curtains – made of the same coarse linen as their clothes and everything else on this godforsaken planet. At least the itching in his wound from the beast in the hills was better. He'd shown it to the herbalist, who'd dosed him with yet another poultice and a foul oral preparation.

Bryar stirred and opened his eyes. His head moved slightly as he took in the room, the candles, the absence of other people. "Where are we?"

Good. His voice was clear, if not strong. "Can you manage soup?"

"After you tell me what happened."

He stopped his pacing to put an assessing hand on Bryar's forehead. Clammy. "Fever's broken. You're one tough bastard."

"Damn it, Kiril. Tell me."

A coiled spring. The man's muscles bunched and tightened, as if he contemplated hopping up and shaking the truth out of him.

He perched on the edge of the bed. "We're hiding out at a herbalist friend of Leo's. Name and location are deep dark secrets. You remember the fight?"

"Parts of it."

"I'll bring soup." With that non sequitur, Kiril headed for the door.

Bryar's voice followed him, demanding the facts. "I want to know —"

"Later."

Kiril let the leather flap fall closed behind him and strode down a corridor. In the kitchen, the herbalist's wife labored over a cookfire, stirring something that released enticing, meat-rich aromas.

"So? How's he doin'?"

"Says he can eat some soup."

"Broth. Hang on." She ladled clear liquid into a mug. "Not too much at once. Husband'll be along to clean the wounds subsequently."

His mouth quirked. He liked this place and these people with their casual, determined efficiency. "I'd rather not be around for that."

"You'll be around. Husband may need you to hold 'im down. Get you gone, an' be sure to come back later for your own portion."

"I'll do that. It smells wonderful."

The compliment brought a tight smile to the woman's face. Whatever he thought of them, they clearly didn't trust him, not even enough to reveal their names. She turned and resumed her work at the cookfire.

Well, he got it. While he had no idea how Leo and his cronies had dispatched Duncan's body, anyone involved could find himself in a whole shitload of trouble if the truth of the previous night became known.

Back in Bryar's room, he eased his erstwhile patient into a propped position. Bryar allowed Kiril to feed him, but waved him away after five spoonsful. "Can't. Queasy."

"Not surprising. Lack of food, shock. Plus, it seems you put up one hell of a fight."

"I have a right to know what happened, Kiril."

He let his posture relax, bowl and spoon occupying his hands, conveying – he hoped – the impression that what he had to say was of no particular consequence. "The fat man tried to take the cell. You fought and stopped him."

Bryar waved his good hand impatiently. "I remember that. And?"

"And he's dead."

Bryar's eyes went blank. "I never... To kill another person... No. It can't be true." Abruptly he slid down on the bed and rolled away, his head abutting the frame supporting his hand.

Any show of emotion ran counter to Kiril's years of military training, but he got that a musician who had killed a man might seek some kind of release, might even want to cry. But he needed Bryar to heal, not wallow in guilt.

"You didn't kill him. I did."

The moment the words fell from his mouth, Kiril wondered what the hell he'd just done. After witnessing the flogging in the square, he had a decent idea how Borgonne treated its criminals. If they failed to make good their escape...

Shit.

"I don't believe you," Bryar growled into the bedclothes.

"Listen. After you collapsed – yeah, the knife was in him. But when I got it out, he came for me. You're clear, man. You didn't kill him."

"You're lying. I remember enough of it," Bryar muttered.

"Defending yourself. Forget it. Getting you well's the first priority. One way or another, we need to disappear. Every minute we're here puts people at risk."

Bryar was silent for long minutes. Finally, he turned onto his back again, his face devoid of expression. "I don't understand why you would lie," he said formally. "But thank you."

Kiril shrugged. "More broth?"

"In a while. Where's the cell? When can we leave?"

"The cell's safe. We leave when you're able to climb up into the hills. No point even trying before that."

"Then help me." Bryar jerked forward, pulling himself upright and disturbing the arm support. "We'll see how strong I am."

"No such thing." The voice came from the door. The stranger entered carrying a tray with bottles, vials, and rags. "Over-exertion would weaken you, not build your strength. You'll need all the reserves you have left to heal this mess."

The man was hefty and determined. With no trouble at all he settled Bryar back on the pillows and claimed the bandaged hand.

Kiril saw Bryar's look of alarm, quickly suppressed. Treating the wound was going to hurt like stink. In the hills, Bryar had fended off infection from the beast's attack with alcohol and herbs. This was worse.

"Tell me about my hand," he said between clenched teeth as the stranger unwrapped the bandages.

Kiril sat on the other side of the narrow bed, clasped Bryar's shoulder, and managed to meet his gaze. There was no way to sweet-coat what had to be the worst possible news for a musician. "It's not pretty. The knife took two of your fingers."

Bryar's head jerked toward the remains of his hand just as the herbalist applied an alcohol-soaked rag to the sewn-up stumps of the fingers. His face took on a greenish tinge in the moment before he fainted.

Kiril glanced up at the herbalist. "For the best," the other man said.

He watched the application of alcohol, then herbs in a poultice, asking questions about the remedies and taking mental notes against the day he might have to do the same.

Bryar didn't move.

Chapter 38

Bryar had been imprisoned – or that's how it felt, anyway – in the featureless room for three days, rebuilding his strength, enduring the ongoing treatment of his wounded hand. With nothing to do but pace and watch the sun's patterns move across the bed, he had more time to think than he wanted.

He had killed Duncan. Kiril lied. Why the cocksure, obnoxious man would lie about something like that, he couldn't work out. He had to learn to live with himself. All the songs he sang, the stories he told of great quests, conquering heroes... many of them involved bloodshed, but none of them spoke of the mental anguish afterwards, the constant awareness of what you had done, justified or not. The taking of life.

Guilt haunted him. Kiril, and the herbalist in a roundabout way, assured him that Duncan's death should be considered a boon, not a tragedy. The blow had been struck in self-defense. The evidence made it clear that he bore no blame.

Yeah. Right. The burden of his actions weighed on him to the extent that he almost welcomed the twice-daily agony when the herbalist dowsed his fingers in alcohol before rebinding them.

His hand. He'd never play the chitarre again, or the flute. The singular grace of music was no longer his. He would never again release harmonies over the land like a benediction, reflecting the beauty of the seasons, the hills and fields...

He'd made it onto his feet on the second day, stiff from the fight and subsequent confinement, desperate for mild exercise to loosen his overtaxed muscles. Kiril turned up regularly, never saying where he'd been. He made no secret of his concern about their continuing presence in Orlan, and proved to be a master nag, keeping Bryar going as he grew stronger. Reiterating his spurious claim that the murder lay on his conscience, not Bryar's.

On the third afternoon, as the sun dipped behind other buildings, throwing the room into shadow, Kiril told him to prepare to travel to the hills that night. "Things are getting hot, and we can't afford to wait any longer. Leo's arranged transport to the start of the trail. From there, we're on our own."

Bryar's response required no thought at all. "Good. I'm ready to go." Fleeing the white room, the memories... even the thought of scrambling up the steep access path one-handed wasn't a deterrent.

"We'll get out of range of their cops, then take it easy."

'Cops' meant policemen, a word from Terra... and from Orlan. But his other concern outweighed any musings about shared vocabulary, and even the risk of arrest. "I'm strong enough. The Aura, though... the shield's weakening more quickly. My head's stuffed like a drinking skin overfilled with water. Joss said that's how it felt to him on this side of the hills."

Kiril frowned. "If it's going to harm you, we can always unmask the cell."

Bryar shook his head. "Once we get into the hills, I'll be fine. If it weren't for the effect on the Weavers, I'd have asked you to unmask it right from the beginning, to hamper Gauvain." Asking Kiril for anything chafed, more so the realization that he controlled the power cell once again. His theft of the cell had started the chain of events that led to their current precarious situation.

No help for it – yet. Bryar's despairing laugh came out more of a snort. "I just hope the protection weave's weak enough for me to light fires. This hand's useless."

"It won't stay that way." Kiril swung from the bed and made for the heavy leather curtain covering the door. "See you later. Lots of things to attend to." The curtain swayed, and he was gone.

Bryar continued pacing, reflecting. The swelling Auric energy in his head and the impending trip home told him he still wanted to live. Without the Aura, compounded by Tai's loss... he really hadn't been sure.

Kiril hoped to god they'd meet up with someone from the Motherhouse in the hills, because he wasn't confident he'd be able to get Bryar back home on his own. His companion teetered on the edge of depression, putting their whole expedition at risk, although Kiril grudgingly admitted Bryar's survival skills ranked on a par with his own. Even though he understood the root of the man's despair, it drove him to distraction. Other people made music. It wasn't catastrophic, like the world would end because of two maimed fingers.

Basic conflict between soldier and musician, he supposed. A musician couldn't be expected to cultivate the kind of mental toughness that led a man to kill when he needed to.

Then again, how would he react in the same circumstances? That bar fight – another knife, an accident. He'd been little more than a kid, hadn't even known the guy. Springing as he did from the upper management caste, the whole episode had been buried and forgotten. It bugged him that it still disturbed his dreams.

Shortly after dark they'd moved to a stable on the western fringe of Orlan, taking a circuitous route through quiet residential neighborhoods, Bryar's hand hidden under his sheepskin vest. They hadn't encountered any police on the way, only distrusting glares from the occasional citizen. But then everyone frowned in this place.

Leo arrived, short-tempered, in the depths of the night. He hitched the lone horse – a beast that for some reason fascinated Bryar – to a ramshackle cart, holding the nag's head while they climbed into the hay-filled bed. Kiril felt Bryar's involuntary recoil when his left hand accidentally brushed against the side wall of the cart. "Suck it up," he muttered.

"Go to hell," Bryar hissed. Good. If they annoyed each other, they were more likely to keep going. More likely to get home safely.

Assuming they made it to the hills. Leo's state of high alert did nothing for his own nerves. Kiril touched the knife strapped to his ankle, one he'd stolen months ago from some little hamlet west of Stanstead.

"Did I tell you?" he said conversationally as he tucked a blanket, then hay, around Bryar's legs. "Seems they found a body in a bad part of town, prostitutes and drug dealers. Pretty sure it was that friend of Gauvain's. Douglas?"

"Duncan." A quick gesture with Bryar's good hand told Kiril he'd caught on to the casual deception.

"Yeah, that's right. They're assuming a sale of a whore gone wrong. Damned aristocrats."

Bryar snorted.

Kiril swung aboard and nudged Leo, who set the horse moving at a slow clop.

Once they passed the last of the town's outlying buildings, Leo stood to look up and down the road. Obviously relieved to find no one following them, he drove the horse at a faster pace, jostling the men in the back enough to preclude conversation beyond the occasional curse. The rhythm of the animal's feet and the faint rustle of a mild breeze crossing the fields filled the otherwise still night.

Leo got them to the trailhead at daybreak. Unlike the approach from the Midland, on this side the hills rose directly from the plain. The access trail snaked up from a weed-choked clearing. Steep, rocky, and largely barren, supporting only occasional stunted conifers, the abrupt ascent marked a forbidding contrast to the dry brown earth of the plains, punctuated only by patches of green where weeds dared establish themselves.

Kiril jumped to the ground and stretched before lifting down their packs. Bryar clambered down without assistance and wandered around the clearing, rolling his shoulders. Leo secured the horse to a leafless bush, then circled the cart and extended a hand; Kiril shook it.

"I'll stay here awhile before returning," Leo said. "There are always plants to be harvested if you know where to look. Some are at their best when very young, and they provide an effective decoy. Everybody knows I collect herbs." He turned to the looming hills. "It looks to be a hard climb. Be patient, and be careful with the bandage. Don't overtax yourselves."

"I'm aware of all that." Kiril shoved aside a pang of annoyance when he realized the old man was fussing because it mattered.

A new feeling, that. To be the object of caring.

Bryar walked over to Leo. "Goodbye, and thank you. We wouldn't have succeeded without your help."

"The world will be better," Leo said. "Gauvain... he is not evil, but his lust for power overrides his judgment. Having met the two of you and Willow, I trust your Motherhouse to deal with the cell appropriately. Travel safely. And should you see Miss Willow, please give her my best wishes."

"Sure." Kiril suppressed a grimace at the assumption he had any association with the Motherhouse. He helped Bryar with his pack and donned his own. "Take care of yourself," he said with a final nod to Leo, and turned toward the trail.

"You have the cell?" Bryar asked from behind him.

Kiril didn't answer, but shot a contemptuous glance over his shoulder.

"I'd prefer to carry it myself."

"You're not strong enough."

"When I am."

Bryar managed the climb better than Kiril had expected, but by the end of an hour of relatively slow progress they were forced to rest. Looking out over the plain, he saw Leo's cart making its way toward the city. The tower loomed in the distance, a black menace against the brown dirt and red brick of Orlan.

Bryar settled on the ground behind a boulder, out of sight of Borgonne. "I'm grateful for your support," he said. "But so help me, if you try to abscond with that thing again, I'll hunt you down and kill you."

"You couldn't kill a fly." Kiril lounged against the boulder, enjoying the break.

"When you've done it once, what's one more? When your land and your way of life are at stake?" Bryar's voice was hard as nails. He meant every word.

"How many times do I have to say it? You didn't kill him."

"Much though I appreciate your trying to shield the truth from the poor, weak minstrel, it won't work."

He heard the underlying bitterness in Bryar's voice, but chose to ignore it. "Believe what you want."

"That isn't what I want." Bryar turned away and took a long pull from his flask. Then he sat up straighter, his head cocked.

"Hear something?"

He smiled, grimly, for the first time since they entered the hills from the Midland two weeks ago. "Sense, not hear. Quinn. She's coming."

Chapter 39

Kiril had watched Bryar's strength improve hourly during the three days of hiking through the hills, making him aware of the rock-hard muscles in the man's legs and back. The persistent frown of pain had vanished, replaced by a face carved in granite. Bryar neither smiled nor scowled. He moved forward like a machine, with no show of emotion.

Three days on the trail had done nothing for their overall cleanliness. They were scruffy as hell. Although they took advantage of streams to wash, their clothes were becoming rank.

At the herbalist's, they'd cleaned Bryar up, but after all the trauma his skin was too sensitive for shaving. While a beard didn't bother Kiril, Bryar sported only a few scraggly hairs where the red mark covered half his face, creating an odd, incomplete appearance.

This morning gave every indication of being the same as the previous ones. They had camped well up a slope, where vegetation was sparse and the morning mist thinner. From their altitude Kiril could track the trail as it meandered around the hills before plunging into a valley to cross a swollen river.

His companion was the same also – taciturn to the point of rudeness. By now Kiril accepted the silence between them. As long as they got back to the Midland safely, he wasn't complaining.

Over a brief stop for food at midday, Kiril had no sooner taken a bite of dried fruit than Bryar spoke, his first voluntary words since they climbed out of Borgonne. "I'll take the cell now."

He replied around the chewy dried abricoe clinging to his teeth. "There's no need." Possession of the cell meant security. It assured he wouldn't be abandoned in the hills, where he'd be helpless without an Auric connection.

Bryar reached over and snagged his pack.

"Just a damn minute —"

Bryar shook off his hand as if he were a fly. "Get this straight. I'm taking the cell. We'll swap packs so we don't risk breaking the shield."

Kiril watched his few possessions land in the scrub at their feet. Then Bryar upended his own pack. "Here." He tossed over the empty bag and crammed his belongings in with the dirt-packed cell.

Kiril hadn't expected it. But the look on Bryar's face reminded him that as long as they traversed the hills, he didn't have a single card to play. He bit back his retort, repacked his possessions, and finished the fruit.

That evening, he studied his traveling companion across the fire. All along, despite the battles first with the beast, then with Duncan, he had viewed Bryar as no more than a pretty boy who spun tall tales. He'd missed the reality.

The man stirring the thin soup was no pretty boy.

In an effort to establish fellow feeling and ward off the unease that crept up his spine as darkness encroached, he tossed out, "You'll be a hero when we get back."

"Pass over your bowl. This is as edible as it'll ever be." Bryar reached across with his uninjured hand.

Kiril handed him the dish and accepted a serving of the soup. Bryar had trapped some kind of ground animal that afternoon, killed, skinned, and cleaned it, mostly one-handed. Kiril hadn't caught anything, to his embarrassment. In fact, he had twisted an ankle in the attempt.

"Must be good, knowing your people are going to worship at your feet," he prompted.

Bryar ignored him, spooning mouthfuls of soup and staring at the fire.

Tomorrow they faced a steep descent into the valley that now, in the early evening chill, sent those creepy tendrils of mist up the trail. Kiril could hear but not see the river below them, with a waterfall off to the right, and was glad they hadn't attempted to go any further. The footing promised to be treacherous, and the mists imparted an eerie, other-worldly atmosphere.

In fact, the hills gave him the creeps, as they had since his first abortive attempts to cross them when no matter what he did, he found himself within a few kilometers of where he started. Sure, the scenery was magnificent but... maybe it was just the absence of people. He'd never spent so long without teammates, bunkmates, fellow crew members around him. Even in the Midland, hamlets rarely were more than a day apart, and nothing about the in-between stretches had given him the willies like the hills did.

If he were fanciful, he'd say a spell gripped the land. Fanciful or not, he wouldn't want to be lost in these mountains.

He dunked a piece of waybread into the bland soup. After forcing it down, he tried again. "You fought well. You deserve the accolades."

"Yeah." Bryar set his bowl aside and stood. As he walked around, stowing his utensils and their meager food supply, Kiril once again sensed the power behind the supposedly mild façade.

Without explanation, Bryar stood a little straighter, holding himself stock-still, then turned away and moved at a near run down the trail.

"Where're you going?" Kiril pulled the packs closer, guarding the cell.

"To meet them." Bryar disappeared around a turn.

"Who?" he shouted, but received no answer. He waited.

Not five minutes later a call split the quiet. *"Bryar!"*

Kiril sprang to his feet and limped around the bend in time to see the magnificent dark-skinned woman, Quinn, launch herself at Bryar and hang on for dear life, her legs wrapped around him, hands clinging like talons to his back and neck. Her feet hit the ground and... Kiril's mouth dried up. She kissed Bryar in a way Kiril hadn't been kissed... ever. He couldn't force his eyes away.

An older man came up the path in Quinn's wake. He waved and walked over to where Kiril stood rooted. "Might as well move on. Those two will be checking each other out for a while yet. Remember me? Dal."

"Sure. Good to see you again." Kiril turned and strode back to their camp, the Healer following. For all the awareness Bryar and Quinn showed, locked together like that, he and Dal could blast off and fly unnoticed to the moon. If this planet had a moon.

"You've hurt your leg."

"It's nothing." He'd done his best to hide the limp. He didn't need mollycoddling.

"It's never nothing. Have you eaten? We caught a couple of rabbits earlier."

Kiril gestured at the pot they'd used to cook the soup, thinking as he did that what they called rabbits bore only a passing resemblance to the pictures he'd seen on Terra. "Go for it. We just finished."

"But you're still hungry, so this will be welcome. I have a turnip and savory seasoning."

Dal moved with efficiency, so Kiril sat back and rested the aching ankle. Dal was the oldest of their merged party by a good ten years, yet he showed no fatigue. He simply got on with the task at hand.

"You crossed the river in these mists? Strikes me as dangerous."

"Not really. The stepping stones are a little slippery, but flat enough to keep your balance. Quinn knew we were close," he added as an afterthought. After tossing herbs and the chopped turnip into the cook pot, Dal sat and started skinning the animals. "Probably we should dry and smoke one of these. No telling what we'll find tomorrow. How's the ankle?"

"How'd you know it's my ankle?"

"I've been doing this for a long time. After a Healing, I expect you'll be able to walk comfortably. You two must be eager to get home."

Home? "It's not my home."

Dal glanced up and seemed to look right through him. "If you say so."

Bryar and Quinn joined them. Quinn shivered and reached toward the fire. "I'm soaked through, thanks to the mist. *Diou*, but I hate being out here."

My sentiments exactly. It didn't help Kiril's peace of mind that the blaze, seemingly of its own accord, grew stronger. He'd never adjust to the way the Weavers just *did* things like that.

Dal stood, poured water over his hands, then rubbed a plant stalk from his pack between them. "Okay, Bryar, let's see."

"I'd rather not." Whatever warmth he felt for Quinn, the affection didn't extend to the Healer.

"But you will. I'm not messing around here."

Bryar sighed and squatted in front of Dal, who carefully unwrapped the outer bandage. The two inner bandages were clean, Kiril noted, so there had been no seepage since Bryar last dunked the remains of his fingers in an alcohol solution, grimly suppressing any reaction to what had to be an agonizing ritual. Dal untied the bandages and studied Bryar's hand.

"Pain?"

Bryar shrugged.

Quinn nudged him. "We didn't come out here so you could be stubborn. You know Dal's going to Heal you. Why not let him do it?"

Grudgingly, he said, "It hurts."

"Movement?"

Bryar flexed the stumps and winced. He'd lost two joints of his middle finger, one of his index finger, and had a nasty gash where the blade failed to sever his ring finger. Kiril hadn't seen the wounds in days, but he saw no sign of infection or putrefaction.

"I approve your use of alcohol, but now we can go to a less harsh remedy. As soon as I've eaten, I'll do a Healing. Don't shut me out on this," Dal cautioned, his voice level. "You think you don't care how they heal, but you do. Or you will, eventually."

"Bull-merde," Bryar snapped. He rose in one smooth movement. "This hand's useless to me. It doesn't make any difference what happens to it." Holding in check a tension so fierce even Kiril could sense it from his place across the fire, he turned and started toward the trail.

"Bryar."

He froze.

"You will join us, you will eat more soup and help me stretch the meat for drying, and we will do a Healing. I will compel you if I have to. Clear?"

"Damn you," Bryar hissed under his breath.

"Do I make myself clear?" Dal's voice brooked no dissent.

"Yeah." Tight-lipped, Bryar returned to the fire and sat next to Quinn. He allowed her to re-wrap the fingers while Dal made a production of merging and sorting their supplies, turning everyone's attention to the food.

Shifting the focus away from the music man, Kiril thought. Giving him a chance to regain his equanimity after Dal's tongue-lashing.

Following their meal, which passed largely in silence, Dal undertook the Healing for his ankle. He wrapped it in an ice-cold poultice, not explaining how he created the chill temperature, then sat dead still in the weird way of Healers, his hands cradling the injured joint. Perhaps ten minutes later he nodded and muttered, "Good." Standing and stretching, he added, "Keep the poultice on overnight. You should be well in the morning."

It felt fine already. Kiril remembered his broken leg, which had healed in record time. He might even be forced to start believing in their magic.

Dal gathered a ground blanket and a handful of vials and pouches of herbs, then addressed Bryar. "There's a level area a little way along the trail. Let's go."

Bryar sat by the fire, cross-legged and hunched over, Quinn's hand on his back. He made no move to rise.

"Now."

"Go on," Quinn murmured. "Please."

Without a word, Bryar rose and followed Dal. From Kiril's perspective on the ground, it looked as if they vanished in the mists. He shuddered.

Quinn sighed. "If Dal's moved them away, it probably means it will be long and ugly. I wish I could help."

"You're no Healer."

"That's for sure. Tell me about the fight." She didn't ask, she commanded.

"Talk to your boyfriend."

"No doubt you failed to notice he's not very communicative. It's important I get unbiased information, Kiril."

Game on. It hadn't taken long for the energy between them to crackle with hostility. Sparring with Quinn was one of his rare pleasures in this benighted place. "Then perhaps you should try asking nicely, instead of acting like a commanding general dealing with a peon. You need an attitude adjustment, lady."

Night had fallen during his Healing; she'd become little more than a shifting pattern of light and dark as the fire sputtered, but he heard her intake of breath.

"I would be grateful," she said, her voice tight and sarcasm dripping from every word, "if you would grant me the wondrous boon of explaining how my friend was injured."

"Sure. Happy to." Satisfied that he'd won a round, he leaned back on an elbow and gave her the short version, using the variation in which he, not Bryar, killed Duncan.

She didn't buy it. "Bryar says otherwise."

"He passed out. He doesn't have a clue what happened."

"Why are you making this up? He'd be better off facing facts, not hiding behind your skirts."

Skirts? He mentally scored her a point. "That's how it played. Believe it or not, I don't really care." He nonchalantly stood and experimented with the sore ankle. Not a twinge.

Quinn made a rude sound, then spread out her bedroll. She unearthed Bryar's and laid it alongside hers. "I suppose I should thank you. Bryar says you got him out of that place."

"I wanted to escape myself. It was a package deal."

"Now that, I believe. Look out for number one, right?"

"Sometimes that includes being there for others. Get over yourself. I don't need a steady diet of your insults for the next seven days."

"You are such a jerk."

In answer to that he pulled out his own bedroll, spread it on the other side of the fire, and turned his back on her. For a few minutes she rustled around, preparing the camp for the night, then sounds faded into nothingness. He couldn't remember the last time sleep came so easily.

Chapter 40

Quinn had slept against Bryar's back, her arm thrown over him, but woke to find the bedroll beside her empty. Through the overnight mists engulfing their campsite, she could make out Dal crouched by the fire, poking it to life. Kiril appeared to be asleep. She struggled out of her bedroll.

"Where is he?" she whispered.

"Gone toward the river."

"Thanks."

Moisture from the heavy mist glazed the path; her feet slipped occasionally as she crept along the trail. She almost missed seeing Bryar. He stood off the trail on a small bluff looking out over the waterfall, which cascaded into a pool upstream of the ford. He'd drawn his right arm back as if to throw a stick.

Not a stick.

Quinn flung herself at him, grabbing his arm before he could launch the little wooden flute into the water. As he stumbled back, his hand went slack. The flute tumbled onto the moss at their feet.

He shook himself free. "By all that's sane, Quinn. You nearly pushed me over."

At least that hadn't been his intention.

"Sorry." She nudged the flute with her foot. "You've carried this for twenty years. Everywhere."

"Yeah. Easy to pack."

Bryar had other flutes, but something about this little guy had always appealed to him. Quinn didn't know if it held a story, but she couldn't let him hurl it into the waterfall.

Making a bid for normalcy, she changed the subject. "How's Ezra's weave holding up?"

His gaze locked on the pool below them, he said, "It doesn't make any difference now. We're out of Borgonne."

"It matters to me. I'm a Scribe, remember. How it works and how long—"

Bryar wheeled on her, his face set in rigid lines of hostility. "I'm well aware of what you are. For how many years? Twenty-five? And in all that time, you haven't learned a damn thing about leaving people alone. Always digging, poking—"

Her temper surged to meet his. "Just stop right there. You know me better than that."

"Do I? Then how is it you don't know me at all?"

Quinn growled low in her throat, too frustrated to speak. She watched Bryar walk away from her, but he didn't leave. After a moment he turned back, rigid with his struggle for control. "In the hills, it's hard to tell. It was breaking up before we left Borgonne."

He'd answered her question. She forced the temper from her voice and replied in kind. "That explains why you kept fading in and out. Arwen and I weren't sure if the weave was disintegrating or if you'd been wounded."

"Looks like both, doesn't it?" He turned away.

Quinn closed the gap between them and touched his arm. "But which came first? And were the two related? Did the injury affect the weave? Talk to me, Bryar."

The instant the words were out she knew she should have kept quiet. His expression, when he faced her, chilled her to the bone. He was... empty. Even the restoration of the Aura wasn't sufficient to counter his losses, starting with Tai, and now his music.

Frustrated, she dug her fingers into her tight curls, gripping hard. "I love you."

"I love you." But you'd never prove it by the flatness of his voice.

"None of us can predict the future. Are you so sure you won't play again?"

"Yeah, I am."

"I don't agree. Maybe... well, could they build artificial fingers to fit over the...?" She gestured at his hand.

She got the full force of his bitterness. "Stumps, Quinn? Is that the word you can't say? Did you see them last night? *Stumps.*" He waved the bandaged fingers in her face. "This hand won't make music again. The flute's useless."

In an effort to provide a more hopeful picture, she changed tack. "How about giving it away, like the Bard who came to your village when you were a kid? Pass the music on to—"

"*Stop!* Just stop."

Bryar grasped her arm with his wounded hand. For an instant, she actually thought he might strike her. Instead he pulled her down on the moss and curled up against her, the two of them nested together as they'd been so many times before in happier circumstances. His powerful body shook under the weight of his broken heart.

Quinn shut up, held him, and let him work things out his own way. But later, when they returned to the camp, she surreptitiously slipped the flute into a pocket, thinking that another might convince him where she had failed to.

When they came around the bend in the trail, Dal and Kiril were chatting comfortably and munching on waybread over the cold remains of the fire, evincing no urgency to travel. That surprised her; she had assumed Kiril's modus operandi involved getting a kick out of being a constant irritant.

"Ready? Let's go," Dal said. He stood and slung his pack onto his shoulders. Kiril followed suit, rather more leisurely, as if this were just a pleasant walk in the forest.

Quinn tore off a chunk of the waybread and handed it to Bryar before shoving the rest into Dal's pack.

Bread in hand, Bryar turned and left the campsite. "Get a move on," he shouted from farther down the trail.

Quinn fell into line, aware of Kiril following, his eyes on her. Of the many disconcerting things about him, his unabashed study of her unnerved her the most.

Chapter 41

Quinn had never been so glad to see home. She'd left almost two nine-days ago, and had just endured seven of them dealing with Bryar's depression and Kiril's smart-aleck comments, all while sharing the responsibility for the power cell's delivery to the Motherhouse.

Afternoon sun poured down on them, spring already hinting at summer. Sunlight filled the bowl of the valley and the kids must be on a holiday, based on the numbers of them swarming around. Quinn welcomed the warmth and resented it in equal measure, as it made her itch with the grime of travel.

They turned the corner onto the green. Arwen emerged from the Centra, heading their way. Quinn watched Bryar scan the chaotic scene, his bearing rigid, probably looking for Mari. Failing to spot her, he faced Arwen and snarled, "Not now."

"Where is it?" Arwen cut to the essentials.

"In the pack. Once I unload my stuff, it's all yours."

"I'll be waiting."

"Send someone. I'm not your messenger boy."

Arwen's gaze sought Quinn's. She nodded; Bryar's mood was nothing new. He'd been silent or had spoken in curt sentences since the morning by the waterfall.

At the snap of Arwen's fingers, one of the apprentices appeared. "Phron, accompany Bryar to his quarters. When he's removed his belongings, bring his pack to me. No dallying, no side trips. Understand?"

"Yes, ma'am." The boy couldn't be more than thirteen, the youngest that kids were accepted at the Motherhouse, but Arwen already had him trained.

Bryar glowered at them both, then stomped off to the Bards' lodge, Phron at his heels.

"I must hear about this," Arwen murmured. "Do you want a break first?"

"A bath, some decent food, a nap?" Quinn suspected her chance of any of these was slim.

Dal had crossed the green in the direction of the Healers' lodge. Kiril gave them a nod as he took off in the same direction, toward the guest lodge. "Getting a bit ripe there, Featherstone," he said in passing. From somewhere he'd unearthed her seldom-used last name.

"You're filthy," she called to his back. "Go to the village. Get a shave."

Kiril turned, walking backwards, and shot her a wicked grin. "Some women like a man with a beard," he responded.

A couple of the older apprentices tittered. When she glared, they ran away, giggling. She felt heat on her face and hoped her skin was dark enough to hide it.

"Come with me," Arwen commanded. "We'll have food sent to my workroom."

And so the heroes return, she thought grimly. No fanfare, no rest, not even a bath, and the cell entrusted to a child. Better, she supposed, than having them fawn over Bryar. He couldn't have borne it.

At least she had a chance to update Arwen, in private.

But when she entered the workroom from the stone corridor, a younger woman sat off to the side, uncharacteristically still.

Tai.

Quinn swallowed her surprise. "You've surfaced."

Tai shrugged. "It was time."

"We could have used you here sooner."

"I wasn't around."

So like Tai, always a law unto herself.

Quinn narrated the story as she understood it, pieced together from what Bryar or Kiril had let slip, from their arrival and Bryar's meeting with Leo to the knife fight, which cost Bryar two fingers, and then their eventual escape from Borgonne. "So far he isn't forthcoming. I'm not sure who killed

Duncan, but my money's on Bryar – although why Kiril would lie about it is beyond me."

"Did you have any trouble with Kiril?" Arwen asked.

"No, surprisingly. Bryar had the cell, and no one contested that. Either he's playing some deep game or he's decided it isn't worth it."

"You don't trust him," Arwen said.

"Some things never change." Quinn snorted, then offered Tai a half smile. "Here. Take this." She rummaged in her pack and pulled out the flute.

Tai ran her hands over the diminutive instrument. "Why would he fight Dal about Healing, Quinn? Why is he inflicting this torture on himself?"

"I've been mulling that over." Obsessing, more like. "If I had to guess, I'd say guilt. He believes he killed Duncan. Whatever the justification, that's got to be tough to live with. When you add in losing his music, he's taken one blow too many."

"That's nonsense. Bryar hasn't lost his music. He's just... sidestepped it for the moment. We'll restore it."

Quinn smiled at Tai's confidence and started to respond, but broke off at a double knock at the door. Phron stepped in. "Here it is, ma'am." Another knock sounded as he dropped the travel-grimed pack on the floor next to Arwen's table, and a woman from the kitchens arrived with caff and an assortment of snacks. She and Phron left together, the woman squeezing the boy's shoulder encouragingly. Even for an innocuous errand, being ordered to Arwen's presence was certain to start butterflies fluttering in the stomach of the hardiest apprentice. Quinn grinned at the woman's show of solidarity.

Tai stood, clutching the flute. "Mental-emotional Healing's tougher than physical, but between Dal and me, he'll get help. I'll hang on to this awhile, until the time's right."

Quinn watched the younger woman cross to the door. She had long been unclear what was going on between Bryar and Tai, and concluded it was a close, if unexpected, friendship. She knew Bryar inside out, but Tai had always been a mystery, forming occasional alliances but seldom friendships. Her disappearance had hit Bryar hard, but the idea of either of them committing to another... well, none of her business.

"Tai?"

"Hmm?" Tai turned to Quinn, her eyebrows raised.

"Bryar's vulnerable right now. Be kind."

Tai's pixie face twisted in a wry grin. "We come from different perspectives. For you, he's still the kid you grew up with. Don't worry." She nodded to the older women and slipped out the door, closing it quietly.

A tiny smile danced around Arwen's mouth. "If anyone can put that man together again, she can."

"What did she mean?" Quinn was honestly bewildered. She harbored no illusions where Bryar was concerned.

Arwen's voice was kind. "What she means is that to you, Bryar's a friend. To Tai, he's a mate."

"They may be lovers, but—" The words sank into her like weights anchoring her to a shifting surface. "Mates?" she echoed.

"Exactly. I could throttle Tai for disappearing, although I understand why she did it. She'll be the platform on which he reconstructs himself, and he won't even know she did it. He needs her, Quinn, as difficult as that might be for you to accept."

Mates. A fissure in their tight group. She made herself grin. "Do you suppose we're finally growing up?"

Arwen laughed out loud, something that never happened. "If so, it'll be interesting to see what form growth takes in you, my dear."

The smile faded. "I just want to get further into the Aura. To learn the truth of our origins. You know that."

"I know you believe what you say. Your friends had all they wanted, too, until... well. Time will reveal."

"Don't prognosticate." The hint of a deeper bond than simple attraction between Willow and Joss didn't sit well, either. Quinn poured caff and helped herself to a pastry – a seed pastry, reminding her again of Willow, off in Hallan. With Joss.

She suddenly felt very alone.

"Tell me your story," Arwen said, settling behind her work table. "Then we dispose of that."

Both women looked to Bryar's pack, sitting slumped and innocuous on the floor.

Bryar wasted no time in his lodging. After cleaning out his pack and handing it over to the young apprentice, he hastily stowed his belongings, plucked a clean tunic from the wardrobe, and headed for the baths on the ground floor. No music came from the common room, and the upstairs suites were deserted. If all the Bards were off traveling, Arwen and the council must be confident the crisis was over. Life was returning to normal.

For most of them.

Residents of the local village handled many of the tasks necessary to run the Motherhouse, including laundry and housekeeping. They had been alerted; he found a tub of warm water waiting. Bryar kicked his dirty clothes into a pile and immersed himself, ignoring the soap for the moment, enjoying the lassitude that overcame his muscles now that he didn't need to try anymore. He wished it were hot enough to scald away the last four nine-days. With the injured hand resting on the side of the tub, he leaned back and closed his eyes, letting the peace of his native element permeate his being.

Every one of Ezra's predictions had played out. From shielding his Entrée, to the intensive physical training, to the cost. Innocently, he'd believed he'd already paid the price for this mission when Tai disappeared, but no. An ache, such as happened when he played the chitarre too long, shot from the nonexistent tip of his index finger up his arm. He clenched his teeth, not because it hurt but because he couldn't massage it away.

He opened his eyes and studied the light bandages covering the remains of his fingers. Dal would remove the stitching soon, perhaps tonight. Then he faced a lifetime learning how to live without music. He pinched his eyes closed again, shutting out the new reality for a few precious minutes.

The door creaked.

"Occupied," he called out. The Bards' lodge held only two bathing rooms, so interruptions weren't unusual.

The door latched closed with a gentle click.

"Washing when your fingers are still bandaged must be a challenge," a soft voice said from beside the tub. "I'll help."

Bryar's eyes flew open as he jerked upright, sending a wave of water onto the floor.

It couldn't be.

It was.

Tai. For all the world as if she hadn't vanished from his life on the bank of a river, leaving him to cope alone. She perched on the side of his tub and ran her finger along his hairline.

He almost believed she was real.

"Tai." He heard the rasp in his voice. The word, which summed up so much, had barely passed his lips since he'd left Ezra's; it was as if he spoke it for the first time.

"Bryar." She said his name as a simple fact, as if the world was set to rights by its utterance, and took his wounded hand in her own. "Can you put it in water yet?" she asked.

"What?" he blurted, jerked back to reality. "No, I mean yes, but I don't—"

"I know about the fingers," she said, silencing him. "No secrets, ever again." She shoved up the sleeves of her tunic and fished a sponge from the water. Claiming the bar of soap, she pushed on the top of his head, dunking him, then massaged lather into his hair. After another dunk to rinse, she ran the sponge along his body, his arms and legs, down his torso...

Sweet Sustainer.

He was helpless under her hands. He'd be happy to stay that way into eternity.

Except –

"By all the blessings in the world," she said, "but you are a beautiful man."

She ignored his manhood and washed his right hand, kissing each fingertip. She turned to his left hand.

"Don't." He jerked free and plunged his hand underwater. It was an illogical, stupid move. As soon as she bore witness to his maimed fingers...

"Bryar, it's me." Tai lifted his hand, removed the sodden bandages, and gently worked the soap into his skin. When she finished rinsing, she repeated the ritual, kissing the tip of each finger.

He watched, torn between horrified and... and what? He, the master of words, had no way to describe the emotions her actions spawned.

"The water's almost cold. Let's go." Tai planted herself at the end of the tub and held out her hands. He took them and allowed her to pull him to his feet. As he clambered out of the water, she claimed a towel from the stack. "Let me do this for you."

Tai started with his hair and neck, rubbing with the cloth, kissing where she had dried. She worked her way down his back, over his buttocks... drying, kissing. His muscles clenched as he fought for control. Up his left arm to his chest...

Unable to bear it another instant, as she must be fully aware, he snatched the cloth from her, tossed it aside, and pulled her to him. The bliss he'd thought was gone forever swamped his nerve endings as Tai molded herself against him, her mouth responsive under his, her hands on his back, working lower.

Bryar broke away, gasping. Nothing emerged when he tried to speak but, reading his message, she crossed the two paces to the door and peeked out. "All clear." She grabbed a second towel from the shelf, tossed it to him, and bolted from the room. Modesty wasn't a big feature of life in the Bards' lodge, but he managed to tie the cloth around his waist before rushing up the stairs after her.

Tai stood on the far side of his bed.

"There's so much you need to know," he said, pleased that his voice sounded remarkably calm, given the way his body hovered on the verge of exploding.

"Later. If you're sure." She wasn't as contained as she pretended; her hands trembled. But she circled the bed and yanked the cloth from his waist. With a fluid movement, she pulled her tunic over her head and let it drop to the floor.

Her skin was molten silk. His missing fingers forgotten, he drowned in the sensory exultation that was Tai.

Quinn caught up with Dal that evening as he crossed the green from the Healers' lodge, heading for a gathering of older apprentices around a fire pit out behind the Centra.

"How's Bryar?" she asked.

"I'm guessing, good, but I haven't seen him. How are you, Quinn? You looked a little the worse for wear this morning."

"Fine." She dismissed Dal's comment with a hand gesture. "What do you mean, you haven't seen him? You were going to do a Healing—"

"Tomorrow will be time enough. Probably better, in fact."

She didn't give up the point. "But you were in a hurry to return to Stanstead."

Dal stopped at the corner of the guest lodge, watching the kids around the fire. These apprentices were older, soon to graduate to their journey year with their whole lives ahead of them. Had she ever been so carefree?

"I do want to get back," Dal said. "Charlotte's waiting for me, and by now they'll have selected a village healer. My work is there, training the new healer and Missy."

"Then why haven't you worked with Bryar? You could be on your way tomorrow."

"Do you really think Arwen would sanction my leaving? The cell's in our possession. The sooner it's sealed and rendered harmless, the better."

"And you'd be a part of it again?" To her own ears, she sounded more bitchy than curious.

"Most of us would, with stronger safeguards. Bryar's an inspiration."

"But I don't understand..."

Shut up, Quinn. Keep your problems to yourself.

She was standing on the edge of the green with her back to the fire pit. A figure appeared out of the dusk, walking toward the dining hall from the vicinity of the Bards' lodge.

"There he is. I need to—"

Dal gripped her shoulder, stopping her. "Look more closely."

Not Bryar alone. A pixie of a woman clung to him, tucked against his side.

"Oh."

Dal turned her to the fire and took her hands. "Trust me on this – Bryar's got better medicine than anything in my repertoire. And you know it. He neither needs nor wants you right now."

Quinn squeezed his hand before turning toward the Scribes' lodge, swamped by the feeling of being old, useless, and alone.

Chapter 42

"You're not concentrating."

True enough. Quinn had passed a restless night and wasn't in any condition or mood to study the intricate diagrams spread out over Arwen's workbench. She started over, tracing the pattern, considering the implications of each step.

Plotting the weave to screen the power cell was Scribes' work, with Dorcas, Ezra, and Tai adding their expertise. Weavers from other guilds might contribute energy to the binding, but wouldn't grasp the intricacies of the completed template. The success of the test on the stone, before the catastrophe that cost Willow so dearly, had convinced them it was possible. But this time the safeguards for the eight Weavers to create and seal the weave had to be foolproof. Nobody would come to harm again.

Nor would they trek to Stanstead. The binding would be executed here in the valley, but far from the Motherhouse complex. The call for volunteers had been posted that morning.

"I'm sorry, Arwen, I can't focus." Quinn tossed down the quill pen she used to keep her place in the diagram. "It looks stable, but..." She shrugged.

"I want this finished. The cell's secure, by which I mean nobody like Kiril will find it. But if, for instance, Gauvain decided to try, the wards aren't sufficient to fend him off." Arwen's voice reflected more determination than confidence.

Quinn smacked the paper in front of her. "I'll fetch caff. Hopefully it will wake me up."

As she walked next door to the dining hall, she ruminated on the forced change in her view of Bryar. Faced with incontrovertible facts, she grudgingly acknowledged that the Bryar she'd carried in her mind no longer existed. Although he still bore traces of the boy she grew up with, he had developed into a complicated, conflicted adult, with a man's concerns and needs.

Needs she didn't fulfill.

Theirs had never been a romantic attachment, but losing the connection they'd shared since childhood wounded her. The lonely sense of being unnecessary refused to go away.

Back at the workroom, she found the weaving diagrams rolled and tossed against the wall behind Arwen's chair, and Bryar himself, perched on a stool looking rested and alert. He stopped mid-sentence and shot a wry smile her way. "Reporting for duty."

She retrieved a third caff mug from the supply Arwen kept in a cupboard – the result of forgetting to return them, she suspected – and poured while Bryar picked up their interrupted conversation.

"He consulted a herbalist in Orlan. By all that lives and breathes, I've never seen anything like it. A monster in the flesh."

"What are you talking about?" Quinn demanded. "Monsters?"

At Arwen's nod, Bryar briefly recapped a tale of a giant lizard attacking Kiril in the hills.

"Did it harm you as well?" Arwen asked.

"I got a few scratches."

"And they healed properly?"

"Yes, but it sank its teeth into Kiril. That's what worried me, the saliva. What was that thing? Neither of us was prepared."

"I'm not sure." Arwen leaned back, cradling her caff mug. "This is merely conjecture." She paused.

A room of secrets. Quinn glanced at Bryar as he nodded his understanding, his eyes fixed on Arwen.

"All right. The spells were woven into the hills long ago, well before my day or even Ezra's. Given how the civilization of Borgonne evolved, we have reason to be grateful. Weavers have always been able to cross, although few knew it. But no one else. Kiril found that out, to his dismay, when he tried to abscond with the cell."

Bryar chuckled. Quinn's head jerked up; he hadn't made any sounds that could be interpreted as happy in a long time.

"Here's one possibility. The spell viewed the two of you as interlopers. With your protective weave, Bryar, you probably confused the energies in the hills, a Weaver and yet not a Weaver. The spell let you go through, but with your Weaver status masked, it might have attacked you as easily. As it happened, it found Kiril first."

Bryar nodded. "Suppose the hills had blocked me?"

She shot him an exasperated look. "We'd arranged backup."

Naturally. Arwen left nothing to chance.

"But why only a single attack?" Bryar asked. "Why didn't another lizard attack us, or some other fantastical beast?"

"As to that," Arwen said, "I wonder if the spell on the hills itself is degrading, much like Ezra's weave. Or like certain Healers' workings, which also decay and require renewal to maintain their potency. Or perhaps it was pure luck."

"You said Kiril's wound itched. Like a healing itch, just before a scab falls off?" Quinn shifted on her stool and sipped the rapidly cooling caff before continuing. "Is it possible the animal infected him?"

"I want Dal to check out both of you," Arwen told Bryar. "You and Kiril. You were wrong not to tell him about the attack." At Bryar's silence she added, "I understand, circumstances dictated otherwise. But see to it now. You're getting the stitches out anyway, aren't you? My sources say Kiril's still here, so take him along. It may or may not be important, but we mustn't risk leaving it to chance. By the way, is the protective weave completely gone?"

"Almost. A few remnants. I'll be happy to be rid of them."

"If Dal can't do it, check with me."

"Yes, ma'am." Bryar stood. "Is there anything else?"

Arwen sighed. "A great deal, but this comes first. There'll be time later for a proper debriefing. And Quinn has work to do, if she chooses to wake up this morning."

Bryar grinned, hauled Quinn to her feet, and wrapped her in a bear hug. "You damn near saved my life in the hills," he said quietly. When she was silent, he murmured, "You're a part of me, Quinn. Always will be." Then he released her and was gone.

Arwen retrieved the diagrams and spread them out. "As I predicted," she said, "that girl is his salvation. I never expected him to appear this stable so soon, though I fear the worst is yet to come."

Quinn stared at the closed door, shaken and determined not to show it. She tightened the screens defending her mind, hoping to avoid one of Arwen's inquisitions. "Let's see the diagrams." She set the caff mug on the tray and readied herself to work.

As the sun pushed toward its zenith, Bryar perched on a stool in the small consultation room, recounting the tale of the lizard's attack. Dal listened, arms folded over his chest, simmering with annoyance. Kiril, lounging against a wall, occasionally threw in a comment.

"And you didn't think you should mention this?" Dal threw at him when he finished. "Even domestic animals can leave hidden infections. To entrust your health to a village healer was folly. You may not have known that." Dal pointed to Kiril before turning to Bryar. "But you assuredly did. Let me see."

Since it delayed offering his maimed fingers to Dal's attention, Bryar hauled his tunic over his head willingly enough. Kiril pushed up his sleeves.

"All of them."

At Dal's glare, Kiril sighed, but stripped off his garment. Despite the underlay of muscle, he was too thin. But then Kiril had always been slender.

After giving Bryar a cursory once-over, Dal waved him away and signaled for Kiril to replace him on the stool. He studied the marks of old bruises and scrapes peppering Kiril's skin, then rested the wounded arm on a small stand. The attack had been vicious, and although the skin had mended, the site of the lizard's bite still appeared red and inflamed. Not gently, Dal prodded it. Kiril's body tensed. Bryar picked up on the other man's unease when Dal placed a hand on the scars and grew still.

"Is this one of your famous Healings?" Kiril's voice conveyed a little less cockiness than usual.

Bryar shook his head. He spoke quietly. "No, not a Healing. He's probing the wound under the skin." He reflected that Dal had in fact earned Kiril's trust a long time ago, taking on the treatment of his broken leg and burns following the crash that marooned him here and coincidentally delivered the nightmare of the power cell into their land.

Both men watched and waited.

Dal opened his eyes and crossed the room to the supply cabinet, where he retrieved a short knife and a basin. He busied himself with a rag and alcohol, cleaning the blade. "This won't hurt too much. Not as much as the original, anyway."

"There's something in there?" Kiril's voice was factual, but a tinge of panic had crossed his face, so quickly suppressed Bryar would have missed it if he hadn't been looking for it.

"Infection. Minor, I hope, but if it isn't tended to, you risk it becoming systemic. You don't want that. Take a breath." With one hand holding Kiril's arm against the table, Dal sliced into the site of the punctures. Blood flowed from the gash, and a greenish ooze that emitted a faint, putrid odor. Kiril stared at the wound. Frowning, Dal caught the fluids in the basin. "I'll do tests on this. We'll let it bleed for a minute to clean it out." He placed the knife in a mug of alcohol and pulled more supplies from the cabinet. Then he pressed on Kiril's arm in a way that brought the bleeding to a stop and applied a few drops from a vial to the open wound. Kiril winced. As Dal set two stitches to close the incision, Bryar noted that he had paled. So, Kiril had a weak spot. He feared illness, didn't like blood or needles. Bryar supposed he had been too traumatized himself to notice, in the hills.

Dal deftly wrapped a bandage around Kiril's arm. "Come back daily until we clear you. I won't always be here, but someone will. Anything else?"

"Nah, I'm good." Kiril stood. "Meet you for lunch?" he asked Bryar.

Bryar almost declined. Then he suffered a twinge of guilt. He owed the guy. "Sure."

Kiril gone, Dal turned to him. His scratches merited only a cursory survey. "I'm not worried, but get to the healing rooms if you experience redness, severe itching, or even just a sense something's not right. Now your fingers."

Tai had bandaged them, at his insistence. "So you won't have to see them," he'd told her.

"So they'll stay clean until Dal gives the okay," she'd contradicted, and kissed the bandages. She never cringed.

Dal untied the neat wrapping and studied each finger, probing for sensitivity or any hint of infection. "Are you getting any phantom pain or other feeling?"

"The other day. I felt it... as if my finger was there, and it itched. I was desperate to scratch, and I couldn't."

"We'll hope that will die out. Nerves take time to heal. Talk to me or another Healer if you need a weave to screen it. After I remove the stitches, I'll want half an hour for a depth Healing. Fortunately, the cuts were clean, and the repair work could have been more skilled, but it's not bad. Hold on. This may be uncomfortable."

Dal snipped and pulled at threads, and Bryar tried not to look at the ruins of his fingers. He had always taken care of them, maintaining their strength and limberness so they danced over the strings of the chitarre, the holes of a flute, on command. They gave pleasure or formed fists. And now they were gone.

Gone. His mind still refused to accept the stark reality.

"So, you and Tai," Dal said as he worked.

"What about us?"

"Nothing. Tai's a fascinating person. When she first came here, it took me a while to sort out if she was a boy."

"Yeah." Bryar wasn't ready to discuss Tai.

Dal looked up. "Talk to her. It'll be easier than talking to anyone else, I suspect. Has Arwen given you a grilling yet?"

Bryar scoffed. "No, just the surface. She's more concerned with securing the cell."

"You're not to volunteer for the circle. I trust you understand that." Dal made a final snip, tugged gently to free the thread, and straightened.

Bryar frowned. He hadn't planned to put himself forward, but he couldn't turn away now. He wanted to be present for the denouement.

Dal gripped his right biceps and shook. "It's for medical reasons. We don't know what happened to Ezra's shield. You say there are still traces, so I conclude there may be long-term effects. You'd put yourself and the others in the circle in jeopardy."

"Surely they'll let me be there, at least."

"I expect so. Speak to Arwen. Now, come with me." Dal lead him to a cot in one of the healing rooms. "Lie down, relax. Your body has suffered far too much trauma. While I'm at it, perhaps I can remove the remains of Ezra's weave."

"Dal…"

"Hmm?" Dal's back was turned as he readied himself for the Healing, working herbs into his palms.

Bryar glanced around to be sure they were alone. "Are you going to…" He took a breath. "I'm kind of messed up… I mean, after the fight and —"

"Killing a worthless individual?" Dal smiled grimly at Bryar's obvious shock. "I don't believe Kiril's version, either, but it shows a positive quality in him he keeps well hidden. And remember, the Mage would have killed you. We'll need a few sessions to free you, but yes, I'll start now."

Bryar allowed his limbs to go slack as he wondered if Dal knew how little sleep he'd had the night before, or why. The memory of Tai hovered over the lingering image of the quivering knife, there in Gauvain's study. Dal lightly brushed his left hand, and he gave himself over to the healing energy seeping into him.

He woke up to find Tai nudging his shoulder, telling him that Kiril was waiting to join them for lunch.

Stepping into the sunlight, he felt more clear-headed than he had since the application of Ezra's weave. Tai walked close beside him. The bandages were gone, leaving the stumps visible for all to see.

And that reminded him to track down Mari and tell her about his hand. Her less than perfect father – but Mari wouldn't care, any more than Tai or Quinn or Willow. They formed his true clan, with or without fingers.

Chapter 43

Quinn looked up from the diagram on the sheet in front of her and rubbed her eyes. The weave had become too complex for her to confirm its utility in her mind; she needed the backup of paper and pen.

They had combined standard Healers' techniques for sealing off poisoned or wounded parts of the body with newly developed templates accessing directional energies. The result had been welded to Ezra's protective template, itself more intricate than any she had ever conceived on her own. Ezra's schema drew on the life force, which was irrelevant in the context of the power cell, but its basic structure would give the rest of the weave stability.

Quinn worried that the resultant working might be *too* complicated, so that the Weavers in the circle would find it impossible to complete their individual assignments.

No, she told herself. The template was dense, but not difficult. The intricacy lay at the intersections, where earth melded into air, air into fire, fire into water, water into earth. Given the dissimilar energies, creating stable joins to unite them had been the most challenging task of her career. Even with their most experienced practitioners stationed at the cross corners where the directional energies merged, the connections presented serious challenges.

Amazing that we dared to try it last year.

A fear-driven decision, she saw now. Since then, their knowledge had grown exponentially. Events of the past autumn and winter had opened their eyes to the reality of a force they had seen as benign – and controllable. Its power awed and scared her in equal parts. A renewed appreciation of the Aura tempered Quinn's work. She respected the dangers but itched to experiment with new techniques. First, though, they'd deal with the power cell.

Quinn was grateful for the grueling schedule and unrelenting expectations. With no time to analyze her own feelings, she tumbled into bed each night so exhausted that she actually slept. In all her years as a Scribe, she had never driven herself so relentlessly.

It was paying off, though. Only a nine-day after their return, she could no longer see any way to improve the weave. Arwen agreed, so the time had come to meet with the volunteers.

Only she, Arwen, Tai, and Dorcas grasped the scope and detail of the proposed template. The design was such that participants in the binding dealt only with their own directional energies while maintaining the flow and building the currents, then shared in gathering up the eight strands of focus into a protection template that would be indissoluble – or so they expected.

Giving up on her faltering concentration, she left her lodge and walked through a warm spring shower to the river. Kiril stood near the riverbed, his wet tunic clinging to him, tossing stones into the tumbling water.

Not her idea, seeking out Kiril. Arwen's command.

Quinn used the high trail that paralleled the riverbank, so she saw his face in profile as she approached. After traveling through the hills with him, she was accustomed to an expression of amused contempt on his face. Finding the smirk replaced by worry surprised her.

What did he have to worry about?

"Lousy weather for a swim," she commented as she came up to him, speaking loudly above the rushing water. Even Bryar avoided the river in its full spring spate.

"Not planning on it. What's up?" Kiril tossed a final stone, then propped a shoulder against a tree.

"We need your help." No point dragging this out.

"How?" His eyes ranged over her, but they were masked, waiting to hear what she would say.

"You've heard about the circle to seal the power cell."

He grinned. "Then hide it where nobody will find it." The grin faded. He turned away and tossed another pebble into the torrent. "You can stop worrying about me. I'm not interested."

Good to know, if it was believable. "Why not?"

"I have other plans."

"Really? What?"

"You care? I'm touched."

Her lips tightened. "The Midland's a big place, and no doubt you have *some* useful skills."

It was insulting, and she knew it. Kiril straightened, rolling his shoulders before re-establishing himself against the tree, arms folded. "I managed for a long time without your help, in the middle of winter, too. I don't need you to vet my plans." His unemotional tone failed to mask his irritation.

"You're still here."

"The food's good." He shrugged. "We didn't come out of that little adventure in the best shape, remember."

That much was true. The planes of Kiril's face were sharper, his body under the wet tunic bordering on gaunt.

"I guess I owe you thanks for saving Bryar. But why make up a story about killing that man?"

"Duncan? Big fat guy, but stronger than he looked. Thank god Bryar exposed the cell. If he'd accessed his voodoo, we might both be dead. Although on the whole," he continued as if reflecting on a recipe, or a new approach to plowing a field, "I think he was the type who'd torture before finishing you off. I pictured a lot of suffering in our future. So why wouldn't I kill him?"

"Because Bryar had already done so. Why lie?" Then she dismissed any possibility of noble intent. "Oh, never mind, I get it. For the glory. You figured he'd return home a hero. You wanted a piece of that. Right?"

"Believe what you choose." He maintained the relaxed posture. But something lurked behind his eyes. More was going on here than she could figure out. Or cared to.

"It's irrelevant, it just muddies the folk history. I'll find it in the Aura anyway."

"What do you people want me to do?"

Business. Solid ground. "We're confident in the technique, but we need a person without Entrée present, in case."

"To pick up the pieces if the whole exercise goes kablooey on you?"

"You'll be our fallback man."

"Pack mule? Messenger boy?"

"Got it." Quinn derived a perverse pleasure in confirming his derogatory assessment of his role.

"Sure. Happy to help. When?"

"Tomorrow afternoon in the conference room for planning, then rehearsal the next morning."

"I'll be there."

Quinn started to turn away, her message delivered, but hesitated. "Kiril —"

"Yes, darlin'?"

She cringed at the casual, contemptuous endearment, but kept her face from showing it. Her eyes hard, she said, "If you do anything, one single thing, to sabotage this, I'll see your guts spread out in a field for the crows. Got it?"

He stretched and turned a full-bore grin on her. "I like crows."

Quinn wheeled and stormed off, muttering 'bastard' under her breath. When she was ten paces down the trail, he called after her. "Hey!"

She stopped, her hands balled into fists. "What?"

He was serious. "Stop worrying. I told you, I don't want the cell. Do what you please with it."

She turned, her smile feral. "I will believe that when the Southlands freezes over."

Her pace measured, she left him there, furious at herself. How did he get to her that way? Why did she let him?

Dal joined Quinn for lunch before the team meeting. She usually enjoyed his company. Restrained and cerebral, he aligned well with her own preferences. About ten years her senior, he had been Willow's mentor and lover during her journey year, when Quinn worked with Ezra at his compound and Bryar battled through his last months of training, the first time the three of them had been separated since they all arrived at the Motherhouse. She trusted Dal and would turn to him with a problem before most others.

Not that she had a problem. Or so she assured herself.

"I suppose you've recruited nearly the same crew as last time," he said as he cut into his chop.

"New volunteers in the north and south, and Judith won't be participating."

He nodded. "Shock and burns, last time. I heard she volunteered."

Quinn chewed and swallowed. "She did. She's powerful, but elderly."

"Even so, she wanted to be a part of it. I hope you let her down gently."

"Of course. What do you think we are?" She paused to tone down her blatant irritation. "The fact remains, we need our most reliable Weavers for the cross-corner positions."

"Quinn? Is everything okay?" Little ruffled Dal, but he paused with a bite halfway to his lips, looking askance.

"Sorry." She reached out to touch his hand. "I didn't mean that. This last nine-day was hard."

"In ways you didn't expect. Listen to me." Dal rested his knife and spoon on his plate and speared her with a look. "You're suffering, and it isn't necessary. Not when help's available."

"All I need is a break. And to have this binding over with." She dismissed his concern with a little wave of her free hand before shoveling a spoonful of mixed root vegetables into her mouth.

Dal shook his head. "I know you better than that. Don't let this go too far, okay? Life has changed. Your job is to come to terms with it."

Quinn poked at her remaining vegetables. "I'm fine."

"You're not. If you were going to be in the circle, I'd force the issue. At the least, you risk hurting Bryar if you keep on this way."

"It's nothing to do with Bryar," she blurted before taking time to consider her words. She never gave that much away.

"I think it is. You've chosen a solitary path, which suits you, but only because of the support of your friends. Now they've gone in different directions, and you're lost."

Fighting an almost visceral fear of exposure, she didn't answer.

"I know what I'm talking about, Quinn," he continued in his quiet, aristocratic voice. "The same thing happened when Mari was born, remember? And because I'm much like you, I recognize the signs."

She never enjoyed being in the spotlight and liked less the idea that anyone saw through her carefully constructed barriers. Dal put her separation under a magnifying glass, forcing her into the open.

Don't blame Dal.

Still, she couldn't handle any more pressure on top of the intensity of the template work. "Stop. Please." The 'please' was formal, spoken for the sake of manners, not a plea.

"I beg your pardon. Be careful, that's all. Tell me who's joining the circle."

The rest of the meal passed in the exchange of Motherhouse news – never called gossip, because it reflected the caring everyone shared for other Weavers. Whether you got along with somebody or not, they were part of your tribe, understood how it felt to be different, and bore the burden the Aura placed on them all.

Chapter 44

Bryar sat off to the side of the conference room. At the table were the eight chosen to build the template, along with Quinn and Arwen. Even from across the room, he picked up Quinn's mood; she wanted to yell or punch something, but she wouldn't. She never did. Frustrations built up until she descended into sarcasm, dissolved into very private tears, or took off on one of her rare journeys. The last time he'd seen her so tense was when Willow insisted on volunteering for this same circle, but that had been fear. This was different.

Next to him, Tai held herself still, her Aura-enhanced senses alert. Like him, she must detect the palpable tension in the room.

Tai's right hand wrapped around his left, the incomplete one. Although she was a Scribe, the comfort flowing from her touch was such that he'd begun to wonder if she manifested Healer's skills as well.

The last to arrive, Kiril strode in and dropped into the vacant chair beside Bryar. They exchanged nods.

Arwen called them to order and began the explanations. Bryar's only job was to be there and aware. All things considered, he was glad Dal had excluded him from consideration for the circle. Despite Tai's ministrations, he felt an odd fatigue, as if a reservoir of Aura-infused energy inside him had been drained away. Willow sometimes experienced the same depletion after an intense Healing.

Perhaps he'd take Tai to Ezra's for a while. He needed space to heal. And to learn to trust she wouldn't leave again.

Her reasoning had been straightforward, for all that he didn't agree with it. Their burgeoning relationship claimed too much of his focus. She wanted him to succeed, and wanted him to survive even more. "I'd become a distraction," she had said, late on the night she'd first returned to him. "And I suspected you would build on grief, or anger, or however you responded to my disappearance."

"You worried your grandparents. It wasn't only me."

"I spent several nine-days with them before I came down here. They always believed I was safe and well. Arwen was the worst. She gave me a tongue-lashing that just about blistered my hide."

"Don't go again."

"Never."

Replaying their conversation, one of many that interspersed their lovemaking, Bryar lost track of the meeting. When Tai elbowed him, he snapped to attention to find the circle working in pairs as Arwen and Quinn hovered, assessing the progress. Odd flows in the Aura permeated the room as the other Weavers learned their weaves and experimented with sections of the currents. Like being in training again, he mused, but the unfamiliar, conflicting energies made his heart beat faster.

On his other side, Kiril fidgeted. "Got to stretch my legs."

"You're not needed," Quinn said, turning from the table to glare at him. "Go ahead, get out of here. Just turn up tomorrow morning."

"Oh, I'll be there. Wouldn't miss it."

Bryar swore Kiril planned his actions to irk Quinn. If so, he succeeded. She turned her back on them, her shoulders rigid, as he exited the room.

"Want to escape, too?" he whispered to Tai.

"I'd like that."

Bryar cleared their departure with Arwen, and the two of them made their way out of the building.

"Where to?" he asked.

"The river?"

"Rivers carry bad connotations where you're concerned." He was only half joking.

She grinned. "Best get over it, then. I'm looking forward to hiding from the world in my secret place. With you."

"I bet Rebecca knows about your secret place." He kept his hand on her shoulder as they strolled, needing the contact. "Probably Ezra, too."

"That's okay," Tai said comfortably. "As long as everyone keeps up the pretense."

They followed the bluff above the river for half an hour before stopping in a grassy clearing. The day spun above them, warm and cloudless, carrying the scents of spring. Bryar stretched out, his head on Tai's lap and her fingers in his hair. "I doubt I'll ever recapture what I had," he said, words he had hardly dared articulate even to himself. "The innocence. An uncomplicated life, but all I needed."

"But you knew it wasn't entirely real. Not after how you were raised."

"I hope never to face anything like this again." The smile faded as he rolled onto his stomach and let his good hand brush the short grass. "I guess I'd grown out of childhood memories. The ones from Borgonne are fresh, and I've got the souvenir, don't I?" He wiggled what was left of his fingers in the warm air.

"Hush. Your day isn't over."

"But it's all changed." He twisted, hooked his arms around her slender waist, and pulled her down beside him. "I never wanted to be a hero."

Tai spoke into his shoulder. "Too late. I bet the other Bards are writing songs about you already."

"The other Bards should find another way to amuse themselves. I'm just a man, Tai. Some people may thrive on confrontation and risk, but I don't count myself among them."

"No, you're better than that," Tai said, her voice serious. "The real hero is the one who doesn't want to do it and does it anyway. You're a good man."

Simple words, but through them a touch of healing flowed into his battered heart.

"But to thrive," she continued, "you need to do what you do best." She shoved his arm out of the way and sat, pulling him up beside her. "This is yours."

She pulled his old flute from her day pack.

Time stopped.

He closed his eyes, blocking out the impossible temptation.

"Experiment with the fingering. This one's going to be a challenge," she added, raising his left hand and kissing the place where his second finger had been. "But by changing the angle... I've played around with it, and I believe it's possible."

He barely registered her words as he fought against the wave of fear twisting his gut. He'd turned from what he had been, and she was thrusting it back at him. Daring him.

He looked away, into the depths of the turbulent river. "Tai, I don't think I can. If I fail... it'd be a double loss. Taking even the memory of what I had."

"If you succeed, you give birth to music again. And if it doesn't work, you still have your voice. And I'm a pretty good accompanist."

Bryar stared at the instrument, then, as if mesmerized, he took it from her. With his eyes closed he explored the flute with his fingers, locating the familiar holes, not daring to attempt the fingering. Not yet.

"If you stay in the low register?" Tai asked.

Could he? With Tai here, everyone else far away, there would never be a better time to try. Bryar swallowed, then began to experiment. Awkwardly, he managed to cover the three left-hand holes.

The resultant note emerged clear and pure, ascending into the trees.

Another note, and another. Tears pooled under his eyelids; he ignored them.

The beginning of a melody evolved, more in his mind than in the air as he fumbled to open and close the holes. It was much too soon to work on more complex fingering. But that still gave him a full octave, majors and minors and the haunting Phrygian mode he built into the music he kept for himself, to be played on riverbanks, crossing moors, speaking to the land.

He let the notes die away as reality sank in. Didn't she know it was fake? Couldn't anyone see the ugliness he carried? The horror of the knife jutting from Duncan's abdomen intruded, destroying the sweetness of the music.

He'd never be free to create beauty again. He'd lost the right.

Bryar jerked the flute from his lips. Shaking, he sprang to his feet. "I can't." His voice rose, filling the air over the tumultuous water. "Why are you doing this? Why don't you leave me alone?" He hurled the flute as far as he could, then watched stunned as it fell into the river.

Only dimly aware of Tai's stricken expression, he tore down the trail away from the Motherhouse. Borgonne and the tower had changed him. There was no going back. And damn her anyway, for tempting him with what was now forever proscribed.

Tai appeared at Quinn's door the next morning, early.

"What...?" Not quite awake, it took Quinn a moment to recognize the state her fellow Scribe was in. "Come in, quickly. What's happened?"

Tai's face was ashen. No sooner had the door closed than tears flooded her eyes. "He threw it away. But I found it in the corridor outside my suite just now. But he threw it away, Quinn. He threw it away."

Quinn blinked at the raw emotion underlying the young woman's words. "I'll make tisane. We have work to do later." She rested a pot of water on her cookfire and began sorting through her stock of herbs.

Tai's outpouring of grief was short-lived; her training took over. "You're a Scribe, and you know him so well," she said, her voice rough. "My thinking's just completely muddled."

"Start by telling me what he threw away." Quinn thanked the Sustainer she'd prepared last night for the morning's work. What spare time she had allowed herself would go to getting sense out of Tai.

"This." Tai reached into her day pack and pulled out the flute.

Quinn took the instrument and looked it over. "A little the worse for wear, I'd say." She set it on the table.

"It's been in the river. How did it end up in the Scribes' lodge? And why is he so angry?"

The water simmered. Quinn added herbs and brought the pot, with two mugs, to the table. "Tell me what happened. There's no time for hysteria."

As they sat, the young woman calmed, perhaps responding to the methodical, businesslike tone in Quinn's voice. "We went to the river. I gave him the flute, and... he played. Only the lower octave, but as lovely as I've ever heard. It got to him, too, I could see it in his face. Then he started shaking, and shouted at me that he'd never make music again, and I shouldn't force him to. He hurled the flute in the water and stormed off. I haven't seen him since. But just now I found this on the shelf beside my door." She touched the little instrument almost reverently. "What does that mean? And why did he say he'd never make music? He was making music."

Tai was on edge. Scribes were analysts; few of them gave way to emotion. Tai might be a law unto herself, but once she got over the shock, she'd draw on a reservoir of calm logic before taking action. Probably unexpected action, knowing Tai, Quinn reflected as she poured the tisane. "Drink this."

Tai did. "I'm not a fool," she said after downing half the mug. "This happened so suddenly, that's all. The connections aren't clear. The whole ordeal the other side of the hills must weigh on his mind, but he has to create music again. He needs it. And it's possible, at least with the flute. Shouldn't music help him?"

Quinn sipped her own tisane, thinking. "People who undergo traumas behave in ways that seem irrational, or so Willow says. Healers have techniques to ease them back into normal life. I expect Bryar's thoughts are as muddled as yours. Could it be some kind of self-imposed punishment for killing Duncan?"

"Did he?"

"I don't know. I'm not sure we'll ever know. Why Kiril would lie about it makes no sense, unless he expected to gain by it. Bryar struck with the knife first."

"And passed out. There are no witnesses to what happened after that."

"One way or another, he fought with the intent to harm."

"Only to save himself."

Quinn smiled at the younger Scribe's stubborn defense of Bryar. "Maybe that doesn't matter. Go wash your face, Tai. We've got the circle mid-morning. Hopefully, he'll turn up."

"This is weird." Tai managed a smile. "I've never been at a loss for words. I may not talk much, but I always know what to say if I choose to. Now I don't. It's like he's a stranger."

"But remember, Bryar's the same man, even though we can't begin to imagine what he's going through. We'll get it sorted out."

She handed Tai the flute and hustled her from the room.

At the door, Tai stopped. "Quinn? Where did the flute come from?"

Quinn smiled, remembering Bryar's facility in the water. "Think about it."

Awareness lit Tai's eyes. As soon as she was gone, Quinn thrust her feet into sandals and set off to find Dal.

Chapter 45

The circle met in a field south of the Motherhouse, past the trail circumscribing the valley. Bryar kept to the fringes, wishing he hadn't agreed to take any part in this. But last night, Quinn had asked that he help monitor the weaves at the junctures with the west, where she was most unsure of them. That was the problem with shared history. It made it damn near impossible to say no. So here he stood, waiting for the work to begin.

Leaving the flute for Tai to find – via one of the messenger kids and the porter at the entrance to the Scribes' lodge – was childish, but he hoped she would read it as he intended, an apology of sorts. She hadn't deserved to be the victim of the sudden, all-consuming rage that had engulfed him yesterday. From her perspective, things had been going well. The truth, barely admitted even to himself, was... he could never create music again. That he had done so terrified him. Nobody so soiled could justify participating in the purity of creation. He was no better than the bullies who had haunted his childhood.

He'd kept to himself for the last two days, and intended to continue to do so. He didn't need their expectations, their expressions of caring. Not a one of them, his former friends, Tai... none of them could begin to understand what a polluted person he'd become. For the only time in his life, he found himself thinking he might be better off without his Entrée; then he could dissolve into the Midland somewhere, and be left alone.

Sun flooded the field, the new green of the grasses and herbs showing chartreuse in the light. The eight participants organized themselves into a circle surrounding a pack filled with dirt and a rock roughly the size of the power cell. With the rock hidden from view, they needed to use their Entrée techniques, in whatever form they took, to feel their way to its surface. Just as they would do when they worked with the real thing.

Tai's laugh rang out over the field, drawing his focus. He could watch Tai forever, her quicksilver nature, the way she connected with everything she touched...

An undeserved delight. He looked away.

As the others grew still, most of them settling into a light trance, Quinn accosted him. "You okay? You don't look okay."

Nothing like Quinn rampant to snap you back to reality. "I'm fine. Were you appointed mother hen today?"

She rolled her eyes. "I must be living right. First I get Kiril's attitude and now yours. Are you ready? We'll be starting in a few minutes."

"I still don't see why you need me. Every Weaver in the Motherhouse is out here. There's no shortage of monitors."

"Nevertheless." She shot him a thin smile and rested her hand on his forearm. "After what happened to Willow, we aren't taking any chances. Besides, you're entitled to share in this."

"I brought the thing here. Do you want my blood, too?"

She held him at arm's length, digging in her fingers, and glared. "I heard you were in a bad mood, but that was uncalled for. I'm not the enemy."

He relented, but only marginally. "I know you aren't. But you could find better targets for your fawning."

Shaking off her hands, he turned away, seeking a place in the grass to settle, sufficiently distant not to cross the circle's energy with his own, close enough to track the currents as they wove them into a template. All the while his skin twitched as Quinn's eyes bored into his back.

From his chosen spot, he looked across the circle and saw Tai studying him, a tiny frown line between her brows. Then Dal claimed her attention from his position in the northeast. An unexpected, and totally unwarranted, stab of jealousy shot through him.

Tai, Quinn, and Arwen moved around the circle, checking the fitted leather harnesses that bound the hands of the participants to one another. No risk of the circuit breaking this time, although he wondered about the effect on the work if someone else went into convulsion, as Martin had done. A couple of them had looked nervous earlier, but now they all had entered trance and awaited the command to begin.

Bryar sat cross-legged and watched as Arwen and Quinn stepped aside and turned control of the circle over to Dorcas, the Scribe in the southeast designated to monitor the weave and energy flow through the emerging template.

Kiril dropped onto the grass beside him. He looked drawn; his voice lacked his usual insouciance. "Guess we'd better make ourselves comfortable. They won't want us prowling around and messing with everyone's concentration."

They had skulked through alleys, fought the beast in the hills. There should be more of a bond between them. But one of them had killed Duncan. Three nine-days since the fatal fight, days that Duncan would no longer enjoy food or companionship or the touch of sun on the field. Days without the magic of the Aura. How do you make reparation for such grievous harm done?

Short answer? You don't.

Bryar gave a bark of a laugh. "You'd have to stick a knife in someone to mess with a deep template weaving."

"We both know a lot about that. The sticking the knife in part, I mean."

"Go away."

"Nah. Like it or not, we've got this connection. Can't just shake it off."

If only Kiril were wrong.

The working began. On the surface, nothing appeared to happen, but Bryar detected the movement of energy as eight powerful men and women manipulated the Aura to their will. Most of them had participated in the circle a half year ago, but these were more robust templates, more difficult to manipulate, or so he'd gathered.

"Is it happening?" Kiril kept his voice quiet.

"Yeah. Slowly."

As the sun rose higher, Bryar's mind drifted. Dorcas's command to release, when it came, startled him. The weave formed a sparkling net in the air before it draped into place, subsumed by the pack hiding the stone. The sheer quantity of bound energy drove a shiver up his spine. Then the group sagged to the ground, helping each other release the leather bindings on their hands.

Arwen entered the circle, dug in the pack, and removed the target stone. It was coated in dirt, with a few smaller rocks stuck to it. Bryar guessed the working hadn't been clean, the energies insufficiently directed to isolate the irregular surface. That shouldn't be a problem with the smooth planes of the energy cell. She tugged at a rock; it held fast. She smacked the edge against a rounded boulder barely visible under the grass; the rock remained locked to the larger stone. Then she handed it to Dorcas, who explored it, seeking traces of the weave, before passing it on.

The members of the circle rested and compared notes. Everyone stayed on the ground, no doubt dealing with the probable side effects of headaches, weakened muscles, and foggy brains. No matter the clan, Weavers everywhere drew on earth energy after intense work.

Ready to escape, Bryar scrambled up. "You coming?" he asked Kiril.

"Nah. I'm their designated dogsbody. Here to haul the carcasses home again."

Bryar strode toward the path leading to the Motherhouse. If anyone noticed him leave, well, he really didn't care.

Arwen barged in on him that afternoon. After a solitary lunch, he was lying on his bed, studying the patterns in the plaster ceiling. As a Scribe, she wasn't welcome in the Bards' lodge, but she had never considered that the rules applied to her. Not when she was on a mission.

She started speaking before she was fully in the room. "You missed the debrief."

He didn't move. "Why bother? Nothing went wrong."

"There was a wrinkle, a place the weave failed to seal properly at the southwest intersection. We needed all the water and fire clan we could round up to work out how to fix it. Damn nuisance. It means another practice before we risk binding the cell. Your input would have been valuable."

"There are plenty of other water clan Weavers. Don't push, Arwen."

"Get up." It was an order, not a request.

"No."

"By the Sustainer. It's hard to believe you've become more of an obnoxious brat than you were when you were fourteen. You have responsibilities. Now *get up.*"

Her expression, her tone, were iron. The way she intimidated him, he could be fourteen again. Bryar sat and swung his legs over the side of the bed.

She loomed over him. "Look at you. Unshaven, unwashed, slovenly and surly. It's past time you completed your Healing. You're disrupting the whole Motherhouse."

Indifferent, he shrugged. "Then I'll leave. I can't say I give a damn."

Arwen slapped him. In twenty-five years, he'd never heard of her striking anyone. Stunned, tears flooded his eyes, and his wounded hand moved automatically to his stinging face. *Sustainer*, but the old woman packed a wallop.

Then she launched into him. "You are a senior in the Bards' guild. The younger members look up to you. You've upset both Tai and Quinn – and it's pretty hard to knock a Scribe off balance. And to crown things, you're also Romarin's father, a fact you seem to have forgotten. I gather you've hardly said hello to her since you got out of the hills." She snatched up his left hand and shook it. "Do you think she wanted to hear about this from gossip?"

Arwen kept her voice tightly modulated, in keeping with the controlled fury on her face. "Given what you've been through, we expect your mind to be wounded. But to refuse Healing? That is unacceptable. Whatever your fingers represent to you, they're not a punishment. A reminder, perhaps. A way to become closer to Tai. Or maybe this whole episode will teach you to be more realistic about life in the

Midland, instead of wandering the roads in a fool's paradise. Ever since you were a boy, you've constructed this make-believe world full of sunshine and rainbows. Wake up, Bryar."

She paused to catch her breath. Bryar sat still, stunned by her polemic as much as the slap. They stared at each other for a long minute. Then Arwen whirled and stalked to his door. She stopped on the threshold and pointed at him. "You will visit Dal, immediately. He's expecting you. And you will dine with Romarin this evening. I won't let you hurt her by your lack of attention."

With that, she left.

Arwen was certain to send someone to drag him to the healing rooms if he failed to show up on his own. After seeing Dal, he'd go to the village for a shave out of respect for Mari, but... He wrinkled his nose. She was right, he needed to bathe. His skin emitted the sour pong of a night terror that had woken him in a cold sweat.

Arwen had cast some variety of mental compulsion on him, he suspected. After Ezra's experiments with the shield, he recognized the subtle shift in his personal energies. So although he had no wish to submit to a Healing, or wash, or even see Mari, he flung himself off the bed and pulled a clean tunic from his wardrobe, preparatory to a trip to the bathing room. He only hoped he'd be able to dodge memories of Tai in the process.

Chapter 46

Dal wasted no time and displayed no sympathy. "Come in and lie down. This may not be pleasant, but try to relax."

His nerves on edge, Bryar snarled, "I'm here, but it doesn't mean I like it. Watch what you say, and don't threaten me."

"Let me put it this way." Dal, as always, appeared the image of calm, but underneath Bryar sensed the hard determination of anger. "You managed to hurt two people I value. You have the Motherhouse agitated, Mari confused, and you may be threatening the success of the binding on the power cell. Why should you expect me to be gentle?"

"Just get it over with." Bryar crossed to the cot in the plain healing room and perched on it, his arms folded across his chest.

"Sandals off. Is there anything physical I need to deal with?"

"Sure," he sneered. "How about giving me new fingers?"

"Why would I do that?" Dal threw his attitude right back at him. "Tai tells me those you have will do you well."

"People are throwing around opinions when they don't know what they're talking about. She heard a dozen notes on a primitive flute. I'm in a better place to judge than she is."

Words shot like arrows across the room. "I doubt that. Did she tell you she's been working on alternate fingerings? And experimenting on the chitarre to see what chance you have of playing it left handed? Everything you need is right in front of you, and you're too much of a coward to take it."

"Stay out of my business, okay? My choices are no concern of yours."

"You say that because your perspective's shot. And when you hurt our friends, it becomes my business. I like you, Bryar. I don't intend to go through life thinking of you as a fool. Now, tell me if it's the loss of your fingers or the death of a man that twisted you in this knot. Or do you want me to probe? And bear in mind, I'm in no mood to probe gently."

Merde. Everyone in his world picked today to rant at him.

But at least Dal's harsh words had cut through the temper that erupted with no warning. And what he'd said about Tai... "She'd do that? Tai's working with my instruments?"

"Not yours specifically. But that's how she is. Curious, as stubborn as every Scribe I've ever met, and for some reason more fond of you than she should be."

The room settled into silence. Healing rooms were designed to minimize distractions. This one had a high window for light, white walls, and an aroma in the air Bryar couldn't define but associated with comfort. Dal fiddled with containers on a small table against the opposite wall. Despite his professed irritation, he'd always trusted Dal implicitly, as a teacher and a Healer. A man who listened without bias, who conveyed truths without sugar-coating or pity. Perhaps the time had come to talk.

The silence thickened, shutting out the world like an embrace. A safe place.

"This anger. It comes out of nowhere."

Dal turned to him but didn't approach. "That's one effect of traumatic events. It's not actually out of nowhere. Your mind is struggling to cope with normality, now that the trauma's over. I could have told you this, as could any number of people around here, if you weren't so busy either sulking or biting their heads off."

Bryar closed his eyes and felt himself slump as the fight drained out of him. "When Tai came back... I believed the worst was over." He kicked the sandals across the room and stretched out on the cot. "It's not, is it? I feel like I can't get clean. Killing... it's almost as if losing the fingers is fit reparation."

"I thought it might be something like that. I never met Duncan, but I've heard enough about him from Arwen and Ezra. The world isn't lessened by his departure from it. I'm just grateful he never got his hands on Willow."

Dal sat on a stool next to him, and the Healing began. Dal smoothed his energies, after a short while muttering, "By the Sustainer, Bryar. How have you lived with this much disruption? I'm surprised you've been able to eat or sleep."

"Not a lot of either." Dal's technique was already affecting him; he could detect his own rhythms, the gentle tide of energy flowing smoothly through his body. After a while, influenced by the tranquility of returning to alignment, he lost touch with the outside world. He ceded control and sank deep inside himself as Dal commenced the real work, watching through an inner mirror while the other man pulled up each memory, each reaction he'd tried to bury, healed it or discarded it, and moved on.

After a while he slid toward sleep, but the dreams stayed at bay. Dal methodically sought, tied off, and healed his wounds.

He'd enjoy sharing supper with Mari, he reflected as he drifted in the soft fog of semi-consciousness. And Tai... she completed him, and her very presence, loving him, was a miracle worth celebrating. Duncan – even Dal couldn't heal that pain away, and it appeared he didn't intend to try. Maybe with time...

Protocol dictated that you stayed in a healing room until the Healer gave permission to leave. Bryar woke to find the window dark and a single light globe floating in a corner, casting a soft illumination. His stomach suggested that he had slept through supper.

As he rolled to sit up, movement caught his eye. Tai stood and gave him a tentative smile. "Dal says there's no need to check with him. You must be starving, and there's custard for dessert. They promised to save some."

He'd never understand how the kitchen kept track of all the irregular meals for Weavers coming, going, in crisis, or simply hungry when they weren't scheduled to be. He hadn't enacted his morning ritual in days, but he sent a silent thank-you to the Aura for food, for Tai. Grief pulsed in counterpoint to the wonder of life, and probably always would, but at least he felt human again.

Tai waited at the door. He strapped on his sandals, then followed her out into the spring twilight.

"Mari!"

Bryar tracked his daughter down after breakfast the next morning, just before she entered her classroom. Mari had inherited his own sturdiness; she wasn't slight like Willow. Her hair was a darker blonde, and she was tall, already Willow's height. No sprite, his Romarin, but solid and sensible, and less than happy to see him. When she didn't hurl herself into his arms, he felt the hurt.

He'd never written a song about her, or about the experience of fatherhood. Now he wondered why not.

She sidled over, eyeing him suspiciously. "Hi, Dad."

"I'm sorry I missed supper. Dal did a Healing, and I slept right through."

At fourteen, Mari tended to the dramatic. She treated him to a sigh with enough power to echo across the valley and back. Not for the first time, he speculated that her future might be as a Bard rather than a Healer. "You could have come this morning."

"Are you as afraid of Arwen as I am?"

A smile twitched her lips at the image of her father cowering before Arwen's wrath. Had she been brought up before the stern head of council for some infraction yet? Probably not something he wanted to inquire too closely about.

"Maybe a little," she allowed.

He sensed her wariness. She'd trusted him, and he'd let her down. And she was old enough to expect reparation. "So no, I didn't really have a choice. Someone told you, I hope."

"Well, yeah. But—"

He touched her arm. "I should have seen you sooner. I'm a jerk."

She didn't deny it. But then, at the moment she could be a three-year-old again, furious with Willow for dragging her away from a tempting, but potentially deadly, clump of flowering herbs. Arms akimbo, she stamped her foot on the paving stones at the building's entrance. "Nobody even tells me what's going on. At least, I ought to know more than them." She gestured behind her at the classroom building.

"I agree. I was injured, Mari."

"Yeah, they told me that much."

"Some physical, and some that screwed up my head."

That gave her pause. She asked, "Like when the other circle blew up and Mom lost her connection? We don't get to study that stuff until we're, like, eighteen. But you've still got the Aura. You're fine."

"Not quite." He raised his maimed hand.

"Oh." Mari stared. "They said... but I didn't think..." Her eyes welled.

"Give me another chance? Supper tonight?" He used the hand to take hers.

"Sure." The anger had dissolved. Mari sounded hurt, but not mad. "Only I wish you'd come to see me sooner."

"I wanted to. But I was in a bad place, and I might have said something hurtful. You deserve better."

A tear leaked out and trickled down her plump cheek. "Your beautiful hand. That must have been *awful*."

"I'm getting over it." He wiped the tear away.

Unexpectedly, her tears forgotten, Mari shot him an appraising look. "Can you play?" She lifted their joined hands and studied his fingers. "I bet you can. It'll be like learning all over again. Maybe we'll practice together, only I'll get to teach you this time. Do they still hurt?"

"Not so much. A twinge now and then. Meet me at the door of the dining hall this evening?"

"They say you're having lots of sex with Tai. She's weird."

At the abrupt non sequitur, a laugh wrenched from Bryar's chest. He hadn't expected to ever laugh again. "I'll tell you about Tai later."

A hug – one she reciprocated, to his eternal gratitude – and his daughter raced off to her class.

That afternoon Quinn went on a search for Bryar. Since their return to the Motherhouse, he had avoided her. They used to be able to talk, sometimes for hours. They'd loved and fought and supported each other, every step of the way. The silence between them troubled her.

She checked the usual haunts – the Bards' lodge, the dining hall, the practice rooms. Mari had joined him for supper the night before, but no one had laid eyes on him today.

After scouring the Motherhouse complex, she set off for the one remaining place he was likely to be. Only a crisis like the lost flute would tempt him into the river in full spate – at least she hoped he'd retained that much sense – but she understood his need for his element and suspected she'd find him along the bank. She headed downstream, hoping she had guessed the right direction and keeping her eyes open for his blond head.

She spotted him by the river's edge, below the trail that followed the high bank, very near where she had located Kiril only a few days ago. Standing unmoving, he stared at the tumult at his feet.

Quinn almost called out, then stopped herself. From her vantage point, she had a good view of his face in profile. The etched lines she'd first noticed during their long hike through the hills hadn't softened; his expression was harder, more intense.

She saw it in his stance, too, once she knew to look for it. His bare arms and legs were hard, muscular, and he held himself as if poised to take whatever the world threw at him. A man's body, carrying his own burdens, dealing with his own losses.

Quinn leaned against a nearby tree trunk and tried to make sense of the changes.

Bryar had always been the lighthearted one, the peacemaker. He was intent about his vocation, but joyous in its execution. He'd brought laughter into her life, a conviction that living, for all its vicissitudes, was worth the effort, that each day bore the promise of happiness and discovery. Through the support they gave each other, the delights of lovemaking, the many years of closeness they shared, in her mind he had remained the boy who wanted only to be carefree.

That boy was gone. And the man who stood below her was a stranger.

Watching the emotions cross his face, pain, resignation, determination, she wondered if she would ever know him so well again.

Bryar.

Diou, but she cared for him.

Quinn carefully worked her way down the slope. Still without looking away from the river, he spoke as if he'd been aware of her all along.

"We've always been straight with each other." His voice was flat.

"Yes." Standing by his side, she waited.

"So I can trust you to level with me."

"Yes, of course. What is it, Bry?"

He turned and looked her in the eye. His face shed a little of the hardness. "Tell me this. Am I worthy of her? Now, after everything?"

"Her?" Quinn thought fast. "Tai? Sure. She's sort of lost right now, after the flute thing, She's —"

"Not Tai. Mari."

At last she saw the worry behind his stony expression. But how could he doubt? Mari adored him. Nobody could cast him as less than a great father.

"Yes," she said simply. "You are."

He didn't quite smile, but some of the rigidity left his face. "Thanks." He returned to his contemplation of the river.

Quinn recognized his desire to be alone. She touched his shoulder and began the solitary walk back to the Motherhouse, sending her own request to the Aura to help him regain something of the joy that had filled his life before.

Chapter 47

Bryar sat at a distance from the practice circle that morning, alert for problems but otherwise keeping his own counsel. Dal ignored him, or seemed to. Arwen's eyes caught up with him periodically, assessing. Quinn had given him a quick hug in the dining hall but now left him alone. Tai used their unique radar to read that he was fine sitting on the grass by himself; she went about her work, but glanced over occasionally. For the moment, solitude suited him. Dal had wrought as profound a shift, in its own way, as the trauma of the fight, the lost fingers. He needed time to pull himself into an integrated whole. For almost the first time since his days in Borgonne, he believed it was worth doing.

Clouds had rolled in overnight, a thick blanket of stratus that guaranteed rain before the day's end. Because everyone in the field had brought a waterproof cape, the smell of lanolin overrode any more pleasant springtime aromas. The overcast skies threatened the mood of the group – or maybe he imagined it. An atmosphere of grim determination enveloped them as they formed a circle around the decrepit pack.

Arwen approached him, taking care of business. "Pay attention to the southwest, water-to-fire seam. Both water junctures gave us problems, but that's where you'll be most valuable."

"Will do."

As she returned to the circle, Kiril sank to the ground next to him. He looked worse today, as if the skin of his face stretched more tightly over the bones. "Damned if I see what good I do here. But following orders."

Bryar nodded, grateful that Kiril rarely said much; he wasn't in the mood to chat. "We learn early not to defy Arwen."

"She's one kick-ass woman."

Bryar had never heard the expression, but it fit. "You okay?"

"Hell, yes. Ready to be done with this witchcraft stuff, though."

After a brief flurry of last-minute instructions, the members of the circle began the working.

It took longer this time, and raindrops sprinkled them before Dorcas called the end. The group dropped as a unit, more needful of grounding in earth energy than the first time. Arwen extracted the target stone. As she studied it, Tai joined her. The two Scribes talked and assessed the weave around the stone, their expressions serious but not grim.

Kiril stood, dusted his hands on his trousers, and left the clearing. Bryar watched him go, then scrambled to his feet and walked over to Quinn, where she knelt between the Weavers in the north and northwest positions. "What changed?"

She rose and unconsciously mimicked Kiril's action, brushing the grass and dirt from her hands onto her trousers. "Not much. Minor adjustments of the template, mainly in the northwest. I think it's just that everyone's still worn out from last time."

"I didn't pick up on any problems in the west. It felt uncomfortable, but tight."

"Good."

"But if they're tired...?"

Quinn sighed. "Between the weather and the fatigue, we may delay another day or two. Not ideal. You okay?"

"Better."

He left her and squatted beside Dal. "Thanks."

"It's my job."

"Nevertheless. I feel human again."

"Next time, don't wait. I'll expect you every few days as long as you're at the Motherhouse."

He hadn't planned on leaving... not consciously. But Dal had been exploring his mind and now had knowledge of things no one else did. "Ezra's. It would be good to go there."

"Take Tai with you."

He just might do that.

Three days later the circle met again, days in which he hung out with Mari, cultivated the bond between himself and Tai – and spent time in private, far along the river bank, with the little flute, which she'd returned to him after Dal's Healing.

He could do it. He could bring the music back. It hurt. Physically, he had to condition the stumps of his fingers, teach them to bend to his will, to apply the right amount and angle of coverage to the holes. The emotional pain was greater as he brought alive again the music he had rejected, wincing at the many missed notes, rejoicing at the occasional perfect ones, working to rebuild himself.

When the memory of Duncan rose up to stab him, Tai held him, her small, lithe body his sole point of stability.

One day he would be whole again. But never innocent. That had been snatched from him forever.

The circle convened on a muggy morning under a bank of thinning cloud as the sun fought to burn through. Steam rose from thirsty ground in the morning warmth. In the three days since the practice, the field and the forest surrounding it had greened out, bursting with new growth.

Bryar sensed the tension in the group. This one mattered, and although there had been no hint of similar problems, everyone remembered Willow's fate – and Martin's.

Kiril paced by the fringe of forest. Even he picked up on the stress... or was he up to something? He'd claimed, more than once, to have no further interest in the cell, but his word wasn't reliable.

Bryar approached Arwen. "I'm concerned. Kiril's too restless."

She glanced in Kiril's direction. "Ethics be damned, I'll be linking a binding on him until we're done. I want him here, but I'm not going to trust him. Not this time. There's too much at stake."

A threat to their way of life, now contained in an old bag. She, Quinn, and Tai wore identical packs, two of them decoys. He settled in his usual place, his mind alert to the hodgepodge of energies around him.

Things started to settle down. Kiril joined him, and Beatris appeared on his other side. She had attended the first, abortive attempt to bind the cell, and Bryar wasn't surprised that Arwen wanted an extra Healer present this time as well.

The energies became more unified and focused as Arwen led them through a final review while Tai and Quinn circled, assisting the participants with the harnesses linking their hands.

Worry more than anticipation hung in the air. The failed first try had taken much longer than a practice session with a stone. Despite the training and rehearsals, no one could be sure what to expect.

At a signal from Dorcas, Tai placed her pack in the center of the circle, and the working began.

From his vantage point, Bryar kept an eye on the joins where water met earth and fire, and otherwise monitored the growing weave. Nothing popped out to concern him, but he did notice that the weave took longer to organize and solidify, almost as if the power cell itself fought it.

Might well be. He didn't imagine the thing was cognizant, but it certainly had potential for harm.

Kiril shifted occasionally, as if he couldn't find a comfortable position. He looked worse than ever, drawn and white.

Bryar glanced at Beatris, but her entire focus was on the circle. When this was over, he'd make sure Kiril got to a Healer. However stubborn the man might be, even he must realize something was wrong.

After an hour, he began noticing signs of strain on the faces of those in the circle. At two hours, the Healer in the south dropped to her knees, and others appeared shaky. But the contact remained unbroken, and the weave was unifying. Although he lacked the skill to follow all the threads, he sensed that, so far, the work progressed according to plan. The sun broke through. By two and a half hours, most of the Weavers were sweating, either from sustained effort or the heat of the day. Physical suffering marked all their faces.

But the circle held. Several more knelt, but never released the currents coursing through them.

They had been at it for nearly three hours when Dorcas uttered the call to gather up the threads they controlled, seal them, and drop the resultant weave over the power cell.

As soon as the weave shimmered into the pack, the collective energy dissipated and the entire circle collapsed. Quinn and Tai speedily released the hand harnesses. Dal looked gray. Dorcas twisted away as soon as her hands were freed and vomited. Others dropped prone on the ground; more than one sobbed. Beatris moved among them, assessing and offering drops from one of the ubiquitous bottles Healers carried with them.

Kiril rose and vanished.

Bryar stood, shook life back into his feet and legs, and approached Arwen. "No problems in the west," he said quietly.

"That was my biggest worry, where the weave is concerned. Since Kiril's taken off, would you go round up another Healer?" Dismissing him, she turned away. "Tai, pass out the energy cakes, please. And water. Everyone, hydrate."

Dorcas shook her head, but with a note of humor despite her pallid skin. "And throw up again? Give us a little time to recover."

Bryar took off along the trail back to the Motherhouse, resolved to commandeer the first qualified Healer he came across. He was moving quickly, focused on his task, and almost didn't notice the man collapsed, unmoving, at the side of the track.

Kiril. The bloody fool.

After checking he still breathed, Bryar straightened him out, making sure his air passageway would remain clear, and left him by the path. He'd need to find two Healers, not one. And with six of the resident Healers in the field, that might be a challenge. He doubted there were more than ten in residence.

He pushed on, hoping and expecting to find everyone in the dining hall. While the members of the circle required Healing, they would ultimately be fine. But he was worried half sick about Kiril.

Chapter 48

Late that afternoon, summoned, Bryar paused at the door to the healing room, then tapped on the doorframe and entered.

He suspected that no one had paid much attention to Kiril in the days prior to the sealing. He'd drifted around the Motherhouse complex, saying little, never intruding. Bryar had long assumed some hidden motive behind his actions. Half of him trusted Kiril, based on their shared time in Borgonne, while the other half couldn't put aside his efforts to claim the cell for his own purposes, purposes involving power and control, or so Bryar suspected.

And now this.

Kiril lay limp under a light covering. He had wakened, but didn't move. His sweating face had taken on a greenish tinge, and his eyes were vacant. Beatris hovered over the cot across from Daren.

"Dal's not here?"

Beatris shook her head. "He needs to be. We hoped to give him more time to recover. Kiril's record mentions a bite. What can you tell us?"

Bryar recounted the attack in the hills. "Dal told him to come in every two days, so I guess he was worried."

"And rightly so. This is odd."

"But Kiril... he's...?"

Beatris, a cheerful woman of middle years who tended to plumpness, looked grim. "All day with the circle, and now this to deal with," she grumbled. "I've never seen anything the like. Daren?"

"I concur, and I want to bring Dal in. Whatever that animal carried in its saliva, it's outside my experience. I don't believe this is a problem for Healers, but he'll have a better idea of where to turn next."

"And Arwen?" Beatris asked.

"Not yet."

Bryar breathed a sigh of relief. He instinctively didn't want Arwen in the healing room. Her forceful presence was too overpowering. "How soon before we can trouble Dal?"

"Tomorrow, for his sake," Daren replied. "He's not that young, and the circle hit him hard. But if he hears of this, he won't stay away."

"And would that result in lasting harm?" Beatris asked.

Daren slouched against a wall, eyeing the inert man on the cot. "Merely assessing, no. But we cannot, under any circumstances, ask him to Heal this."

"We need his expertise." Beatris was insistent.

Daren capitulated. "I'll go find him." He left the room.

Beatris busied herself with the assortment of herbs and remedies on the small table against the far wall. Bryar walked over to Kiril and took the man's hand.

And dropped it. A strange energy pulsed there, such as he'd never experienced before.

He stepped back and watched the older woman. "You should rest."

"More than I'm up for anymore, it's true. But good work was done this morning. History will remember. Bryar, how are you?"

"Okay. Better. Can I help here?"

"No, but I'd like you to stay, unless Dal says otherwise. Our patient rests easier with your presence."

Bryar couldn't detect any difference in Kiril's energy, but he believed Beatris. She turned from him and resumed her work with the medicinals on the table. Bryar found a stool and waited.

Daren returned with Dal a little before the evening meal. He looked better, but still far from well. Fatigue played across his face and flattened his gaze. He went straight to the cot and began an assessment. After a few moments, he jerked back and muttered, "Stupidity."

"There's no record of him returning for further treatments," Daren said.

"No, and I didn't follow him. I should have. We might have stopped this thing before it got a hold. But the pus from the bite was a standard infection, no trace of anything like he's experiencing now. And with the cell —"

"We had enough on our minds. And it takes a fool to ignore his own health." Daren sounded frustrated, and more than a little worried.

Bryar felt the force of the words in his own situation, and wanted to add that for a man unfamiliar with their methods of healing, it might also require a level of trust Kiril hadn't yet acquired. But he merely said, "What is it?"

Dal sank to the floor next to Bryar's stool, leaning against the wall. "I'm guessing the animal that attacked Kiril was part of the spell on the hills. When it bit him, something of the spell's energetic imprint entered his body. And now it's attacking, just as if it were still fighting to keep Kiril from crossing the hills."

The room fell silent. "There's some logic there," Daren said. "But is anything like that even possible?" The horror of the implications registered on his face.

"What do we do?" Beatris asked.

Dal sagged where he sat, graphic evidence of the stress and exhaustion of the day. "I wish I knew."

The next afternoon, Bryar could almost see the thoughts surging through Arwen's mind as she frowned at the man lying on the cot.

The Healers kept Kiril alive. Arwen had spent the morning in the healing room, probing. Nobody knew how to combat the energy that seemed to be tearing him apart.

"The way I sense it," Arwen said, her voice cautious, "whatever the beast infected him with is in direct opposition to his own life force."

"Agreed." Dal spoke from a stool on the other side of the cot. The hours since the sealing of the power cell had only partially restored him; fatigue blanketed his face. "And as such, because it's the result of some kind of weave, I don't have the tools to Heal it. I'm at a loss."

"I guess we keep on with what we're doing." Arwen's voice sank, as if the events of the preceding day had depleted her. "Between Scribes and Healers, we'll come up with a treatment plan. We'll probably have to involve Quinn."

"Tai." Bryar spoke quietly; the name arrived on his lips without volition.

Arwen shook her head. "Not Tai. Walk with me, Bryar. I need to discuss something with you."

Not again. 'Discussing' with Arwen usually meant being given a task he didn't want, or a challenge he'd struggle to accomplish. But arguing never got him anywhere. He held aside the heavy curtain for her to exit.

"Bryar." Dal's voice stopped him as he exited the healing room.

He turned back.

"Check in with me this afternoon. Let's say the hour before supper. I intend to be damn sure you're not infected with the same thing."

"I'll be here. Thanks, Dal."

Bryar caught Dal's encouraging half smile as they left, an acknowledgment that he had started down the long road to full healing. Gone was the underlying surliness, and if at times he still needed to escape them all, he considered that a part of his recovery, a part of being human.

Arwen didn't speak until they were crossing the green. "Tomorrow, you and Tai are leaving for Ezra's."

"That's fine with me. Why?"

She almost smiled – except Arwen never smiled these days. "You don't believe it could be for your own benefit?"

"From someone else, maybe. From you, no."

Tai came around the corner from the Scribes' lodge and walked toward them. "You wanted me?" she asked Arwen.

"Yes. Can you be ready to leave for Ezra's tomorrow?"

"Sure. I miss Granddad and Rebecca. Why?"

Bryar laughed out loud.

Arwen's mouth twisted in a wry grin, no doubt remembering the apprentices they had been. A little of the heaviness left her brow. "You're taking the cell. Kiril's out of the picture for now, but be warned, it still isn't safe from Gauvain. And that man will believe he's powerful enough to undo the binding. I don't doubt for a moment he'll go after it again. Once it's disposed of, he won't find it."

"But Ezra's – it's pretty obvious," Bryar said. "If he sends his thugs, that's the first place they'd look."

"My hunch is, since he can't track it he'll come himself and try to trick us into revealing its location. I have a plan, which I'm not going to reveal to you. I'd never put Ezra at risk by hiding it there."

"The Old Man..." Bryar mused. "Being around him helps."

"Peace," Tai added. Just the one word. She reached for his hand. "We'll be better there."

"I don't like leaving Kiril, though."

"There's nothing you can do," Arwen said. "Try not to worry. If he can be saved, we'll do it. I hope..."

Whatever Arwen hoped, she kept to herself. "See me in the morning before you leave. The cell's packaged up and ready for you. Don't waste time, and be alert. Ezra's standing by to handle the next step in its disposition."

Arwen strode off in the direction of the Centra.

Bryar watched her go, then turned to Tai. "Good?"

"Good."

No one could doubt the importance of securing the cell, but he caught Arwen's underlying message. His work was done. It was time to rest, and heal, and rebuild his life.

"It won't always be easy," he said.

"That's why we travel together."

Together. His new favorite word.

From the forest behind the Motherhouse a single thrush sounded a call, then half a hundred of them joined in, breaking the midday peace. Bryar's fingers tightened on Tai's as he stood listening. G, C, a handful of harmonics, a simple, happy chord filling the clear air above them. The clamor died down as the birds settled, but his mind heard the notes, the beginnings of a tune...

Her small hand clasped his and tugged. "Let's head to the river."

The river. His element, where the most profound healing began. "Good idea."

They walked hand in hand toward the sound – the music – of the rushing water.

To My Readers

Hello, and thanks for choosing *The Bard*. The story continues with book 3, *The Scribe*.

If you enjoyed this book, well, I don't need to tell you how much reviews mean to writers.

To keep up with my writing, whether fantasy or romance, visit my website, http://lizanncarson.com.

Happy reading,

LizAnn

About LizAnn Carson

It's interesting, trying to condense who you are into a paragraph or two. For openers, I live with one husband and two cats, on the west coast of British Columbia, in a city that's large enough to have all modern conveniences, but not so large as to have hours-long traffic jams or heavy duty pollution. I can follow a trail to my local supermarket, or I can be downtown in twenty minutes.

Yes, I spend most of my time writing (and editing, formatting, critiquing for other writers, battling computer problems, and occasionally tearing my hair out). But beyond that, I enjoy a variety of crafts. I love the new craze of coloring books for adults. Recently I have been learning to play early music (Baroque and earlier) on my baritone ukulele – it works! I walk a lot and enjoy weight training. Once, a long time ago, I owned a yarn shop, and for a while I taught English as a Second Language. My career, on the other hand, was in the world of computer systems development.

You'd be very welcome to drop in at my website: http://lizanncarson.com.

www.ingramcontent.com/pod-product-compliance
Lightning Source LLC
Chambersburg PA
CBHW030316200626
46816CB00006BA/1810

* 9 7 8 0 9 9 4 9 0 3 6 7 9 *